The Counterfeit

OTHER BOOKS AND AUDIO BOOKS
BY ROBISON WELLS:

On Second Thought

Wake Me When It's Over

The
COUNTERFEIT

A Novel

Robison Wells

Covenant Communications, Inc.

Cover image by Sami Sarkis. Copyright Photodisc Green/Ghettyimages Inc.

Cover design copyrighted 2006 by Covenant Communications, Inc.

Published by Covenant Communications, Inc.
American Fork, Utah

Printed in USA
First Printing: July 2006

11 10 09 08 07 06   10 9 8 7 6 5 4 3 2 1

ISBN 1-59811-116-7

To Dan, who breathed new life into this book more than once.

Acknowledgements

This book, more so than either of my others, has been a collaborative effort. It's taken two and a half years and at least fourteen rewrites—including a nasty hard-drive failure where I lost everything (and learned the hard lesson of backing up my files). The plot is completely different from what I originally planned and almost unrecognizable from what I was writing even a year ago.

And I got a lot of help. Most prominently, my brother Dan acted as both my brainstorming partner and harshest critic. In one of the drafts, he summed up a conversation I'd created—one that I'd thought was poignant and touching—with the simple phrase: "Holy lame." He was also tireless in his advice and ideas, and he saved me more than once from throwing out the whole manuscript.

Likewise, I'd like to thank the staff of Thai Village, the restaurant where this book was written and rewritten. And if you stop by, I'd recommend the Masman Curry and the Chicken Satay. They're Thai-riffic!

The French translations were courtesy of Micah Bruner, Scott Carlson, and Katie Hansen, and I assume they did a bang-up job. (I can't be sure, since I don't speak French, but it certainly looks good.) Thanks also to those who proofed the French.

A special thanks also goes out to Covenant, who guided me through a difficult revision—particularly Angela, Kathy, and Robby. I'd also like to thank the art department for the wonderful cover.

And the big list: thanks to my wife, for never killing me in my sleep; to my great support group at The Official Time-Waster's Guide; to President Steve Marsh for his valuable explanation of Church organization in the San Juan Islands; to the good folks at Weyerhaeuser, purveyors of wood; to Cameron and Birgitte Ruesch; to the River Oaks 8th Branch; and to Stephanie Fowers, Katie Hansen, Micah Hausen, Ben Olsen, Stephen Shimek, and Koseli Christensen. And if I left anyone out, rest assured that whatever it was that you did, I was so emotionally moved by it that I felt a simple acknowledgement wasn't enough—you're forever in my heart, or whatever.

The Counterfeit

Prologue

HE LEANED BACK in his chair, his body turned slightly to one side as he gazed at the item on his desk.

It wasn't fear that kept him from picking it up. He'd conquered his fears long ago. Besides, he wasn't one to be swayed by irrationality, and he certainly wasn't dealing with people who would make allowances for cold feet.

He slowly rubbed his face, perhaps subconsciously hoping that the paper would be gone when his eyes reopened. The note was expected, of course. It had been expected for several months and was simply the culmination of countless hours of effort. It was a date, nothing more. A decision had been made, and he would do his part.

He picked it up. The folded paper was soft and thick, like a page from an old book. It was bent in thirds and sealed with wax—old-fashioned, perhaps, but so were the note's authors. In the center was a circle, drawn roughly in black ink, and in the center of that was a dot. The Black Sun.

From another room he could hear the sound of a television anchorwoman describing the failing economy. Stocks plummeted. Inflation soared. He raised the note and tapped it absently against his chin as he listened to the news story. There was nothing new—just the same information recycled again and again—and it wasn't as though he hadn't known it all before he heard it. Only a handful of people on the planet had a better understanding.

He looked back at the note. A surge of rebellion pounded through his body as he thought of it. It had been decades since he'd had to answer to anyone about anything—and this was so big, and his superiors so unrelenting. Taking a deep breath, he stretched his neck and pushed the anxiety from his mind.

He slid his thumb under a corner of the note and let the seal crack apart. He brushed the flecks of red wax that scattered across his desk into his hand and then tossed them into the wastebasket before he unfolded the page and began to read.

Tuesday, August 1st.

He glanced down at his watch. August wasn't very far away, and he had much to do before it came. The schedule would have to be hurried.

Standing, he walked the note down the hall and shredded it personally. Not everyone in the organization knew of his plans. Not yet.

CHAPTER 1

June 23

I waited anxiously in a back corridor of Abravanel Hall. I was supposed to meet her for lunch, but apparently I'd written down the wrong time. I'd expected her rehearsal to end at noon, but that had been twenty-five minutes ago, and the orchestra was still going strong. I'd brought a book to read, but really had no interest in it and left it unopened in the front pocket of my suit coat.

From where I sat on the hallway floor, I could see Rebekah on her feet in front of a music stand. Even though she wasn't playing, she was listening studiously, occasionally jotting down a quick note on her sheet music.

We'd been dating since autumn, following a rather atypical courtship process during which she'd been kidnapped because of something I'd given her, and we'd both nearly died. Because of that, life wasn't exactly the same for us as it was for most people our age. Where the typical guy my age might have a busy schedule juggling a job, a girlfriend, and finishing his degree, I had a busy schedule juggling a girlfriend, endless streams of interview requests, and hour after hour of meetings with a federal prosecutor.

Rebekah seemed to handle it better than I did. She'd thrown herself into her music, even more so than she used to. In a twisted kind of way, her notoriety as That Girl Who Got Kidnapped seemed to open a lot of doors in the concert-violin world—not that she was a novelty act, but everyone suddenly had heard of her and realized how good she was. There's no such thing as bad press, I guess.

She lived in a big house in Spanish Fork Canyon with her mom and sister. I lived in a small basement apartment with two roommates. She drove a BMW. I drove an old Chevy. She'd traveled the world, and I'd been to Disneyland every summer of my life, with the exception of the two years I spent on my mission. Even while there, as I tracted the streets of Nebraska, my mom sent me photos of the family vacation, along with some Donald Duck stationery. Rebekah and I were from two different worlds.

My roommates told me she was out of my league. Figuratively speaking, she was the first-round draft pick in the majors, and I was fighting for a fourth-string position on the high school junior varsity. My roommates also listed a dozen other reasons why it wouldn't work out—everything from my utterly forgettable looks to my occasional snoring. A girl like Rebekah, they said, wasn't interested in a snorer.

And yet we continued to date. Somehow, even though terrorists had stopped shooting at us, and our lives no longer hung in a tenuous balance, she still liked me.

The conductor said something—too quiet for me to hear—and the orchestra disbanded for lunch. I gathered my things and stood.

She was beautiful, and while I certainly admit a bias, my assessment had nothing to do with being blinded by love. She was nearly as tall as I was—taller on Sundays or at concerts. Her hair was sandy blond and wavy, and today it was pulled back into a simple ponytail. She wore a white, collared shirt and a knee-length khaki skirt. She carried her sheet music with her and an old, worn book, and she was flipping through its pages as she walked.

"Hey," I said, waving as she emerged from the room.

She smiled. "Eric."

"How'd it go?"

"*C'est nul!*"

"What does that mean?"

She laughed and held up the book for me to see. "It means that I think I'm in over my head. It's French."

"I don't believe it for a minute."

"No, really," she said, looking back down at the pages. "I haven't really read any French since my freshman year at BYU, and I think I forgot more than I should have."

"What's the book?"

"A biography of Camille Saint-Saëns." After seeing the blank look on my face she added, "He composed the piece I'm performing tonight."

"Oh yeah," I said, nodding. She'd been talking about Saint-Saëns for months, but I'd never seen the name in print. I would have sworn it was spelled San Saw. "Don't worry about it—it'll come back to you. Speaking French is like riding a bike."

Rebekah grinned. "And how do you know this?"

"Everything is like riding a bike. A bike that tastes like chicken."

She looked at her watch. "We need to be back by five today."

I pushed the front door open for her. "There's a problem with that, actually."

"What?" She looked concerned. "You're still coming to the concert, right?"

I nodded. "I'll be there, but you'll have to find something to do by yourself this afternoon. Agent Harrop called."

Her shoulders fell. "Again?"

"Someone else from Washington is in town today, and they want to talk to me."

"Not me?"

"I'm the lucky one today."

"Who is it?"

"I don't know. Harrop never tells me anything."

"I'm getting so sick of this."

There'd recently been a rumor that Rebekah and I might not be safe. Neither of us put a lot of stock into it because the FBI had informed us of similar rumors at least six other times, and they'd all turned out to be false alarms. Even so, every morning I had to call Special Agent Jeff Harrop, my personal knight in shining armor, and tell him my schedule for the day. He would agree to some activities and nix others, and generally be a pain in the neck.

I didn't really like that my noble protector was named Jeff. Nobody tough is named Jeff. There's Jeff, the sleepy guy on *The Wiggles,* and Jeff, the sissy mannequin on *Today's Special.* And finally there's DJ Jazzy Jeff and the Fresh Prince. And that's it. No more famous Jeffs.

I wanted a bodyguard named Mad Dog.

I opened the door for Rebekah, and we stepped out into the warm afternoon air. "I need to leave pretty soon. I'll be at the courthouse, so I can just walk back here."

She frowned. "Still have time for lunch?"

* * *

Rebekah and I sat together on a bench behind the Church Office Building, eating peanut butter sandwiches and apples. I didn't have a job, so I couldn't afford anything better. (I had a hard time finding a job that would tolerate my hectic court schedule.) And despite the fact that Rebekah grew up astronomically rich, her family was living under the constant worry that the FBI would seize all of their possessions. They were having to learn frugality.

She picked up her half-eaten apple and took another bite. She chewed slowly and thoughtfully, and I pretended not to stare at her.

"Are you ready for next week?" she said, fourteen beautiful chews and a dainty swallow later.

"What's next week?"

"You know, the big one."

"You mean for Isabella?"

She nodded.

"I guess," I answered. "I haven't had to think about my story for months—I've got it all memorized by now. Half the time, I'm not sure if I'm remembering what actually happened, or if I'm remembering what I said in a deposition or an interview or an affidavit."

She laughed a little bit and nodded. "I know what you mean."

I unscrewed the cap on my water bottle and drank the last few swallows. "Rebekah, I don't know what to do at the trial. It'll be easy testifying against Paul Arbogast—he was trying to kill us. Isabella wasn't—she hated us, but she was trying to help."

"She didn't hate *us*."

"Well, she hated what she was doing. She hated helping us. But she still did."

"So say that," Rebekah said, sitting up and scooting a little closer to me. "You're not testifying against her. You're just telling what happened. If the jury thinks that she's guilty, that's their choice. You telling the truth isn't what would put her in prison."

"What did she even do? Her only crime is working for your dad, and no one has even established that he's a terrorist. No one knows *what* he is."

Rebekah's eyes turned down for a moment. "That's what I'm hoping. They can't convict her on terrorism charges if they can't prove she's a terrorist."

"It would help if she'd say something once in a while. Sitting silent in a jail cell for five months doesn't make you look innocent."

Rebekah nodded. As much as we denied it, the truth was pretty clear. If Rebekah's dad, and Isabella, his personal assistant, hadn't been involved in anything illegal, why didn't they come forward? Every day that Isabella remained quiet was a day closer to Rebekah being marked as a terrorist's daughter.

"I wish Arbogast's trial was first," she said.

"Me too."

"Do you know who they want to talk about this afternoon?"

I shook my head. "I assumed Isabella. I don't really know, though."

Rebekah took another bite of her sandwich, and thought.

I looked down at my watch. "I need to go."

"You'll be back tonight?" She smiled hopefully.

"Wouldn't miss it for anything."

CHAPTER 2

I LEFT THE courthouse at 7:15, giving me forty-five minutes to walk the five blocks to Abravanel Hall. It was a breezy night, and the sidewalks were nearly empty.

Rebekah's concert was going to be a big deal. She was an incredible violinist but rarely got a venue that would showcase her talents. Of course, I don't know Mozart from Monet, but she assured me that this performance was important. She wasn't the star of the show, but she was a featured performer, and her photo was on the second page of the program.

I turned off of Main Street and onto 100 South.

It happened fast—faster than it happens in the movies. One second I was walking, looking down at my feet and thinking about Rebekah, and the next second I was face to face with death, and there was a knife at my stomach. There was no time for anything.

I don't know where he came from—I hadn't been paying attention—but his left hand was suddenly gripping my shoulder, and his right was violently rocking the knife back and forth.

I struggled against him, my first blows panicked and worthless. It didn't deter him—he kept ramming the knife into me. And for some reason, all I felt was a dull pressure. I mean, every time he shoved I nearly fell over, but there was no piercing pain, no blood.

I looked into his face. His wide eyes were angry and frightened, and I'm sure that mine mirrored his on both counts. I took a step back and threw a punch. He dodged it easily and yanked the knife back, tearing a jagged hole in my suit coat.

The knife was long and wide, with a serrated edge and a wicked point. He held it lightly, sizing me up and ready to lunge. I thought of my options. I could stand and fight, but there wasn't much I knew about self-defense. I could run, but the thought of turning my back to him terrified me.

Suddenly, he glanced at something over my shoulder, took one last look at me, and fled.

The FBI arrived a moment later. A man who was dressed almost exactly like Agent Harrop grabbed me by the shoulder and hurried me into a defensible corner until a car arrived. It only took a few seconds before I was helped into the back of a black sedan.

My attacker was gone. The FBI agent was yelling into a radio, and other people were yelling back at him. Our car pulled away from the curb, and I tried to start breathing again.

I guess the rumor was true.

CHAPTER 3

WE DIDN'T GO far. One FBI agent drove, and the other—the one who had appeared out of nowhere—sat in the back next to me. The driver turned the car once to the right, and once to the left, and then pulled into a no-parking zone across from Abravanel Hall.

The agent next to me hopped out of the car and jogged across the street.

I was panicked and confused, and there was a foot-long tear across the front of my suit. I'd kept a book in my pocket—something to read while waiting for Rebekah—and it was gouged and shredded. Numbly, I reached between the seats and handed it to the driver.

"Who was that?" I asked, hardly daring to speak.

He looked at me in his rearview mirror. "What have we been telling you for months?"

"If it was a real threat, why did you let us walk around and be by ourselves?"

"We didn't."

I thought for a minute, blood rushing in my ears. "How long have you been following us?"

"A long time."

"Is someone chasing my attacker?"

He shook his head. "Not *that* many agents were following you. Our instructions were to secure you and Rebekah. We got a good look at the suspect, though. We'll find him."

I gazed out the window. Through the tall, glass windows of Abravanel Hall I could see streams of concert-goers socializing as they climbed the long stairs to their seats. Rebekah was going to miss her big show.

"Wait," I said, suddenly annoyed. "Why did you call him a suspect? You watched him do it."

He let out a small, tired laugh. "Habit, I guess."

"Well, good. Because he's not a suspect, he's the guy who did it. He's not an accused stabber—he's a stabber."

"I'll remember that."

Fifteen minutes passed before Rebekah appeared, walking briskly next to the FBI agent. He was carrying her violin case. She wasn't wearing her usual black concert dress and high heels—the agent must have insisted she change clothes. They hurried through the courtyard in front of the hall, and then jogged across the street, ignoring the signs that warned about crossing the train tracks.

The agent opened the car door for Rebekah, and she jumped into the backseat.

"Are you okay?" she asked, her face flushed.

I nodded and showed her the hole in my suit coat. "My book stopped the knife."

She hugged me and I hugged her back; I didn't realize how much I'd been trembling until then. We'd both been through this kind of thing before, but that didn't make it less frightening.

The agent got in the passenger seat and turned to face us.

"Buckle up. We're going to the airport."

"What?" we both said in unison.

"Orders from on high," he said dryly. "We're getting you out of here."

* * *

The driver, Agent McCoy, stayed with the car. It was Agent Reuben, the man who had come to my rescue and fetched Rebekah, who led us to the plane.

For a smaller jet, it wasn't anything to speak of. I'd only seen private jets in movies, and expected something nicer, with leather seats and thick carpet. This plane, however, was much like any other—a bunch of seats with gray upholstery, facing forward. I suppose the FBI doesn't have an enormous budget for this kind of thing.

Rebekah and I sat toward the center of the plane, right on top of the wing. There was no fight attendant and there were no other passengers. Agent Reuben sat two rows ahead. He seemed perpetually annoyed. He was a short man, with black hair and a grim look. He didn't look very old—probably in his early thirties. His face was kind of chubby, even though the rest of him wasn't.

"Where are we going?" I asked.

"Honestly," he said, buckling himself in as the jet engines roared to life, "I have no idea. We're taking off, and while we're in the air, we'll be told where to go. It makes us harder to follow."

Rebekah frowned. "So we *are* being followed."

"Like I said, I have no idea. It's a precaution. Right now, we don't know who's after you, and we don't know who your attacker was."

"I can guess," I offered.

"Well, I can guess too," Reuben replied. "But what good would that do?"

Rebekah and I had never flown together, although we'd tried once. Back in December, when everything was at its bleakest—when we'd just escaped a car crash and a shooting and a burning building, only to realize that this was the pattern our lives would probably follow if we didn't go into hiding—we'd accepted a pair of plane tickets and a pair of fake passports from a mysterious party.

We'd never made it onto the plane. We got to the airport, checked in, and got chased by a man with an Uzi. Sometimes life is like that. Not often, but sometimes.

On the FBI plane, I tried to figure out where we were heading by looking out the windows, but couldn't tell much, other than that it was getting dark and we were flying north.

Halfway through the flight, the copilot came back to talk to Reuben. They chatted for a while with serious faces and low voices, and then the copilot went back to the cockpit and closed the door.

"So?" I asked.

He groaned. "So what?"

"Where are we going?"

"We'll be landing in about an hour and transferring to another plane."

"To go where?"

"It's a secret."

"Who are we going to tell?"

Rebekah leaned forward. "Agent Reuben, can you find out if my mom is safe?"

He rolled his eyes and took a deep breath. "I'm on it like a hobo on a ham sandwich."

Reuben unbuckled his seat belt, sighed, and stood up. He spent the rest of the flight in the cockpit.

* * *

By the time we transferred planes, it was dark and cloudy. I didn't recognize anything, other than the fact that we were at an airport in a somewhat large city. Visibility was low, and I couldn't see much of the skyline.

Rebekah and I climbed into the cramped backseat of the tiny propeller plane, and Agent Reuben took the front. Rain was falling, and he was soaked.

"All right," he said, buckling himself into his seat. "The pilot isn't a government employee, so we're not going to be saying anything about who we are or what we're doing, got it?"

"Where are we going?" I repeated for the hundredth time.

"I'll tell you when we get there."

Rebekah leaned forward. "Where are we now?"

"The airport."

"I know that," she said, annoyed. "I meant what city?"

"I knew what you meant."

"What's the big secret?" I asked.

"You're not getting this, are you?" he said, turning around to face us. "Eric, you were stabbed. Who knows what it'll be next time. A bomb? Poison? Snipers? You're in the custody of the federal government. The Witness Protection Program."

Rebekah's face went white. "What?"

As though on cue, the door opened and the pilot climbed up and into the plane. Reuben gave us a look, indicating that he wanted us to keep quiet, and then turned around.

"Well, I don't know what the urgency is this evening, folks," the pilot said, putting on a pair of headphones and adjusting some instruments. "But it'll be a choppy ride. Weather's only gonna get worse."

He wasn't kidding. By the time we got permission from the tower to finally get off the ground, rain was pounding the little plane. There was no lightning or thunder—there were no flashes of any kind—just a long, steady stream of water. A few minutes into the flight the pilot shut off the windshield wipers. When Rebekah protested, he said that they weren't doing any good anyway—we couldn't see a thing.

I held her hand, and she squeezed mine every time the plane bounced, which was almost constantly. There was no flight attendant to relay safety instructions and tell me how to buckle my seat belt, but for the first time ever, I wished there was. It had been so difficult getting into the tiny plane that I knew getting out would be worse—and judging by the rain, we'd be landing in a flood.

"Is this safe?" I asked. Even Reuben looked uncomfortable.

"Well," the pilot said thoughtfully, scratching at the stubble on his chin, "it's not as safe as being on the ground, I suppose, but it's a mite safer than being in a car."

"But you can't see anything."

"This is the twenty-first century," he laughed. "Eyes ain't half as good as instruments."

He began pointing to the various gauges and lights on the compact dashboard, explaining each and every one. Rebekah offered the occasional polite "Really?" and "Wow." Reuben ignored him. I tried to think about something other than flying, but then I could only think about getting stabbed. Or bombed, or poisoned, or shot at.

It didn't make any sense. Felix hated us, but he didn't have any good reason to kill us. Yes, we'd thwarted his plan for attacking Internet commerce, but he was still pouring counterfeit money into the economy, and the dollar had lost value, just as he'd hoped. He'd spent two decades building up the enormous fake-money reserve, just waiting for the right moment to spring it on the public. His hope was that several-hundred-million-dollar's worth of fake money would shake America's faith in the dollar. And when no one believed in their money anymore, the money would be worth nothing. Crazy, yes, but no one had accused Felix of being sane.

Businesses were handling it the best they could. Stores offered discounts for using checks or credit cards. Even coins were preferred to bills, as no one had ever found a good, cost-effective way to counterfeit a quarter.

The government was responding to the threat in the way that the government responded to things: Congress was asking for more funding for the intelligence community. Some of that money also went to public service announcements, in which big-name celebrities encouraged the public to have faith in their money. Dustin Hoffman had a spot eating at a diner and leaving a twenty-dollar bill on the table; Julia Roberts paid five bucks for a bag of Doritos at a gas station.

And yet the dollar was dipping steadily. As far as we could see, Felix's plot for complete economic equality via countrywide bankruptcy was beginning to work. I suppose he might send someone to kill us just because he didn't like us, but it still didn't make much sense.

There was another possible reason, though. Perhaps someone was trying to stop us from testifying. And there were two possible suspects our unknown pursuer could be defending.

First, we were testifying against ex-Special Agent Paul Arbogast. He'd been working for the FBI, although his secret allegiance was to Felix and the Novus Ordo Seclorum, and he tried on several occasions to turn Rebekah and me over to his terrorist leaders. But there was no reason for Felix to fret over our testimonies—Arbogast had been caught red-handed. Whether we were on the witness stand or not, there was a mountain of evidence against him.

The other option was Isabella, the former personal assistant of Edward Hughes, Rebekah's father. Isabella was currently in prison, but she wasn't talking. We were supposed to testify against her, too, but Rebekah and I were certain that her father would never try to kill us. He'd risked Isabella's life, after all, just to ensure that Rebekah was safe. The thought that he would kill his own daughter now just to save Isabella from prison was ridiculous.

The sound in the little airplane was deafening—both from the overworked engine and from the huge drops of rain pelting the fuselage. Rebekah said something to me, but I couldn't understand a word of it. She turned and yelled it into my ear, but I still only got part of it. So I kissed her. That probably wasn't what she was asking for, but I figured it couldn't hurt.

The pilot tilted his head and shouted something equally unintelligible. I didn't ask him to repeat it because it would do no good.

We could see runway lights. There weren't many of them, and they were faint, but when everything else is black, even faint lights stand out. I felt the engine's power drop, and I swear the airplane fell a hundred feet. My head hit the ceiling, and Rebekah let out a yelp— loud enough to be heard clearly over the noise. The pilot laughed.

To say that the landing was bumpy would be an understatement. The engine shuddered and squealed. We ricocheted off the tarmac, bouncing a dozen feet into the air. The little plane yawed back and forth a bit, the pilot let out a few choice words and a yeehaw, and we skidded to a stop six feet before the runway ended and mud began.

Agent Reuben looked as shaken as Rebekah and I, but he rubbed a hand across his face, shook the tenseness from his neck, and spoke. "Well, kids, we don't have an umbrella, and there's no car waiting. We've got about a quarter-mile jog. Just follow me." He turned to the pilot. "You've been paid?"

He laughed and slapped Reuben's shoulder. "I wouldn't fly on a night like this if I didn't have cash up front."

Reuben wasn't kidding. We left the plane and immediately began running, getting pelted with stinging rain as we went. Reuben led the way, hurrying down a short hill and across a parking lot that had once been made of dirt and was now two inches of slime. Rebekah ran in front of me, and I watched her slip twice as she picked her way frantically across the impromptu pond. I slipped five times, but I'd volunteered to carry her violin case, and I blamed it on that.

We turned onto a semipaved road. Densely packed pines stood on both sides, affording us a little protection from the rain, but the ground was still a mess. To my right I could see a broad field with several small cabins lined in neat rows. Lights gleamed in a few of the windows.

Ahead of me, Rebekah paused. As I caught up with her, she pointed in the distance. "Look."

Despite the pouring rain and darkness, it was undeniable. "A marina?"

"Where are we?"

"I don't know," I said, shivering slightly. Rebekah's long blond hair was plastered to her face and neck, and her clothes were soaked through. "Let's hurry." I took her hand and we ran again.

The road curved along the side of the hill, and more buildings became visible. A large steepled church rose to my left, and buildings dropped off to my right. I glanced down the steep slope and saw that the water—dancing and glistening in the rain—was only thirty or forty feet below us.

Suddenly, the dirt ended and the wide path was paved with cobblestones. Reuben swung over to the left and under the wooden awning of a white, three-story hotel. Without waiting for us, he wiped his muddy shoes on the doormat and entered. Rebekah and I followed, grateful to be out of the rain.

The building was old—probably on the historic register for one reason or another. There was a fireplace, but unfortunately no fire had been lit. The check-in desk was made from old, dark wood, and antique furniture lined the lobby.

"Here," Reuben said, turning to us. He handed us each a room key. "Head upstairs and get dried off."

He turned back to the plump woman at the desk. "Are there towels in the rooms?"

"In the bathrooms," she answered, and then, speaking to us, "We have bathrooms on each floor. This time of night, they should be available."

"Great," Reuben said, running his hand through his black hair. About a quart of rainwater ran down his back. He followed us to the stairs. "Take a shower and get some sleep. I don't think we have any dry clothes for you, so you'll have to make do until tomorrow."

I had a million questions to ask, but my mind was numb from the cold and I had trouble picking just one. So I simply nodded. Rebekah answered with a shiver.

"Meet me out front at eight in the morning. We'll get some breakfast and figure out what's going to happen."

I nodded again. Maybe I was just tired. I put my arm around Rebekah's waist and pulled her close to me, hoping a little shared body heat might help. She was far colder than I was.

"Anything else?" Reuben prompted anxiously.

"Are we safe here?" I finally asked.

He pursed his lips and nodded. "For now. No one could have followed us. Like I said, we'll figure things out tomorrow." He turned to leave, and then added, quietly and condescendingly, "Don't go talking to people here, but if you have to, at least don't tell them your names. Okay?"

CHAPTER 4

THERE WAS A knock at the door. I opened one eye, glanced at the clock, and wondered why anyone would be bothering me at six-thirty in the morning. The first rays of sun were peeking through the window.

The knock came again. I sat up slowly and then stumbled over to the door. The springs in my mattress echoed a few times around the world, probably startling people in nearby rooms.

"Good morning," Rebekah said, smiling sheepishly. "Did I wake you up?"

"No."

"Liar." Her face fell. "Sorry."

"It's fine," I said, and motioned for her to come inside. I pulled the blankets up over the bed and pretended that it was neatly made. Rebekah sat down on the uncomfortable antique chair in the corner of the room.

"Did you sleep okay?" I asked.

She shook her head. "The shower's nice, though."

"It looks like your clothes dried out." Her shirt was wrinkled but dry, as were her pants. My suit was still damp and clung to my legs.

"There's a hair dryer in the women's bathroom," she said, smiling. "I used that."

I had to admit—not that it takes much for me to admit this kind of thing—that she looked surprisingly good for having gone through what we did. Her blond hair was neatly done, pinned here and there in a casual style so pretty that it looked like it had taken her hours. But there were dark circles under her eyes—evidence of a lack of both sleep and makeup. I didn't mind at all.

I wouldn't recommend getting stabbed as a relationship builder, but the past twenty-four hours had only cemented my love for Rebekah. The prospect of losing her . . . I didn't like to think about it.

"Washington," Rebekah said as I finished making the bed.

"What?"

"We're in Washington—State, not D.C."

"How did you find out?" I moved to the window and fiddled with the lock.

"I went downstairs," she said simply. "Asked the front desk."

The window slid open jerkily, and I stuck my head outside. There was a low, moss-covered roof a few feet below, and firs and ferns were growing every place where a building didn't get in the way.

"Where in Washington?" I asked, pulling my head back in.

"It's an island, actually," she said, standing up. "Come here."

Rebekah led me out of the room and down the hall. A narrow, screened doorway opened onto a long balcony that ran the length of the entire hotel.

Directly in front of us were two elegant gardens, with a trellised walkway between them leading out to the marina. To our left another long, white building stood, with the words *Roche Harbor Lime and Cement Co.* It jutted out into the center of the marina, built on what was either a man-made peninsula or a perfectly formed natural pier.

"The island is mainly for tourists now," Rebekah said, breathing in the clean morning air. "The woman at the desk said that it'll be really busy in a few weeks."

I sat down on a green wooden bench. Rebekah joined me.

"All in all," I said, "there are worse places we could have been sent."

"Who knows how long we'll stay, though."

She leaned against me slightly.

"Your birthday's in three days."

She smiled. "I know."

"I bought you a present. It's even wrapped."

"Really?"

"Next time we're back in Utah, I'll give it to you."

* * *

At ten minutes to eight, Rebekah spotted Agent Reuben walking in from the parking lot. He'd just climbed off of a BMW motorcycle, which seemed a little odd, though I suppose if our FBI protectors looked liked FBI protectors then it wouldn't be a secret.

He was wearing a red turtleneck sweater and looked more like a fisherman than a government agent. She waved to him, and he motioned us down from the balcony.

"Sleep well?" he asked. It seemed like he was hoping I would answer no, so I replied with a "never better."

"There's a restaurant over here," he said, motioning to the Lime and Cement building. We followed him down through the trellised walkway and then turned left. The restaurant was on the far side, with floor-to-ceiling windows on three sides, each with a different view of the harbor. Rebekah and I both ordered large plates of eggs, bacon, and hash browns, famished from a night of bad sleep and no food. Reuben asked for smoked salmon and a bagel.

We selected a table in the corner, near a small heater and a wall-mounted television.

"Was the hotel all right?" he asked, staring up at the TV. CNN was giving the morning news.

"It was fine," Rebekah answered.

"Good, good, good." The waitress brought him a cup of coffee, and he took a sip. "Okay. Everything is all set. If you haven't figured it out already, you're on San Juan Island, about twenty miles off the coast of Washington, in Puget Sound. Basically, you're between Seattle and Vancouver." There weren't many people in the small café, but he kept his voice low anyway.

"Are we staying here?" I asked.

"For the time being."

Reuben proceeded to lay out the situation. We had fake names (she was now Jennifer and I was Hugh), and we were just tourists on the island. No elaborate cover story, no fake jobs at a convenience store. He simply gave us a stack of fake IDs, a couple FBI credit cards, and told us to change our hairstyles. I was supposed to grow a beard, and Rebekah was supposed to cut and dye her hair—Agent

Reuben had already made her an appointment at the salon. From the look on her face, you'd think it was the most distressing thing she'd heard all week.

Our accommodations weren't quite ready, Reuben told us, so I would be remaining in the hotel for the time being. Rebekah had a house out in the woods, which he assured us was safe and used only by top FBI officials. When they found other housing, I'd get moved.

Finally, Reuben tossed a couple dollars on the table for a tip, and stood.

"Wait," Rebekah said, her nerves showing. "Do we have a car? How do we get to the house?"

"I gave you a map," he said, glancing toward the door. "It's in the envelope. Your car keys are there, too. Jennifer, yours is the black Honda Civic out front. Hugh, yours is the little green thing parked next to it." He smiled wide and hurried out the door.

"Little green thing?" I asked, watching him disappear. "That can't be good."

Rebekah sadly ran her hand through her hair, as if it were the last time she'd ever see it.

CHAPTER 5

THE LITTLE GREEN thing turned out to be a moped—a 1970s era, rust-tinged bike that was more closely related to a footstool than a motorcycle. It lacked the macho factor that comes from a Harley or a Kawasaki, and it was even too dilapidated to score me points for kitsch or camp. It was a little green nightmare with a cracked mirror and a torn seat. I named it Maurice.

Rebekah had a Honda Civic, black as obsidian, with only ninety-two miles on it. The seats were leather and heated, the cup holders ample, and the stereo system top-of-the-line. I made a mental note to have words with Reuben the next time he showed up.

"We can share the car," Rebekah said, crouching down to get a better look at Maurice—he was hard to see from five feet away. If nothing else, he'd recently received a nice fresh coat of rust to cover up the paint.

"We don't live close to each other."

"We're pretty close," she answered, standing back up and looking embarrassed by her good transportational fortune.

"It's at least a mile or two," I said, picking at the foam bursting from Maurice's seat. "Besides, I like riding motorcycles. I used to own one."

"That's not a motorcycle." She pursed her lips, glancing back and forth between the two vehicles. "Why don't you take the car?"

"Right." I pulled the car keys from the envelope Reuben had left us. The key to the Honda had a remote control that could pop the trunk and set off a car alarm. The key to Maurice was on a sun-bleached *I love to shop* key chain. I handed Rebekah her keys and the envelope.

"I'll follow you," I said, climbing onto the little moped and putting the key in the ignition. Maurice sputtered, his engine making a floppy, thumping noise, then wheezing out a raspy puff of exhaust.

"How about I follow you?" she asked, looking doubtful, as though expecting me to change my mind, push the moped into the harbor, and join her in the car. When I didn't, she broke into a smile that had all the earmarks of a soon-to-be laugh and handed me the sunglasses that had been perched on her head.

So I had a little green nightmare and girl sunglasses.

The drive was pleasant enough. Once we got going, Maurice's floppy thumping turned into a marbles-in-the-dryer kind of sound. Rebekah had told me that San Juan Island was home to bald eagles and all manner of wildlife. I watched the trees around me, knowing that they were completely devoid of critters—I was scaring them off long before I ever arrived.

Maurice or not, I had to admit that this situation was bordering on the ideal. Rebekah had been cooped up too long by school and depositions and pesky terrorists. I'd spent the last five months watching my back, wary of everyone around me—and the last two days had increased my worry exponentially. A remote island, with false names and no worries bigger than a noisy moped, was the perfect solution.

My main hope was that Rebekah would find a lounge chair and lie in it for a few weeks before trying anything adventurous. I'd spend my days reading and my evenings watching baseball on TV. But in the few short minutes we'd had after Reuben left us, Rebekah had talked unceasingly about hiking and boating and fishing and clamming—I didn't even know that *clamming* was a word, but she wanted to do it.

After several miles, I turned onto a long, straight road, with a large farm on my right and a forest on my left. A man was standing on the side of the road, mending the barbed-wire fence. I waved to him, and he halfheartedly shook his wire cutters in reply.

A small, black mailbox marked the road that led to Rebekah's house. I slowed Maurice down (not that he'd been going very fast anyway) and turned off the pavement and onto her drive. The road was steep, dropping down through a forest dense with pines and madrona trees. Looking between the foliage, I got the occasional glimpse of ocean and deducted she must be living right on the water's edge. And then I saw the house.

It was a good thing that as a poor college student I didn't pay a lot of taxes. Because if I did, I just might have had to write a letter to the editor, complaining about the egregious misuse of government funds in the Witness Protection Program.

Maurice and I rounded a bend in the road, and I nearly crashed watching the four-story edifice materialize out of the forest. Maurice choked on something and died.

Rebekah pulled up behind me, stared for a few seconds, and turned off the car.

"Is this the right place?" I asked, hopping off of Maurice's uncomfortable seat and walking to her door.

"The address was right on the mailbox," Rebekah answered, every bit as bewildered as I was.

"Try the key."

"Maybe I do have a job—I'm going to be the housekeeper." She fumbled with her keys to find the right one, and I followed her up the large stone steps.

"It's a lot like your house back home," I said, running my hand along the details of the carved wooden door—it was decorated with flowers and vines and birds. There was a small owl with big eyes right over the doorknob.

"A little, I guess."

Rebekah's father had had plenty of money, and she'd grown up in no less than a mansion. She'd always been told that he'd been involved with some kind of international business, and the money rolled in every month—lots of it. Her father had never been there to spend it; that was handled by Rebekah, her sister, and her mother. He only showed up every six months or so, sometimes coinciding with a holiday, but usually coinciding with nothing. He'd spend three or four days eating dinner with the family at fancy restaurants, asking the girls about school, and telling tales about Pakistan and South Africa and Japan.

Rebekah found the key and pushed the heavy door open. The interior was no less impressive than the exterior; the entry was bigger than most living rooms and was awash in antique furniture and artwork. I could only imagine they were all fake—government spending had to have some limits, didn't it?

Inside the front door was an array of buttons and LCD displays. The first—a large one with blinking lights—was obviously security. But there were others for temperature and humidity, and one of the panels seemed to be monitoring the power system.

I found a few pages' worth of notes on a short wooden table. The first page detailed the alarm system, which, I was pleased to learn, was top-of-the-line.

The next page was marked *Emergency Contacts,* which looked normal enough. It listed Fire, Police, and Ambulance. I had to wonder how quick any of those services could reach us. No fire engine I'd ever seen could make it down that winding road—maybe they just wanted to know when there was a fire so they could come watch the place burn.

Poison Control was listed, as well as something called Marine Toxins. The Coast Guard was next, in case I was sitting in the house, next to the phone, and got attacked by pirates.

At the bottom was written, *Speed Dial #1: Grandpa.*

"Grandpa?" I asked.

"Agent Reuben said he was the first speed dial."

I nodded and looked back at the list, while Rebekah walked farther into the depths of her new home.

The last line read, *Speed Dial #2: Hugh.* I wished my hotel was a little closer.

* * *

Rebekah and I left Maurice at her house to watch over the place and guard it from intruders. I pulled out the map Reuben had left, and in the time that it had taken me to plot an accurate course to Friday Harbor, Rebekah was already there. One benefit of living on a tiny island is that most roads will get you where you're going.

Friday Harbor was the biggest town in the entire complex of islands, but that wasn't saying much. It had a high school and a hardware store, but the majority of the lots were occupied by restaurants and real estate offices, obviously catering to tourists. At the waterfront, a marina—less picturesque than Roche Harbor's but larger and more active—housed boats of all sizes, as well as the ferry dock. Basically, Friday Harbor was on one side of the island, and Roche Harbor, where my hotel was, was on the other. Rebekah was somewhere in between—a mile and half (or so) from Roche, and probably eight or nine from Friday.

The sidewalks were dotted with tourists—fashion-unconscious parents, annoyed teenagers, and unruly, sugar-stained children—looking for souvenir visors and made-in-China Friday Harbor refrigerator magnets.

Naturally, Rebekah pulled right over—come rain, snow, sleet, or dark of night, the shopping must be done. I didn't complain too much—it was after eleven and my suit pants were just barely beginning to dry. Besides, I had something important to do in town.

The first store we entered was a moderately sized gift shop and video store, attached to a supermarket. Yet while the store technically sold both clothing and groceries, a Super Wal-Mart it wasn't. The prices were high, no doubt a result of shipping costs across the Puget Sound, and the selection was small.

I'd already plunked down my official FBI credit card to buy three logo T-shirts—one for Friday Harbor, one for San Juan Island, and one on the clearance rack from Butte, Montana—when Rebekah found me and told me about the real clothing store upstairs.

The clothes were definitely higher quality up there. For one thing, most didn't have logos, except for the most expensive, which traded souvenir place names for Tommy Hilfiger flags.

Rebekah insisted that I try everything on, which I did—very reluctantly, and only because I knew that I would then get to watch her model everything she was buying. She did, and I enjoyed every minute of it.

Eventually, we had to leave. It took about twenty-five minutes of walking, but we found Christy's Island Salon—only a block away from the clothing store. Rebekah squeezed my hand and paused at the door.

"It'll be okay," I coaxed.

"You don't understand," she answered, staring fixedly at the salon. "I've never had short hair. Ever since I was a little kid, it's always been long."

"I think you'll look good," I said, trying to be supportive, despite the fact that I found her wavy, blond hair one of her best features. "Which is not to say you don't look good now. You look good now. You'll look . . . I meant, you look *great* now. And you'll look great after . . . the . . . you know, with your hair." Unfortunately, I have trouble complimenting a woman's physical appearance. No problem appreciating it—just problems talking about it.

Rebekah grinned. "Really?"

"Oh yeah," I nodded emphatically. "Everything I just said—you can double it."

She smiled, her cheeks flushed.

"Triple it," I continued.

"If you say so," she said, worry dimming her sparkling eyes. "I'll see you in a couple hours?"

I looked at my watch. "I'll be back. We'll go to dinner or something."

"I hope you recognize me."

"You'll look beautiful."

She smiled warmly, the tiny dimple at the corner of her mouth appearing for an instant.

"Where are you going?"

"Oh, you know me," I said, glancing up and down the street. "Shopping."

* * *

Back in December, just when it was looking like the terrorists were going to win and we'd both go to jail, framed for several crimes we didn't commit, I thought Rebekah got shot in the back. I had good reason for it, of course. It's not like we were sitting around the dinner table and the notion just popped into my head. No, we were at the airport—the targets of a very large man carrying a very loud Uzi. Bullets were smashing into things all around us—windows, walls, floors, security guards. Even the Don't Joke About Bombs signs were getting shot up. Rebekah was running just ahead of me, scrambling to get out of the line of fire and into the shelter of a gift shop.

Suddenly a puff of white had erupted from her coat. She'd fallen to the floor, just behind a magazine rack.

I thought she was dead.

For those of you who haven't had that kind of thing happen before, imagine this: you're driving somewhere and you realize that you didn't turn in that year-end project at school. You then remember that you left the gas running at your house, and the birthday candles were still lit. Then you get pulled over. Do you have that image firmly implanted in your brain?

Watching Rebekah get shot in the back was absolutely nothing like that.

I felt like *I* had been shot, except it hurt worse than if I'd died. I felt like there was no point to anything anymore—all we'd done, every miraculous escape we'd made, and every drop of good fortune had been for nothing. It was a loss, a failure. I felt like standing up, walking over to the nice man with the Uzi, and telling him he'd missed a spot.

I didn't, of course. Rebekah was fine. The coat she was wearing was big and puffy, and the bullet had gone in and then out, leaving her unscathed.

And here we were, getting chased. Again.

So, when Rebekah went into the salon to get her hair cut and dyed—a desperate attempt to keep her alive—I didn't walk next door to Duke's Sporting Goods to check out the latest fishing rods. Instead, I walked a few blocks down the road, hung a left, and looked at jewelry.

Rings.

I'd seen the shop while we'd been driving and had decided it was the one. Once inside, though, I found nothing that really suited my tastes or Rebekah's. The jewelry was mostly made from beads and hemp. I didn't even know if that was legal.

I explained what I was looking for to the nose-pierced woman behind the counter, and she said there were no traditional jewelry stores on the island, but I might want to check the new antiques store around the corner. I made a fairly unfunny joke about new antiques. She pretended to think it was witty, and I left.

* * *

I cracked open the door to the antiques shop, the building looking like it was older than most of the wares—the hinges sounding twice that.

A female voice called out as I entered. "Hello?"

"Hi," I said, my eyes adjusting to the darkness.

"Just take a look around," she said. "Let me know if you have any questions." The shop was densely packed with furniture, books, lamps, and all sorts of other old things. The air smelled musty, like rotten wood and mildewed paper.

I scanned the cramped space for jewelry. There seemed to be no order to any of it.

"Are you looking for anything in particular?" A young woman appeared from the back room, tying her hair back into a ponytail as she walked. She looked at me and paused.

"Uh, yeah," I said, finding myself slightly embarrassed about discussing my engagement plans with a girl so near my age. "Jewelry."

She was staring at me.

"Jewelry," I said again. "Rings, actually."

"What kind?"

"Engagement." I must have turned a little red, because she politely tried not to smile.

"I have a few things," she said, weaving her way through the stacks of antiques to a small glass case by the window. Inside were four rings.

"This is the only solitaire," she said, pulling a ring from the case. The gold was tarnished with age, but the stone was huge. I didn't even bother asking the price. I had a little savings back home—money I'd use to reimburse the FBI for putting the ring on their credit card—but certainly not enough for that one.

For the same reason, I passed over the next as well—three smaller diamonds, though still undoubtedly pricey.

"What's her birthstone?"

"I don't know," I said. "Her birthday's the day after tomorrow."

Her face brightened. "Really? Perfect. June is a pearl." She reached into the case and withdrew the third ring—a small, shimmering pearl on a simple band. It wasn't much—certainly less than Rebekah deserved—but I gave my nod of approval.

"I purchased this at an estate sale just last week, over on Orcas Island," she said, carrying the ring to the counter. "It's over 120 years old."

"Really?"

She told me several more interesting facts about the ring's origin, its former owners, and the jeweler who'd made it. I nodded and occasionally added a "wow" when the conversation required. My mind, however, was far, far away from the antiques store.

I slipped the small, carefully folded paper bag containing the ring into my pocket, then I headed out the door to find Rebekah. She'd just come out of the salon as I turned the corner and was looking up the street toward me. I'd never envisioned Rebekah with anything but the long golden locks I had come to adore, but even with her new short, dark hairstyle, she was stunning. After spending the rest of the afternoon and evening exploring the quaint little town together, I drove Rebekah home, fired up Maurice, and drove back to the hotel, envisioning the moment when I would present the ring to the love of my life.

CHAPTER 6

Sᴜɴᴅᴀʏ ᴍᴏʀɴɪɴɢ ᴄᴀᴍᴇ bright and early. Though the sun didn't rise outside my window, it rose in what I had figured was the northwest. I've always considered myself to have a better-than-average sense of direction, but I realize now that that was based on my use of landmarks; in Utah I only needed to look for the mountains. Out on the island, the biggest landmark, the water, could be seen in every direction. I decided I probably ought to invest in a compass.

I took my small travel bag, which contained everything I owned, and headed for the bathroom. The shower was occupied. Instead of going back to my room and waiting my turn, I snuck to the floor below and used their bathroom. Perhaps this was a perfectly acceptable thing to do, but I felt guilty the whole time, wondering if statisticians had calculated the exact ratios of hotel guests to showers, and if my trespass threw the whole system off balance. Some poor guy would be waiting all day for hot water just because of me.

But then, as I headed back up to my room, tripping over a six-inch bulge in the hallway carpet and catching myself on the out-of-plumb wall, I realized that no one who understood math could have been involved in the operation of this hotel.

The morning air was clean and fresh. I wasn't the first person up and about—the marina was already bustling, and I passed at least a dozen people as I strolled to the parking lot. Maurice was just where I'd left him—no one had picked him up and walked off. There was dew on the seat, which I tried to wipe off with my hand, but which I knew would leave a big wet mark on my backside anyway.

For some reason the air didn't smell salty. In books and movies, whenever people are near the ocean it smells salty, and people talk about the salty breeze or the salty taste in the air. Granted, we weren't technically on the ocean—we were on the Puget Sound—but even so, the Sound was saltwater. The air smelled good—clean and fresh—but I was expecting salt.

It took Maurice some coaxing to get him up the hill and out of Roche Harbor, but eventually he conceded, and we zipped the mile and a half over to Rebekah's house. Shortly before I slowed to turn onto her dirt drive, a bug flew in my mouth and I nearly choked and died.

Rebekah looked gorgeous, as usual, despite her now short, brown hair. She complained that her new skirt was in need of ironing—the furnishers of her mansion had apparently been unable to afford an iron after buying all the fine art and priceless antiques, and paying the electric bill for the heavy-duty power lines that fed into the house.

I guess she was right about the skirt, but I hardly thought it mattered, and I began to tell her so.

"Rebekah," I said as she closed the front door and walked down the steps toward me. "I . . . you . . ."

I had originally meant for that to be a real, honest-to-goodness sentence, complete with verbs and everything, but they never materialized.

She pressed a button on her car-key remote and the Honda headlights flashed. "What?"

"How are you?"

"Good." She opened the driver's-side door and climbed in.

I took the passenger seat. "Sleep well?"

She shrugged. "Not great. Not horrible, though."

I really should have made that first sentence work. The conversation would have gone much better.

"So . . ." I began, looking for something to say that was more interesting. "I think I swallowed a bug."

Rebekah offered a quick courtesy frown to show she felt terrible about it. "Was it a big bug?"

"Not like a butterfly or anything, but it was bigger than a gnat."

"Like a bee?" She turned the key in the ignition.

"Maybe, but I don't think it stung me. A fly maybe."

She grinned and sang, "I don't know why he swallowed that fly—perhaps he'll die."

"I just might."

"I'd prefer it if you didn't." She put the car in drive, and we wound our way up and out of Rebekah's private forest.

Despite Agent Reuben's warnings about anonymity in the Witness Protection Program, Rebekah and I had determined that we would still keep our ties with the Church. As vital as it was that we hide our identities, it was equally as vital that we hold onto the essentials. We needed protection, and the FBI could only do so much.

The branch building was set on the outskirts of Friday Harbor, tucked out of the way on a small, wooded hill. It was small—no more than a chapel and a handful of classrooms—looking very unlike the mammoth Utah churches I was used to. Still, there was something very comforting about the building.

The area's Church meetings were a little unusual. The San Juan Islands, by their very geography, make any kind of organization a logistical nightmare. The local chamber of commerce states that there are around 200 islands in the San Juans. Some claim that there are as few as 172, while others put the estimate near 700. Even if you go with the smaller number, however, home teaching has got to be a pain in the neck.

The meetinghouse was as normal a building as you ever saw. What made the branch stand out from other Church buildings was that there was a phone in the chapel.

Every Sunday, three other congregations on three other islands got together in members' homes, or at the local library, and connected to sacrament meeting via teleconference. It was a little disconcerting at first, but it also had a very stone-cut-out-of-the-mountain-without-hands feel.

Rebekah and I sat in the back of the chapel, hoping to remain unnoticed and uninterrogated, and we failed miserably. Almost everyone came up to us and shook our hands, introduced themselves, and invited us over to dinner. We reluctantly gave them our fake names, and, when asked about our backgrounds, tried to change the subject. I had seven different people explain the mechanics of teleconferencing Church meetings, just because it was the easiest way to get off topic.

That afternoon, we went back to Rebekah's house. I grilled some chicken, which tasted excellent, and I baked some potatoes, which I burned. We spent most of the afternoon on the back deck, staring at the water and talking. Her massive house was right on the edge of the water, and the three-tiered deck led down to the Puget Sound and a private floating pier. The water lapped against the rocky shore, and the birds chirped in the surrounding fir trees.

"What are we doing here?" Rebekah asked, gazing out at the water.

I reached over and took her hand. "Waiting, I guess."

"How long?"

"I don't know. Who knows how long they postponed Arbogast's trial."

"It could be months."

It could be years, I thought. Trials weren't nearly as speedy as advertised.

"Oh," she said, hopping up from her chair. "Hold on. I want to show you something."

Rebekah jogged up the steps and back into the house. She was only gone for a few seconds and handed me something when she returned. It was a small, triangular antique, made from metal and wood, no more than six inches on each side. Across the bottom was a row of letters—seemingly random—and at the top, centered on the peak of the triangle, was a tiny hand crank.

I looked up at her. "What is it?"

"No idea. It was on the mantelpiece. Look—the letters are interchangeable." She reached down and removed the first one—a *U.*

"So it's like some kind of Scrabble game?"

"I don't know," she shrugged, putting the *U* back. "But when you turn the crank, pins come out the bottom." She demonstrated, rotating the small handle. Just as she'd said, a series of small pins emerged from the letters—each no more than a quarter inch long.

"What's the point of that?"

"I was thinking maybe it's some old way of writing braille," Rebekah said, sitting down. "You arrange the letters to spell a word, then set it on paper and turn the handle. The pins punch a pattern in the paper."

"But there's only, what, twelve letters?"

She nodded. "I messed with it for a while yesterday, but couldn't get it to spell anything useful."

"We ought to take it on *Antiques Roadshow.* Maybe it's worth a million dollars."

Rebekah laughed and leaned back in her chair. "I doubt it."

I played with the letters for a few minutes, trying to make a word, but the choices were awfully limited. Finally, I held the triangle up and showed Rebekah my wordsmithery.

"*A Semi Fun Tipi?*" she said, smiling.

"You know," I answered. "It's a tipi, but it's not as fun as you'd hoped."

"Here," Rebekah laughed, motioning for me to give the machine to her. She rearranged the letters for several minutes before showing me her creation.

"*Fat I Minus Pie,*" I read. "What does that mean?"

"It's diet advice: 'Fat? I minus pie.'"

She set the triangle down and took a sip of lemonade.

"There's an antiques store in town," I said. "We ought to take it in there just to see. I mean, it's not like it's ours, but it'd give us something to do."

Rebekah nodded, gazing out at the Sound. "It's pretty here."

"Yes it is."

Eventually, the sky dimmed, the clouds lit up in brilliant reds and oranges, and the sun went down.

I think I might have proposed right there if I hadn't left the ring back at my hotel.

* * *

We began our exploration of the island the next day. Leaving the car at Rebekah's house, we walked up her steep drive and onto the main road. The forest was thick on both sides, the air was still and quiet, and we strolled happily toward the end of the road. I had no idea which direction we were going—I was still confused by the lack of good landmarks. The sun was high overhead, offering no clues as to which horizon it was headed to.

Every so often, we caught a glimpse of a house hidden deep in the woods, but the only real sign of Rebekah's neighbors was an occasional mailbox at the mouth of a dirt road. Eventually, a public path split off from the paved street, and Rebekah and I descended a rough slope to the water's edge. We were in a rocky, windblown cove.

"Have you noticed," I asked, "that the air doesn't smell salty?"

She paused briefly and sniffed. "Should it?"

"You always hear about how the sea smells salty. Here we are, on an island surrounded by water—"

"All islands are surrounded by water," she pointed out with a grin.

"Not islands in the street."

"Isn't that a Dolly Parton song?"

"Or islands in the kitchen."

The sun peeked out from behind a cloud, and Rebekah pulled her sunglasses down over her eyes. "It doesn't smell salty because this isn't the ocean?"

"Is that a question?"

"I thought you were going to explain why it doesn't smell."

"No—I don't know the answer," I said. "I was just commenting."

"Oh."

"You'd think, even though Puget Sound isn't the ocean, it's still saltwater—it ought to smell salty."

"There aren't a lot of waves," she offered.

"Does that matter?"

Rebekah shrugged and picked up a handful of small stones. She tossed one out into the shallow water and watched it sink. "How's your hotel?"

"Fine, I guess," I answered. That didn't sound happy enough, so I added, "It's fun to be in such an old building."

"Sorry I got the house."

"Are you kidding? The hotel's great. Teddy Roosevelt stayed there once."

One by one, Rebekah threw the rest of the stones, trying to hit a small piece of driftwood floating several yards from the shore. I sat on a rock and made a moderate effort not to gaze too long at the tiny dimple in her cheek, or at the eight inches of smooth, creamy skin between the cuff of her capri pants and her shoe, or at the way her tendons moved as she craned her neck.

She scratched an itch on her elbow and managed to make the action look both sophisticated and alluring.

I liked Rebekah.

Back in the good old days when my main concerns were trying to wake up on time and not fail statistics, back when terrorism was the furthest thing from my mind, I thought Rebekah was great. I remember staring at her every morning in class as she entered the room and took a seat a few rows ahead of me. I used to believe that she was some fairy-tale princess trapped in the dull existence of a college junior. My roommates told me it was infatuation. I told them that that word was not necessarily pejorative. And frankly, if I was infatuated back then, then I don't know what kind of Olympian, revolutionary kind of infatuation I was in now. Because now made my old infatuation look like mild interest—like the difference between really loving artichoke dip and really loving breathing.

Having hit the driftwood two out of fourteen times, Rebekah turned and motioned for me to follow her. We held hands and walked along the beach.

It wasn't a beach in the traditional sense—instead of sand and surfers, there were a lot of rocks and dead seaweed. My family had only two vacation spots: Disneyland, with an occasional visit to the beaches of southern California, and Disney World, with the occasional visit to the beaches of Florida. My mom was kind of a fanatic. Rebekah, who had traveled a considerable amount more than I, told me that sandy, warm beaches were the exception, not the rule. I told her that she spent too much time in England and not enough in Hawaii.

And then she went on and on about the beaches in India, and I wished that I had some interesting vacation experience to compare it to, but I didn't. So I told her about the time that my younger brother kicked Sleeping Beauty in the shin while we were waiting in line for Mr. Toad's Wild Ride.

The path led along the shoreline, past thick fir trees and ferns, to a large outcrop of mossy rock. Signs indicated that it was a popular place for clamming, though another sign said to only dig for clams if you intended to eat them. Since I intended nothing of the sort, I sat down on a log and admired the view. Rebekah sat next to me.

"I wonder where my mom is," Rebekah said absently, watching the water lap the rocks.

"Did you write a letter for her?"

Rebekah nodded. "I already mailed it to Reuben—I drove into town late last night. Did you send one?"

"Not yet. What am I supposed to say? I can't tell them where we are."

"Just say that you're safe and fine. Your mom will be dying to hear from you."

"I know. I need to."

Rebekah picked up a seashell and turned it over and over in her hand.

"Today's my birthday," she said.

"I know. I already sang to you." I'd arrived at her house early, with take-out pancakes from the café in Roche Harbor. I'd asked them to make a smiley face with the toppings, and they'd happily obliged. Maurice had built-in storage under the seat, but it wouldn't fit much more than an apple, so I was forced to hold the Styrofoam breakfast containers on my lap. When I got to Rebekah's house, I found that the bacon mouth had shifted over to one side and one of the blueberry eyes had disappeared completely—it looked more like a pirate than a smiley face. Still, I delivered the holiday breakfast, sang "Happy Birthday," and made her wear a party hat.

"It was beautiful singing, too," she said, laughing and bumping me with her shoulder.

"I try."

She tossed her seashell into the shallow water and picked up another. "Did you get me a present?"

"I already told you," I protested with mock indignation, "I bought you one back in Salt Lake. You can have it when we go home."

"What is it?"

"You'll have to wait and see."

"Are you serious?" Rebekah threw the second seashell, took my hand, and looked into my eyes. "You wouldn't tell *me?*" She batted her eyes playfully.

"Are you kidding? You're the last person I would tell." I let go of her hand and stood up.

I pretended that I was standing up because I was trying to avoid her feminine wiles. The truth, though, was that I was standing up because I didn't want her to notice how jumpy my knees were getting, and how much sweat was beading up on my forehead. I dug my hand into my pants pocket and wrapped my fingers around the ring.

"That's fine," she sighed. "I guess I don't need any presents. You only turn twenty-one once, but that's okay." She pretended to sniffle and wipe her eyes.

"Look on the bright side. Now you're old enough to drink."

"Or go on a mission."

"But probably not both." I pulled my hand out of my pocket, the ring clutched tightly in my fist.

She laughed. "Probably not."

"What makes you think I got you anything, anyway? Maybe I forgot, and you're just making me feel really stupid. That would sure make for an awkward situation."

"I know you got me something."

"How?"

She slipped her arm through mine, and we continued to walk the trail. "Because when I got my hair cut, you came back with a bag, and you didn't tell me what it was."

"If you must know, that was dental floss. I have gum disease. Thanks for bringing it up."

"Really?"

"Yes."

"Then why did the bag say 'Spring Street Antiques'?"

"You're certainly observant."

She grinned. "I try."

I stopped walking and turned to face her. "You probably wouldn't believe that it was antique dental floss?"

"No."

I was trembling.

"Rebekah?"

"Yes?" She waited, smiling and expectant. I don't think that I'd ever been so nervous.

I opened my hand and held up the ring. "Rebekah, will you marry me?"

She said yes, we moved to Fiji, and had seven kids—four girls and three boys—and an Irish Setter named Bandit.

At least, that's what should have happened.

CHAPTER 7

I HELD UP the ring for what seemed like decades, watching Rebekah's face go from pale to ashen to white. Her eyes bore into that little ring as though she was staring at the world's rarest species of cockroach—she was a frazzled mess of shock, intrigue, and horror.

"Eric, I . . ." She glanced up and looked in my eyes. I stared back, wondering how the sparkle had been replaced so quickly with panic, and what I was supposed to say next.

I didn't know what to say, so I kept on standing, holding the ring.

"It's just that . . ." she stammered, looking back at the ring. "I wasn't expecting . . ."

What was I supposed to do? Ask again? Put it back in my pocket and finish the hike?

"Can we sit down?" she asked, and immediately dropped to a large rock. It wasn't large enough for two, though.

I stood for a minute, still holding out the ring like an obedient but ignored butler. Rebekah stared at the ground.

"Here," I said, taking a step toward her. I took her hand and placed the ring in her palm.

She was visibly crying, though silently. I took a seat on a bumpy log, directly in front of her.

"It's beautiful," she said, her voice shaking. A big tear rolled down her cheek and hung for a moment on her upper lip. She wiped it away.

"Rebekah," I said, "I love you. I know that this isn't ideal—that nothing in our relationship has been ideal—but—"

"Eric," she said, her voice faltering. "I love you too. It's just . . ."

She slid the ring onto her finger. It might have been a half size too big, but I couldn't think of a more glorious sight. And then she took it off.

"What?"

Rebekah stood up, so I did. She wrapped her arms around my neck.

"Eric, I can't think of anyone I'd want to marry more than you," she whispered quietly in my ear, her breath hot. I hugged her back as though I'd never get another chance. "It's just that—I don't know—I just need to think."

Now, I'm no expert on gender relations, but I'd been thinking about my proposal every day for months—and I'd been told that women are much more likely to think about marriage than men. Why she would wait until right now to think about it, I have no idea. Of course, that's not what I said.

"That's fine," I assured her. "Take as much time as you need."

* * *

We walked home in a mostly awkward silence, and even though Rebekah held my hand almost the entire way, she stared at the ground. I kept thinking of things to say, but none of them sounded good, so I didn't. I felt like things were hanging in a precarious balance—if I tried tipping them one way, they might swing the other.

Even as we left the main road again, winding back down through the forest to her house, she remained quiet.

I had to let go of her hand to take the house keys out of my pocket, and the balance tipped.

"Can we talk?" she said quietly.

"Sure."

"Eric, I love you. I can't even tell you how much. I can't imagine being married to anyone else."

Maybe things were tipping in my favor.

"But," she continued, "I can't imagine being married at all right now."

"Why not?"

She shook her head. She was still holding the ring and playing with it between her fingers.

"Pearl is my birthstone," she said, changing the subject with a forced smile. Her cheeks were stained with tears.

"I thought you'd like it."

"Did you pay for it with the FBI card?"

I nodded. "But I have money in savings back home. I'm going to pay them back."

"It's beautiful."

We sat for a few more minutes. She looked at the ring from all sides, held it in both hands, but never slipped it back on her finger.

"Why not?" I asked again.

Rebekah exhaled loudly and wiped her eyes.

The fir trees around the house were thick and tall, keeping the driveway and front door in almost permanent shade. I wished for sunlight—anything that could give me a little hope.

"Eric," she said, "we're in the Witness Protection Program. People are trying to kill us. I want to marry you—I would love to marry you—but I can't right now. . . . I just don't want something to happen."

I put my arms around her. "Rebekah, I don't want to lose you."

"You won't."

We hugged for a long time. Rebekah cried. I did my best not to and almost managed. Finally, Rebekah let go and stepped back.

"Here," she said, holding out the ring.

"Keep it," I urged. "For now. Just think about it."

She nodded. "I will. I just need some time to pray and to think. Will you keep it for me?"

"You keep it," I replied. "It's yours."

Before she could reply, I turned and walked toward the house. "I need to get the keys to the moped. I left them on your table."

I unlocked the door, jogged inside, only half breathing. Things had not gone at all like I'd hoped. I'd played the scenario out in my head a hundred times, but it never occurred to me that she'd give no answer at all—neither a "yes" or a "no." In some ways, I felt like leaping for joy—she'd said that she wanted to marry me!—but in other ways I felt like my heart had been crushed and stomped on.

I grabbed the keys and headed back. When I got to the porch, Rebekah was standing next to Maurice.

"I'm just going to put the ring here," she called out. "I want you to keep it for me."

As she bent over Maurice and lifted up the seat to access the pint-size storage space underneath, there was a sudden flash of light, and I fell backward through the door. As my head hit the stone entry floor, I heard a pop—loud enough that my ears stung.

I sat up, gravel and leaves dropping to the ground in front of me. Maurice was gone, replaced by the scent of burning gasoline and a cloud of pungent, oily smoke.

Rebekah was gone too.

I scrambled to my feet and dashed down the steps. My head hurt and my ears were ringing, but I ignored them. I ran to where Maurice had been. I could see his carcass lying behind the Honda, twisted and black. The Honda was scratched up the side, its doors dented and windows cracked.

"Rebekah!" I yelled, but as soon as the name left my lips I saw her—lying on her side in the deep ferns by the side of the road.

She was still awake when I reached her, though just barely. I called out to her, yelled at her, held her face between my hands, and looked her in the eyes—demanding that she stay with me. But Rebekah quickly slipped from consciousness.

CHAPTER 8

I RAN INTO the house. Yanking the alarm instructions off the fridge, I pounded the panic code into the keypad by the front door, alerting whichever security team that something had happened. I then grabbed the phone, a bottle of water, and a stack of towels, and ran back outside.

I hit speed dial #1 as I ran. After one ring, Reuben answered.

"Agent Reuben?" I said, nearly shouting into the phone as I dropped back down by Rebekah's side.

"Eric?" he said, sounding groggy and confused.

"Yes," I yelled. "Get over here! Rebekah's hurt."

"Rebekah's hurt?" he repeated.

"Blown up. Exploded. Whatever the word is. Get over here and bring an ambulance!"

"Rebekah?"

"Yes," I snapped. "Is this connection bad? Rebekah's lying here on the ground, bleeding to death!"

Reuben swore, then assured me someone would come immediately. He told me to stay by the phone, then hung up.

Rebekah looked bad—worse through my eyes, which were tear-filled and burning. She was bleeding from everywhere. Her shirt and pants were splattered with red. I noticed a two-inch-long shard of jagged metal sticking out of her leg and guessed Maurice's shrapnel was the cause of most of her wounds. Her right forearm—the hand that had been holding the ring and that had opened Maurice's tiny storage space—was a mess of blood and burned skin.

I'd received the first-aid merit badge in Scouts. I'd even had to splint twisted ankles before and rescue a swimmer who'd gotten hypothermia during a lake swim, but all of my knowledge vanished. With each new wound—as I glanced from her bleeding forehead to her blistered fingers to the way her left leg was bent unnaturally beneath her—panic overcame me, and all rational thought was swept under the relentless tide of dread.

I had towels for applying direct pressure to wounds, but would I just be pushing the shrapnel deeper? Would pouring water on the burn help or hurt? I knew there was something I wasn't supposed to put on it—what was it? Did I raise her head or her feet? Did I move her at all?

I had no oil and I had no companion, but I knelt there in the ferns and gave her a priesthood blessing.

CHAPTER 9

IT WAS FOUR minutes by my watch until the paramedics arrived. It was an eternity of darkness and smoke and burns and blood.

I didn't bother trying to get our cover stories right, let alone our aliases. Before they'd even checked her pulse I was well into the description of what had happened, why I thought it happened, and who I thought placed the bomb.

"I once saw a paramedic give a sick guy an IV," I nervously told a policeman as we watched the two paramedics work. "Are they going to give Rebekah an IV? Would that help?"

"Hold on," he said, quickly assessing the situation and shouting commands into his radio.

"*IV* is an acronym," I told him. "It means 'intravenous.'" My heart was pounding, and I felt dizzy.

"Thanks," he said, nodding, and then crouched over the blackened remains of Maurice.

"*Intravenous* is derived from Latin," I continued. "It means 'in the veins,' or something like that."

"They've got it," a cop snapped. A paramedic pulled a syringe from the box.

"Getting a shot is like an IV," I said, rubbing my hand across my cloudy eyes. "But it's not intravenous, because it's not in a vein."

"Do you need to sit down?"

I told him I didn't. Then I passed out.

* * *

When I woke, everything was quiet and dark. The air was cool but not cold, and something was in my arm.

It took Herculean effort, but I lifted my head, focused on my right hand, and tried to get my brain to work. An IV.

I knew what that was.

I was in a hospital, in a bed. There was a table next to me, on which sat a big mug of water with a bendy straw, and on the far wall was a TV. A baseball game was on.

Mariners 3, Dodgers 2.

"Hello?" I said. My mouth was dry, and my tongue felt big.

There was a slight shuffling sound to my right. "Are you awake?" I turned my eighty-pound head and saw Agent Reuben standing up.

"The Mariners are winning," I said. Small talk was the best my brain could manage.

"The locals will be happy."

"I don't like baseball."

"How are you feeling?"

"Why am I in the hospital?"

"Shock. And you hit your head. You have a slight concussion."

I paused, piecing things together. "Where is Rebekah?"

Reuben rubbed his face and sighed. "She just got out of recovery. They've got her in the ICU."

"Recovery? She was in surgery?"

"This was her third. You've been here almost thirty-six hours."

"Where's here?" I sat up. My head spun.

"St. Joseph Hospital, Bellingham, Washington."

"How did we get here?" I swung my legs over the side of the bed. My feet were already cold, and the tile floor was freezing.

"Rebekah was airlifted," he said. "We requested this hospital specifically. The paramedics took you to the clinic in Friday Harbor, but then we asked them to move you out here—just to make security easier."

I slowly stood up.

Reuben looked confused. "Where are you going?"

"The ICU," I answered. I pulled the blood-pressure monitor off my finger and steadied myself by grabbing the IV pole.

"I don't think you should."

"Too bad." I took a tentative step. I didn't fall down and die, so I considered it a success.

"Here," he said, scrambling around me. "Let me call up there and see if you can go."

"Out of my way, Reuben." I pushed past him and opened the door just as a nurse appeared.

"Um . . . are you feeling better?" she asked, surprised.

"I'm heading up to the ICU."

"You can't right now. Let me get the doctor in here to see you."

Agent Reuben nodded to her and tapped his badge. "It's okay. We'll only be a minute."

She argued a bit, but eventually conceded on the condition Reuben push me in a wheelchair. I was halfway to the elevator before he caught up with me and made me sit.

"Tell me what happened," I said as we got in the elevator and Reuben pushed the button.

"There was a bomb. It was hidden inside your moped and linked to a radar detector."

"Radar detector?"

"Yep," he said. "It's an old trick of the Irish Republican Army. They'd connect explosives to a radar detector and hide them in a car. The victim could be driving around with the bomb for days before it went off. You'd be driving, and if some cop had his radar gun turned on—the bomb would detonate."

"Why?"

"It's fairly untraceable. They can set the bomb and leave. They'd be long gone before anything ever happened—out of the country, usually."

"So, some cop set a speed trap somewhere near the house, and it set off the bomb?"

Reuben nodded. "That's what was supposed to happen. Presumably to you, since Rebekah doesn't ever ride the moped. You'd be all alone, out on the highway, and the bomb would explode right under you. Scary, eh?"

I tried to act tough, but I couldn't think of anything courageous enough to say, so I just nodded.

"Not that Rebekah wasn't a target too. Our techies are tearing apart her car, looking for anything they can find. Of course, it doesn't matter now—she won't be going back to the island."

He rolled me down the hallway, past nurses and patients and waiting families. If what Rebekah had told me was true, she had spent exactly three days in the hospital in her entire life. First, when she was nine, she was in a skiing accident in Switzerland which landed her a hairline fracture in her lower leg. Her father was rich, so the doctors kept her under observation for two days. The other hospital visit came in the form of food poisoning while she was visiting her father in Pakistan in 1998. The Pakistani doctors pumped her stomach, and she slept off the event in an Islamabad clinic while her father went back to work.

And here she was, in the ICU, after three surgeries, because of me.

"Reuben?"

"Yes?"

"How is she?"

"See for yourself," he replied grimly. We turned the corner and entered the ICU. Reuben flashed his badge at the nurses' station and then again at the armed guard watching Rebekah's room.

Inside, the lights were out, leaving only the blue glow of computer monitors to illuminate her face. There was a bandage wrapped around her head, looking something like an exercise head-band. A thick square of gauze was taped to the left side of her neck, and a small, red spot had managed to soak through. She had a thin tube in her nose, and a thick pipe of heavy plastic in her mouth. Tape was all over her face, holding two tubes in place. Two smaller cuts—one on her chin and one across her cheekbone—were secured with butterfly bandages.

The rest of her body was covered in blankets, but I assumed it looked about like her face.

"Is she going to be okay?"

"The short answer is yes," he said. "Thankfully."

"The long answer?"

"The first surgery removed some of the shrapnel. The second was for her hand. I don't know what this last one was for. The prognosis is good, though."

"What's that tube in her mouth?"

"It helps with the breathing," Reuben said. "One common side effect of being close to an explosion is something the doctor called pulmonary barotrauma. In the army, they used to call it blast lung. The explosion creates a sudden, massive change in air pressure—it rockets up to incredible levels and then dips back down into a vacuum. The result is that any air-filled organ gets battered like a balloon under an elephant's foot."

"Her lungs don't work?"

"They will," he said, his voice not sounding as optimistic as his words. "Right now they're pretty bruised. She's lucky, though—the pressure change will usually cause a lot of other bad things—bowel perforations and a whole lot of painful stuff. So far, there's no sign of anything like that."

I sat there in my wheelchair and stared at her. It should have been me in that bed, with a tube down my throat and a perforated bowel, whatever that was. Someone had tried to kill me, but had hurt Rebekah instead.

Reuben laughed sadly. "She got a haircut."

"A lot of good it did her."

* * *

We returned the wheelchair to the nurses, and Agent Reuben went down to the cafeteria to get some dinner. I walked back to my room, nodded to the guard standing watch, and crawled back into bed.

I think I would have lain there and bawled if I hadn't found someone sitting in the chair next to me.

CHAPTER 10

I KNEW HIM instantly, not because of the one time I'd met him before—he'd done his best to change his appearance considerably—but because I'd been looking into those eyes every day for the last six months. Rebekah's eyes—eyes that her mom said she'd inherited from her father.

He'd shaved the goatee, which made him look younger than the last time I'd seen him, and he'd dyed the gray out of his hair. He still wore the same coat he'd worn back in December—a long, gray trench coat that looked like it had seen too much wear.

I stared at him for several seconds, and he stared right back, his face unreadable.

"A trench coat in May?"

The side of his mouth broke into a grim smile—revealing the same dimple his daughter had. I wanted to punch him in the teeth for having the same genes as someone so innocent.

"You remember me," he said.

"It's not an easy thing to forget. You, a big shiny gun, and a dead man on the floor."

"He had a gun in your stomach before I shot him."

"Sorry I didn't send a thank-you card."

He paused, thinking. The half grin and dimple remained on his face, but there wasn't any humor in his eyes.

I reached over and picked up the big mug of water. "How did you get past the guard?" I took a long suck on the straw. The water tasted like it had been sitting there the entire thirty-six hours, but I pretended like it was excellent, and like I wasn't at all bothered that my girlfriend's terrorist father was sitting next to me.

"Fake ID," he replied, as though I was absurdly stupid for not knowing the answer. "Homeland Security is such a mess—nobody knows who has jurisdiction over anything. Wear a high-ranking badge and look like you know what you're doing, and you can go anywhere."

I took another sip.

"How did you know we're here?"

He shook his head. "What you should be asking is why I came."

"That's easy," I said. "Your daughter got blown up and nearly died because you and your buddy are trying to save the world."

"My buddy?"

"Felix Hazard."

"Ah."

He leaned back in the chair and thought. He wasn't at all like I'd expected. His voice was soft, his demeanor calm. His face was lined and careworn; I imagined that running a terrorist organization could be a real hassle sometimes.

"Do you know why you've been living on the island, and why Rebekah is now in the ICU?"

"'Cause Felix is trying to stop us from testifying against Paul Arbogast."

"Are you joking?" His face remained unchanged.

"Uh . . . no."

"Do you remember Felix at all?"

"More than I'd like to."

"Do you remember David, the tall man who ran the counterfeiting operation in Utah?"

I used to call him Wool Coat, not David, but I knew him. "Yeah. He smelled like bananas and cigarettes."

"What happened to him?"

"He chased us into the airport. He tried to kill us. The police shot and killed him."

"Do you think that Felix expected David to survive that attack? Do you think he told him to go into an airport—with increased security since September 11—and shoot up the place, and somehow thought he'd manage to escape?"

I shook my head and took a sip from my mug. I wished I had some other way to look calm and relaxed, but I was lying in a hospital bed. The mug was it.

"Felix doesn't mind that Paul Arbogast is going to jail. Felix won't shed a tear if Arbogast is sentenced to life—or death. In a secret society, you're only worth anything if you're secret. What good would Arbogast do for the N.O.S. if he was acquitted? The FBI would still watch him like a hawk. No, he has served his cause faithfully, and he's dutifully going to prison. Felix expected nothing less."

"But," I said, defensively, "if he wasn't trying to stop us from testifying, then why *is* he trying to kill us?"

"Revenge." Edward Hughes spat out the word, and it echoed a few times around the room.

"For what? He won."

"He beat you, true. His counterfeiting attack has begun and has been going strong. But he didn't win."

"Why not?"

"Because it's *not* working."

He paused, waiting for me to speak, but I decided to just let him go right on talking. I had nothing intelligent to contribute.

"He and I hatched that plan—you are aware that I was involved?"

I nodded.

"We came up with it back in 1982. We were young idealists who turned to the KGB, not because it offered anything, but because we needed an outlet. It was the system we hated. But the Soviet Union was a joke—it advertised socialism and delivered bureaucracy. We invented a way to achieve true equality—Novus Ordo Seclorum—'A new order of the ages.'" He smirked, as though something he'd said was funny.

"The counterfeiting," I said. "Isabella explained that to me. Release huge amounts of fake money into the economy, businesses will stop accepting cash, and the people will lose faith in the dollar."

"And since the dollar is only worth what we think it is, the entire country goes bankrupt."

"But the plan seems to be working just fine. The economy's in a slump."

Edward nodded thoughtfully and then continued. "Consider how long ago we came up with that plan. Did you know that, since 1982, the use of credit cards has increased almost 1500 percent? VISA had only been in existence for four years—and virtually no one had heard of debit cards. We never anticipated that type of revolutionary change in the economy. The truth is, Felix's attack is already failing. It was doomed from the start."

"No," I objected, confused. "Don't you watch the news? Some small businesses have already failed. The dollar is at its lowest value in decades."

He put a finger to his chin. "But do you think the economy will collapse any time soon? In the next few months?"

"No, but if things keep going the way they're headed, it could collapse within a year. At least, that's what they said on CNN."

Edward smiled—the first full-on smile he'd shown since we'd been talking. It wasn't a joyful smile, though. It was the happiness that comes from satisfied revenge. "First, Eric, you need to realize that CNN is a waste of time. They report whatever is sensational and shocking. If there is some horrible change in the economy, they'll talk about it and interview factory workers who have just been laid off. But the next day they'll be more worried about a celebrity trial or a meaningless rise in gas prices. It gets them ratings. The worst thing a news agency could report is that everything is fine and there's nothing to worry about. As much as people complain about negativity in the media, nobody wants to watch good news. It doesn't sell."

He glanced down at his watch, his smile fading. "The second thing you have to remember about CNN is that they know nothing. Sure, there's occasionally some plucky reporter who will uncover a real fact, but ninety-five percent of what makes it on the news comes from carefully crafted press releases. Everybody—businesses, law enforcement, government—they all decide exactly what is going to make it into the news."

"So the real news is that the economy is fine, and that we're all worrying too much."

Edward shook his head. "The real news is that the economy won't fail. Felix's attack won't lead to complete anarchy, and it can never lead to total economic equality. However, there will be a depression to make 1929 look mild."

"So he wants to kill me just because of that?"

Edward sighed as though the weight of the world was on his shoulders and he wanted me to know it.

"To some extent, that's true. As you know, Felix is not exactly even-tempered, and he doesn't forgive grudges. He's an ideologue, and people don't become ideologues by compromising. But, on the other hand, you two—you and Rebekah—were and are just pawns. Felix was only interested in you by association, and he only pursues you because of Rebekah's relation to me."

"He's after us because of you?"

Edward took another look at his watch and stood up. "Felix doesn't like you, but he hates me. You may have messed up his plans, but he knows that I'm going to stop them completely. Instead of being intelligent, he thinks that killing Rebekah will dissuade me from doing what I need to do. He's wrong."

"Wrong about what?"

He didn't answer but straightened his tie and ran his hands over his tired face. "I haven't been able to see her. How does she look?"

"Not good. She's had a lot of stitches. Three surgeries. She has a breathing tube."

Edward grimaced and rubbed his eyes. He suddenly looked very old.

"They told me she should heal completely," I said. "Other than some scars. The doctors are optimistic."

"He almost killed her."

"He was trying to kill me."

Edward shook his head. "This isn't your fault, Eric. Don't think that it is. You've never done anything but try to protect Rebekah." He walked to the window and peered out through the blinds. "No, Eric, this isn't your fault at all. Felix is to blame for what happened to Rebekah. He ordered that the bomb be planted, using something as indiscriminate and random as a radar detector. He didn't care who he killed—you, her, it didn't matter." He turned and took a step toward the door.

"Where are you going?"

"I'd like to take a look at my daughter. Although I doubt I will be able to."

"What's to stop me from telling the police you were here? The FBI will be back in a minute."

"Why would you tell them?" He was looking at the door, not at me.

"You're Public Enemy Number Two, next to Felix."

"Have I ever done anything to hurt you? Or Rebekah?"

"No."

"And, on the contrary, have I done everything for you? Did I send Isabella Hakopian to offer assistance? Did I expose myself to world-wide defamation when I saved your life?"

He turned and looked at me, his face calm, but with a fiery anger in his eyes. "Under the watchful eye of the Federal Bureau of Investigation, my daughter was nearly killed. She's under my care now. I'll be watching, and nothing like this will happen again."

* * *

Agent Reuben returned carrying a blue cafeteria tray loaded with a sandwich and chips. He dropped it on the table and then fell into the chair. I sat silently, watching him. He hardly paid any attention to me. Instead, he wearily rubbed at his eyes and the bridge of his nose.

I could tell him. I could spill the beans right here. Edward hadn't been gone for more than two minutes, and there was a good chance they might find him. The hospital had security cameras; they could play back the tapes and discover which doors he'd used. They could watch his movements and trace him back to a vehicle—maybe get his license plate number and have police all across the state looking for him. They'd set up roadblocks at the Canadian border and watch the airports. I could tell Reuben right now.

Agent Reuben yawned loudly and turned to face me. His face was pale, and his lips were pursed thoughtfully. He began digging in the pocket of his suit coat. "Take a look at this." He extracted a sealed plastic bag and tossed it to me.

It was nothing special. A spark plug, and a small one at that. It was worn and scratched, and obviously old, but there wasn't much to set it apart from any other spark plug I'd ever seen.

"What?" I asked, turning it over and over in my fingers. It was about an inch long.

"During Rebekah's first surgery," he said, his voice emotionless, "the doctors took that out of her abdomen. It nicked her liver."

I gazed at the chunk of metal that had previously been a vital component of my moped and tried unsuccessfully not to think about the kind of force needed to launch a spark plug like a bullet.

Reuben rubbed his face again and stared at me. I saw something almost like compassion in his eyes. Finally, he stretched his neck and began unwrapping the plastic off his sandwich.

I set the spark plug on the table and stared at it for a long time.

CHAPTER 11

I SPENT ALMOST two weeks in the hospital, despite the fact that I pretty much felt fine. I still had the occasional headache, and I'd get dizzy if I stood up too quickly, but I was in far better shape than everyone else in the surrounding rooms. The nurses still came in once an hour and asked if everything was okay. I'd say yes and they'd leave, probably wondering why the doctor was refusing to release such a healthy patient.

Agent Reuben explained that the FBI's resources were limited, that it was easier for them to keep an eye on us while we were both in the same hospital than if I left and Rebekah stayed. I would have thought that our funding would receive a boost, since their previous methods obviously weren't working; apparently not. But Reuben assured me that changes had been made that would provide for a little better help. If there was one good thing to be said about the FBI, they'd done a good job of damage control. There was nothing on the news about the attack in Salt Lake, and there wasn't even much talk about Rebekah and I being gone. I'd watched CNN eight hours a day in the confines of my hospital room, and I'd only heard our disappearance mentioned twice, and both times the commentators cited it as a wise decision on the part of law enforcement that we'd been taken into the Witness Protection Program. The FBI representative was still tight-lipped, refusing to even talk about Rebekah and me.

I knew, though I didn't tell Reuben, that there was a second security team—provided by Edward Hughes—watching us now. Whatever else that could be said about Edward, I didn't doubt his ability to protect his daughter. The FBI was restricted by legal limitations; Edward didn't have to worry about that kind of thing.

Normally I would care about that, but this was Rebekah.

If there was one benefit of staying in the hospital, it was that my beard was coming in a little bit better. It had finally made it past the maddeningly scratchy stubble stage—and was slowly becoming a longer, softer beard. Reuben asked me to dye it, and I told him no.

Rebekah had woken up the day after I had. Since she still had the breathing tube in, they kept her sedated most of the time. My days were spent sitting by her side, watching the lights flash on machines, holding her hand, and waiting for any sign of change while CNN droned on and on. The doctors told me they were pleased with her recovery, but I really didn't know what to make of that. In a hospital, good news was relative.

Eight days after the attack—three days after I'd even had so much as a headache—the doctors removed Rebekah's breathing tube. Unfortunately, they kicked me out of the room to make room for her pulmonary team and all of the FBI agents who wanted to hear her first words. Five hours later, I finally got to see her.

When the nurse led me back into the room, I immediately noticed that the bandage had been removed from Rebekah's head, revealing a thin red wound just above her eyebrow. The rest of her forehead was dotted with tiny pink spots. Her hair, needless to say, was a matted mess, having been flattened against her skull for over a week. There was still tape residue on her cheek and upper lip from the various tubes that had been removed. She smiled, and I've never, in all my life, been more grateful for anything.

"Hi," I said, taking her hand and sitting down on the stool next to her.

"Hi." Her smile was warm but her voice almost nonexistent.

"How do you feel?"

"Been better."

"What did the doctors say?"

"You know more than me," she answered. Her voice was so soft she was practically mouthing the words. "My lungs are pretty bad. It hurts to breathe."

"You don't have to talk."

She smiled again, a tear running down her ashen cheek. I squeezed her hand.

"The doctors are optimistic," I said, feeling tears well up in my own eyes. "You have the lung problem—you know that. It could last for a few weeks or a few months. For now they want you to rest and relax—you probably shouldn't be going jogging anytime soon."

We both forced a laugh at that comment, and she mouthed, "No jumping jacks."

"You had some bleeding in your abdomen that could have been a lot worse than it was. You had a bunch of stitches—I don't know how many—because they repaired your liver and I don't know what else. They said that all of that should heal perfectly—no problems."

She nodded, bracing herself for the bad news. "What about my hand?" She raised her right arm slowly off the bed. Thick, white gauze still covered everything up to her elbow.

I took a deep breath. Rebekah was a concert violinist—not something you can do with one hand. "I don't know. Your hand got the worst of it. The doctor told me that the explosion kind of tore the skin, so the burns got deep down in the muscle. They're going to keep a close eye on it, but there'll be scar tissue, and it'll probably affect movement in your fingers and wrist."

She paused for a long time. She was fighting back tears. Finally, she squeezed my hand one more time and smiled. "I'm glad you're okay."

"Your hand will get better," I assured her, and then, straining to find something more comforting to say, I lowered my voice. "And we'll both be okay from now on, Rebekah. We have more than the FBI watching us now."

"Who?"

"We probably shouldn't talk about it much," I whispered. "But your dad was here. He said that he's going to make sure the N.O.S. stays far away."

She didn't say anything.

"Look," I continued, repeating the arguments that Edward had used on me. "We don't know anything about him or what he does. All we know is that he's always protected you. He sent Isabella."

Rebekah sighed and leaned back into the pillow.

"I love you, Rebekah. We're going to be okay."

She just nodded.

* * *

The next day I left the hospital. Reuben and I drove back to the island. In Anacortes, a small town on the mainland, we boarded a ferry that took an hour to reach Friday Harbor.

I was heading back, he told me, simply to wait. Rebekah's condition had been downgraded and her release was imminent. I was supposed to wait in the house until they could find a more suitable place. I protested, of course. The house couldn't have been all that safe, given the fact that we'd nearly died there, but Reuben assured me I'd be fine. As long as I stayed inside, he said, no bomb could hurt me—it was essentially a bunker.

It was strange going back. The driveway was clear and clean—there was no sign of the Honda Civic or of Maurice's remains. Reuben's motorcycle was parked near the front door, and we pulled in next to it.

"So," I said, as we approached the door. "I just wait?"

"You just wait."

He unlocked the massive front door and let me in. Closing it behind me, Reuben pressed a few buttons on the security keypad.

"The pantry's stocked, so you don't have to go buy any food, and the house is secure."

"I have a hard time believing that."

"Eric," he sighed. "I know that you guys got attacked here, but I promise you'll be fine in the house. This building has been owned by the FBI for decades, and it's much more than just a house. Did you notice that during the explosion none of the windows broke? The glass is bulletproof—two inches thick. There's sensory equipment all over the place in here."

"Really?"

He nodded. "We blew it with the moped—that's our fault. But I guarantee this house is safe. We know what we're doing."

* * *

I spent six days doing exactly what I had originally planned when we first came to the island—I lay around in the big family room, doing nothing. In the hospital I'd bought a book of crossword puzzles—I'd narrowed it down to that or a Gameboy—and I figured I could use the downtime to improve my vocabulary.

Feeling somewhat literary, I pulled the antique Scrabble triangle off the mantelpiece and played with it again. I didn't come up with anything better this time around. *Pa Unifies Tim* was one variation of which I was particularly proud, because *unifies* is a big word. But I didn't think Pa could unify Tim, since Tim was one person—already unified.

I never got anywhere with it, but I kept it by my bedside and fiddled with it every night before going to sleep. And I usually fell asleep quickly.

I was thoroughly impressed with the house and its amenities— being the kind of luxurious estate it was—and I found myself spending a lot of time outdoors on the three-tiered deck. The top deck had the barbeque and a hot tub, which I wished I could try out. The second had a table with a big umbrella, and the third was empty. And more often than I should have, I wandered down there to watch the water. From that deck, stairs ran down the steep hillside to the water below to the narrow pier that extended out into the Sound—just in case the government gave Rebekah a boat to go along with her mansion and car.

At night I watched TV. CNN kept right on with its explanation of the failing economy and the drooping dollar, but still never mentioned Rebekah or me, and the fact that she had nearly died.

On my seventh day back on the island, I got a phone call. I clambered off the couch, careful not to overturn the bowl of guacamole that had been resting on my stomach, and turned down the volume on the TV. Whoever was on the phone, I didn't want them to know I was watching reruns of *Charles in Charge*.

"Hello?" My corn chips were mostly crumbs, so I crumpled the bag and threw it in the trash.

"Eric." Like every other phone call I'd received in the past week, it was Agent Reuben.

"Oh, hi. How are you?"

"Eric. What've you been doing today?"

"Not much. I'm thinking of taking up gardening. Any idea where I can get a cheap tiller?"

"You're kidding."

"Yes."

"Great."

Cradling the phone between my shoulder and ear, I walked to the cupboard and pulled out a new bag of tortilla chips. I don't think I'd eaten anything remotely healthy since I'd left the hospital.

"Any word on the bomber?"

"Yes," he said, lowering his voice. "But if I tell you, it doesn't mean you can ignore all the security precautions."

"Of course not."

"They've traced him to a small town in eastern Montana. We have high hopes."

"It's a him?"

"To be honest, I hadn't thought of him being anything other than a him."

"But could it have been a her?" I dipped a chip in the guacamole, but it broke in the bowl and I had to messily fish it out.

"It could have been, I guess, but it isn't. It's a him. They have his picture on the security cameras from the ferry dock."

I licked the green dip off my fingers. "How did you trace him?"

"He came to the island in a rental car—a silver Lexus. We got the plates, found the car, and traced him."

"That's stupid."

"Most terrorists are. He used a fake ID but had to reserve the car with a credit card. He wasn't hard to find."

"So you have him?"

"Almost. He was seen in town, and we're staking out several of his old hangouts."

"But you're not worried?"

"Like I said, this doesn't mean that you ought to shave your beard and get your picture in the newspaper."

"Who is it?"

"That's classified."

"You just told me how you found him, where you're looking for him, and how you're going to catch him. So just his name is classified?"

"Eric," he said, sounding a little annoyed, "I didn't call you to talk about him. Listen, I'm going to hand the phone off. This is doctor's orders."

"Huh?"

There was a brief static on the other end, and I heard muffled voices. I used the opportunity to take a quick sip of water.

"Eric?"

It wasn't Reuben's voice. On the contrary, it was the only voice that would make my mouth drop and dribble water down my shirt.

"Rebekah?"

Her voice was soft and raspy, and her words were punctuated with a faint, high-pitched wheeze. "They don't want me to talk much."

"No kidding," I said, sitting down on the tile kitchen floor because my legs just didn't feel like functioning anymore. "You don't have to talk if it hurts—I'll come see you. I'll leave right now."

"Agent Reuben says you can't," she said, her voice cracking.

"Are you okay?"

She was crying. Breathing problems or not, I could hear the tears in her voice. "I'm okay."

"Does it . . . I . . . When can I see you?"

"Soon, they told me."

"I'm going to talk to them. I'll come and see you."

"The doctor says I have to hang up."

"I'm glad you called."

"Me too."

Agent Reuben came back on the line. "Eric?"

"Still here," I sighed. "I'm going to head over there."

"No, you're not."

"Why not?"

Reuben gave me all sorts of reasons, and I rebutted them all. Eventually, it all boiled down to Reuben repeating the words: "It's not my decision." Regardless, I was standing by the front door, keys in hand, ready to hop on his motorcycle and leave. The only thing that stopped me was Reuben's final admonition: if—and there was a slim possibility—the N.O.S. was watching me, then I would simply lead them to Rebekah. It wasn't a great reason, it had a lot of logical holes, and I could have easily argued. But I didn't.

Even so, I left the house. Renewed by a sense of safety (with the FBI hot on the bomber's trail) and a desire to do something Rebekah-related, I went outside to search for the ring.

The work was slow and ultimately unproductive. The house was surrounded by dense forests with uneven, rocky terrain. And I had no idea how far the explosion had thrown the ring. Still, I searched on my hands and knees for the better part of two hours. Eventually, a light rain began to fall.

I went inside to look for a raincoat. I walked downstairs, and downstairs again—the house actually had four levels—and began looking around. The first closet I opened was filled with extra blankets and pillows—in case the protected witnesses had big slumber parties, I guess. The second was stocked with emergency supplies, which made more sense. Not only were there first-aid kits and hundreds of bottles of water, there was a small defibrillator hanging on the wall.

The third and final closet, in the back of a spare bedroom, held what I needed—coats. Parkas, windbreakers, lambskin coats, and anoraks hung from the closet rod, and boxes lined the floor. I browsed through the selection, trying to decide which one looked the most waterproof.

As I was standing to leave, one of the parkas fell from where it hung, revealing a door. I had a hunch that Narnia was behind it somewhere.

I shoved all of the coats out of the way to get a better look at the heavy, steel vault. Just like the front door of the house, it was decorated with birds and plants, all molded into the cold metal. A big, fat owl sat in the center, perched on a block of stone.

There was no doorknob, just a small ten-key electronic pad on the wall. I messed with it for a minute—trying the authorization code for the alarm system—but nothing happened.

Agent Reuben had said there was sensory equipment all through the building—maybe there was more than that. After all, it was the government.

The rain was getting heavier, and I had a ring to look for. I pulled on a windbreaker and jogged back upstairs. The Lion and the Witch would have to wait.

CHAPTER 12

I NEVER FOUND the ring. I spent five hours on the muddy hillside, but found only two signs of the explosion. Half of the moped's headlight was resting under a fern, and a small chunk of metal was lodged in the trunk of a tree.

Two days later Reuben came to visit. He didn't say much, and I pestered him with question after unanswered question. The most I could get out of him was that it was time to go. I scooped up my clothes and all of the outfits Rebekah had bought herself in Friday Harbor, and her violin, and we left.

We took the ferry to Anacortes, and then drove inland, but instead of turning north toward Bellingham and the hospital, we turned south toward Seattle. Something was on Reuben's mind, but he wasn't saying anything.

Reuben pulled the car into the airport.

"Where are we going?" I said for the hundredth time.

Silence.

"We're going to the next place we're hiding?" I suggested. "Where's Rebekah?"

Nothing.

"Is she out of the hospital?"

Reuben sighed. "Eric, you're a good kid."

"What's that supposed to mean?"

* * *

It was a private jet—similar to the one we'd flown in on, but it looked a little sleeker and more expensive. Reuben carried the bag with Rebekah's clothes, and I carried mine. We climbed the steps.

Agent McCoy was right inside the door.

"Hello again," I said, confused.

"Eric."

He pointed for me to continue down the length of the plane.

It looked far more expensive on the inside. The seats were plush and leather, with lots of leg room. There were some separate rooms in the back of the plane, it appeared, and McCoy directed me to sit at what looked like a conference table in the center.

"Where are we going, McCoy?"

"Hold on a minute."

I waited.

I actually waited for forty-five minutes before anyone returned. Peeking out the windows, I could see the ground crew getting the plane ready for takeoff.

Finally, another vehicle arrived—a Cadillac with tinted windows. The door opened.

Huh?

A man came up the stairs and boarded the plane. I panicked. *Should I tell Reuben or McCoy?* Wait—they were talking to him already. Did they know who he was?

He entered the room, smiling apprehensively, as though he was well aware of how strange this appeared.

I stared at him. "Edward."

"Eric."

I glanced at Reuben, who was standing back by the door. He looked back at me but didn't respond. McCoy sat down at the table with us.

Something was seriously wrong. "What's going on, guys?"

Reuben stepped outside and then popped his head back in. "Mr. Hughes—they're here."

I looked out the window.

A van. Out climbed two women. They helped a third out—Rebekah.

I looked back across the table. "Edward, what are you doing?"

He glanced out the window and then looked at his watch. "Early."

I stood and hurried to the window, watching as Rebekah was helped out of the van. One of the women was dressed as a nurse, and the other wasn't—she was in a business suit. I looked at her closely. Dark hair, olive skin, scowl. Isabella Hakopian.

CHAPTER 13

REBEKAH WAS AWAKE, but barely. The nurse explained that the doctors wanted her sedated for travel.

The nurse and I helped her to the back of the plane, where a room was already equipped with a bed and medical equipment. I sat next to her for a while, because she was real and alive and I loved her, and outside the door were three men and one woman I could never begin to understand. Sitting next to Rebekah grounded me in reality. The rest of the plane was like some kind of elaborate joke.

"Rebekah?"

She opened her half-closed eyes and turned her head to look at me. She was lying in the bed, propped up by a mountain of pillows—under her back, neck, arms, and knees.

"Eric," she said, her voice incredibly soft. She broke into a wide grin. Her face was speckled with tiny cuts, and a larger one—the one forming a scar, pink and smooth—crossed from her eyebrow up to her hairline.

"Are you okay?" I sat as gently as possible on the edge of the bed and took her hand—her left hand. Her right hand was still wrapped in bandages.

Rebekah nodded, her thumb stroking mine.

"We're leaving," I said. "I don't know where we're going."

She nodded sleepily.

I held her hand and stared into her eyes for several minutes, just breathing her in. She was scarred and pale, and I could tell just by looking at her face that she'd lost a lot of weight—not that she had much to lose. But I could see in her eyes that she was the same Rebekah. I loved her. And I told her.

"I love you too," she whispered. She squeezed my hand and then tried to turn and move a few of the pillows. I stood to help her, and then she motioned for me to sit down in the newly created space next to her.

Rebekah cocked her head and grinned. "Your beard's getting really thick."

"I hate it," I said, sitting down next to her.

"Me too." Her voice was barely audible.

"What do you remember?" I asked. Without the pillows, she shifted some of her weight and leaned on me. I could have spent the rest of my life just like that.

"Remember?"

"About the accident." We'd only had a handful of chances to talk since the explosion, and the subject of my proposal had never come up. I'd been reluctant to mention it, since the last thing she needed right now was added pressure, but I kept hoping she'd say something.

"Nothing," she said, shaking her head. "They've told me a little, but the last thing I actually remember was talking to you. Agent Reuben told me that there was a bomb in your moped."

She completely ignored the proposal, and I let her. There'd be more time.

"Right," I nodded grimly. "The bomb was meant for me. Sorry."

She smiled. She would have laughed if she'd had an ounce more energy. "Where were you?"

"I was in the house," I said, guilt dripping from every word. "Getting my keys. I got knocked down, but that's all. It should have been me."

"No."

"Have they told you what's going to happen?"

"You mean about transferring?"

I frowned. "They told you that you were being transferred?"

"Isn't that where we are now?"

"Didn't you see who was in the other room?"

She looked confused. The medicine was taking over. "I don't really remember."

It could wait, I decided. I couldn't explain something that I didn't understand.

I changed the subject, watching her eyes cloud over. "How do you feel?"

She exhaled loudly and forced a smile. "It hurts . . . a lot. That's the main thing. It hurts everywhere. My stomach, my legs . . ."

"Will you be . . ." My voice faltered. "I mean, can you walk?"

"Yes," she answered. Her eyes were closed. It was like she was on autopilot. "My left leg hurts to walk—" She let out a little laugh, her first real laugh. "I don't like to, but I can."

"What about your hand?"

Her eyes opened a sliver, and she raised her right arm off the bed.

"Is it bad?" I asked.

"It hurts," she said.

"Will it get better?"

She made a motion with her head that might have been a nod, but might have just been her dozing off. She was asleep.

I heard the engines start, and we all strapped into our seats—there were two chairs in Rebekah's room. The nurse and I stayed.

Rebekah was asleep before the jet got off the ground. An hour into the flight, McCoy appeared at the door.

* * *

Edward sat across from me, his legs crossed comfortably as he sipped a drink. I had a drink in front of me as well—water—brought by Agent Reuben, who didn't look happy to be serving drinks. McCoy sat at the table next to Edward, while Reuben sat comfortably in a chair at the end of the room. Isabella, looking a little paler than the last time I'd seen her, sat next to McCoy.

I didn't drink my water. I let it sit on the table, watching beads of condensation form on the outside of the glass, hoping that one of them would run down over the edge of the coaster and stain the tabletop. That'd show him.

"I'm sure you have a few questions," Edward said, smiling smugly.

I shrugged my shoulders. "I don't know what to ask, Edward. This is kind of like being told, 'Your entire world is a lie. Any questions?'"

Edward took a quick drink and then rested the glass on his leg. "I've been watching you, Eric. You're a smart kid. I'm sure you've figured out some of this tale already."

"Why don't you just start at the beginning?"

He frowned and rubbed his chin. "It's a long story."

"Then just explain the following: Where are we going? And why does the FBI not seem to want to arrest you? Are *you* in the FBI?"

Reuben laughed. Edward smiled condescendingly. "I am not, nor have I ever been affiliated with the FBI."

Confused, I cocked my head. "Well, you're affiliated with Reuben and McCoy. That's kind of like the FBI."

"Kind of," he answered. "But not really."

I was scared, and I was trying not to show it. I turned to Isabella. "And aren't you in jail?"

She smiled.

Edward cleared his throat, signaling that he was ready to begin his story and was done with questions. "Eric, my time is very valuable, and I can't afford you much of it. You and my daughter have already cost me precious resources during a particularly busy time of my work."

I frowned. "Sorry to be an inconvenience."

"Consequently," he said, ignoring me, "I am going to explain a few things, and then I'm going to expect you and Rebekah to follow a few rules."

"What rules?"

"We'll discuss those later."

"If I'm agreeing to something, I'd like to know what I'm agreeing to."

He smiled and clasped his hands together, his fingers interlaced. "Effectively, you are agreeing to my protection. You are agreeing that you cannot be ably guarded by the proper channels, so you are seeking protection elsewhere. You are agreeing to live."

I thought of Rebekah in the other room and how I wished this was all a bad dream. I nodded.

Edward smiled and took another sip of his drink. From the expression on his face, it seemed like he'd just negotiated a major business deal.

"Eric, are you familiar with the writings of Bernard Mandeville?"

"No."

He tutted and shook his head, as though I were the reason the world was going downhill. "'The Fable of the Bees.' It was first published in 1705. It's a long poem—very simple, really—discussing a hive. Each bee is greedy, doing whatever he can to satisfy his own appetites, and yet, through the mysteries of social mechanics, the hive thrives:

> *Millions endeavoring to supply*
> *Each other's Lust and Vanity . . .*
> *Thus every Part was full of Vice,*
> *Yet the whole Mass a Paradice.*

I shook my head. "I don't understand."

"Let's say there are three companies, each selling chocolate. If none of them is interested in riches, what happens? They make the candy according to their family recipes, making batches of the stuff in their kitchens and selling it at moderate prices to anyone who is interested. Sound all right?"

"Sure."

"Let's say one of them gets greedy. He wants more money, a house on the hill maybe."

"Or a private jet," I added.

He smiled. "Exactly. Or a private jet. So, how is he going to get more money? He needs to increase demand for his product. How does he do that?"

"He makes better chocolate," I answered.

"Excellent idea. He takes the old family recipe, he hires a famous Swiss confectioner to recalculate the ingredients, and business starts coming in. But then what happens when the other candy makers start losing business?"

"They make better chocolate too."

"Right. One of them does. He boosts his recipe to make it better. But the third candy maker can't seem to get a better recipe. His chocolate is good, but nothing terrific. What can he do?"

I shrugged.

"He lowers his prices by twenty percent. Suddenly, a lot of people realize they're not looking for amazing Swiss chocolate—they just want a decent candy bar at a low price. He makes twenty percent less on each bar but is suddenly selling forty percent more bars. The others follow suit—continuing to perfect their recipes and lower their prices."

He paused, waiting for me to speak. I obliged. "It's just simple market forces."

"It is simple, but when people think about the market, they use very positive terms—'healthy competition' they call it—when what they're actually talking about is greed, lust, envy, avarice. Those are the necessities that force low prices and improved products."

I raised my hand. "So what does this have to do with anything?"

"It should be obvious," he answered with disdain. "I realized this later on. Felix and I were so enraptured with the idealism of it all that we hadn't figured vice into the equation. What happens if the country goes bankrupt? According to Felix, the rich and the poor will be forced by their circumstances to adopt an equitable lifestyle. But it won't work. It wouldn't ever work. People, no matter how poor they are, still want to be just a hair less-poor than their neighbor. Not only is greed essential to a free society, but it can't be gotten rid of."

"So you left Felix and the N.O.S."

Edward nodded, then finished with his odd little poem:

> *Then leave Complaints: Fools only strive*
> *To make a Great and honest Hive.*

I gestured around the room at the lavish amenities of the private jet. "It looks like you didn't have trouble embracing wealth."

"I never hated wealth," he said, shaking his head. "I hated the things it causes: poverty and suffering and war."

The entire thing sounded rehearsed—a sales pitch that he'd given so many times that he didn't even have to think about it.

"So, greed is unavoidable, but you're still fighting against it?"

"I'm not fighting against anyone, Eric. I'm a businessman, despite what the media and the FBI say. However, you make a good point. Greed *is* unavoidable, but it's the cause of war and death. How can you stop it?"

He took another sip of his drink and smiled, perfectly comfortable and completely pleased with himself.

I indulged him. "You figured it out."

"I figured it out."

"How?"

"Felix and I worked for the KGB while founding the N.O.S. Felix had done the actual information gathering—I never did. I had connections back in the Soviet Union, so Felix would get the intelligence to me, and I'd relay it to others.

"As you know, in 1991, the USSR was dissolved. The various states went their own directions—most of them with money troubles. I saw an opportunity. I didn't discuss it with Felix. I knew him too well. He would never agree. But I knew that his plan was flawed at its very center. His economic attacks could never work, because no one can be forced to be virtuous. Since I knew all this, I had no trouble taking the money."

"What money?" I asked. I finally took a sip of my water.

"*All* the money. Everything that we'd been counterfeiting for nine years. Back then it was easy—we had a small organization at the time, nowhere near what Felix has now. I gathered up the counterfeits we'd been stockpiling and left the country."

"How much money was it?"

Edward laughed. "Plenty. Just a hair under three hundred million dollars."

"And you just put it in a suitcase?"

"The United States expects things to be smuggled in, not out. It was difficult, but Customs never found a single bill. And with the exchange rate what it was at the time—with a high dollar and a painfully low ruble—the money, even though it was fake, was worth far more over there than it would have been over here."

"But couldn't they see the money was counterfeit?"

He grinned. "People in Kazakhstan are not nearly as discriminating."

"What's in Kazakhstan?"

Edward took another drink—a long one, rolling the liquor thoughtfully over his tongue before swallowing.

"This will sound strange to you," he said. "So hear me out."

"What am I going to do?" I replied. "Fly away?"

He looked pensive for a moment, as if he were carefully weighing his words. "Nuclear weapons."

"What?" I shot a glance at McCoy and then at Reuben. Neither of them was jumping up to arrest him.

"That's what was in Kazakhstan. That's what I spent my money on."

"You bought nukes?"

"Just listen. I went back to the USSR and worked with my contacts there. They put me in touch with some people who got me in touch with some other people. I didn't buy nuclear weapons per se—I didn't carry a warhead home in the back of a pickup truck. On the contrary, I formed a business of sorts. My money was spent almost entirely on personnel and infrastructure—that was the hard part. Getting fissile material was relatively easy."

I was still gaping.

"Like I said, I'm a businessman. I saw an opportunity and I seized it. The small, formerly Soviet states had scientists and technicians who were all suddenly unemployed. Kazakhstan had no need for nuclear weapons without the Soviets calling the shots. Many people were interested in what I offered. Not only was it a paycheck, but it was a chance to do a little good in the world."

"Good?" I interrupted.

"Of course good!" he snapped. "Here's an easy one for you: ever heard of MAD? Mutually Assured Destruction?"

"Yes."

"What is the whole point of Mutually Assured Destruction?"

"That no one will ever fire their missiles because they know that the other side will just fire theirs too, and everyone will be dead."

"Yes. The U.S. never fired at the USSR because they knew the USSR would fire right back. The system was completely safe. No one could ever launch. But suddenly, with the Cold War over, there was an imbalance in the system. What happens if you fire nuclear missiles at a country that doesn't have any?"

"A lot of people die."

Edward nodded emphatically. "A lot of people die, and you don't. You win. Only when rival nations have nuclear weapons will they both be safe—they both need to have them, that's the key."

He finished off his drink in one final gulp.

"So that's what you do?" I asked. "You sell nukes?"

"Put plainly, yes. Are you familiar with Pakistan and India's ongoing wars?"

"Oh, sure. Who isn't?"

Edward sighed. "Pakistan was formed in a rotten little era of world politics when Britain was freeing its former colonies. The British made a mess of half the world in the process. They partitioned territories along all sorts of absurd boundaries, leaving border disputes wherever they stepped. Kashmir, a territory on the borders of India and Pakistan, has been disputed for decades, and Pakistan and India have fought each other viciously for it. Some estimate the civilian casualties alone at 500,000."

Edward continued, "India has had some nuclear capabilities since 1974, and in the space of three days in May of 1998, they tested five weapons." His eyes sparkled for a moment, and he smiled as he spoke. "Pakistan responded, that very same month."

I was beginning to understand. "You helped them?"

"Yes. I am a businessman, Eric. I suppose you could call me an arms dealer. I work with governments as an advisor, offering them the services of my scientists and, if need be, nuclear material to get their own programs up and running."

"And you get paid very well for it," I added.

"This is the way to end war," he said. "The world functions on greed. People will always do what is best for themselves. No country, knowing that their enemy has nuclear weapons, will go to war—it's simply not in their best interests, and nations always act solely out of their own interests. If everyone has weapons, no one will fight—no one will be able to fight. Look at Pakistan and India—they haven't gone to war since 1998. Sure, they've had a few skirmishes—shooting across the border once in a while, but they've stopped invading. The deterrent works."

The deterrent works. It was an awfully callous way of saying my girlfriend's dad sold nukes.

CHAPTER 14

THE PLANE FLIGHT, wherever we were going, was long. I spent most of it in Rebekah's room. It was Edward's decision, because he said he had to get back to work, but it was just fine with me. Rebekah slept, and I watched her. And I prayed.

Finally I fell asleep.

When I woke up, absolutely nothing had changed, except that—according to my watch—eleven hours had passed. I looked out the window. We were flying above the clouds. Rebekah was still asleep.

I tried to do some quick math in my head and failed miserably, but I was pretty certain that eleven hours in a plane, leaving from Seattle, doesn't really take you anywhere within the United States.

I left Rebekah's room and wandered back out into the conference room. Edward was sitting at the table, his tie still snug around his neck. Isabella was typing on a laptop, and McCoy was bringing dishes to the table. I didn't see Reuben.

Edward looked up. "I was just about to have Isabella fetch you."

"Are we almost there?" I asked.

"No, but it's time for dinner. You slept through lunch."

"How much fuel does this plane have?"

"Enough. We stopped in New York. You slept through that, too." He gestured for me to take a seat. "How's my daughter?"

"She's okay, I guess." As I sat down, McCoy entered with plates of food. It smelled good but looked awful.

"We're heading to England," Edward said, unfolding his napkin and placing it in his lap. "There's no sense in it being a secret. I have a home there, and you and Rebekah will be my guests."

"For how long?"

"As long as it takes."

"Until what?"

"Until you are safe to return," Edward said, gingerly cutting his thin steak.

"Who decides that?"

I hadn't touched my dinner, partly because I was too annoyed to eat, and partly because my steak was raw. Edward gave it an Italian name, but I wasn't fooled. It was just steak, raw. I wondered if Betty Crocker's Cookbook had a recipe for it. *Directions: Open package, put steak on plate. Serves two.*

I set down my knife and fork. "Can I just ask one question?"

"What?"

"Are you insane? I mean, have you seen a doctor about this?"

"Eric—"

"No," I interrupted. "Rebekah's in the other room half dead. You're out selling nukes. The FBI knows about this, and they're fine with it."

He thought for a moment and then sipped his wine. "The FBI doesn't know about it." He set down the glass and picked up his knife and fork.

"What about. . . . Huh?"

He placed a piece of steak on his tongue, chewed thoughtfully, swallowed, and then called to McCoy. He appeared in an instant.

"Bring Agent Reuben in here, would you?"

McCoy nodded obediently and disappeared.

Edward wiped his mouth while he waited. "If you're learning anything today, Eric, I hope it's that you don't know everything. What you don't know is, in fact, so much greater than what you do, that I'm amazed you dare open your mouth."

Reuben entered.

"Agent Reuben," Edward said, standing up. "Please tell Mr. Hopkins where we met."

Reuben looked uncertain of what he should say. I didn't blame him.

"Go ahead," Edward assured him.

"Islamabad," Reuben answered. "Seven years ago."

Edward smiled and nodded, gesturing for Reuben to sit. "Reuben was working as a project manager on a pipeline. Fresh out of business school—MBA at Princeton—and they had enough confidence in him to ship him off to Pakistan. He was referred to me by someone in my organization, and I hired him."

"Wait," I said, my brain particularly annoyed with this line of conversation. I had assumed that Edward had some kind of connection with the U.S. government and had worked out a deal with them. Apparently not. "So Reuben . . . you've infiltrated the FBI?"

He shook his head. I could tell he wanted to smile but didn't because the boss was there. "No. I am not affiliated with the FBI."

"What about the house? And the credit cards? And the medical bills?"

"They're all in my name," Edward replied. "I've owned the house for years. I designed it, in fact, from the foundation up."

"So . . ." I never quite formed a question. There was too much weight from my life crashing down on top of me.

"You want the truth?" Edward asked.

I nodded, wondering why I was suddenly dizzy.

"You are not, and have not, been in the custody of the federal government. Agent Reuben, along with all the other law enforcement personnel you've met in the past month, work for me."

"And the FBI doesn't even know?"

"Are you kidding?" Reuben snorted. "They're searching for you high and low."

"They think we've been kidnapped?"

"Not to hear them tell it," Edward said, smiling smugly again. "They've assured everyone that you're perfectly fine. Even your parents think you're in custody."

"Why?"

"You both disappeared out from under their noses. And the next day . . ." He pointed to Isabella.

She smiled. It was the same old snide Isabella I knew and didn't love. "I escaped," she supplied graciously.

"Isabella escaped. The timing was perfect. And Eric—have you seen anything on the news about her escape? You watch TV constantly."

I was beyond confused. "No."

Isabella spoke. "That's because, at this very moment, a lot of people are falling over themselves to not look like idiots." She paused and took a sip of her wine. "You and Rebekah are missing, I escaped from prison—it looks pretty bad for the FBI. And since December, the public has been screaming at the government to *heighten* security—to increase the intelligence budget and ensure that nothing like that ever happens again. And then the Novus Ordo Seclorum successfully attacks you—stabs you—and the next day Isabella Hakopian escapes from prison. Do you know what this proves?"

"What?"

"That when all is said and done, the FBI, the CIA, and the NSA are not as concerned with the nation's security as they are with their own jobs. If they announce that I'm gone, pictures of me will be plastered on every TV screen in the country—maybe getting me recaptured. But a thousand people in Washington D.C., and a hundred law enforcement agents in Utah, will get fired for incompetence."

I took a bite of my steak. I didn't care what it tasted like. Isabella disappeared the day after we did, leaving the FBI with a truckload of egg on their collective faces. The best they could do, if they wanted to save their jobs, was to act like it was all part of the plan, and hope to get us back alive in time to testify.

Someone was getting fired for this one.

The smile faded from Edward's face, and he took another sip of wine. "You were stabbed, Eric. One of Felix's men tried to kill you, and the FBI did nothing about it. In my opinion, you both should have been taken into protective custody back in December, but the government didn't do a thing about it. They were only too happy to parade you in front of the cameras. Nothing builds national pride—or boosts approval ratings—like seeing two American kids outwitting terrorists. You two were a windfall for the intelligence community. If you hadn't have been on *Good Morning America,* making Felix look like a clumsy idiot, people would have been terrified. You took the terror away from the terrorists because you fought them and survived—and won."

He folded his napkin and continued. "And every time I saw Rebekah on TV, talking about how you'd figured out everything about Felix's schemes, I knew that he was watching the same TV show, getting angrier and angrier. They should have put you in custody. I decided to take matters into my own hands."

"Wait a minute," I said, trying to sort things out in my head. There was a lot to sort out, and I had a lot of questions and no idea which one I should ask first. "Let me get this straight. When you first came to the hospital, you said that you weren't happy with the FBI's protection of us, and that you were taking matters into your own hands."

"Yes."

"But that whole time, we hadn't been under the FBI's protection at all—we'd been under *your* protection. It was under *your* watchful eye that Rebekah got attacked."

He nodded, his face changing almost imperceptibly. "Yes."

"Then why did you say all that about the FBI's incompetence?"

"Because I needed to talk to you. And because, at that time, I wasn't ready to tell you everything."

"So it was your fault that Rebekah was hurt, not the FBI's."

He stared back at me, his eyes cold but calm. "I don't believe you're in any position to be doling out blame, Mr. Hopkins."

CHAPTER 15

ENGLAND WAS PRETTY much like I expected. Great big, busy London surrounded by rolling hills and idyllic countryside. Rebekah sat next to me on the drive, fully awake, but almost in a state of shock. I'd explained everything. If we'd been in the same car as her father, I'm sure there would have been palpable tension. Which is probably why we weren't.

Isabella drove us. She seemed to have no trouble whatsoever with the left-side-of-the-road driving, but it terrified me to watch. At every intersection I thought we were going to die.

"So you escaped," Rebekah said, her face flushed.

Isabella looked in the rearview mirror. "Yes."

"How? He helped you?" Rebekah's voice was getting stronger but still had a raspy whistle to it.

Isabella looked back at the road. "No. I escaped. The fact that it coincided with the attack on Eric is merely a fortunate happenstance."

"How did you do it?"

"Rebekah, I am good at what I do, or your father would have never hired me."

Rebekah glowered, staring out the window. The past twenty-four hours had confirmed her worst fears—elevating them, in fact. Her father wasn't just a terrorist—he was an arms dealer selling weapons of mass destruction to the highest bidder. And he had worked with Felix. And he'd worked for the KGB. I could only guess what this news was doing to her.

"Where are my mother and my sister?" she asked, suddenly remembering what Reuben had said weeks before.

"They really are in the Witness Protection Program. The real one. When you two disappeared, the FBI feared the worst, as they should have."

"So they're okay?"

"They're living in a small town in rural Kansas, as I understand it."

Rebekah held my hand and took a deep breath. I'd been listening to her breathing the entire car ride, and it didn't sound good. All the bandages I'd seen in the hospital were gone, except for the wrappings on her right hand, but her left hand was shaking noticeably.

I hate to admit it, but I'm glad Rebekah was upset; keeping an eye on her medical condition and trying to help her stay calm was the only thing keeping me from buckling under the pressure. We were in England, for crying out loud, living with a criminal. We were doing things based on his time schedule, staying with him for who knew how long. I had no lofty goals for my life—I'd never dreamed of being a doctor or a lawyer—but I certainly wanted to live normally. Little house, white picket fence, kids playing in the yard, big-screen TV.

But that's not how it was happening.

We reached Edward's house. Apparently the nuke business was very profitable.

It was near the center of town but was surrounded by both a high stone wall and an enormous. . . . I don't know if you'd call it a lawn or a yard or a garden. It was as big as four city blocks, with gardens, hedges, and fountains here and there. In the center of the plot was an old, brownstone manor house. It was three stories high, slightly blocky, with neoclassical pillars and pediments.

Isabella pulled through the gate, following Edward's car up to the front entrance. The doors to Edward's sedan flew open and he jumped out, striding quickly up the imposing stone steps. Rebekah tried to do the same, to follow and confront him, but her legs wouldn't carry her that fast, and he couldn't hear her muted shout.

Rebekah sadly turned back toward me and held my arm, and we walked slowly up the rest of the stairs and through the front doors. We were in a grand hall with marble floors and an enormously high ceiling. Edward was nowhere to be seen.

Rebekah turned to Isabella, who was coming in behind us. "Where did he go?"

"I'm sure he has very important things to attend to."

"And his daughter isn't one of them?"

Isabella set down the bag she'd been carrying and walked off toward the far door. "You're awfully ungrateful, considering he saved your life."

Rebekah moved to follow Isabella but knew she couldn't keep up. A housekeeper entered from a side room and took our bags. "This way, please."

"I can't believe it," Rebekah muttered, more to herself than to me.

I took her hand. I didn't know what to say, but I was sure she ought to be resting. "Come on."

She bit her lip and nodded, then we followed the housekeeper.

CHAPTER 16

OUR ROOMS WERE every bit as luxurious as the rest of the house. I had an enormous bed, which had probably been made four hundred years before. Artwork covered almost every inch of wall space. I don't know enough about paintings to know if they were valuable, but they were amazing to look at. And from my window I had a postcard view of the gardens and town. It was like living in a movie.

Rebekah slept most of that first day but then decided she was done being sick. A British doctor, an old man with slate-gray hair and a trimmed beard, visited Rebekah the first night, and a physical therapist showed up on the second morning and never seemed to leave. They worked with Rebekah in the grand hall, or out on the garden terraces, walking and stretching and checking general body mechanics. On the fourth day they walked the perimeter of the grounds. A respiratory therapist came in the afternoons. With all the therapy, Rebekah and I had very little time together. Not that I'm complaining—she was getting better.

On our seventh day in England, Rebekah had finally had enough. I was sitting in front of the TV, ignoring the news and reading a British magazine, circling all the words I didn't know. Rebekah appeared in the doorway wearing a T-shirt and shorts, and carrying a backpack over her shoulder. It was obvious that she'd spent the last month indoors—her legs were milk white. Not that I was looking.

"What are you doing?" she said.

"Do you know what *widdershins* means?"

"Are you going to be doing that all day?"

"Doing what?"

"Being bored."

"Probably. Your dad needs to buy a foosball table or something."

"We're going out."

"Out as in out? Outside? Out the front gates? Out to eat in a place where they have real food and normal people?"

"We'll start with outside," she said, a grin washing over her face. "We'll see what happens from there."

I tossed the magazine onto the end table and stood. "Are you feeling up to it?"

"The doctor told me I'm supposed to exercise," she answered mischievously.

"Yeah, but he was talking about your wrist. Are we going bowling?"

"We'll see."

Suddenly our strange fortress-prison dissolved into nothing more than a mere residence as we walked out the front door, down the stone steps, and onto the graveled drive that led to the front road. There were no guards standing at the gate, nor were there hounds patrolling the grounds. When we reached the end of the property, Rebekah merely pushed a white button on the gate's intercom, and the wrought-iron cage swung open, and all of Britain lay before us.

Of course, I wasn't dumb enough to think we weren't being watched. But we had a considerable amount of anonymity here, and we were half a world away from the last known location of Felix's assassins. But there was more to keeping us safe than geography, I was sure.

"You cleared this with someone, I assume," I said as we strolled toward the small town.

"I told Isabella," she answered. "She's probably following us. I don't care."

The sky was bright—far brighter than it had looked from inside Edward's house. Maybe the windows needed washing.

"Have you been here before?" I asked.

She shook her head. "We visited him in England every now and then, but always at hotels in London—I never knew he had a house here, much less that huge place."

"So you don't know where we can find some good food—something I'm familiar with?"

"British food isn't as bad as you think it is."

"Your dad's food is bad."

"It's not British. I think it's mostly French."

"I think it's mostly rich-people food. Who eats raw steak?"

"A lot of people."

"A lot of rich people."

"I was a rich person," she laughed, "and you know what we used to eat all the time? Grilled cheese sandwiches. Just because we were rich didn't mean we knew how to cook."

"You could have hired a chef."

"And he probably would have made us eat raw steak."

I nodded in agreement with her wise deduction and then turned my attention back to the amazing sights that surrounded me. I'd lived the majority of my life in Utah, a state which is world-renowned for its beauty—having more national parks than any other state in the country, and snowcapped peaks, barren deserts, rock formations of every shape and color, wildlife galore, and yet nothing I'd ever seen compared to the idyllic beauty of this small Midlands town. Stone cottages roofed with earthy tile and speckled with creeping vines lined the road on the left, while a narrow canal ran on the right. Sheep grazed in a pasture on the far side, and large oaks and elms spread wherever they were given enough room. Everything looked old—but not antique. It was old and comfortable, like the entire country was your grandparents' house.

We crossed a small footbridge over the Trent and Mersey Canal, and Rebekah found a low stone wall on the opposite side. I sat next to her.

"How are the lungs?" I asked. I'd been intently listening to her breathing as we'd walked—her breaths were shallow, but it didn't seem to be bothering her.

"They're okay," she answered. "I just need to rest for a minute." She pulled the backpack off her shoulder, set it on the ground, and leaned forward to take a long, deep breath of air.

I rested my hand on her back, feeling the rise and fall of her body. All in all, things could have been a lot worse.

After a few minutes she straightened back up and stretched her neck. We sat there for a long while, Rebekah performing her breathing exercises and me offering silent prayers of joy that she was alive.

"Look at that," Rebekah said, pointing south at a malformed patch of clouds hovering over a row of squatty brick homes. "What does it look like to you?"

"A cloud."

"No, come on," she said, her shoulder leaning into me. "It's like a Rorschach test—whatever you see reveals your true character." She glanced at me and grinned, then looked back into the sky.

"Well, in that case, it looks like a completed homework assignment and a nicely cleaned house."

"Really?" Rebekah laughed, and then replied with mock seriousness, "To me it looks more like a church. Flowers out in front."

"Oh. Well, I saw the church too, of course. But it's more like a temple, with the scriptures next to it, and a Boy Scout who's helping old ladies cross the street. A heavenly choir is hovering just above, and—do you see that little tuft to the left? That's Michael the archangel."

She pulled the backpack up onto her lap and began fiddling with the zipper. "What does it really look like?"

"A frog that's been run over by a truck, maybe? What does that say about me?"

She looked back at the cloud. "Oh, good. I thought it looked like spilled pudding. A dead-frog nature is worse than a spilled-pudding nature any day."

"Does that make you a glutton or a litterbug?"

"Which is better?"

"Depends, I guess."

Rebekah pulled a bundle wrapped tightly in cloth from the pack. She untied the top. "My father's chef told me that this is what they call a ploughman's lunch."

In the bundle were two large pieces of crusty bread, a few chunks of Cheddar cheese, and pickled onions.

"Well, it's no steak tartare," I said, grateful to see recognizable food for once. "But it'll have to do."

Rebekah didn't eat much, mostly preferring just to drink from her water bottle. She was sicker than she let on, and our walk was probably more than she should have done. I ate my cheese quickly—it was better than any cheese I'd had in America—and gnawed on the hard bread for a while.

"Do you think we'll ever get back to normal life again?" Rebekah asked, gazing down at the pressure bandage still on her wrist. "I mean, what about school? The last six months—even when we haven't been hiding from terrorists—haven't been normal."

I finished chewing a small piece of bread and took a quick sip of water to wash it down. "Oddly enough, you've also been dating me for the last six months—coincidence?"

She laughed. "No, I mean it. Do you think we'll ever get to the point when we can go back to school and get jobs and have a life that isn't closely watched by the press and guarded by the FBI?"

"I don't know. My only real knowledge of terrorists comes from action movies. Something blows up and the main characters kiss and they all live happily ever after. Not too long ago something blew up, and we kissed, and we've been sitting in court for half a year. Is that how it's supposed to work?"

"Maybe we're in the sequel now," she said, smiling and standing up.

"Then let's blow something up and kiss again and get it over with."

I put my arm around her waist, she kissed me, and we walked.

"Here's how I see it," Rebekah said, looking down at the road rather than at the shops. "We're currently not in the custody of the United States government, right?"

"Right."

"Well, then, everything that's happening right now is technically against the law."

"If we were in the Witness Protection Program, Felix would probably have killed us both by now."

She nodded emphatically. "Oh, I understand that. And we've had no choice in any of this. I'm just saying that whenever we get out of this and go back and testify, we'll have to start all over and have a hundred interviews and depositions about being here in England with my father. It'll be the same thing over again. Six months ago I had a house and a car and a family who was relatively normal, and no one cared that I got up in the morning and went to school, and no reporters sat outside the library and waited for me to leave so that they could ask just one more question. I could go to the mall without having to get approval from the FBI. Are we ever going to get back to that?"

I pondered it for a minute. I'd thought of all these things too, of course, but had never come up with an answer. "Well, eventually, I guess. Look at disasters that happened ten years ago—does anyone even think of them anymore? For all we know, twenty years from now our experiences will be the story of a video game."

She forced a grim smile. "That doesn't seem to make it any easier."

I shrugged. "Then what do we do? We could move to Nepal, and no one would ever recognize us, but would that be a big improvement?"

"Probably not."

We walked on for a few dozen yards and stopped at a church-yard. The building was old, its stone face worn by centuries of wind and vines. The cemetery surrounding the church was a mix of old and new—some of the headstones looked older than the church itself, and some, with crisp edges and polished surfaces, looked as recent as last week.

"I get tired sometimes, Eric," Rebekah said, leaning against the trunk of a spindly willow at the side of the road. "Look at these tombstones. These people probably did great things—fought in wars, maybe—and no one remembers them. It's almost like it never happened. I sometimes wonder why we even bother anymore. Let Felix do his thing and let my dad do his thing, and let's you and me just get on with our lives."

I stood and thought, staring at the graves.

"Get on with what, though? Life is about the struggle."

She didn't respond.

I didn't know what else to say, and rather than try, I changed the subject.

"Look at that." I pointed to a tall headstone several yards away. It was over five feet tall, shaped more or less like an obelisk, with a large, square base. "You see that symbol at the top—a twelve-pointed star, and underneath the circle with a dot in the middle?"

"Yeah?"

"I've seen that thing half a dozen times in your dad's house. It's on the pillars in the great hall, and in a painting in the dining room, and it was on a book lying on his desk."

"Must be some local design," she said, strolling over to look at the grave. I followed. Its occupant, Renée Proust, died in 1834. "It could just be a variation on the cross—there are all sorts of different ones in these old cemeteries. Some have circles."

"Probably," I agreed.

"Anyway," Rebekah said, turning to me. "Sorry I'm being depressing. We ought to get back."

CHAPTER 17

THE WALK BACK up to the house was a little bit worse than the walk to town, and I offered more than once to call for a car or to carry Rebekah piggyback. She didn't weigh much before the explosion, and after four weeks of bed rest and nausea, she had really shed the pounds. But while The Event (the bombing, the explosion, or as Rebekah called it, the "accident") had weakened her physically, it had drastically strengthened her resolve. She had no intention of asking for help. If she asked for help, then the terrorists had won.

When we got back to the house, Rebekah went straight to bed. After making sure she was attended to by the finest housemaids in the house (there were only two), I made my way back to the great hall and looked for the symbols from the cemetery. I did this not because of my clever sleuthing skills, but because I'd run out of things to do. The pillars were obviously made of stone—brownstone, to be precise. They featured twelve-pointed stars, and circles with dots in the centers. Ha! I'd cracked the case. Elementary, my dear Watson.

With my ingenious Matlockery complete, I retired to the TV room, where I sat on an antique couch watching the BBC and eating ginger cake—a gift from the cook. I turned on the TV just as a news program was ending and another was beginning; someone had just finished talking about the conflict between the Labour Party and the Conservatives, and a new reporter was now beginning to discuss the pollution level in the Thames and its effect on the tourist industry. I turned to the game beside me.

When I'd been gathering up my things on San Juan Island, I'd absently tossed the antique Scrabble game into my suitcase, and I now lay on the couch playing with it. It had a soothing, sleep-inducing effect. What it really needed was more letters.

I kept expecting something to happen when I turned the crank, but nothing ever did. Presumably, the right word combination would affect it, but for the life of me I couldn't figure it out. The best I could do to crack the code was: *If I Input Mesa.* I thought maybe something would happen then. Nothing did. Nothing ever happened. I fell asleep with the pile of letters on my stomach.

When I woke, two fingernails were poking me in the shoulder—two well-manicured, sharp fingernails. Isabella Hakopian stood above me dressed in a blood-red business suit with her hair pulled tightly back. It was the old Isabella I knew and disliked.

"Eric," she said, still jabbing me. "Wake up."

"What time is it?" I asked, looking around for a clock.

"Eight-thirty," she said as I sat up. "Can you come with me?"

"Where are we going?"

"Outside." She reached down and picked up one of the Scrabble letters.

"That's the second time today that someone has come in here and told me that."

"And your point is?" She dropped the letter back onto the couch.

I stood up, checking my mouth for drool. "I don't have one."

"Then please come with me."

I followed her out of the room and down the long corridor toward the back of the house. Her high heels clacked along the marble floor, echoing through the empty halls. Most of the lights were out, and even though the sun hadn't quite gone down, the place was dark and gloomy.

We turned off the main hall and went down a narrow spiral staircase to the floor below. We were in a library, a section of the house I hadn't yet seen. Isabella opened a set of French doors and led me out onto a wide stone patio.

I sat down on a bench. She didn't, so I stood back up.

She folded her arms and looked out across the gardens. "We need to talk."

"Apparently."

"Mr. Hughes thinks that it's time you understood a little more of what he does. You're still in the dark about a great many things, and they need discussing."

I thought for a moment and then scratched my itchy beard. "Yes, I am in the dark, and yes, they need discussing, but Mr. Hughes doesn't think it's time to tell me. You do."

She turned and stared at me.

"A few minutes ago you *asked* me to join you out here. Then you said 'please.' Either prison turned you soft, or you aren't sure of what you're about to do."

Isabella stammered momentarily and looked back at the gardens.

"Sorry, Isabella."

"Tell me what you know."

"About what?"

"Edward."

"Plenty, but not nearly enough. I know he's an arms dealer and he thinks he's saving the world."

"But he's not a criminal, right?"

I paused. Her question almost seemed posed for her own benefit, not mine. "I suppose it depends on your definition. In my book, selling weapons of mass destruction to the highest bidder doesn't seem like an activity of a law-abiding citizen."

"You obviously don't understand what we were doing," she said sharply. "He wasn't in it to make money. If he only wanted money then he would have turned to Saudi Arabia or Iran or any number of countries who would give half their GNP to get a nuclear weapon. What we did was choose countries on the brink of an arms imbalance—we sought *them* out, not the other way around."

I nodded. "Yeah, Edward explained his philanthropy to me. If it's not about the money then what is all this?" I gestured out to the darkening gardens and the house behind us.

"He wasn't anti-money. He just had a higher cause as well."

"Why do you keep talking in the past tense?"

Isabella paused and then turned to step down off of the patio and into the garden. I followed.

"I saved your life, Eric," she finally said, her arms still folded and her voice low. "More than once. I went to jail for you, and I have a bullet wound in my stomach because of you."

It wasn't exactly the truth. She'd gotten shot and had gone to prison because she was following Edward's orders—orders that had everything to do with Rebekah and nothing to do with me. Still, whatever the reason, she had saved my life. "Are you going to ask for a favor?"

Isabella stopped and looked at me. She wasn't enjoying this, and that only made me wish I was. "You have to understand that I have been loyal to Edward from the beginning. I have been in his service for over six years, and I have never failed to do anything that he asked of me. I have met with heads of state, and I have smuggled scientists across borders, and I . . . I have never hesitated to ensure the success of his vision."

"And you went to prison for six months."

"Yes," she answered hotly. Her voice was low and fierce. "Six months in jail I kept my mouth shut. You know why there were so few witnesses for the defense? Because I never said one word to my appointed lawyer or the FBI or anyone else. Not one word, for six months."

"Why did you do it?"

"Because I knew . . ." She suddenly appeared very flustered and gestured quickly and nervously. "Because I knew that Edward would get me out of there. He has power, and he uses it. I was going to be rescued, just as I had rescued you."

"And he did," I said. "He got you out of jail."

"No! *I* escaped. I've broken men out of Pakistani prisons before— getting myself out of an American cell was nothing. Just time and patience."

I didn't know where she was going with any of this. Isabella usually treated me as a fool, only occasionally elevating me to the status of idiot. I'd never been her confidant.

"Maybe that was his plan," I offered. "He knew you could get out, so he let you do it."

Isabella took a deep breath and sat down on a garden bench. This time I stayed standing.

"I've thought about that," she said. "And yes, that's what he's told me."

"Then what's the problem?"

"He's lying. He has a new assistant, Mr. McCoy. That's fine, I guess—maybe Edward had no idea how long I'd be in prison, and obviously he needed an assistant in the interim. But it's his attitude. He was surprised to see me—shocked, actually."

"I was surprised to see you too."

"He doesn't trust me anymore, Eric. There are things he isn't telling me—big things."

"How do you know?"

"Because I've picked up enough to learn that there's a project he's working on, but it's nothing we've ever discussed."

"It's been six months."

Isabella began pacing, and I felt a drop of rain hit my arm. "You know how long it takes to do what we do? We worked with Pakistan for three years. We've been with Japan for six, and we're probably still a year out. No, this is something that's recently begun and will soon be over."

"How soon?"

"Tuesday night. That's six days from now."

"Why are you telling me this? Talk to Reuben or McCoy, or anybody."

Her voice was quiet but intense. "There isn't anyone I can talk to. I can't leave without being followed, and I can't use the phone without being listened to."

Another raindrop hit me on the cheek and trickled slowly down into my beard. "Then let it end and be done with it."

"You don't understand. Something isn't right."

"Here's an idea. Maybe he thinks that you didn't really escape from prison—maybe you made a deal with the FBI, and you're collecting information on him."

Isabella chose to ignore that comment, and I shook my head because I really *didn't* understand. If she wanted my opinion, none of this was right. But she didn't want my opinion—she wanted a favor.

"So," I said, wiping the water from my face, "what can I do for you?"

She reached into her purse and pulled out a small bundle of papers secured with a rubber band. "As far as anyone knows, you and Rebekah are in the Witness Protection Program. No one is looking for you, other than Felix—and Felix probably thinks you were moved to the suburbs of Minneapolis or somewhere like that. Obviously, the FBI doesn't place witnesses overseas."

"Right, so no one is watching us." The rain was coming more aggressively now. Isabella's expensive suit might be ruined, but she didn't seem to mind at all. A few more minutes of water on my wool sweater would probably have me smelling like the county fair, but I was intrigued by Isabella's disregard, so I stayed.

"I, on the other hand, have escaped from a federal prison and injured an officer in the process—"

I interrupted. "Really?"

"Oh grow up, Eric. The police are after me, and since the FBI rightly suspects Edward's organization is international, they've sent my picture to every agency they're on good terms with."

"You could grow a beard."

"I have passports for you and Rebekah, and cash. I need you to go to Paris."

"Excuse me? In case you hadn't noticed, Rebekah's not exactly in tip-top shape. She should be in bed, surrounded by doctors. Why should I drag her to Paris?"

"Because you have no idea what Edward's doing."

"Neither do you."

She looked down at the ground, flustered. After several seconds, she raised her head and stared into my eyes. "I don't know what he's doing. But I do know what he's capable of. It's bad."

"A lot of things are bad."

"This is worse."

I tried to read her face, but didn't get much other than rain and anger. Her gaze was fixed, and she was either completely confident in what she said or an amazing liar. "You're serious?"

She answered with a solemn nod.

"When?"

"Tomorrow."

* * *

Rebekah's hair was still wet from the bath when she opened the door. "Ever been to Paris?" I said, smiling a big, dumb smile.

She looked confused but laughed. "Good morning to you too."

"How long do you think it would take for you to get ready?"

"For what?"

"For a long train ride, part of which will be underwater. Hence the question, have you ever been to Paris?"

"Huh? Paris?" She ran her fingers apprehensively through her dyed hair and looked at me quizzically.

"I'll explain on the train."

Her hand fell from her hair and went straight to her hip. She was concerned. "Has someone approved this?"

"Very much so. Don't worry—I'm assured that it'll be all trains and taxis and lots of time to rest."

Rebekah grinned. "I'd swim the English Channel if it meant getting out of this place."

* * *

It was actually two trains, and they were expensive. The first we picked up in Wolverhampton. Isabella drove us to the station in a big, black car with big, black windows. She wore a British-looking hat and sunglasses. She didn't say a word to Rebekah, and Rebekah hadn't yet bothered asking what the occasion was. I got the feeling that the reason wasn't important to her, just as long as she got to get out of the house. I also got the feeling that Rebekah expected this to be some kind of romantic day trip, planned by me. As pleasant as that sounded, I knew she'd be disappointed.

We left Isabella at the car, and Rebekah and I walked arm in arm through the station. I might as well have been in Shanghai for all my proficiency with the local dialect, but Rebekah helped translate and we ended up with two first-class tickets to London.

Since we only had a single backpack for luggage, the small compartment ended up being fairly spacious. Rebekah sat by the window, eager to soak in the fast-moving countryside.

"So," I said, after twenty minutes of chitchat about weather and trees and rolling hills and sheep.

"Yeah?" Her gaze was glued to the window. She was wearing a casual summer dress—light blue, made from thin, loose fabric. She tapped her sandaled foot absently in rhythm with the low rocking of the train.

"Have you ever been to Paris?"

"Three times," she said. She turned to look at me, grinning. "Once when I was seven, and twice when I was fifteen. We need to stop at a chocolate shop—you've never tasted anything like it."

"Sounds good to me. Why twice when you were fifteen?"

"I had to do a report for my high school French class. Flying me to Paris for a week—twice—was my father's version of helping me with my homework." She paused. "So, why are we going?"

"I thought you'd never ask."

She looked back out the window but kept smiling with the corner of her mouth. "I figure that it has something to do with Isabella. It took an hour of arguing with her to let us go into town yesterday. I don't think she'd give us money and let us leave the country unless she had some ulterior motive."

"You won't like it," I warned. Surprisingly, this warranted the biggest smile of the morning, which quickly turned into a laugh.

"All the news we get anymore is something I won't like. I'm getting used to it—it's almost like a game. For the past twenty minutes I've been trying to think of the worst possible thing it could be, just so that whatever it is seems better by comparison."

I chuckled. "How very optimistic of you. What did you come up with?"

"She wants us to try escargot," she said simply, and then laughed.

"What could be worse than that?"

"Not a thing," she said. "So, what is it?"

"She wants us to spy on your dad."

Rebekah's smile faded quickly. I'd told her she wasn't going to like it. "What?"

"Isabella pulled me aside last night. She said something is wrong. Your dad doesn't trust her anymore."

Rebekah thought for a moment, and the tapping of her foot stopped. She raised her hand to her chin. "This hardly seems like our problem."

It was gone. Every bit of playfulness and humor had left her. She'd hit the brick wall of reality in a speeding train, and instead of worrying about eating buttered gastropods she was worried about spying on a nuclear arms dealer.

"Isabella couldn't go," I answered. "Everyone is watching her."

"But why us?"

"Who else?"

"No," she said, standing up and trying to pace in the cramped compartment. It was about two steps in each direction. "Why did she want *us* to do it? Why not one of the however many other . . . um . . . What do you call the people that work for my father?"

Terrorists was the first word that sprang to mind, but I didn't say it. "Employees?"

"I guess." She was visibly flustered. Her pale skin was turning red, and her breathing was getting shallower.

"Why don't you sit down?" I offered.

"I don't want to sit down."

I knew better than to press her about it. Instead, I tried to change the subject.

"Listen," I said in my most reasonable voice. "Isabella asked us to go and find out who is attending a meeting at a certain place and a certain time. All we have to do is snap a few pictures and e-mail them to her, and then we get to spend two days roaming Paris. I thought it'd be fun."

Rebekah didn't say anything. She was too busy running a marathon in two-step increments.

I pulled a folded map out of my back pocket. "They're all meeting at a restaurant near the Pavilion day la Ray-eena." I was making an unintentional mockery of the French language. "It's by the Place dess Vose-guess. It's pretty close to all of the touristy stuff—Noh-ter Dayme and the Loove. I thought you might like to go see it all."

Rebekah stopped, a reluctant smile breaking across her lips. She sat down next to me and took the map.

"Pavillion de la Reine, Place des Vosges, Notre Dame, and the Louvre." Her accent was perfect, I assumed.

"I'm glad you speak French."

She laughed quietly and shook her head. "I don't, really. A couple of years in high school and a couple of classes my freshman year."

"I took four years of Spanish in high school, and all I can do is count to ten and say *taco*."

Rebekah grinned. "I think my French is a little better than that."

"So you'll do it?"

"It's a little late to say no, but I think I'll survive it," she said, leaning up against me. "What did you mean by two days?"

"Two days. That's what Isabella wanted. So that on the off chance your dad goes home on the chunnel train, we'd be going home at a different time. Isabella already booked us two rooms at some hotel."

She frowned. "I didn't bring a change of clothes."

"I didn't think of that," I said, feeling a little guilty.

Rebekah took my hand. With her shoulder against mine, I could feel her rapid breathing, and I could tell she was trying to get control of it.

"Isabella doesn't even know his schedule?" she asked quietly.

"She doesn't know anything, apparently. She said that since she's been back the only real responsibility she's had is to take over the staff's payroll."

"Hmm."

I looked out the window, watching the scenery fly past.

"How do your lungs feel?"

"They hurt."

* * *

The countryside had disappeared somewhat, and we were no longer in postcard England, but in a city of seven-odd million people. London was cramped and tall, the denizens having chosen to build up instead of out. Having just seen the countryside, with all its comfortable greenery and peaceful pasture, I felt like opening the window and screaming at the Londoners that there was a whole other world out there, just waiting to be urban sprawled.

In London we switched trains, moving from the boxy, dated cars we'd been riding in to a big, flashy, white thing with racing stripes and a sleek nose. It was the Chunnel train—three hours from London to Paris—and it cost only slightly less than an airline ticket. Rebekah and I had, once again, first-class tickets—and with a first-class ticket on an expensive train, in a part of the world that really knows the definition of class, we were living the high life. We had enormously comfortable chairs that once again offered spectacular views of the country, and, eventually, half an hour of concrete tunnel. We were fifty feet underground and under I-didn't-want-to-guess-how-many feet of water.

And then we were in France, and then we were in Paris. Rebekah slept nearly the entire time, but only after ordering a wide variety of cheeses from the dining car. As we rumbled across France I watched Rebekah sleep; thought about Edward, Isabella, and Felix; and ate Brie and Camembert.

Throughout the entire trip, all I discovered was that one of the problems of traveling by rail is that trains don't go past well-known landmarks or quaint, culturally iconic villages. Modern trains, by their very nature, stick with other trains, the effect being that the views—especially as we approached Paris—were mostly of other trains, or row after row of tracks, or of the parts of town that no one wants to live in, because, well . . . they're by the tracks.

CHAPTER 18

IT WAS HECTIC getting through Gare du Nord, the train station in Paris. We were crossing international borders, after all, and though the wait wasn't as long as it would've been at the airport, it wasn't particularly short. Our standing in line only exacerbated Rebekah's chest pain. Despite sleeping nearly three hours on the Eurostar, the trip was more excitement than her weakened body wanted, and she had a difficult time regulating her breathing.

I bought a travel guidebook in the station at a shop with a big sign reading *We Speak English.* The book cost about twenty euros, and I happily forked over the multicolored money. I had no idea what it equated to in dollars—I just know that I gave the girl behind the counter two brown bills, one pink one, and a handful of coins. All the money was bright and cheerful, and it looked more like it belonged in a Monopoly set than a wallet. The girl gave me my change, along with a heavily accented, "Enjoy your time in Paris."

We waited on a stone bench outside Gare du Nord, me flipping through maps of the city, and Rebekah lying down, her head resting on my leg. After several minutes she opened her eyes.

"Have you figured it out?"

I nodded halfheartedly. "Kind of. The hotel is too far to walk to—I'm pretty sure it's about three miles. I hate the metric system."

She smiled, closing her eyes again. "Get used to it being different. They use a twenty-four hour clock here, too."

"Huh? So do we."

"I mean that four o'clock in the afternoon isn't four o'clock—it's sixteen."

"Sixteen o'clock?"

"I guess so. You know—like the military."

"Speaking of that, what time is it?"

She cracked her left eye open and peered at her watch. "Two-fifteen. Fourteen-fifteen, I guess."

"That's a pain in the neck."

I read the same map over and over, the web of red and green and yellow lines not making any sense no matter how hard I tried. I'd lived in three cities—Salt Lake, Provo, and Omaha. None of them had a subway system, so this was all new to me.

"It looks like we can either take this orange line down to this yellow line, and then walk, or we can take this green line up to the light blue line. It's longer that way, but I think it goes right by the hotel."

Rebekah rubbed her face and sat up. "Let me see."

I showed her the routes again and she laughed.

"The only problem," she said, "is that this light blue line isn't a subway—it's a river."

"Really?" I looked closely at the travel guide. "So our hotel is in the middle of the river?"

"What's it called?"

I reached in my pants pocket and retrieved the address Isabella had written out. "Hôtel des Deux Iles. Fifty-nine Rue St-Louis-en-l'Ile." I slaughtered the pronunciation. A French policeman would probably come and arrest me for crimes against the culture.

"St-Louis?" she replied excitedly. "That's the name of the island. It's not the famous one—well, it might be famous, but I don't know anything about it—but the other island is the one with Notre Dame. I bet we'll have some great views."

"Cool," I said, turning back to the book. "So I guess that means we take the orange line to the yellow one."

"How much money did Isabella give you?"

I dug in the backpack and produced a roll of bills wrapped in a rubber band. "I have a little change in my pocket, too."

She flipped through the euros while I read about the dark blue and dark green lines. Both were express trains, and both were going in our direction; but I had no idea how often they stopped, and I feared we might end up on the one-way express to Spain.

Rebekah stood up and walked toward the street, waving her hand to a taxi. I grabbed the book and backpack and followed.

"Can we afford this?" I asked.

"How much do you think a euro is worth?"

"No idea. . . . Five per dollar? Six?"

"Not quite." She grinned and opened the door of the cab. "I think we can afford the taxi."

* * *

The hotel was, as Rebekah had predicted, on the island east of Notre Dame. Just the ride through town was worth the price of the trip. It was quintessential Paris. Even before we passed any landmarks, the streets and houses and apartments were historic and amazing. Everything was old and architecturally magnificent. Every now and then, between narrow buildings, we'd catch a glimpse of the Eiffel Tower or the Arc de Triomphe, or one of the many other things that makes Paris, Paris. It made me want to pull out a sketch pad or an easel or a camera—and I don't have an artistic bone in my body.

Salt Lake City was founded in the mid-1800s—about the time that Paris was just winding down. While pioneers were planting the first trees in the Valley, the French were illuminating the world with art, architecture, and culture. I'd heard there were Utah leaders currently striving to make downtown Salt Lake City "a little bit of Paris." They had a long way to go.

Rebekah and I sat in the back of the taxi, me staring dumbfounded out the window and she grinning uncontrollably. I held her hand, and the world of terrorists felt a million miles away.

The cab driver dropped us off in front of the hotel, a five-story building made of white stone and fronted with a green canvas awning. Black lanterns flanked the front entrance. Rebekah gave the driver several of the bills and said, "Enchanté de faire votre connaissance." The driver chuckled at her attempt to speak his language and waved as he drove away.

"So this is it?" Rebekah asked, red-faced from the exchange with the driver.

"What did you tell him?"

"That I was happy to meet him," she said defensively. "It was a perfectly acceptable thing to say."

"Absolutely."

"Do we have reservations?" she asked, putting on her business face, obviously done talking about her French.

I nodded and opened the door for her. "Isabella said she set us up with two rooms. It's supposed to be prepaid."

The interior of the hotel was simple but refined. Red upholstered furniture sat in the center of the room, flanked by a glass coffee table. The walls were striped with cream and white, making the ceiling look higher than it was—the lobby was actually fairly small.

A middle-aged woman in a black pantsuit sat at a desk just inside the door.

"Bonjour," she said, looking up from her computer. "Je peux vous aider?"

Rebekah, flustered, attempted to answer. "J'ai fait une . . . um . . . reservation."

"You are American?" the woman asked.

"Yes."

"Welcome to the Hôtel des Deux Iles. Under what name is the reservation?"

"Hugh Waltz," I answered. "w-a-l-t-z. There should be two rooms."

She typed the name into her computer and then opened a desk drawer to retrieve our keys. "Yes, Mr. Waltz. Your rooms are up the stairs and on the left—one room has a view of the street and the other has a view of the courtyard."

She gave us some more information about room service and had me sign. I hated having to sign anything with my fake name, and I stared at the paper for several seconds before scribbling the words out. She never looked at the form, but filed it in her drawer and then returned to working on the computer.

"What time do we have to be at the meeting?" Rebekah asked as we left the lobby and climbed two flights of stairs.

"Eight," I answered. "Or, uh, twenty o'clock."

She took the last few steps to the landing, paused, and then looked at her watch. She was out of breath.

"That's four and a half hours. You mind if I get a nap?"

"Not at all," I lied. Here I was in Paris—the most romantic city in the world—with the girl I loved and hoped to marry, and she wanted to sleep.

I helped her to her room—tiny, but nice—and made sure she was comfortable. She took the small, portable oxygen tank from the backpack, lay down, and tried to breathe.

* * *

While Rebekah slept, I wandered the streets. Notre Dame was close, but I decided to save that for later since I knew that she'd want to go. So instead I headed north across the Seine. With my trusty guidebook under my arm, I made my way from sight to sight, first a museum—which looked like it belonged at Disneyland, snuggled somewhere in between Sleeping Beauty's castle and the Snow White ride—then on to a church, and finally to the Hôtel de Ville.

I paid ten euros and joined a tour group. The hotel was grandiose and ornate, one of the buildings that show up in calendars and James Bond movies, the type of building that doesn't exist in America. It was a town hall of sorts, built in the late nineteenth century after the original had burned down in 1871. Its courtyard was the sight of many terrible events—it was there that the assassin of Henry IV was executed, with horses pulling him limb from limb.

It was also in that courtyard that thousands of Parisian women had gathered, showing their support for the French Revolution. Incited by rumors of soldiers desecrating the tricolor flag, and angry about the price of bread, the women had marched to the Hôtel de Ville. And, with the aid of national guardsmen, they succeeded in storming the building, killing several of the royal guards. They got the undivided attention of the king.

At the end of the tour I stopped in a small shop that looked like it catered to tourists. I bought a bottle of soda—orange, though I didn't recognize the brand—and a package of what looked like cookies. It wasn't the kind of snack my dentist would approve of, but he wasn't there.

I paid for the food (one gold coin with a silver border, one silver coin with a gold border, and a bunch of little gold and copper ones), and to be honest, none of it was any good.

* * *

Rebekah looked better when I returned to the hotel. She'd slept and showered, and even though she didn't have any other clothes to change into, she looked great.

It was clear that she hadn't fully recovered. The scar on her forehead was still pink and obvious, and her skin was pale. And the weight she'd lost made her look painfully thin. But she was up and walking, and that was good enough for me.

We strolled the streets, doing our best to blend in with the touristy crowd. Isabella had given me a digital camera, and we stopped here and there, taking pictures and generally having a marvelous time. I didn't really need a reminder of why I'd fallen in love with Rebekah, but it was nice for it to feel normal again.

I had an ulterior motive for this trip. With Rebekah away from all the troubles back in England, I might be able to talk to her about my proposal. Hopefully she wouldn't always associate engagement with explosions and pain, and we'd be able to come to some sort of resolution. I'd told her I didn't want to lose her, and then I almost did. The bombing did nothing but strengthen my resolve.

We were going to be in Paris for two days. The first day was for spying on her father, and the second for sightseeing and romantic strolls. The marriage discussion could wait one more day.

Rebekah and I got an outdoor table at a café called Le Poivre, across the street from Le Grand St-Julien, the restaurant where Edward would be meeting with his supposed partners in crime. His eatery was listed in the guidebook as one of the finest dining experiences in all of Europe, whereas ours wasn't listed at all. However, it also said St-Julien was renowned for its cold oysters in aspic, and poached pigeon with lentils. I was perfectly content to eat at the cheap place.

The sun was getting low in the sky, and Rebekah and I had long finished our meal, but we remained at the table, talking and waiting.

Someone approached the St-Julien doors. I pointed the digital camera, pretending to take Rebekah's picture, but actually zoomed in on the restaurant. Rebekah looked at my watch and logged the time of the picture. We'd been doing the same thing for the better part of an hour.

"Can you believe we're here?" Rebekah said, leaning forward and speaking excitedly.

I nodded and looked up the still-packed street. I'd never been to Europe, but this was almost exactly as I'd imagined it'd be.

She pointed at the buildings across the street. "This neighborhood—the Marais—was totally taken over by the people during the French Revolution. This is where the people met and talked and rallied."

I nodded and gestured to another possible suspect. I photographed him and she jotted a note.

"Why did it start?" I asked. With my fork, I played with the remnants of an apple tart on my plate. I'd been too full to finish it.

"Didn't you have to learn about it in history?"

"I was supposed to. I remember vague stuff—three estates, something about a congress or something."

She put on a look of mock disapproval. "What grade did you get in that class?"

"I don't remember. Not an A."

"There were a bunch of reasons," she said, smiling. "They were inspired by the American Revolution, and philosophers were proposing all kinds of new ideas—Rousseau and Voltaire. They talked about a social contract between the people and the government. Basically, the people agree to be governed and the government agrees to be fair. It was revolutionary stuff."

"Literally."

"Right."

We took another picture. It was five minutes to eight.

"And here's a little-known fact: the American Revolution led directly to the French Revolution."

"You just said that," I answered. "They saw our example."

"Well, that's just part of it. The French bailed us out during our revolution, sending troops and ships—but it nearly bankrupted France to do it. They were having money problems anyway, but then we owed them a lot of money and couldn't pay it back. Living conditions in France got worse and worse, which upset the people."

"They revolted because of the price of bread," I replied, showing off the fact I'd learned that afternoon.

"Their money problems also helped America again—France desperately needed money, so they sold the U.S. the Louisiana Purchase."

"Really?"

"There's another one," Rebekah said, pointing toward the restaurant. We snapped the photo.

"Rebekah," I said. "You're a nerd."

She laughed, a little color flowing into her pale cheeks. "You're the one who's good at math."

Edward appeared a few minutes later, stepping out of a black cab, dressed impeccably in an expensive suit. Rebekah had talked for an hour about how she needed to have her back to the street so he wouldn't recognize her, but as he walked she stared at him. He never glanced in our direction.

Twenty minutes later we left the café.

Rebekah was silent most of the walk back to the hotel. It was almost as though seeing her father had spoiled everything—we were far from danger, and then we were close again.

We stopped on the Pont Marie Bridge and looked out over the Seine.

"Rebekah," I said, trying to figure out the best way to phrase what I was going to ask.

"What?" Her voice was quiet and tired.

"Why don't we just run?"

"Don't say that."

"Things may never get back to normal."

"I don't want to think about it."

"We're going to have to sometime."

"Eric," she said, turning to face me. "Just drop it, okay? I don't know what to do."

I nodded. "Okay."

Rebekah began walking again. I followed, wishing I had something comforting to offer.

She stopped and turned. "He's my father."

"I know."

"He's not a criminal." There were tears in her eyes.

I didn't answer.

"He's . . ." She stood there, trying to think of something to say. She couldn't. We walked all the way back to the hotel and upstairs to our rooms. At her door I hugged her good night, and she hugged me, and we didn't say a word.

After making sure she was tightly locked in, I went downstairs and got directions to a nearby Internet café. I e-mailed all the photos to Isabella, along with the time log. Edward looked like a criminal to me.

CHAPTER 19

I DREAMED ABOUT many things that night, every one of them peaceful and every one of them happy. I dreamed about Rebekah and being back home, and I dreamed about Thanksgiving dinner in a completely terrorist-free reality, and I dreamed about way back on my mission in Nebraska, when it was nothing but spirituality and corn on the cob all summer long. My dreams were the type of warm, innocent flights of fancy that would make great musical montages accompanied by Johnny Mathis music. Family, calm, Rebekah. No terrorists.

I was shaken out of my dreams with all the reality that the devil could muster.

"Eric! Eric, wake up!"

It was a woman's voice, but not Rebekah's. When my eyes popped open, taking in my French surroundings, they focused on a very haggard Isabella right in front of me, and a very anxious Rebekah throwing all of my stuff into the backpack.

"What's going on?" I asked groggily. I sat up in bed and grabbed my shirt from the chair by the bed. I may have been rudely interrupted, but I knew Rebekah and Isabella well enough that I didn't want to slow their actions, whatever the reason was.

"I got your pictures," Isabella said. "We have to get out of here."

"Rebekah?" I asked, finally noticing her tear-stained face.

She only nodded and continued to zip up the bag.

"Come on," Isabella ordered. "Get dressed. We need to get out of this hotel."

Rebekah forced a smile and handed me my shoes. The women left the room, and thirty seconds later I joined them in the hallway.

My hair was a mess, but I figured that bedhead was probably not a major concern right now. Besides, Rebekah's was nearly as bad.

"What was in the pictures?" I asked as we rushed down the stairs.

"Rebekah," Isabella said, ignoring me. "Go to the desk clerk and tell her you'll be staying two more nights."

Rebekah gave her a strange look, but only for a moment. Isabella and I stepped outside, and I heard Rebekah begin her broken French.

"So?" I said, looking back through the windows. Isabella's eyes were on the street. Over her shoulder was an obviously heavy gym bag.

"It's bad, Eric."

"You know who the people are?"

She nodded, scanning the faces of the tourists and Parisians already out for the morning. "Every one of them."

"Are they from some other country? Are they buying nukes? Terrorists?"

"No."

The door opened and Rebekah joined us. She was wearing the same clothes from the day before, and it suddenly struck me how impractical sandals were for running. Then again, her lungs were far more restrictive than her shoes.

Isabella checked us over with a frown. "You look like tourists. That's fine for now, but when we get out of the city you'll need some more native clothes."

"Where are we going?" Rebekah asked, taking my hand.

"Somewhere we can talk," Isabella said. "After that . . . I don't know." She was obviously flustered and tired. If she'd made it all the way from England to arrive early in the morning, she'd certainly been up most of the night.

She picked a direction and began walking. Rebekah and I followed. Her gait was much too quick for Rebekah, and I wanted to say something but didn't. We crossed the bridge, headed north, and soon found ourselves winding down the narrow streets of the Marais.

"What's going on?" Rebekah demanded as we walked.

"We have two problems, but I don't know which is bigger."

"What are they?"

"The first is my fault," Isabella said, "and it's more applicable to you two."

"What?"

"I gave you the passports—the same passports you used back in Washington."

"So?"

"So, someone has been watching for them."

Rebekah stopped. "What? Who?"

Isabella, who wasn't used to admitting she was wrong, didn't stop. Rebekah and I were forced to keep up with her. "I don't know. But they've been tracked."

"Was it the FBI?" Rebekah asked warily. "Or Felix?"

"More likely Felix," she conceded. "The passports were flagged at the train station, and somebody accessed the information."

I couldn't believe Isabella had been so stupid. "Any chance it was the FBI?"

"It doesn't look like it. We know that Felix was on the island, and he most likely discovered your false identities. The FBI never could have."

Rebekah didn't bother trying to keep her voice down. "Are you trying to get us killed?"

"I said it was my fault," Isabella replied simply. "This is why I told you to register two more nights at the hotel. If you get traced there, Felix and the N.O.S. will wait for you to come back and we'll be long gone."

I shook my head. "Long gone to where?"

Isabella stopped at an intersection and scanned the cross street up and down. "For now, we're just leaving." She picked her direction and started to walk again.

Rebekah was out of breath and having trouble keeping up. I grabbed Isabella's arm.

"You need to slow down."

Isabella rolled her eyes but slackened the pace.

"What's the other thing?" Rebekah asked.

"A hunch."

"About the photos we sent?"

"Yes."

"Who were they? Who was he meeting with?"

"Hold on." Isabella turned suddenly and trotted down the long flight of stairs of a metro station. We had to wait for the train, so

Rebekah pointed us to an empty corner. We sat on a filthy metal bench, letting her get her breath back.

Isabella whispered as she spoke. "Look at these." She unzipped the gym bag, withdrew several sheets of paper, and held them out to us. "Do you know who any of these people are?"

Both Rebekah and I shook our heads. We already knew that none of the people we'd seen the night before looked remotely familiar.

Isabella pointed at the first, an older man in a tan coat. "Robert Belmont Hamlin. He's old money, now living just outside of Exeter. This one is Friedrich Simons of Frankfurt. He all but owns the public works of western Germany." She gestured to the next page. "James David Mills, recently listed as the fourth wealthiest man in Europe. Paul Stoddard of New York City. His corporations control almost half of Manhattan. Emil Gobert. For all intents and purposes he's calling the political shots in North Africa."

"And the woman?" Rebekah asked.

Isabella nodded grimly, tapping the photo. "Harriet Webster Kincaid. More money than all of them."

"But who are they?" I said, taking one of the pictures and staring at it. "Where did their money come from?"

"People with this kind of money don't *do* something to get this kind of money. They're not the founders of Wal-Mart or General Motors. They have money because they've always had money, and now there's so much of it that it can't help but grow exponentially."

"So?" Rebekah said, obviously annoyed. "Where's the danger? They're rich—so what?"

"They're not just rich. Money equals control. Why did people first go to America?"

"I'm sure you're going to say money."

"Yes. You're taught in grade school that the pilgrims came to America for religious freedom, but it's only mentioned as a sidebar that they were working employees of massive trading companies. They settled not to find truth, justice, and the American way, but to mine for gold and to grow silk. Why did Columbus sail the ocean blue? Money. Why did William Randolph Hearst start the Spanish-American War? Money."

"So what?" I said, confused. "Of course rich people control things. This isn't exactly big news."

Isabella pursed her lips. "This is different, Eric."

I could hear the rumble of the subway train as it approached. Suddenly, Rebekah stood. "Wait a minute."

Isabella took the papers back, folded them neatly, and inserted them into her bag. "What?" I asked, as I noticed Rebekah's expression.

Her face was pale and contorted. "We're not running from Felix—we're running from my father."

Isabella stood, calmly watching the train platform. "Both, technically."

I was confused. "What's the difference?"

Rebekah's face was red. "The difference is that one is temporary and one is permanent. We can run from Felix and get protection from the FBI. But we can't run from my father, can we?"

Isabella shook her head. "You know too much."

Rebekah was shaking. I took her hand and tried to calm her down.

"Think about it," Isabella snapped, her voice barely audible. "Do you think he told you any of that stuff expecting to ever send you back to your old life? He knew that the FBI would question where you'd been and that you might tell them everything."

Rebekah was ready to hit something. "We only know all of that because he told us. It's not our fault. I just want things to get back to normal."

"It's not my fault, either. I wouldn't have told you."

"Wait a minute," I said, trying to quash the coming fight. "Why are *you* running? For that matter, why are you coming to us? Couldn't we all just go back to Edward's house—he doesn't know we were in Paris. He doesn't know that we know about his friends."

"We still don't know about his friends," Rebekah said, exasperated. She pointed angrily at Isabella. "You won't tell us what's going on."

The metro car came screeching into the station, and I could barely hear Isabella's response over the din. "I know who they are," she said, almost shouting. "And I'd rather take my chances running from them than living in the same house with them." With that, she tossed the heavy gym bag to me and turned toward the platform.

"At least tell us where we're going," I said, taking Rebekah's hand and following.

Isabella held up her hand, indicating that we'd discuss more later, and we crammed into the subway.

CHAPTER 20

THE SUBWAY CAR was crowded, and Rebekah and I sat quietly together, packed in tightly with a group of tourists and commuters. Isabella sat across the aisle—too far away to talk quietly, and there were too many people nearby to talk loudly.

I held the gym bag on my lap. Isabella had her small, leather briefcase, and Rebekah held the backpack. She clutched it tightly and stared into space.

"You okay?" I asked, my voice barely above a whisper.

Her lips curved into a sad half smile, and she shrugged. "I don't know what to think."

"Neither do I."

She thought for a long time. Meanwhile Isabella, always wary and on guard, was scanning the faces of the passengers.

"Eric," Rebekah said. I felt her shoulder lean into me as she quietly spoke. "I need you to be on my side."

"I am on your side," I answered quickly. "Always."

"This isn't right."

I nodded. "I know it isn't, but I don't know what is."

"We need to pray."

Isabella was watching us talk but surely couldn't hear the conversation.

"When we get off the metro, we'll find a place," I assured Rebekah. I thought for a minute and added, "I've been praying like crazy since I woke up, but it doesn't seem to be helping."

"Me too." She leaned her tired head on my shoulder.

"How are you feeling?"

"Been better."

"If we end up getting on a train, you can sleep. I don't think we're going to be doing more walking. Of course, if you and I decide not to go with Isabella, you can just go back to the hotel."

"Right."

The subway car slowed to a stop, and the crowd was rearranged. Several of the people sitting next to us left, and as more people boarded, Isabella moved next to me. I thought she might say something, but instead she just continued watching the passengers.

A large man in a tight T-shirt sat opposite us and began eating a floppy sandwich. Next to him a family of American tourists gathered around a guidebook, studying their next sightseeing tour. Two young Frenchmen stood by the door, dressed for work.

Halfway down the car, on the far side, was a skinny young woman with black, curly hair. She was talking on her cell phone and looking at the floor.

"Rebekah," I said, pointing toward the girl. "Do you recognize her?"

Isabella immediately interrupted. "Why?"

Rebekah gazed for a moment and then nodded, looking relieved. "She works for the hotel. I think she's housekeeping—emptied the trash in my room last night."

A French voice came over the loudspeaker announcing something, and the girl looked up—and stared right at me. Isabella noticed it as well. The instant our eyes met, the girl glanced away, and then she turned her entire body to face the other direction.

"You've seen her before?" Isabella asked sharply.

"When did she get on the train?" I asked.

"The same station we did," Isabella answered.

"I've seen her someplace else," I said.

"Are you sure?" Rebekah asked.

I nodded. "But I can't remember where."

Isabella calmly looked at the floor and spoke in a whisper. "Stop staring at her. At the next stop, Eric, you get off. If she stays on, Rebekah and I will get off too. If she follows you off, get back in here."

I agreed and took a deep breath. I felt Rebekah's hand touch mine.

"It might not be anybody," I said.

Isabella's answer was short and grim. "But it could be."

The next few minutes were long and nerve-racking. Despite Isabella's warning, I watched the girl from the corner of my eye. She stayed on the cell phone and never looked back. She played with her hair twice and rubbed her eyes once.

I felt the train begin to slow, and I slung the shoulder strap of the bag over my arm. I felt Rebekah squeeze my hand, and then I stood up. The girl didn't watch.

A moment later, the doors popped open and I pushed through a crowd of people—as casually as possible—to get out. I walked a few yards and waited.

I looked back at the subway. Rebekah was staring at me through the windows. She and Isabella stood, ready to exit. I strained to see the girl, but there were too many people. I jogged a couple feet, hopping up some steps to get a better view. I didn't see her anywhere—it seemed that everyone in France had dark hair.

I turned back to the windows—Rebekah was waving frantically. Without thinking, I elbowed my way back through the throng and onto the subway. It was more crowded now, leaving the three of us standing.

"She left?"

Rebekah nodded. "Right after you did."

"I lost her," I said. "Where did she go?"

Isabella tapped my arm, her voice almost inaudible. "There."

The girl stepped back onto the train, at the far end of the car, just as the doors slid shut.

Without any further discussion, Isabella pointed toward the other end of the subway, and we maneuvered clumsily through the standing passengers. I stepped on someone's foot, and I'm sure we got more than one dirty look, but I didn't care.

"Any idea who she is?" Rebekah whispered as we reached the end.

I took a breath and glanced over my shoulder. She was still on her phone, not watching us. "She doesn't look like a . . . whatever. What are these people? Terrorists? Criminals?"

Isabella ignored me. "She's been on that phone since she boarded. She knows we're on to her, so she's probably calling for backup. Since this subway only goes one direction, she'll be telling someone to meet her farther down the line. The more time we give her, the less likely it is that we can get out of here without a fight—so we're getting off at the next station."

She glanced over her shoulder at the girl, and then turned back to us. "We have two options. If we're lucky, we'll get off this car just as another is arriving in the station. If so, we can board that and head another direction." She paused and thought for a minute.

"What's the other option?" Rebekah asked.

Isabella offered a reluctant smile. "We outrun her."

I shook my head. "Rebekah can't run."

"I know."

"So?"

"You two get out of here. I'll make sure she doesn't follow you."

Rebekah looked worried. "Where do we go?"

"Get out of the station, but watch the entrance. I'll meet you."

"What if you don't come?" I regretted the question the moment I said it, but Isabella brushed it off.

"If this girl was the type to cause trouble, she'd have already done it."

Rebekah pulled the backpack over her shoulders and tightened the straps. I looked back down the length of the car and saw the girl, looking back at me and standing next to the door. It was too far to read her face.

I took Rebekah's hand. "I'm going to follow you, okay? You go as fast as you can, and I'll stick with you."

She nodded and took a deep breath.

The train slowed, and I grabbed an overhead rail to steady myself.

Without turning to face her, Rebekah asked Isabella, "How are you going to stop her?"

"Discreetly."

The concrete walls of the tunnel suddenly disappeared, and the train entered the metro station. The loudspeaker came on saying something I couldn't possibly pronounce, let alone understand. Rebekah squeezed my hand and then let go of it.

A bell sounded, the doors sprang open, and Rebekah ran. I hadn't expected a full sprint, but she was fifteen feet ahead of me before I knew it. I took off after her, weaving through the sea of people, dodging garbage cans and pillars. No one looked at us strangely, other than to give the occasional disapproving glance. We weren't anything special—just a couple of travelers behind schedule.

There was no second train, and Rebekah didn't pause to wait for one. She changed course, sliding slightly in her loose sandals, and headed for the stairs. With the crowds thinning, I caught up with her.

She took the stairs two at a time, red-faced and breathing heavily. There was light above us, and I could feel the warm summer air. As we neared the top, Rebekah took a misstep and stumbled, barely catching herself on the railing. As I took her arm to help her up, she began coughing—a shallow, raspy cough that caused her to shudder with pain.

"Come on," I said, pulling her arm over my shoulders. "Just a little farther."

She nodded, still coughing uncontrollably, and hobbled the rest of the way up the steps. When we reached the street I spun around, looking for somewhere we could hide. There was a narrow alley a few dozen yards away. I pointed to it, offered a few worthless words of encouragement, and we walked.

Rebekah nearly fell to the ground when we reached the alley, ignoring the litter and muddy pavement. I helped her into a sitting position with her back against a wall. She leaned forward, resting her head on her knees, coughing and gagging.

I pulled the backpack off her—she was barely responsive as I tried easing it from each arm.

"Rebekah," I demanded. "Talk to me."

She bobbed her head, the coughing slowing, but she was still shaking with pain. I tore open the pack and pulled out her oxygen tank. It was a poor fix, but it might help. Carefully, I placed the mask over her nose and mouth, then adjusted the elastic band. Rebekah leaned back against the wall, her wet, reddened eyes shut tight as she sucked in tiny, rapid breaths.

"Are you okay?" It was the dumbest question I'd ever asked.

After a slight pause, she nodded.

This was stupid. We should never have gone to France. I should have never listened to Isabella. Living back under Edward's care—no matter what he and his friends were up to—was better than watching Rebekah struggle to breathe, collapsed in the filth of an alley.

I looked back out onto the street. We were only a few feet into the alley, but mostly blocked from view by a row of parked and chained bicycles. Crouching low, I watched the entrance.

When I glanced back at Rebekah, she was lying down on her side—almost in a fetal position.

"Rebekah?"

She wheezed. "I'm . . . all right."

"I don't see anyone," I said, looking back into the street. "Isabella should be out soon."

More than twenty people trickled out of the station as I watched. Isabella wasn't among them, but none of them looked alarmed either, which probably meant that no one had started a fight. Still, the girl with black hair didn't come out. Something was happening.

"Should we check on her?" Rebekah asked. It was almost funny—there was no way Rebekah would be standing up for a while, let alone heading back down all those stairs.

"She'll be okay," I answered. "You need to rest. Isabella's tough."

"Eric?"

"Yeah?"

"Can you get me something to drink?"

I looked back at her, her knees and legs grimy with the filth of the alley, and her clothes stained. Her hair was still a mess, and her face was red and splotchy. I didn't want to leave her for a minute—I'd have much rather called an ambulance.

"Water, if you can," she said. Her right hand—still bandaged—was in a fist and pulled tightly against her chest. The left was lying limp at her side.

I knelt down and unzipped the gym bag. Isabella had pulled money from it earlier to pay for the subway. On top were the papers and photos she'd shown us, and I pushed them aside. Beneath them was a thick stack of photocopied maps—blurred and confused, speckled with French. As I picked them up, I saw the money.

"Rebekah," I said, staring and pointing.

She didn't respond. I glanced over at her and saw her eyes clenched shut and her hand balled up in a fist. She was trying desperately to control her breathing.

I took a stack of euros, told Rebekah I'd be right back, and then hurried out into the street. I hoped no muggers lurked in that alley—the bag must've held millions.

There was less foot traffic here than back in the more touristy areas we'd been in. The street was narrow and tall, with apartments and offices rising up five or six stories on both sides of the street. There were no cafés or street vendors in sight, but I spotted a small shop across the road. I waited for a car to pass and then jogged over.

I didn't try to speak any of the French Rebekah had taught me. Instead, I just grabbed a bottle of water and laid it and one hundred euros on the counter. The clerk said something I didn't understand and handed me my change—apparently one hundred euros was a lot of money.

As I stepped outside there was a flash of white—a small sedan sped past and screeched to a halt in the middle of the road. The driver left the car, dashing for the metro entrance.

He was dressed the same as always—tan pants and a polo shirt, and he looked far more like a golf pro than a terrorist. Felix Hazard.

In seconds he had disappeared from sight down the steps to the subway. I ran at full speed back to the alley, almost getting hit by a passing cyclist. I found Rebekah sitting up again, massaging her forehead with her left hand.

"Can you walk?" I asked, hastily unscrewing the cap from the water bottle and handing it to her.

"Do I have to?" she said, pulling the oxygen mask down and taking a timid sip of the water.

I crammed all of Isabella's papers back into the gym bag and zipped it closed. "Yes. Felix just went down into the subway."

Rebekah nearly choked on the water. "Felix? Was that girl working for him?"

"I don't know," I said, putting on Rebekah's backpack. "We have to get out of here."

"What about Isabella?"

"She can take care of herself."

"Eric," Rebekah said, struggling to her feet. "She stayed down there to save our lives. We need to at least warn her or something."

"Rebekah, we could get killed."

"So could she."

"Rebekah," I said again. "You can hardly stand."

She fumbled awkwardly with the mask, finally yanking it off. "Eric, we need to do the right thing. I don't know if we can help her, but we need to try."

I grabbed the mask and oxygen and stuffed them into the backpack. My voice was harsher than I meant it to be. "The right thing might be to run. Maybe the right thing is to survive."

"No," she insisted, taking a wobbly step away from the wall. I reached forward and took her by the arm.

"Rebekah," I pleaded. "You could die."

I could feel her trembling as I held her up. She looked into my eyes—there was pain in hers, and tears. "What good is living if I'm not living right?"

I shook my head. I didn't want anything to happen to her—we'd come so far and been through so much.

"Here," I said, gently forcing her to sit. "I'll go."

"I can go," she insisted.

"You couldn't even make it down the steps."

I dragged some aluminum garbage cans from the other side of the alley to better obscure her location. Finally, I gave her a kiss on the cheek and headed for the stairs.

CHAPTER 21

I CREPT DOWN the steps, slowly, cautiously, and terrified. I knew that anyone watching the stairs would see me before I saw him or her. It had been at least two minutes since Felix had run down the same steps, and he hadn't come up—I didn't know what that meant. Had he found Isabella and were they in the middle of fighting? Had he found no one and exited the station using a different set of stairs? Was he still down there looking, and would I run into him in the next few seconds? I didn't like Felix even from a distance; up close and personal was out of the question.

As I reached the bottom of the stairs I saw that the metro looked exactly the way it had minutes earlier. There were small clumps of people standing around waiting; there were men and women in business suits carrying briefcases and bags on their way to work. There were tourists, looking lost. A guy about my age was playing the guitar by a pillar, singing something in French and making no money.

Isabella was nowhere to be seen, as was Felix or the black-haired girl. I walked nervously through the crowd, looking around pillars and bracing myself for a bullet in the chest or a knife in the belly. I tried to think of some way to better conceal myself but couldn't come up with anything. I had no hat. There was no stray newspaper that I could pluck up to cover my face with. There were no large potted plants that I could hide behind. I was out in the open, and I felt like someone had taped a *Kill Me* sign on my back.

I paused and leaned against a pillar, partly because it was nice to have a wall behind me, and partly because my blood pressure was reaching critical heights. I waited there for several seconds, taking deep breaths and trying to see straight. I closed my eyes and rubbed them, my head aching and my body tired. There was a high-powered fan above my head, and it felt good to have a little air—it wasn't fresh but at least it was moving.

When I opened my eyes, I saw her—Isabella, crouched behind a bench as though she were tying her shoe. There was still no sign of Felix or the girl, but obviously Isabella knew she needed to keep a low profile.

She was watching me, her face looking both disapproving and relieved. (I had a hunch that if I did every single little thing Isabella ever asked of me, she'd still shake her head and roll her eyes.) She mouthed something, and I mouthed back that I had no idea what she'd just said. She pointed subtly, with such a low-key gesture that she may have simply been stretching her hand. Still, I got the message: someone was behind me.

I turned around instinctively. There was a pillar there. Oh yeah.

The station rumbled as a train approached. Isabella watched and waited. I dug into my pocket.

The train burst into the station, screeching and thundering. As the doors popped open and the mass of quietly waiting passengers turned into chaos, I pulled the thick stack of euros from my pocket, yanked off the rubber band, and threw it with all my might over the crowd.

They fluttered above the Parisians for several slow-motion seconds, spreading in the fast-moving air. The bright green-and-orange bills didn't catch the distracted travelers' eyes at first, but when they did, oh, boy! And I thought it had been chaos before.

The mob surged, frantically grabbing for the cash and nearly trampling anyone who got in their way. I looked at Isabella. She nodded—probably the best professional courtesy she could muster—and ran for the far exit. I took a deep breath and dived into the crowd, pushing my way to the stairs and Rebekah's alley.

I paused just once to look back. There was Felix, spinning in circles and swarmed by the crowd as he searched unsuccessfully for Isabella and me.

I took the stairs three at a time, bounding up to fresh air and freedom. Isabella had exited on the far side—probably a block away—and she'd be around. We'd hail a cab and get Rebekah to a hotel with a nice, warm bed and a doctor who wouldn't ask nosy questions.

And then I turned the corner into the alley, saw Rebekah leaning against the wall, her face ghost-white, and the girl with black hair six feet in front of her, holding a pistol.

I remember back in the eighth grade when I'd encountered my first real bully. His name was Ben Olsen, but everyone just called him B.O. He wasn't particularly evil-looking, but he had mastered the kidney punch and once threw a rock at my head. There was one morning, outside of gym class, when he'd made a particularly disparaging comment about my mother's weight. I responded with a solid, "Oh, yeah?" For the next four years I found myself thinking of brutally crushing replies.

Likewise, there hadn't been a day that had passed in the last month that I hadn't thought of what had happened to Rebekah. I had a whole list of things I would have done or said, had I been there when the terrorists were placing the bomb in Maurice's storage space. I'd envisioned exactly where I would have hit them, and what kind of baseball bat I would have used, and what I would have kicked in their faces as they lay groaning in the dirt.

Solar plexus, aluminum, sand. Toxic sand, infected with the hantavirus.

The girl with black hair looked over at me, looked back at Rebekah, and tried to decide in that split second which one of us was a better target for her small pistol. She looked surprised, and she almost seemed nervous. I don't know which one of us she was going to aim at, but it should have been me, and it should have been quicker.

I lunged, leaping a distance far greater than I thought I could leap. She swung her arm around to aim the gun at me, but I was inches away from her and it was all over. She was short and thin, and I tackled her to the pavement without hardly trying. I held her hands in place with mine, and she struggled in vain to point the gun at anything important. She was scared.

I moved my left hand slowly, inching up from her wrist to her hand to the gun. Her grip was like iron, and her knuckles white. I thought about letting go with my right and hitting her, but I didn't. She was stuck where she was, and I didn't want to give her a chance to move.

"Rebekah," I yelled. "Grab the gun."

"Hold on," she answered behind me, and I heard her shuffling to her feet.

"Who are you?" I demanded, looking into the frightened eyes of my would-be assassin.

She didn't respond, other than to shake and turn pale.

"Why won't he leave us alone?" I shouted, my face only inches from hers. "What did we ever do to you?"

Rebekah touched my side and knelt down carefully to wrench the pistol from the girl's hand. The gun was pointed away from all of us, and Rebekah slowly tried to pry finger after finger from the grip.

"Why do you want us dead?" I yelled again. I could feel myself shaking—not with fear, but with anger.

Rebekah nearly had the gun.

The girl shuddered, her eyes pleading. I didn't care one bit, and I showed it in my face. This girl wasn't going anywhere other than to the police, and I'd write a letter to the parole board about how she deserved a nice, damp cell with rats for company.

There was a flash of light and a loud pop. Rebekah jumped, snatching the recently fired gun from the woman's fingers. I hopped to my feet, taking the weapon and pointing it at her. She rolled into a ball.

Rebekah wheezed. "I'm sure everyone heard that."

The sound was still ringing in my ears, and I doubted anyone in Paris could have missed the noise. Keeping the pistol aimed, I moved to the bags and carefully slung them over my shoulders.

"How many of you are there?" I demanded.

She didn't answer, so I repeated the question, louder and with the gun a lot closer.

"Three," she finally shrieked. "Just three."

Her accent was American.

There was a sudden movement around the corner. I swung the gun around, and Isabella nearly dropped to the pavement to avoid the line of fire.

"Who got shot?" she asked urgently.

"No one," I answered, lowering the pistol and then pointing to the girl. "She fired it—probably a signal."

Isabella hurried to me and snatched away the gun.

"We have to get out of here," she said.

"What do we do with her?" Rebekah asked.

Isabella hurriedly checked her watch, dug in her bag, and then had me hold the girl's hands together while she bound them with a zip tie. After doing the same with the girl's feet, we ran.

* * *

Isabella carried the bag of money and her briefcase. She had the pistol in her suit pocket—it was small and easily concealed. I wore the backpack and held Rebekah's arm around my shoulders to help her walk. We were trying to go fast but knew that running was out of the question.

We hadn't done anything to stop the black-haired girl from following us. She might have been easily stopped, but the N.O.S. wasn't made up of spineless young women. If she was working for Felix, then she had to be more than she seemed.

The alley continued for a hundred feet and then branched in two directions. Isabella took a quick glance down both and chose the left. We followed.

Halfway along the narrow back street, Isabella opened a door and ushered Rebekah and me in. It was a service entrance for some kind of business—boxes lined the hallway, all marked in French. There was a faint smell of something good, and I guessed we were in a restaurant.

"What are we going to do?" I asked, my voice hushed.

"We're going to wait," Isabella answered. She quietly opened a door and peeked inside. Satisfied, she motioned us to enter. "Felix will have discovered where we were, and that girl will have told him which direction we went. He'll be watching the streets. We'll wait here until he decides that we must have escaped."

The room we were in was dark and mostly empty. It smelled slightly of mildew, and as my eyes adjusted to the light, I could see it was a laundry room.

"Who was she?" Rebekah asked as I helped her down onto a full laundry sack. She snuggled down into the softness of the bag and relaxed.

"I don't know," Isabella murmured, closing the door all but a crack. "One of Felix's operatives, obviously. I haven't exactly been able to keep tabs on them."

I sat down next to Rebekah. "I remember where I've seen her."

"Where?"

"Back on the island," I answered. "She owned an antiques store. I bought . . . something there."

Isabella nodded thoughtfully. "Well, one thing is certain. She's not good at what she's doing."

"Why didn't she just kill me last night?" Rebekah said softly. "She was right there in my room."

"She probably wasn't supposed to," Isabella answered. "Watching her on the train, I'd guess that she was supposed to track you down and then call Felix. She was probably just keeping close tabs on you while he made a flight over."

I leaned back against the wall and closed my eyes. I couldn't get myself to calm down—I kept reliving the events of the morning over and over. Rebekah looked so pale. The black-haired girl had looked so evil and then so scared. Felix looked just like I remembered, and I hated him.

"How long do we wait?" I asked.

"A few hours, at least."

"What if someone comes in?"

Isabella didn't answer.

Within twenty minutes, Rebekah was asleep, sucking oxygen from the mask. I felt exhausted all over, and every muscle ached, but there was no way I could nap. My mind raced, darting from Felix to Edward to Rebekah. I had no idea what would happen in the next few hours, but one thing was certain: no matter what it took, I would convince Rebekah to run. We'd find a train out of Paris and ride it until we reached a country that didn't watch the news and didn't care about the American economy or Edward's friends or anything.

Madagascar maybe. I'd once watched a PBS documentary about Madagascar and had been fascinated with it ever since. They had great big, funny-shaped trees, and lemurs, and weird bugs. Or maybe we'd go to Australia. I knew nothing about the place, but I figured it was big and open, and we could easily disappear.

Isabella sat near the door, holding the gun in her lap and staring fixedly through the crack she'd left open. Occasionally, we'd hear noise from the hallway, but no one ever came back to the laundry room.

Rebekah slept silently. Her chest rose and fell erratically, and at times it looked like she was fighting for breath. I listened to every inhalation and waited impatiently for her to breathe out.

Isabella stretched a kink out of her neck and unzipped the gym bag. She fumbled through its contents for a moment, and then pulled out a small automatic pistol and a penlight.

"Come here," she said quietly.

I crawled across the floor and sat next to her. She handed me the black-haired girl's revolver, keeping the automatic for herself. I nodded, testing the weight of the gun in my hand. As I gripped the handle I felt both safe and dead, as though simply holding the weapon drained the life from me.

She turned on the penlight and checked a small metro schedule. "I'm heading out into the hall. I want to find out where we are and how we can get out of here if we need to. You stay here."

"Where are we going to go?"

She shook her head, frustrated. "We'll have to wait."

"Can we afford that?"

"Rebekah needs a doctor," she answered. "And I doubt she should be traveling. Even if she could travel, every train station in town is going to be watched."

"The girl said there were only three people from the N.O.S. in Paris."

"She also posed as a member of the hotel staff, which means she probably had access to your personal information. Remember, the hotel made copies of your passports as ID. It might be hard to get out of the country now."

"So we head south," I answered. "We don't leave the country immediately—we head south and buy a car." I pointed to the gym bag. "With money like this we don't need to take the train. And we can wait—maybe get some new ID."

"Eventually. For now, Rebekah needs to rest."

Isabella peered back out the door, and was about to stand when I took her arm.

"Who are they, Isabella? Who is Edward?"

She stared out the door and took a long breath before answering. "He's a member of a secret organization. They only have one goal: control. And their control comes from obtaining and using money."

"Everyone wants money."

She looked back at me. "This is different."

"So you keep saying."

Isabella left and I took her place at the door, keeping an eye on the hallway.

* * *

As the minutes dragged by, I nearly panicked sitting in the dark on the laundry room floor. Nothing seemed real. There was no good reason for us to be hiding in the back room of a Paris restaurant, waiting to be killed. It wasn't fair, and it wasn't right.

Rebekah was sleeping lightly. Occasionally her eyes would open long enough to focus on me or the crack in the door, and then they'd close again. Her breathing was awful.

I opened the gym bag and looked at the photos again. Their faces seemed harmless. Well groomed, perhaps, but they certainly didn't seem all that threatening. I couldn't imagine what Isabella's problem was. Edward was an arms dealer trying to save the world with his crazy scheming—a handful of rich people gathering for dinner hardly seemed worse.

The maps were next in the stack. I'd thought at first that they were photocopies, but on closer inspection I found them pixilated—printed off a computer. I couldn't guess where they led—there was no sign of a road or a city or a mountain. Instead, the maps were a mess of pathways, some curved and some straight. In places the maps looked more like collections of geometric shapes, and in others like the tunnels of an anthill. Across the top of one map was a phrase in French: *Le coeur peut être vu seulement par les yeux de Minerva.* It was punctuated with a small, black circle with a dot in the center—the same symbol I'd seen at Edward's estate. Isabella had made several notes on the map in red felt-tip pen, though they made little sense to me.

There were more papers underneath—photocopies and computer printouts. Some were images and some were text, and most were in French or German.

Oddly enough, Isabella had packed the triangular Scrabble game we'd found in Edward's San Juan Island house. From the look of the letters, she hadn't had any success playing either.

I looked at the money—there was a lot to look at. Most of it was euros, but there were also dollars and pounds. The denominations were large, and the bag was stuffed.

There was a brief movement from outside the door, and I tightened my grip on the gun. I watched, motionless, almost wishing that I could stop the blood from moving through my body—I wanted to be invisible. Then I heard her voice.

"Eric?" Isabella whispered.

"Yeah?"

"I'm coming in. Don't shoot me."

The door opened and closed in an instant, and Isabella slipped inside, crouching next to me.

"Is it time to go?" I asked.

She zipped up the gym bag, giving me an annoyed look as she realized I'd been snooping. She took the revolver from me, set the safety, and shoved it in with the money.

"What is all that stuff?" I asked.

"I've devoted many years to Edward Hughes," she said coldly. "I'm owed at least this much."

Isabella motioned for me to get ready, and I moved back to Rebekah. Her head had fallen at an uncomfortable angle, and I touched her shoulder to wake her. She sat up, stretched, and winced.

"What time is it?" she yawned.

"Eleven," I answered. "It seems a lot later than that."

"It's cold."

Isabella stood. "It'll be warmer outside."

"Are we leaving?"

She nodded. I pulled on the backpack, picked up the gym bag, and then turned to Rebekah. "Can you walk?"

"Yeah. I'm feeling better."

I smiled. "Liar."

"No, I really am," she said, sounding like she was trying to convince herself. The corner of her mouth turned up into a grin. "But let's not run anymore."

Isabella carefully pulled the door open and peeked at the hall. There was noise down at the far end, the sound of many people talking. Isabella whispered and pointed to the door we'd come in. "We'll go back out into the alley, head straight for the street, and find a taxi."

We nodded, following closely behind.

The three of us left the laundry room, making sure we left nothing, and closed the door behind us. Isabella moved quickly to the back door. She was holding the pistol in her right hand and tried the doorknob with her left. The hinges squeaked and we all cringed at the noise. Finally, Isabella pushed the door all the way open and stepped out.

Two shots, loud and fast, rang out like a sickening thunder. Rebekah screamed and I froze. Isabella stumbled, lost her footing, and fell back into the hallway. Time stopped. She was hit in the chest and stomach, her dark suit glistening with blood. The door to the alley swung closed, all of us still inside.

Rebekah jumped, screaming Isabella's name and frantically trying to find something to stop the bleeding. She was yelling, first in English and then in French. "Help! Someone help! Au secours! Appelez la police! Appelez un médecin!"

Isabella's face was white, her eyes halfway open but focused on nothing. Rebekah darted into the laundry room, returning an instant later with a handful of towels. I sprinted to the back door and locked the bolt.

"Eric!" Rebekah shouted, panicked. "There's too much blood. I can't stop it."

I knelt next to her and felt Isabella's neck for a pulse. I couldn't find one.

"We need to leave," I said, my face hot. I felt like I couldn't get a breath.

"Help me stop the bleeding!"

A man appeared at the end of the hall. He took one look at Isabella's body and ran.

"Eric!" Rebekah was desperate.

There was a lot of blood.

"Rebekah," I jumped up and grabbed her arm. "She's gone. We have to get out of here."

"But—" Rebekah was sobbing.

"I'm sorry."

I could hear someone yanking on the alley door, and the dead bolt clanked back and forth. I snatched up the bags again and took Rebekah's hand.

There was another pop and a high-pitched ping. Felix—or one of his friends—was shooting the lock. Rebekah took one last look at Isabella's body, and we ran.

CHAPTER 22

THE HALLWAY FORKED. To the left was another ten yards of corridor ending in white double doors, and to the right was a short flight of stairs leading down. We took the right, since the man we'd seen had taken the left.

The staircase was narrow, as was the rest of the hall. Rebekah took the steps quickly, and I knew she'd pay for it later. At the bottom were two doors—heavy and wooden. I chose one at random, which turned out to be locked. Rebekah yanked open the other.

We were in a small basement café, which looked like it hadn't quite opened for the day. A teenage boy in a white apron swept the floor, and an older woman was setting tables. Both of them looked up at us as we entered.

"C'est fermé," the woman said, bewildered.

Rebekah didn't bother responding. We jogged across the stone-tiled floor and out the front entrance. Seven or eight cement steps led up to street level, but before climbing them I paused, holding Rebekah back. The image of Isabella stepping outside and getting instantly shot replayed over and over in my head.

"What?" Rebekah asked.

"What if someone is out there?"

"We know someone is behind us," she said, breathing heavily. Her eyes were red and scared. I knew she couldn't take much more.

I nodded and then crept up the stairs, peeking over the edge of the sidewalk. Cars were buzzing past, and a crowd was milling around a market just down the street. There was no sign of a disturbance, or any trace of Felix. I took Rebekah's hand, and we hurried out.

I stepped into the street, waving for a taxi. Rebekah stood impatiently on the curb, watching the hotel entrance—if Felix had made it in the back door, he'd probably be right behind us.

After what seemed like forever, though it was probably more like fifteen seconds, a blue cab stopped and the driver motioned to us. I pulled open the door and helped Rebekah in.

The driver looked at me in the rearview mirror. "Où?"

"Where are we going?" Rebekah asked me urgently.

"I don't know," I whispered. "We need to get out of here."

Rebekah stammered for a moment and then said, "Le Musée du Louvre."

The driver nodded and pulled away from the curb.

"Why there?" I asked.

She shrugged nervously. "At least we're moving."

"Look." I pointed out the back window. Felix had burst from the hotel entrance, looking desperately up and down the street. He ran his hand over his face, turning in circles as he searched for us.

The taxi stopped. A group of school children was crossing the road up ahead.

"Nous sommes pressés," Rebekah told the driver.

He laughed and pointed at the kids. "Je ne vais pas écraser les enfants!"

I looked back out the window. Felix had started walking up the sidewalk. I reached into the gym bag and pulled out a fifty-euro note. I handed it to the driver.

"Merci." He began honking his horn and inching forward.

"No!" Rebekah said, cringing. "I mean, non. Euh, ne klaxonne pas!"

I looked back out the window, hoping that Felix hadn't noticed the sound. He was staring right at me. Our eyes locked for a moment, and then the taxi surged forward, only inches from running over the children's teacher.

Felix paused, watching us pulling away, and then he darted into the street. Just as we turned a corner, I saw him get into a car.

Rebekah's fingernails dug into my hand, squeezing tightly as the taxi drove us toward the Louvre.

"What are we going to do?" she asked, whispering.

I leaned forward to the driver and told him to take us to Miami Beach. He looked at me quizzically and then glanced at Rebekah for a translation. She shook her head.

"Miami Beach?"

"I was making sure he doesn't speak English," I explained.

She forced a smile. "Got it."

"So what are we going to do?"

"I asked you first."

I looked out the back window. There was no obvious sign of Felix, but he'd gotten into a white sedan, and there were certainly plenty of those behind us. He could easily have been fifty yards behind us and we'd never know.

"We have to run somewhere."

She didn't say anything.

"I mean, we can't go back to England, and we can't use our passports. We can't even check into a hotel, if what she told us was true."

"I don't know. Why should we believe her? She comes in, out of the blue, and tells us we need to run. We don't know why, except that she thinks my father's involved with a bunch of really rich people."

"So you think we should go back?"

Rebekah let go of my hand and turned to look out the window. "I don't know what I think."

"We could, I guess," I said, grasping for straws. "The whole reason your dad stepped in was because Felix was trying to kill you. He's trying to kill us now—I'm sure your dad would take us back."

She didn't answer. I looked back behind us and tried to spot Felix. I thought I recognized one of the cars, but it was impossible to be certain. When I turned around again, Rebekah was facing me.

"No," she said, shaking her head. She was holding back angry tears. "At least one thing that Isabella said has to be true. There's no way my father would tell us everything he did if he ever expected us to meet with the FBI again."

"So what do we do? Do we go to the FBI? Or the French police, or Interpol?" The question that had to be asked, although I wasn't about to ask it, was what lengths Edward would go to in order to stop us. He was out trying to save the world from nuclear war—were the lives of two dumb college kids worth the risk? Would he allow us to talk?

When I'd said, "Interpol," the cab driver raised his head and looked back at me. Rebekah took my hand again and subtly motioned for me to speak more softly.

"Have you ever been to Australia?" I asked.

"Eric," she sighed, "I need proof."

"Proof?"

"I'm not going to throw my life away and move to the Australian outback just because Isabella's paranoid. This is my father."

I opened my mouth to answer, but she cut me off. "I know what you're going to say, and you're right. But I need something more."

The cab driver cleared his throat and gestured for our attention. "Je ne sais pas si ça vous intéresse, mais quelqu'un nous suit."

Rebekah thought for a moment, translating in her head. "Nous suit?"

He glanced in his rearview mirror and continued. "Dès que nous ayons quités l'hôtel—une voiture blanche nous suit à cinquante mètres."

I looked at her, confused. "What?"

She turned to face me and stole a glance out the back window. "We're being followed."

I was going to hand the driver a stack of money and tell him to get us away, but traffic was getting thicker and slower. Felix could have just as easily followed us on a bike.

"Wait," I said, pulling the gym bag up on my lap. I unzipped the top and handed the map pages to Rebekah. "Can you translate this?"

She read the pages carefully, voicing a word here and there. "Where did it come from? This is Isabella's?"

"Yeah."

I watched out the back window and could see the taxi our driver had indicated. It was hanging back, but matched our course at every turn. With seventy-five yards between us, I could only see a vague outline of the driver and his passenger.

Suddenly, Rebekah leaned forward to the driver and handed him another bill. She thought for a moment, mouthing the words she was trying to remember. "Monsieur, nous allons à L'Arènes de Lutèce."

"L'Arènes de Lutèce?" he repeated, looking more than willing to agree if there continued to be fifty-euro notes involved.

"Oui, s'il vous plaît." She smiled at the driver and then turned to me.

"What is that?"

"I think this is where Isabella was going," she said, pointing to some notes on the map.

"I thought that she was leaving the country."

"I don't know," Rebekah shrugged, tired and agitated. "But at some point she was planning on going there."

"What is it?"

"The entrance to the catacombs."

"What?"

She looked at me for a long time. Her eyes were red—no wonder. They were eyes that had watched someone get shot in front of her only moments before, eyes that had been blind to her father's genuine character for two decades of her life. Her face was almost colorless, except for the large pink scar above her eyebrow, and her cheeks were sunken and thin.

I felt like crying, but I squeezed her hand and offered the best hopeful smile I could manage. "You need a doctor."

"I need proof. He's my father."

I put my arm around her as we drove. The cab driver turned on some loud techno music, and at the next intersection he turned the car toward our new destination.

* * *

L'Arènes de Lutèce was a wide stone amphitheater built by the Romans in the second century. Parts of the stone were scavenged to build other medieval structures, but eventually the entire thing was buried and forgotten. It wasn't excavated until the early 1900s. The tall trees and green grass offered a small chunk of green space in a city that was short on that kind of thing. It wasn't exactly a park, but it was close.

As we drove, Rebekah explained the catacombs in more detail. My guidebook had shown a small portion of them—stacks of bones that had been moved two hundred years before, unearthed from cemeteries and stacked in the old quarry tunnels under the city. But

Rebekah explained that there was much more to the catacombs. There were hundreds of miles of tunnels under Paris—old quarries, sewers, unused basements, and forgotten foundations.

Our plan was simple. We'd hide inside the catacombs, wait until nightfall, and then go for supplies.

The cab driver dropped us off. He'd managed, he told us, to shake the white sedan—and he wasn't to be disappointed by his reward. I handed him a hundred euros and told him to keep the change. I didn't say it in French, but money is a universal language. He smiled and laughed and winked at Rebekah.

She and I split up to canvas the area as quickly as possible. All she knew was that there was an iron grate on the northern side—it had been handwritten on the map by Isabella. It wasn't much to go on.

I watched her as she walked, a little shaky on her feet and obviously tired. I hated that I was taking her down into a filthy tunnel rather than a sterile hospital, but it was better than letting her get killed. I still had no idea what our next move should be—neither she nor I had international contacts like Isabella. We didn't know any foreign languages other than Rebekah's high school French. We didn't know the first thing about hiding in a foreign country. Sure, I could still take her to Madagascar, but would we end up sleeping in the sewers there too? Did Madagascar even have sewers?

"Eric," Rebekah called, waving me over. "I think this is it."

In some places the old Roman stones were secured with modern concrete, and on the north side of the amphitheater, behind the rows of stepped seating, there was a small metal storm drain. Next to it, in the wall of concrete, was the wrought-iron grate—no more than three feet square.

"Look," she said, pointing to the top of the metalwork. "It's all scratched and bent. It looks like a lot of people have pried it open over the years."

I looked around to make sure no one was watching, then knelt down. With all the strength I could muster, I yanked the grate with both hands—it flew from the wall, and I rolled backward onto the ground.

Rebekah laughed. "You don't know your own strength."

"It was just set in there. First thing that's gone right today."

She crouched down and looked inside—we couldn't see more than five feet in. "I hadn't thought of that."

"Isabella had a penlight," I said, pulling the gym bag from my shoulder and unzipping it. "It's in here somewhere."

"Oh no," Rebekah said, touching my shoulder and pointing.

Felix had arrived and was getting out of the haphazardly parked car. Fortunately, there were two-hundred feet between him and us. Without my having to say anything, Rebekah got on her hands and knees and crawled into the hole. I shoved the gym bag in after her and followed. It took some doing to get the grate to stand back up in place, but eventually I managed. Rebekah and I sat in the dark for half an hour, staring up toward the grate and the outside world, but we never saw Felix.

* * *

The three-by-three tunnel ran twenty feet and stopped. At the end, the floor disappeared—terrifying if you're feeling your way in the dark. We paused there long enough for me to dig Isabella's light out of the bag, and then saw that a steel ladder was bolted to the side of the hole. I held the light while Rebekah descended. When she touched ground, I dropped the light to her and began my descent.

It was a long way down. I counted the rungs as I climbed, and came up with twenty-six. The ground at the bottom was hard and cold, different from what I'd expected. Whether catacombs or tunnels or passageways, I'd been envisioning a sewer. In America, not much is under a city. In Paris, what's visible on the surface is only the very latest in thousands of years of architecture. From the dim light that Rebekah shined around us, I could see that the walls were stone—not roughly carved, but constructed, brick upon brick.

"You realize," she said with a nervous smile, "that this is crazy."

"The thought had crossed my mind."

I took the light and discovered we were in a small room of some kind. The walls were colored with graffiti, and I guessed it was all modern—the writings were mostly spray paint and chalk, and a wall-sized, yellow peace sign was emblazoned next to the ladder. Empty bottles and food wrappers littered the floor—this was apparently a popular picnic spot for adventuresome kids.

"Come on," Rebekah said, pointing to an inky black hole on the far wall.

"What?"

"Let's go," she said, walking slowly toward the opening.

"Go where?" I answered incredulously. "We're just hiding here until it gets dark."

"I know, but people come here." She gestured to the debris all over the floor. "I've heard that these tunnels are used by drug dealers, and I don't want to be here when they show up."

Uncertain, I pulled out the map. "How far do you want to go?"

"Not far. But look at all the nooks and crannies here. Let's just find some dead end and wait."

I nodded, staring at the map for a few moments. Truth be told, I was more than a little scared. I was afraid of the unknown—of falling down an obscured hole or getting caught under a collapsed ceiling.

"Come on," Rebekah urged again, taking my arm. "I need to lie down."

The opening in the wall was no more than four feet high and two feet wide, and it looked like it had once been covered by a metal door, which was now covered in thick, brown rust and lying against the wall.

I shined the dim light through the hole. The floor on the far side was uneven gravel and dirt, and the walls bare stone. I paused for a moment, like I was about to climb into the mouth of a lion.

Rebekah led the way. As I followed her, she took the light and shined it ahead of her.

"I need to tell you something, Eric," she said, a few steps ahead of me, picking her way carefully around chunks of broken rock.

"What?"

With the penlight in front of her, and me behind, all I could see was her dim silhouette.

"I don't believe it."

"That we're being chased by Felix again, and are now hiding in a secret passage underneath a Roman ruin in Paris? I can't really believe it either."

She laughed, but there was no joy in her voice. "I don't believe Isabella."

"What part? She hardly told us anything."

"Any of it, really. I don't believe that there are people in this world who control things like that—it's too easy. You know why I think people believe in conspiracy theories?"

"Why?"

"Just because they're easy. You remember the midterm in Dr. Vigil's American Heritage class?"

"Yeah. I remember that I did lousy on the multiple-choice section."

"For the essay portion I answered the question on the causes of the Civil War. I wrote seven pages on that thing, all about slavery and the abolitionists, and do you know what grade I got?"

"An A?" Rebekah got A's on everything.

"A C minus," she said. The tunnel came to a fork and she paused, turning to face me. "Dr. Vigil wrote one word across the top of the essay: *monocausationalism.* When I went to his office to ask him about it, he said that being called a monocausationalist was one of the worst insults a historian will ever hear."

"Academics are weird," I said with an uncomfortable chuckle. I had no idea where she was going with this.

Rebekah smiled. "What it means is that the historian claims that something happened just because something else happened. It's extremely simple cause and effect: the Civil War happened because of slavery, or the Great Depression happened because people were buying stock on margin. But it ignores all of the other causes."

She finished her point and then looked flustered. "Which way do we go?"

I unfolded the map again and she shined the light on it. "There's this dead end to the left," I said. "Around a curve. It looks good." The path to the right headed into an area with a lot of right angles and was most likely a former basement.

Rebekah nodded and headed left. "It's like what Isabella was talking about with the pilgrims. I grew up hearing about how they came to America looking for religious freedom, and that's true—but it's not the only reason. In fact, it's just one of a dozen reasons."

"And this is why you don't believe Isabella?" I asked, confused.

"People believe in conspiracies," she said firmly, "because they don't understand all the causes that go into the big events in history. They can't understand what makes prices rise and fall. I mean, I got an A in economics, and I don't really understand what makes prices rise and fall. So people think that it can't possibly be as confusing as it really is, and they decide that prices rise and fall because a secret society somewhere has secret meetings in dark, smoke-filled rooms, and they've decreed that gas prices will go up and bread prices will go down."

"I hate to sound cliché," I said, "but just because you're paranoid doesn't mean that someone isn't out to get you."

Rebekah laughed softly. "I think I saw that on a bumper sticker."

"I can't claim to be an expert," I said, "but there's a lot of compelling evidence out there. I mean, I'll be the first to admit that most conspiracies are hoaxes, but think of how many of those theories are out there—the JFK assassination, Roosevelt knowing about Pearl Harbor before it happened, the astronauts never landing on the moon. Some weatherman in Idaho believes that the Japanese mafia used Russian weather-control devices to send hurricanes to America. I'm not saying that these ideas are correct—but think if just one out of a hundred crazy theories *was* true. Or if the theory was just half true."

"I don't believe it," she repeated.

"Look at your monocause-whatever example. You were wrong on that essay because you left stuff out, not because of anything you put in. All your facts were right—they were just incomplete. Maybe Isabella was right, but even she doesn't have the entire story."

The tunnel turned sharply, ending in a large, flat wall. Rebekah turned to face me. I couldn't make out her facial expression in the darkness, but her voice was tired and frustrated. "You might be right, Eric. Isabella may be right. But that doesn't mean that my father is one of them."

"Your dad sells nukes," I answered a bit too harshly. "You heard it from his own mouth."

"But he does it because he's trying to save the world. What Isabella talked about was different. You heard what she said—he's part of a group of rich people that control things for their own gain. Does that sound like my father?"

Rebekah didn't wait for an answer. Instead she sat down on the hard earth and leaned against the wall, then turned off the light.

I stood in the dark, not knowing what else to say.

* * *

It was cold in the tunnel, and the air was stale and motionless. Rebekah, perfectly invisible in the blackness, complained on and off about the chill—she was still wearing only a light summer dress. We sat, huddled together in the darkness, but it was only for warmth— Rebekah was withdrawn and distant, as though my comments supporting Isabella's claims had been an attack on Rebekah's integrity, too.

They weren't, of course, but it was no use hiding the fact that I had no great love for her father. Neither did she, though she'd never admit it. He'd been absent all her life, choosing to parent her with a full bank account and the occasional phone call. When she did see him, it was visiting him in Pakistan or South Africa—it was never Edward coming home for Christmas or high school graduation. Rebekah desperately wanted a real father.

I turned on the light to check my watch. Five-thirty in the evening. Rebekah was asleep again, propped awkwardly between me, the wall, and the bags. Her legs were brought up to her chest, and she rested her arms and head on her knees. She didn't look like herself. If I hadn't spent the last month with her, I wonder if I would even recognize her. Her hair, once long, wavy, and the color of honey, was short, uncombed, and brown. She looked frail—not the in-shape girl I'd tried to keep up with when running from Felix. Her face was gaunt, with sunken cheeks, and her left hand was nothing but skin and bone. Her right hand was still in a pressure bandage and in dire need of a doctor's attention.

I turned off the penlight and listened to her breathing. It was shallow and fast—a short, low whistle punctuating every exhalation.

I'd been planning on reproposing to her today. I guess that would have to wait.

I reached into my jeans pocket and fished out the spark plug. I'd carried it with me every day since the accident. I felt it in the dark—hard and small, with no particularly sharp edges. Unlike a bullet or an arrowhead, it shouldn't have nicked Rebekah's liver.

It angered me just to hold the thing, which is probably why I kept it around. Every time I held it, feeling its weight in my hand, I thought about Felix and how much I hated him. I thought about how if anyone in the world deserved a spark plug in the stomach, it was him. I thought about the first time I'd met him in the basement of a filthy house, as I'd awoken from a restless, painful sleep. He had let me go, but he had kept Rebekah.

* * *

I must have dozed off, because I woke with a start, yanking my head up from its drooped position and smacking it on the smooth stone behind me. I yelped and heard Rebekah gasp and sit up.

"What is it?" she said, obviously groggy.

"I hit my dang head," I said, annoyed. The blackness ahead of me was orange and yellow—I was seeing stars, I guess. I rubbed my scalp to make sure I wasn't bleeding.

"What time is it?"

I fumbled around me for the penlight. When I turned it on, the bulb was dim. I kept it on just long enough to check my watch.

"Eight-thirty," I said. "What time does it get dark? Ten?"

"I don't know."

I stretched out my sore arm and rested it on her back. "How are you feeling?"

"I feel like I ran a marathon today."

"While you were sleeping, I was thinking about your wrist—you're going to need to see a doctor. Isabella brought your antibiotics, but it can still get infected."

There was a pause.

"Isabella's dead."

"Probably."

"There's no probably about it. She's dead."

"Yeah."

"Eric?"

"Yeah?"

She didn't say anything, but she leaned a little closer. Her hands were like ice.

"You need something warmer to wear. Want my shirt?" I offered.

She chuckled quietly. "What would you wear?"

"We'll only be down here for a few more hours," I said, doing my best to be chivalrous. "You could have it until we leave."

"Eric, we can't leave."

I'd hit my head, but she was the one with brain damage.

"Are you nuts?"

"Well," she said, forcing a laugh, "it's freezing, and I want something else to wear, but I think we need to stay here."

We'd talked about it, of course, and that was the plan, but I had been secretly hoping that the hours we'd just spent in the dark had convinced her otherwise.

"Eric, I have to know." She was no longer leaning against me, and I imagined she had her my-mind's-made-up look on her face.

"Know what?"

"About him."

"You mean, you want to follow the map?"

Her answer was soft and reticent. "Yes."

"What does it say on it? How do you know that it has anything to do with your father?"

"It was with Isabella's stuff—all the stuff she'd gathered about his friends. And look—" She fumbled for a moment in the dark and then turned on the light. "Those symbols you saw at his estate. They're on the map."

"That map looks about a hundred years old."

Rebekah stared at it, frowning and desperate. "It has to mean something." She turned off the penlight.

"It's really dark down here," I said, quickly thinking of all the reasons why this was a bad idea. "And cold. And there are drug dealers down here, and criminals, and mummies probably—I don't know."

"Mummies?"

"It's a catacomb, right? Besides, we haven't eaten in twelve hours. We don't have any flashlights, and . . . and you're freezing!"

"I thought I could go up and get that stuff," she said.

"Whoa. If anyone is going anywhere, it's not the girl with pulmonary barotrauma who nearly died today. The only place you can go is to a nice warm hotel, with a nice warm bed, and a nice warm bath. After that, we'll think about where else we're going, and we'll find a doctor to look at that hand."

"No, Eric," she said firmly. "I'm willing to entertain the idea that my father is mixed up in something truly evil—something that lacks the 'noble motives' that his nuke selling seemed to have. But I'm not willing to believe it wholeheartedly based on the rantings of one of his ex-employees."

"Hold on," I protested. "Isabella saved our lives how many times?"

"She worked for my dad's secret organization, right? She was put in prison because of Felix's secret organization. Maybe she's so used to that kind of thing that she thinks she sees it everywhere. I had the chicken pox when I was thirteen, and after that, any time I got a little red zit, I thought I had the chicken pox again."

I laughed uncomfortably. "I don't think that's exactly the same."

"It's not that different. She's used to conspiracies because she was part of one. She thinks they're everywhere."

"You're not used to conspiracies," I replied, "because you've led a very normal life. Maybe they're all around us and we don't see them."

She paused and thought. I wished I could have seen her face.

"Listen, Eric." She took my hand, which was pleasant enough, but a sure sign that I wasn't going to win the argument. "I'm not going anywhere until I know for sure that my father is dangerous. I'm not going to get on a train to wherever and burn my bridges with my family—and my entire life!—just because of what Isabella thinks is true. I want to *know* what's true."

I nodded (not that she could see it) and thought about what lay ahead.

"It's not going to be easy," I said, wishing there was some way I could talk her out of it.

"I know."

"And there's no guarantee that we'll find anything. That map is old."

"I know that, too."

I started making a mental list of things we'd need if we were going to attempt this: flashlights, warm clothes, sturdy shoes, food, water. Sherpas. An excavation team.

I stood up. Moving in the complete darkness was dizzying, and I felt myself sway back and forth without any visual references to guide me.

"What sizes do you wear?" I said.

I heard her stand, her sandals crunching the flaky gravel beneath her feet. A searching hand touched my shoulder, and then she hugged me. Her body shook—she was still unsteady on her feet. And she was crying.

"I'm sorry."

I patted her back. I was the most helpless person to be stuck with—she'd have been much better off if I'd died and Isabella had remained. I had no idea how to console her tears, let alone guide her through the fetid underbelly of Paris.

I turned on the dim light. "Here," I said, leaning down and opening the gym bag. I took a stack of the orange fifty-euro notes and stuffed them in my pocket. Digging deeper in the bag I found the medicine Isabella had packed. "Here's a full inhaler. Your oxygen is in the backpack."

"I'll be okay," she answered, sounding almost like she meant it.

"I'll be back soon. If drug dealers come, don't buy anything."

Rebekah laughed, tears in her eyes, and held my hand as she walked me to the ladder. Her penlight was growing dim, and she'd probably spend the next several hours in the dark. I glanced back down into the pit as I reached the top, barely able to discern her face in the darkness. She looked small and cold and alone.

CHAPTER 23

IT WAS GETTING dark outside, but it seemed almost like noonday compared to where I'd been. The air outside the Arènes de Lutèce smelled clean and fresh, and a warm summer breeze blew through the tall deciduous trees that lined the amphitheater. It was like stepping into heaven.

There were very few people around. On the far side of the circular stone arena was a young couple holding hands and laughing. An old woman carrying a shopping bag and using a cane was shuffling slowly up the sidewalk. I could hear the voices of teenagers somewhere, playing some kind of game.

I replaced the grate carefully and silently, easing the heavy ironwork back into place. No one watched me do it, and no one could have heard a thing.

From there, I had no idea where to go for supplies. I doubted France had a Wal-Mart, and I definitely wasn't going to find spelunking attire at Christian Dior. Surely there was some kind of middle ground, but I had no idea what it was—or where. Eventually I just picked a direction and began walking, hoping that stores in Europe stayed open as late as stores in America.

I was filthy, more so than I expected. The streetlights on the Rue Monge cast an orange-yellow glow across the pavement, and I discovered that my hands were black with rust, grease, and dirt. I'd seen Rebekah's legs, smeared with the damp soil from the tunnel floor, and I could only imagine that the back of my jeans was just as dirty. Before venturing into a clothing shop, and probably getting thrown out for being a vagrant, I stopped in at the Monge metro station to wash up. It wasn't at all what I wanted—I would have been happy to never go into another metro ever again—but I couldn't read most of the signs in Paris, and had no idea where to find a suitable public bathroom. The metro was my best option.

The station was nearly empty, and I slipped into a restroom without anyone seeing me. When I was thinking rationally, I had a hard time imagining that I'd run into Felix or the black-haired girl here. After all, she'd said there were only three of them, and Paris had over a hundred metros, let alone train stations and airports. But irrationality was calling the shots today, and I looked at everyone suspiciously. I still didn't know who the third person was, and for all I knew it could have been the drunk man lying on a bench or the aging widow reading the newspaper.

The restroom was dimly lit and dirty. I spent ten minutes washing my face and hands, rubbing water through my hair to get the dust out, and wishing I could shave. My beard was thickening quickly, in desperate need of a trim, and I looked like a serial killer.

I peeked out the bathroom door for a few seconds before leaving. No one was watching me, or talking on a cell phone, or polishing a sniper rifle. I took a deep breath and hurried back up the stairs and out.

I walked for more than half a mile before I found a store suited to my needs. It was little more than a glorified convenience store, but they had racks of clothing in the back and very few customers.

I found two flashlights, one red and one blue, and a package of batteries. Remembering the Boy Scout motto, I grabbed a second pack. I didn't know how long we'd be down in the catacombs, but the last thing I wanted was for our lights to go out when we were miles from an exit.

Rebekah already had medicine, but I picked up a bottle of what looked like aspirin, and a travel-size first-aid kit.

There was a roll of thin cotton rope in the small automotive section, and a picture on the front showed a happy couple merrily tying luggage to the roof of their car. I couldn't think of why I'd want rope, but it seemed like a good thing to have. For the same reason, I bought a butane lighter.

Food selection was difficult. I loaded up on as much bottled water as I figured I could carry and then searched for nonperishable items—

particularly those with appealing pictures on the labels. I took a long, thin box of crackers, and two jars of something that looked like you ate with crackers. I found a can of something with a picture of a duck and bought that. Finally, trying to find something that actually looked appetizing, I bought a loaf of bread and a round block of Camembert.

The clothes selection was sparse, but since we were going to be walking through utter darkness I wasn't too concerned about fashion. I found Rebekah a pair of dark slacks, which were nicer than necessary for a filthy hole in the ground, but the only ones that looked like they'd fit. I also picked out two thick wool sweaters, two T-shirts, a hip-length coat, and several pairs of socks. For myself I grabbed a sweatshirt and hat.

I took my large stack of purchases to the counter and laid them out.

"Hello," I said, hoping that I'd be lucky enough to have an English-speaking cashier.

"Hel-lo," he returned, enunciating carefully and slowly. He was middle-aged, probably in his late forties, and had sixty years' worth of belly. His hair was receding, and he'd deftly combed it over so you'd never notice unless you got within fifty yards.

"Do you know where I could buy some shoes?" I pointed at my feet, which he couldn't see because he was on the other side of the counter.

"Shoes?" he repeated, smiling cautiously. "Oui." He looked back down at the cash register and began ringing up the items.

"Where?"

"Excusez-moi?"

"Shoes. I need a shoe store."

"Shoe store?"

I lifted my foot high enough for him to see, and patted it. "Shoes."

"Ah, shoes. Le magasin de chaussures. Allez à droit sur la rue de l'Epée de Bois, puis prennez la troisieme rue à droit—Rue Mouffetard."

"Uh . . . Mouffetard."

"Oui," he said happily. "L'Epée de Bois, Mouffetard."

He resumed tallying my purchase and hummed to himself. He paused occasionally to take a drink and finally showed me the total. I handed him three orange bills, and he handed me a rumpled mixture of change. Carrying the bags that I hadn't even reckoned having to carry—the water *was* heavy—I stumbled toward the exit.

"Mouffetard," I confirmed, pointing north.

The Frenchman pointed south. "L'Epée de Bois, Mouffetard."

"Thanks."

The Rue Monge was narrow and tall, with five- and six-story buildings lining every inch of it. From what I'd seen of Paris, most of it was like that, with each building butted up against the next. And yet, despite the obvious number of people who inhabited these apartments, the streets were tiny little two-lane things with constant foot-traffic crossing. It was like being at the bottom of a slot canyon and looking up and seeing only a sliver of the sky. I doubted that I'd see stars; however, the street was well lit from every streetlight and shop and the rows and rows of windows. The Rue Monge glowed.

I walked south, following the incomprehensible directions from the clerk, hoping to find something that looked like Mouffetard. I passed store after store, none of which looked ready to close anytime soon. One even sold shoes, but I could see from the window that it wasn't what I was looking for—I doubted pointy-toed stilettos and thigh-high boots with three-inch platforms would help much in the catacombs.

A small café caught my attention, both because the food smelled wonderful and because I heard the waitress speaking English. I left my shopping bags at the front door and ventured inside. There were several small, round tables placed haphazardly around the room, but no other customers. A busboy stood behind the bar, watching a small TV.

A woman, probably in her thirties, tall and tired, greeted me.

"Do you speak English?" I asked timidly.

"Yes," she answered. She looked annoyed and ready to be done for the day. She also looked uncertain that someone with my appearance would have any money.

"I'm American," I said as though that explained something. She nodded as if she got my point.

"Have a seat," she said absently. Her accent was thick, but she spoke without difficulty.

I walked to a table near the front that was positioned perfectly for me to keep an eye on my bags. She handed me a menu, but it was all in French and there were no pictures.

"I need some food to go," I said, speaking slowly and clearly. "I need to take some to my girlfriend."

The waitress smiled as though she doubted it.

"What would you recommend?"

"What do you like to eat?"

"Anything warm."

"Andouillettes à la Lyonnaise?"

I frowned. "Uh, sure."

"Do you eat meat?"

"Yes."

She took the menu back from me and headed toward the kitchen. The busboy pretended to sweep for a minute, then, giving up, took a coin from the till and fired up the pinball machine.

I suddenly felt exhausted, as though my body had finally decided it'd had enough. I leaned forward on the table, my head resting on my hands, and wondered what in the world I was doing.

The TV caught my eye—not surprising, since they were showing a great big picture of me. It was stock footage. January in Salt Lake City. I was leaving the hospital, my arm wrapped tightly in a thick bandage. Rebekah stood on my right and my parents on my left. Behind me were Special Agent Jeff Harrop and Lieutenant Dean from the police department. The shot changed to a few days later, showing Rebekah's first live interview. She was sitting in the studio of the *Today Show* and talking with the hostess.

The screen switched to the anchorman briefly, and he said a few things I didn't understand, but in a moment the mug shot of Isabella appeared over his shoulder. The camera cut to the alley, filled with police cars and ambulances, and then to the front of the restaurant we'd hidden in. There was an interview with the woman who had run the basement restaurant, and I decided it was too risky to watch any more. If this was all over the evening news, I needed to get back out of sight.

"Excuse me," I said, waving to the waitress. "Would you mind changing the channel? Maybe there's a game on."

She shrugged and walked over.

"Where is your girlfriend?" she asked, probably trying to call my bluff.

"The hotel," I answered quickly.

"Oh." She stopped the TV on a soccer match.

I watched her as she fiddled with the knob—she was tall, almost the same height as Rebekah.

"I have a question."

She turned to look at me.

"Do you know where I could find a shoe store?"

"Up the street," she said, pointing north—the way I'd just come.

I shook my head. "Not nice shoes. I need tennis shoes."

"Tennis?"

"Sneakers. You know, like your shoes."

"Oh," she said, finally understanding. "There was a store on the Rue Mouffetard, but they have closed. I believe there's another near St-Germain."

"Is that far?"

She thought for a minute. "Perhaps one mile."

"Nothing closer?" I didn't want to haul all my groceries a mile there and back.

"Not at this time of night."

"Can I ask you a strange question?"

She shrugged, hardly interested. I reached into my pocket and dug out several bills.

"Can I buy your shoes?" They were white sneakers, fairly new. I imagined that she wore them while working since they were so comfortable and she had to stand all the time. Perfect for a long, dark walk.

"You are strange, American."

"Two hundred euros."

"Two hundred euros," she repeated, looking bewildered. "Why?"

"My girlfriend needs shoes."

"Two hundred euros?"

"Yes." I handed her the four fifty-euro notes.

She stared at me strangely and thought. I could only guess what was going through her head, and I was sure none of it was good. After nearly a minute I was ready to stand up and leave.

"Shall I put them in a bag for you?"

* * *

It was awkward getting down the ladder with all the bags. I had to take three trips from top to bottom, and even then I slipped and dropped one sack. The thick plastic cap of one water bottle cracked, its contents spilling out across the floor and making a muddy mess.

There was no sound in the cave, just as before, though I'd almost forgotten how dark it was. With the flashlight I was able to get a better view of my surroundings and what we'd be facing as we delved deeper.

The tunnel varied between five and eight feet wide. In some places the floor was smooth stone or cement, and in others it was packed dirt and gravel. Decaying brick pillars lined the walls, and dusty, rotted timbers stretched across the ceiling. Graffiti was everywhere, from the modern "artwork" we'd seen earlier to ancient scrawl. The words *P. L. Giumard, 1801* were immaculately scribed on a brick wall in charcoal—next to the words was a spray-painted smiley face.

I followed the map carefully, curving to the left as we'd done before, anxious to see Rebekah again. Finally, I turned the corner and found the large, flat wall. She was sitting at the base, curled up in the darkness, and she covered her eyes to block the brilliance of the flashlight. I dropped the bags and sat down next to her.

"Hi," she said, her voice trembling but happy.

"Are you okay?"

"People came by," she said. Her hand touched mine—it was ice cold and shaking. "Probably half an hour after you left."

"Did they see you?" I dug into the bags to find her something warm to wear.

"No."

"Who was it?"

"Young people, I think. I only heard their voices. They were speaking French, but I only caught about half of it. They said they were heading for something—they used a German word, *blockhaus*. It sounded like they do this a lot."

"Probably the same people who left all those wrappers by the ladder." I presented her with the clothing and she looked thrilled. "Do you want to get dressed first or eat? I got us something hot for dinner."

"What?" she asked, holding up a sweater to look at it. It was a dark red one, with thick ribbing and a turtleneck.

"The waitress told me the name, but I can't remember. Androids and mayonnaise, or something."

Rebekah laughed. "Let me put on some clothes first. Whatever it is, it smells good."

The food turned out to be some kind of spicy sausage with grilled onions and fries. Rebekah tore rapidly through her meal, looking content for the first time all day. She was bundled up in the sweater and coat, wearing the black slacks and sneakers—she had also pulled a sock over her bandaged hand, trying to warm it up again. I put on my hat, reining in my too-long hair.

"So do you call these French fries in France?" I asked, holding up one of the potatoes. The flashlight was lying on the ground, pointing up.

"I don't think that they're actually French, though I've heard that here they call French toast *Belgian toast*."

"What about French-cut beans?"

"Those are French. Lyonnaise, they're called."

"That's the word! Androids and lyonnaise."

Rebekah grinned. "I'm sure that's it."

The sausage tasted wonderful, and I ate like I hadn't seen food in months. I even ate every onion, and I hate onions.

"I read something while you were gone, before the penlight went out," she said as she finished her food. "One of the papers in Isabella's bag." She shuffled through the documents before finally selecting one.

"What is it? I don't suppose she wrote down somewhere exactly what's going on."

"That's what I was hoping," Rebekah answered with a laugh. "But no such luck. Instead, it's just more of her weird conspiracy theories—but she's even crazier than I expected her to be." She reached into the bag of money and pulled out an American dollar bill.

"Look at the back," she said, handing it to me.

I shined the flashlight at the bill and inspected it. I knew it pretty well—the phrase Novus Ordo Seclorum came from the Great Seal, and I'd spent a lot of time staring at it. When it was discovered that Felix's group had taken their title from the dollar, several news organizations had written articles about its symbolism.

Rebekah looked at her paper and then quizzed me. "What does the pyramid stand for?"

"If I remember right, it represents that the country isn't complete yet."

"And the eye?"

"It's supposed to be the all-seeing eye of Providence, or something—watching over the U.S."

"And why are there thirteen levels of stone?"

"Are there? That's one I didn't know."

"Guess."

"The thirteen colonies."

"Probably, yeah. And the date at the bottom?"

"I don't know my Roman numerals very well, but I would assume it's July 4, 1776?"

Rebekah nodded and then said with a mocking laugh, "You are 100 percent *wrong!*"

I smiled. "What is it?"

"You're right that it's 1776, but it isn't July 4—it's May 1. On that day, a Bavarian named Adam Weishaupt founded a secret society. In his organization, there are thirteen levels, or ranks—they have crazy names like the Presbyter and the Regent and the Magus. So, they build from 1776, and you rise in the ranks as you go up the pyramid, until you reach the top rank—and guess what it's called?"

"The all-seeing eye?"

"The Illuminati," she said, lowering her voice in mock reverence. "They are fully illuminated by knowledge and see everything."

"Are you serious?"

Rebekah handed me the paper. "According to Isabella's notes. Which is just one more reason why I don't believe any of this."

I chuckled a little as I looked over Isabella's hand-drawn diagram. "I researched UFOs for a paper back in high school and checked out a bunch of conspiracy websites. It seemed like they had tons of evidence like this but never really came to a conclusion or an explanation. It was as though they assumed we knew their thesis, and then they included unexplained diagrams to back it up."

Rebekah smiled tiredly and closed the Styrofoam lid of her dinner box.

"Does this mean that you want to go back to England?" I asked.

She didn't answer for a moment but finally said quietly, "No. I have to know for sure."

I couldn't do anything but agree.

She stretched and yawned. "When are we leaving?"

"How do you feel?"

She thought for a minute, and I almost thought she was going to say she was fine. "Not so good."

"I could use some sleep too."

"I don't know how much oxygen is in these tanks."

"If our luck holds out," I said, unscrewing the lid of a water bottle, "we won't be running again for a while." *If our luck holds out. . . . We haven't had much luck all day.*

"Let me see the map."

I pulled the papers from my pocket and unfolded them. "It'll be a long walk."

Rebekah nodded. She was going to go through with it—I was certain of that. But we both knew that it would hurt.

"What time is it?" She was using her fingertip as a scale to guess the distance.

"A little after eleven. Twenty-three o'clock."

"This could be miles."

"And we don't know exactly how that page matches up with the next—"

Rebekah cut me off with a frantic wave of her hand and scrambled for the flashlight. She had it doused in a moment.

"What?" I whispered, searching in the darkness for her hand. I couldn't find it.

"Listen."

Everything was silent. I couldn't hear Rebekah breathing, and I wondered if she even was. In the complete darkness I thought that I saw lights and shapes, but it was only an optical illusion—images remaining in my eyes from when we'd had the flashlight on.

Then I heard it. It wasn't a voice, but it wasn't an animal, unless birds frequented the tunnels. Someone or something was whistling. It was sporadic, and it certainly wasn't a tune. It was like someone was communicating—signaling someone else.

Rebekah's shoulder bumped mine, and I grabbed her hand. With my right hand, as quietly as possible, I dug into the back-pack.

We heard the noise again, farther away, but distinct and deliberate—
I felt as though I could almost understand what the whistler was saying.

It sounded twice more, one call and one answer, maybe. And then
we sat in the dark, terrified and motionless, for another thirty
minutes. Rebekah squeezed my hand like she was juicing an orange.

"Do you think it's okay?" she whispered after an eternity of
silence and blackness.

"I guess."

She flicked the flashlight back on, obscuring most of the glow
with a T-shirt. Our small corner lit up again, and I saw her face. And
she saw the pistol I was clutching in my right hand.

"Where did that come from?" Rebekah gasped much too loudly.

"Isabella had it. She got it from the girl," I answered. "It was in
the bag."

Rebekah stared at the weapon. It was compact and blocky,
weighing very little and easily concealed.

"Why do you have it?"

"Rebekah," I began, trying to think of the best way to phrase
what I wanted to say.

She waited, but I didn't say anything. "What?"

"I'm not going to let anything happen to you."

"Eric—"

"No, Rebekah. You're too important to me."

She paused, tears coming to her eyes. I didn't know if they were
good tears or bad tears.

I set the gun back in the backpack and took her hand. "Listen, it's
not a great solution. It's not even a good solution, but if someone tries
to attack you, I'm not going to let them."

"Eric, this is what *they* do. Not what *we* do."

"We have to because they do. It's the only way to stop them. If Felix
comes after us with a gun, he's not going to stop because I ask him nicely."

She was shaking her head, staring at the pistol with a mixture of
revulsion and intrigue. "No. Terrorists use guns. Criminals use guns."

"That's why we need one. It's just protection. We're not doing
anything wrong."

Her gaze turned up to me, and I looked in her eyes. Still red and
tired, but resolute. "You know who you sound like? My father."

"What?"

There was anger behind her words, and it caught me off guard. "The only way one country can stop another is if they both have nuclear weapons. If one country gets them, then the other country has to get them."

"Maybe he's right," I answered, trying to hold back my frustration. "Maybe that's what we need to do to stop Felix—start playing it his way."

"Eric, he's evil! We need to do the right thing."

"What do you mean? You mean just let him come up to us and kill us? Even the scriptures say that we have a right to defend ourselves."

She shook her head. The tears were flowing freely now. "I don't want to play their game, Eric. I don't want to stoop to their level."

"And I don't want you to die."

"Eric, you don't understand. I don't want to be like them, no matter what."

"Then what do you want?" I yelled. I jumped to my feet and walked a few steps away.

I wasn't doing anything wrong. I hated carrying the thing around as much as anyone did, but I didn't have any other options. I wasn't in an arms race with the terrorists, I just wanted to protect myself. There was a lot to be said for taking a moral stand, but this hardly seemed like the best time.

I'd never yelled at Rebekah before. Never even raised my voice, that I can remember.

I took a deep breath. "I'm sorry."

I waited for a few seconds, listening to her breathing, which had gotten bad again. When she finally spoke, her words were almost too soft to hear. "I'm sorry too."

I stared into the inky blackness that surrounded us and the tiny shadows that stretched across the wall, chased by the glow emanating from Rebekah's light.

As I gazed, faint letters appeared, painted on the smooth stone many decades—perhaps centuries—earlier. *Insensé que vous êtes, pourquoi vous promettez de vivre longtemps, vous qui ne pouvez compter sur un seul jour.*

"Rebekah," I said softly, hoping to change the subject. "What does this say?"

I heard her sniffle and then stand. She took a few steps toward me. "It's old," she answered, her voice soft and broken. "The syntax is strange. 'Crazy as you are, why do you promise yourself to live a long time, you who cannot count on a single day.'"

CHAPTER 24

I SLEPT FAIRLY well, all things considered. I lay in the dirt, using the bag of money as a pillow. It wasn't very soft, but it helped a little, and I felt something like Scrooge McDuck. Rebekah lay beside me, using the extra sweater and T-shirt as a blanket. Her breathing had returned to normal, and she almost seemed to be smiling. I let her sleep, even long after I'd grown too uncomfortable to lie there. We had a long walk ahead of us, and she needed as much rest as she could get.

Our dead-end tunnel was as stale and dark as it had ever been. As I lay in the dark, aware of Rebekah's sleeping body only from the weak sound of breathing, I couldn't see so far as an inch in front of my face. I was suddenly seized with panic, as though the walls would collapse at any moment. My lungs strained for breath, and I fought the idea of unseen fumes and odorless poisons. What if there had been a rockfall farther back in the tunnel and we were blocked in? We had no canary to alert us to a problem with the air. What if Rebekah's deep sleep was brought on by lack of oxygen?

I sat up quickly, and the movement made me dizzy. I ran my hands along the uneven, damp soil, groping for the flashlight. My hand touched a box—the package of crackers. We hadn't done anything to hide our food, and I was instantly certain we were surrounded by rats, digging in our bags and nibbling at our feet.

I felt plastic. I snatched up the light and flicked the switch. Light. There was no collapse, no rats. Everything was exactly how we'd left it.

I took long, deep breaths and my mind seemed to grow more lucid. We weren't being poisoned.

I found my watch. Six-thirty in the morning. It was Sunday.

We'd been in the tunnels for eighteen hours.

Rebekah woke an hour later, looking like she'd spent the night sleeping in dirt. She insisted that she felt much better, refreshed and ready for a walk. We ate a small breakfast of bread and Camembert. Rebekah swallowed some aspirin, washing it down with a quick gulp of water.

The bottled water was awful. It tasted like some of the grimy well water I'd had back in rural Nebraska, but this came in bottles and cost two and a half euros.

Rebekah wore the backpack, and I carried the gym bag. It was packed a little fuller now, with the extra water and batteries, but I didn't complain. Rebekah's bag held a portable oxygen tank, which wasn't light at all.

As we started off, there was no sign of the whistlers we'd heard during the night. For the first hour there was evidence of visitors to the tunnels, but the farther we traveled from L'Arènes de Lutèce, both the modern graffiti and the litter became less frequent. Instead, we found more and more inscriptions like the one at our dead-end camp—old French poems carved or painted on the stone. At one turn, an elegant cursive *Rene Pabou, 1850* marked the wall. At another, in short, simple script, was *1785*.

In the second hour, we turned onto what the map showed as a vast underground highway. It was long and straight, probably stretching out half a mile in one direction. Even shining the flashlight directly ahead didn't reveal the end of the inky black passage. The ceilings rose high above us and arched dramatically, and the tunnel was wide enough for five adults to walk side by side. There was a slight, but noticeable, downward slope. My last vestiges of claustrophobia vanished, replaced by the sinking feeling that I was walking down the path to the underworld.

Rebekah paused, leaned against the wall, and unscrewed the cap of her water bottle.

"How're you holding up?" I asked.

She'd been silent most of the morning. Then again, I hadn't exactly been a chatterbox. We hadn't resolved anything from the night before. I still kept the pistol in the side pocket of the gym bag, easily accessible, and Rebekah knew it.

She forced a smile. "I'm okay." She took a drink and then wiped her lip with the back of her thumb.

I pointed at a sign across the tunnel. It was modern and stenciled in yellow paint. I'd seen a dozen of these identical markings in the last hour. "Can you read what that says?"

She nodded and swallowed—it looked like it took a great deal of effort just to get the water down.

"Throat hurt?" I asked.

"Chest," she said. "Only a little. The sign says—I think it says, 'This area is off-limits to unauthorized personnel,' or something like that. It's signed by the Inspecteur Général des Carrières. Inspector general of something—I don't know that last word."

Rebekah bent over, stretching, her fingertips touching the ground. I'd never been able to do that.

"I wonder how deep we are," I said.

"Have we been going down?"

"I think so."

"Where are we on the map?"

I pulled the wrinkled pages from my pocket and showed them to her, pointing to the long passage. Next to it were the words *Corridor du Mort*.

Rebekah looked at the map for several minutes. She'd stare for a while, turn the page on its side, and stare some more. I think she was stalling for a longer break.

"What does it mean by 'The heart can only be seen through the eyes of Minerva'?" She pointed to the phrase I'd seen on the map—the sentence marked with Edward's symbols.

"I have no idea."

"That's where we have to go. Who is Minerva?" she asked, mostly to herself.

"There was a Minerva in old mythology—I don't remember if she was Greek or Roman. The goddess of wisdom, I think."

"How do you know that?"

My face reddened. "From a video game. *Epoch of Gods.*"

She laughed. "I guess all that time in front of the PlayStation is paying off."

"You realize that from now on I'm always going to cite this as an excuse to play."

Rebekah grinned and then refocused back on the map. "So we can see the heart of the Illuminati through the eyes of the goddess of wisdom," she said with a frown, trying to reason out the cryptic phrase. "We can understand the Illuminati if we're wise?"

"Makes sense."

She grimaced and laughed, handing the pages back to me. "I guess we won't be finding the heart, then."

"It definitely won't be me."

We followed the Corridor du Mort for another quarter mile before the map instructed us to turn to the right. This passage was much narrower, and the ceiling dropped considerably. In the distance, I heard dripping.

We walked stooped over, careful not to bump our heads on the solid stone above us. The tunnel, instead of being constructed of brick like the others, or even supported with wooden crossbeams, was carved directly through the bedrock. The floor was uneven, and we regularly came across piles of debris where the ceiling had fallen in. It wasn't making either of us feel very safe.

Another turn brought us into an area with higher ceilings, but my first thought was that the floor had dropped out below—it was completely black. As we shined our lights into the darkness, the problem became apparent—water.

I was ready to turn back right there. I hated the water. Back home, swimming was fine as long as I was in a pool, but I shuddered at the thought of swimming in a lake—I couldn't see the bottom, and I couldn't see what was swimming in there with me. Of course, rationally, I knew that we wouldn't come across piranhas or sharks in the tunnels under Paris, but I couldn't see the bottom of this murky mess.

I walked in front, nervously testing every step. Rebekah had changed back into her sandals to keep her shoes dry. I didn't have that luxury, and there was no way I was going to walk in that water barefoot.

It started shallow, barely above my shoes. After ten yards, we were slogging through twelve inches. The water wasn't exactly icy, but the tunnels were already chilly, and I shivered with cold and nerves. Behind me, Rebekah seemed to be doing fine, but she had the bonus of wanting to be there, and the drive to find out what lay at the end. I merely wanted to get in and get out, the sooner the better.

There was about an eight-inch drop, and suddenly the water was above my knees. The passage was curved, twisting left and right, and I couldn't see the end. The map had indicated it wouldn't be far, but we'd already discovered the scale wasn't perfectly accurate.

The higher it got, the fouler the water smelled—like a mixture of old dishwater and oil. It was thick with sediment and slimy to the touch.

"How much farther?" Rebekah asked, a few feet behind me.

"I don't know." I tried to breathe through my mouth—the smell was getting worse.

"I hope you didn't pay too much for these pants."

I laughed and glanced back at her. She'd taken off the sweater and held it above her head to keep it clean. She scrunched up her face and grinned uncomfortably.

And then I fell in.

I'd been running my feet along the floor, feeling my way, but somehow I'd missed the next step—I stumbled forward and fell face-first into the rancid water. I found my footing and sprang upward immediately, spitting and choking.

Rebekah shrieked, and I felt her arms around me, helping me stand. The stench, now clinging to my face and nose—and inside my mouth—was overpowering. I fought the urge to vomit.

Then there was laughter and light.

There's no better cure for nausea than thinking you're going to die. We were surrounded by light and saw the bright beams of three flashlights pointed straight at us.

"Faites attention!" a voice said. It was male and adult. A cop?

I looked to Rebekah for a translation, but she seemed too confused to answer. She'd also dropped her sweater in the water, and it floated heavily on the surface.

She stumbled over her words. "Pouvez-vous parler moins vite, s'il vous plaît."

"Parlez-vous anglais?" the voice asked.

"Yes," she answered. "You speak English?"

"A little," replied the heavily accented voice. "What are you doing?"

"Walking," I answered, checking the gym bag to make sure it wasn't touching the water. It appeared to be okay—it was thick nylon and hadn't been submerged.

"It looks like you were falling." More laughter. "Walk to the left of the passage. On the right there are holes."

"Who are you?" Rebekah asked.

"We are like you. Except that you are wet and we are not. Come—the way is not far, and we will talk."

"Do you think they're cops?" I whispered to Rebekah.

"If they are, I don't think we should run."

I considered it for a few moments and then began walking toward them. They turned their lights out of our eyes, and we trudged on another forty feet. At the end of the passage, a series of ten steps led up and out.

They were waiting for us at the top, three young men in their late twenties or early thirties, and definitely not police. They were dressed in coveralls and wearing miner's hard hats with headlamps. Their clothes were tattered and patched, their hard hats covered in stickers and logos. All three had some kind of facial hair, and one had a tattoo on his cheek. They were all smoking cigarettes while they waited.

"I am Stephane," one of them began, apparently the leader of the group as the others seemed content to let him do the talking. "Where are you going?"

"A little farther in," I answered.

He smiled. "You seem ill prepared for a journey."

"We'll manage."

The man with the tattoo extinguished his cigarette on the wall and then pointed down a side passage. "Come. We will eat and talk."

He led us a hundred yards down the side passage and then into a tight tunnel, no more than five feet high. After a ten-foot crawl, the hole emptied out into a wide room. It was much more modern than the crumbling brick-and-mortar halls we'd traveled down. The floors and walls were rough concrete, and large metal boxes hung on the walls—electrical boxes that had fallen into disuse. Stephane disappeared into another room for a moment, then returned with a cask of wine.

"Sit down," he instructed us. Rebekah and I huddled close together, nervously watching the men as they prepared their meal. The tattooed one knelt in the center of the room and lit a small propane stove. He turned to me, grinned, and pointed at the ceiling. Rebekah and I obediently looked and saw a wide crack in the concrete.

"Vent," he said proudly, as he pointed at the stove. "For the gas."

Well, we might not asphyxiate, but I hardly felt any safer.

"Who are you?" Rebekah asked. "What do you do down here?"

Stephane sat, holding a tin of something on his lap and fiddling with a can opener. "We just might ask you the same question. Obviously, we are regulars here. You are not."

The three men watched us, waiting for an answer. I looked at Rebekah.

"We're looking for something," she finally said. "Perhaps you can help us find it."

"A pretty girl like you shouldn't be in a place like this," Stephane answered casually. He twisted the lid off the can and set it to the side. "But what are you looking for?"

"We have a map," she answered. "But we don't know how to use it—we need to find some landmark to make it usable."

The tattooed one rolled his eyes and set a can of soup on the stove. "Tourists," he muttered. Stephane also looked annoyed. The third man, who didn't seem to speak English, was sitting a little farther off, sipping wine and eating bread.

"Here," Rebekah said, refusing to give up. "Let me show you the map."

Stephane waved his hand. "I assure you, I've seen it. Let me guess—you're tourists from America, and you found a map on the Internet."

"No," she insisted. "Eric, let them see the map."

I dug out the map, unfolded it carefully, and handed it to Stephane.

Rebekah spoke quickly, not wanting to lose their attention. "We were given the map by, well, a friend. It's very old."

Stephane looked closely at the page, squinting in the bad light. The one I'd decided to call Tattoo scooted toward him and looked over his shoulder.

"We know where we are on that map right now," Rebekah continued, "but we're trying to get to the area on the next page. See?"

Stephane quickly flipped through the pages. Tattoo motioned to the silent man, who joined them.

"Where did you get this?" Stephane finally said without glancing up.

"From a friend."

"This map is very old," he replied, pointing to the front page. He turned it and pointed to the other section. "But this map I have never seen before."

Rebekah exhaled heavily, dejected.

Stephane moved next to Rebekah and showed her. "I know these tunnels," he said. "But this section is foreign to me. Perhaps it is because the map is so old—much has changed down here." He turned the map back to the front and pointed to a blank spot. "See, this is where we are sitting now. On your map, there is nothing here. That is because this was built in the 1940s—this was a Nazi bunker, for communications. On your map, this bunker does not exist."

I looked around me at the smooth cement walls. "A Nazi bunker?"

"Yes, the Nazis. It was in these tunnels that the Resistance organized."

"So the map is useless?" asked Rebekah.

He laughed. "No, not useless, but wrong. Look here." He indicated a long, straight tunnel. "This area has been blocked now by the metro."

Her voice was desperate. "Can you lead us to the area on the second page?"

Tattoo spoke up. "We can lead you there, but it is different now. What you are looking for is not there anymore."

"You don't even know what we're looking for," Rebekah said, confused.

"I know these tunnels," Stephane said. "And much of what is on that map no longer exists."

Rebekah shook her head, refusing to believe it. "What if these tunnels are hidden?"

"Why would they be hidden?"

"Just, what if they are?"

Stephane looked at her, intrigued and amused. "What happened to your hand?"

She glanced down at the pressure bandage. "I was in an accident."

"You were burned."

I interrupted. "Can you take us there or not?"

He watched Rebekah thoughtfully for several seconds. "I can take you there, but you must do something for me."

"What?" she asked.

"Let me make a copy of your map."

We sat in the room for an hour while Stephane studiously transcribed our map onto his. Once again, he'd gone into the other room, returning this time with a three-ring binder. He had dozens of maps, all hand-drawn, and each was in a separate plastic sleeve.

As he copied the map, Stephane explained to us that he was known as a cataphile—part of an exclusive subterranean subculture who spent days at a time in the tunnels and catacombs. Tattoo referred to them as "urban adventurers." Tattoo had been at it for three years, Stephane for six. Each of them knew the tunnels by heart, which explained their eagerness to have a copy of a map with unknown tunnels.

"Do you live down here?" Rebekah asked, accepting some duck confit that Tattoo had warmed on the stove.

"No," Stephane laughed. "I have a job and a flat. But we spend time down here—a lot of time." He gestured to the silent man. "Jean-Arnoud has a wife and two children."

"But what about the police?" I said. "We heard that there are drug dealers down here."

"Yes, but it is rare. In three years, I have never seen police," Tattoo offered.

Stephane chuckled, still drawing his map. "Several years ago there were many police. It seems a group of cataphiles were operating an underground cinema in one of the chambers. The police arrested them."

Tattoo nodded. "But they mostly leave us alone—too much trouble to patrol down here."

He offered us wine, which we politely refused, and we offered them some of our Camembert, which they eagerly accepted. It was strange, the five of us sitting in near darkness and near silence forty feet or more beneath the surface. Wherever Felix was, I'm sure he never expected us to be here. Neither did I.

When Stephane finished the map, he brought it back to

Rebekah. Pointing at the upper corner, he asked, "Do you know what this is?"

We both examined the map. He was indicating the small circle with a dot in the center. Rebekah shook her head. "No idea."

He handed the map back to her. "The Black Sun."

"What is that?"

"An ancient symbol," Stephane replied.

"A symbol of what?"

"I do not know. But I've seen it many times." He sat back for a few minutes, thoughtful, and then said, "Come. It is time to go."

We left the bunker the same way we'd entered. I tried to keep track of our movements on the map but couldn't. As Stephane had explained, much had changed. In one corridor, thirty minutes into our walk, the cavern began to shake. The noise was overwhelming, and dust fell from the ceiling. Rebekah grabbed my hand, and we jumped into an indent in the wall, expecting an avalanche of stone. I held her tight against me, watching the bricks overhead, knowing I might have to dodge them at any moment. But as quickly as it came, the sound passed.

"Metro," Tattoo said with a laugh. "We are safe."

Stephane led us farther and deeper into the tunnels, staying eerily silent most of the time. Occasionally Tattoo and Jean-Arnoud spoke in French, but their words were whispers that Rebekah could not translate. The path turned from wide tunnel to tiny passageway to chalk quarry, but all the while our guides seemed to know exactly where they were.

At last, Stephane led us all through a fissure in the rock, down a rickety wooden ladder, and into a small room. The floors were paved in tight, carefully crafted stone, and carved pillars rose to the ceiling.

"We are here," Stephane declared. "Give me your map."

I handed it over, and he marked a spot with a small scratch of red ink. "This is La Grotte du Soliel," he explained. "The Grotto of the Sun."

"How do we get out?" I asked, unsure I could retrace our path.

"You will find the way," he replied with a slight grin. "If you wish to follow us now, we can lead you. If not, you must find the way back yourself."

"We'll find the way," Rebekah insisted. She was putting on a confident face, but I could tell she was nervous. I didn't bother with any false appearances—I was scared.

Stephane nodded and took Rebekah's hand. "Before we go, I want to show you something." He led her across the room to a large carved stone and helped her climb it. I followed, more than a little annoyed that he had touched her.

"Look," he instructed, and pointed to the floor of the grotto.

Rebekah stared for a few moments, and I followed her gaze but saw nothing other than dusty paving stones. Suddenly, she gasped. "Eric!"

"What?"

"Come up here."

I scrambled up behind her. The rock was large but there was no good place for me to stand. She took my hand to steady me, then pointed. In the center of the floor, as part of an elaborate mosaic, was a thick, black circle with a round stone in the center.

"This symbol—this Black Sun—means something to you?" Stephane asked curiously. Tattoo and Jean-Arnoud watched us silently.

"Yes," she answered.

Rebekah offered no further explanation, and the men didn't press her for one. Stephane helped her back down from the rock.

"I must warn you," he said with a wry smile. "You will not enjoy the rest of your journey."

Without warning he kissed her on both cheeks and grinned at me, then the three of them left.

"What was that supposed to mean?" I asked, not trying to hide my annoyance.

She laughed and took my hand. "Eric, it's cultural."

"In America, it's cultural to hate the French."

CHAPTER 25

IT WAS JUST after one o'clock in the afternoon when the cataphiles left us. We weren't hungry, but Rebekah was in pain, so we stayed in the grotto to rest. She took more aspirin and her daily antibiotic, and hooked up her oxygen mask.

We hadn't bothered fishing her sweater from the foul-smelling canal we'd waded through, which made me grateful that I'd bought her a second. She pulled it from the backpack, checking to make sure it wasn't wet, and put it on. It was black, and with her black pants and dark hair she would have vanished into the shadows had it not been for her pale skin.

My clothes had mostly dried, but they still stunk. I felt like I hadn't had a shower in months, and I had never felt such an overpowering need to wash my hands.

Despite Stephane's bothersome exit, I still wished he was there. The cataphiles were our safety net—they knew the ins and outs of the cave, and they knew how to get back to the surface. When they left, they took with them any knowledge of an exit route—and they had shaken our faith in the map.

I took several long drinks of water, ignoring the hard flavor—just grateful for something clean. Rebekah had curled up in the center of the room, using the backpack as a pillow. I lay down next to her—not too close, since I knew I smelled awful, but close enough that I could hear the quiet hiss of the oxygen tank.

I turned off the light to save batteries.

I tried to sleep but couldn't. Instead, I prayed. I prayed long and hard. Longer and harder than I had in months, and yet my prayers seemed to go nowhere, as though the however-many feet of earth between me and heaven were impenetrable.

Life wasn't supposed to be like this. If things were fair, I'd be back in college, staying up late to play games and watch movies. Rebekah and I would date in the normal way, going to restaurants, taking long walks. . . . Occasionally, something really terrible and life-shattering would happen, like me tearing my pants or her getting an A minus.

We could still go to Madagascar. Maybe Australia would be better—they spoke English there, and we wouldn't have to learn a language. We could buy a small cottage in the outback—a ranch, maybe, with kangaroos and wallabies and didgeridoos.

We were currently napping on the Black Sun. Maybe this was all true. Isabella was right and Edward was in the Illuminati. If it was true, maybe Rebekah would finally agree to run. We'd start over.

It was really dark when Rebekah stirred. "Eric?" Her voice was soft, but in the utter silence of the tunnel it sounded like a gunshot.

I jumped. "You're awake?"

"Yeah."

"How do you feel?"

"I'm okay."

"Let me know if you need anything."

"I just wanted to say thank you."

I rolled over. If it had been light, I would have been looking her in the eyes. As it was, I saw nothing but blackness. "For what?"

"For coming with me. For not thinking I'm crazy."

"I never said that," I joked.

She laughed, but I could tell she was getting ready to cry. "It's my fault, you know. It's my father who's messed up. It's because of him that we're down here."

"What your dad does isn't your fault."

"I want him to be someone he's not. That's why we're down here. We're down here because I want to love him and I can't."

I stammered. I wanted to say something comforting, but nothing came to mind. Rebekah had always been the one to give me advice— she kept me happy, and I didn't know how to return the favor.

I felt her touch my arm, and I fumblingly took her hand.

"I wish things were different," I said.

"Me too."

Neither of us could sleep, but we lay there for over an hour. Rebekah's body needed the rest, even if her mind couldn't. Eventually we flicked the lights back on, regaining our bearings in the small room. Rebekah and I both drank some more water, and she nibbled at some cheese. Finally, we slung the bags over our shoulders and headed out.

Two spurs of the tunnel split off at the grotto. The map showed that one turned left and wound senselessly in spirals and twists. The other went straight, with branches breaking off to both sides in a very orderly manner. If the map was right, though Stephane had said it wasn't, then we should go right. We did.

Our philosophy was simple. We'd go where the map pointed, doing the best we could to find the chambers of the Illuminati (if that's who they were). If something had changed—if a Nazi bunker or a metro station got in the way, we'd try to circumvent it. And if none of that worked, then I'd do my best to sell Rebekah on the benefits of another land down under.

We were three minutes into our hike when Rebekah let out a little yelp.

"What?" I said, spinning around. It sounded like she'd spotted a rat.

She didn't answer, only pointed at the walls.

I had been watching the floor—it was uneven and strewn with rocks, and the last thing I wanted down here was a twisted ankle— but I hadn't looked at the walls. I'd noticed that the tunnel was fairly wide, probably twelve feet across, and I'd thought the walls were made of brick.

I turned the flashlight and took a step forward. It wasn't brick.

"There's so many," Rebekah said, horrified.

They were bones, but not skeletons. It was all sorted—arms, legs, and skulls. Where the ribs and vertebrae were, I had no idea. The legs and arms were stacked one on top of the other, with only the knobby ends visible, creating a nearly straight wall six feet high and endlessly long. There were a lot of people here.

"Stephane said we wouldn't like it," I said quietly, gazing at the morbid exactness of the pile. I swung the light around and looked at the other side—all the same. A small, stone plaque was nestled into the bones as part of the wall. I touched Rebekah's arm and pointed.

"Cimetière du Rue Braque," she read. "They moved all the bodies down here."

I took a breath, glancing up and down the catacomb—the bones continued as far as my light would go. All at once the ceiling felt too low, the walls too narrow, the air too cold, and the tunnel too dark. I reached for Rebekah's hand just as she was reaching for mine.

We hurried down the tunnel as fast as Rebekah's lungs would carry us, occasionally noticing a plaque from a new cemetery, or a ghoulish design in the bones—a crucifix formed from skulls, or a skull-and-crossbones. As we traveled, there were signs of the catacombs' age. In places, the perfectly even walls had fallen, spilling out onto the floor. I thought my hand would break from Rebekah's squeezing as we quickly picked our way past the bones.

The map instructed us to turn right at the end of the straight-away, which we did, only to discover that the boneyard continued. There was more disarray here—no one had ever taken the kind of time needed to make smooth walls—these were just piles and piles of the dead.

Rebekah began running, and I followed, the beams of our flash-lights bouncing wildly from ceiling to floor. At every turn I'd pause long enough to check the map and then run to catch up with Rebekah. She once took a wrong turn and had to run back to me— her eyes appeared to be almost closed, but tears were streaming down her cheeks. I grabbed her and wrapped her up in my arms.

"I have to get out of here," she whispered urgently, her eyes clamped shut.

"Come on," I coaxed, "we're almost there."

"I didn't know it would be like this," she sobbed. "I didn't know."

I held up the map. "Look Rebekah. Open your eyes."

Slowly she obeyed, shuddering. She looked down at the paper.

"We're right here," I said. "The room can't be far. One more turn."

She nodded, wiping her eyes. "I'm sorry," she said, trying to get hold of her emotions.

"It's okay. Let's just get there and then get out."

I walked quickly, my arm around her waist. Her fingers gripped my arm tightly, but her eyes were open. More importantly, she wasn't running. We both kept our gaze straight ahead, ignoring the death that surrounded us.

The tunnel took a sharp turn to the left. Just as the map said, it was another long straightaway. But the map showed a small curved tunnel branching to the right. We were there, but there was no tunnel—just more bones, neatly stacked.

"It should be right here," I said, pointing to the wall of femurs.

"Could we be in the wrong place?"

"No. We haven't made that many turns."

"But that can't be right," Rebekah said, running her hands over her tired face. She took a step toward the wall and then turned back. "The guys said that the map would be wrong because it was old, but nothing here has changed. There's nothing new here—no basements or subways—nothing."

"Maybe the map is just wrong."

"But why?"

It was the end of the line. There was nowhere to go, nowhere to look. We were in the right place, and there was no tunnel. No Illuminati.

"Maybe you're right," I ventured. "Maybe Isabella was wrong. The Illuminati doesn't exist."

Rebekah didn't answer but turned slowly in a circle, looking at the endless tunnels and endless bones. And then she looked straight into my eyes, terrified. "What was that?"

"What was what?"

"You didn't hear it?"

I reached out and took her arm. She was breaking down. "Rebekah."

"Shhh!"

I pulled her closer to me but listened. There was nothing but silence. Rebekah was frantically shining the light up and down the corridor. I held her tightly against me, feeling her shake.

"There!" she whispered and turned off her light. I did the same, leaving us blind and surrounded by death.

I strained to hear, but couldn't. I didn't know what I could do to get Rebekah out of there. There was no easy exit, and we'd have to backtrack through all the catacombs we'd just crossed—and another several hours after that.

And then I heard it.

"It's a whistle," Rebekah said, clinging onto me. "It's *the* whistle."

I had no idea what direction it came from, but it was distinct—occasionally high and occasionally low, but noticeable and getting closer. It didn't sound like a person, but it wasn't a bird either.

"What do we do?" I asked Rebekah, my machismo shining through.

"I don't know." Her voice was less than a whisper—it was as though I felt her breath on my face and knew what she'd said.

The noise was close and coming fast.

"Eric," she pleaded.

One more loud whistle, and then a light appeared. It rounded a far corner and came flying toward us, bouncing up and down. Rebekah and I stood, frightened out of our minds, like deer in the headlights.

A bell rang twice, and Rebekah looked at me. I turned on the flashlight.

It was a man on a bike. He rang his bell again and waved. I watched him clench the brakes, the wheels squeaked—whistled—and the bike rolled to a stop.

"Bonjour!" he said, hopping from the seat.

Rebekah let out a long breath. I didn't.

The man was old, probably in his late sixties. He was thin and pale, but wrinkled deeply. He had a short, white beard, and was balding on top. Yet, despite his age, he was quick on his feet, swinging his leg off the bike and giddily shaking our hands.

"Ça fait longtemps depuis que j'ai vu quelqu'un qui est descendu jusqu'ici!"

His hand was rough and cracked, the driest skin I'd ever felt.

"Et alors, qui êtes-vous? Qu'est-ce que vous faites ici?"

Rebekah spoke slowly, still bewildered. "Je ne comprends pas."

"Vous êtes Americains? You are Americans?"

"Yes," Rebekah answered. "Uh . . . who are you?"

"Have you not heard of me?" He laughed boisterously. "Le Catacyclist!"

"You're not French," I said. His accent was wrong.

"Guilty as charged," he chuckled, and then jumped to attention and saluted. "A loyal servant of the queen, I am. Long live the queen! It is still the queen, right? She hasn't, you know, passed on?" He pointed at the bones with his thumb and then shrieked with delight.

Rebekah eyed him nervously. "You live down here?"

"Here and there," he answered. "There and here. Haven't been topside for eight months now, I think. I don't wear a watch, though, so I'm not sure."

"Where do you get food?" she asked.

"Oh, I have friends. Cataphiles. Spelos. People underneath. But what are you doing here? You're new here, and you don't know what you're doing." He grabbed my arm and sniffed it. "You've fallen in the water, and not the good water either."

Rebekah's grip on me loosened, but she kept hold of my hand. "We're looking for something. We have a map." She motioned for me to give it to her, but before I could unfold it, he was waving it away.

"The only map I need is up here." He tapped on his forehead. "It's all here. Should be—I've been down here for fourteen years."

"Why?"

"Why not?" He laughed.

"We're looking for a tunnel that branches off from here," Rebekah said, still showing him the map.

"Lots of tunnels. Miles of tunnels."

"This one is supposed to be right here," she insisted.

"Why do you want this tunnel? Why not another one? Lots of tunnels, lots of bones."

"We're looking for a room."

"Lots of tunnels, lots of rooms."

"We need to find it," she pleaded.

"Whose room is it?" He bent down and picked up a loose bone from the floor, flipping it over and over in his hand.

"What do you mean?"

"All the rooms belong to someone. Whose is it?"

I shook my head and gave Rebekah a this-guy-is-crazy look.

She thought for a moment, searching for an answer. The Catacyclist tossed the bone back into the pile and climbed onto his bike.

"The Illuminati's room," she blurted out.

It didn't faze him. "Whose room is it really?" He nudged the kickstand with his heel and rolled the bike forward.

"It is the Illuminati's room," I yelled. "We need to find it."

"It's not their room," he laughed, pedaling away.

Rebekah let go of me and ran after him. "It's my father's room!"

Without flinching, the Catacyclist pulled the bike around in a tight U-turn. He pedaled back, braking right in front of her and ringing the bell. "Your father doesn't visit much."

She didn't say anything.

"It belongs to your father?" he said, grinning curiously.

"Yes. In a sense."

"In a sense. In a sense, the room belongs to me. In a sense, the room belongs to all of Paris."

"I need to find out if my father is a member of the Illuminati."

He laughed, throwing his head back wildly. "You won't find out in that room, oh no! Not unless your father is much older than you."

I stepped forward. "So you know the room? You know where it is?"

"I know the room, but your father hasn't ever been there. No one ever goes there. No one but me."

Rebekah gasped. "You've been there?"

He smiled as though trying to stifle a laugh. "I've been everywhere down here. But I like that room especially much because it has pretty pictures."

"Can you take us there?"

"You're already there," he cackled. "But you wouldn't want to go in, I'm sure."

"Just show me," Rebekah pleaded.

The Catacyclist set the kickstand and stepped away from his bike. He hopped quickly along, darting from one side of the tunnel to the other, looking. Finally, he waved to us, and scrambled up onto a pile of bones.

"You can hide anything behind bones," he laughed, playfully picking up a skull and tossing it from hand to hand. "Alas, poor Yorick! Nobody will ever look!"

Rebekah grabbed my arm. "You mean we have to climb over?"

"Yes!" he shouted, dropping the skull. "Yes, you have to climb over. Why do you think no one has ever found it?"

She turned to me, a look of horror spreading across her face. "I'm going to need a lot of therapy."

"Not as much as him."

Reluctantly, we followed the Catacyclist onto the bone pile. Rebekah gripped my hand fiercely, partly to steady herself, and partly, I assumed, to see if she could squeeze hard enough to draw blood.

As I walked on the unsteady mass, I tried to imagine I was somewhere else, doing something far more wholesome. I was in McDonald's Playland, tromping through the Ball Crawl. Then I remembered where I was, and what I actually was walking on, and I didn't think I could ever go to McDonald's again.

Rebekah started singing a hymn, the most cheerful one she could think of—"There Is Sunshine in My Soul Today." It didn't make me feel any less like I was walking on the remains of hundreds of Parisians, but it did make me laugh. She looked like she was going to be sick.

"Sometimes I wonder if I'm related," the man ahead of us said, reaching the back wall. "If my great-great-grandfather knew I was walking on his bones, he'd roll over in his grave!" He roared at his own joke and hopped off the back of the pile.

Behind the bones there was a narrow gap between the pile and the wall. As I climbed down I wondered which was worse—walking across the dead, or squeezing down a tight passage, waiting for the pile to collapse onto me. I did my best not to think about it, and I failed entirely.

The narrow passage was probably fifty feet long, and our guide was far ahead of us, scampering toward the room that he alone knew existed. Rebekah, walking ahead of me, turned to whisper in my ear.

"I'm afraid to ask how he found it."

"Don't."

He paused at the end of the passage, proudly waiting to display his knowledge. As we reached him, we saw a wooden door in the stone wall. It was carved ornately with birds and flowers. In the center was an unfinished pyramid—just like on the dollar bill, except with no all-seeing eye above it.

I looked at Rebekah, and the man cleared his throat.

"Presenting for your enjoyment, The Room."

Instead of touching the lock, the Catacyclist lowered his shoulder and slammed the door open. It looked like it ought to hurt, but he didn't seem to notice. The door led down a short series of steps, and then into a perfectly square room. On the floor, like in the grotto, was a large Black Sun, though this one was more ornate. The stone was glossy black, possibly marble, though now covered in dust. The circle and dot were different—roughly hewn from a white rock, making the symbol seem to glow.

"Who cares about that?" he said, moving in front of us to block our view. "Look at the pictures!"

We turned our flashlights up. The wall to our left was an enormous bookcase, stacked tightly with volume after volume. To our right was a frieze of the unfinished pyramid, though once again the triangular eye was missing—there was a cavity in the wall, as though a carved stone had once rested there. On the wall directly in front of us was a mural. The paint was faded and flaking away, but much of the image was visible. It was a battle scene, with thousands storming a castle. They wore the clothes of peasants, but carried the blue, white, and red flag of the French Revolution. The painted sky was dark, obscured by the smoke and fire of the battle. And perched on the castle was an enormous owl with royal soldiers in its talons. Bold script, arching over the battlefield, read "Les Vainqueurs du Bastille."

Strangely, the entire mural was randomly pock-marked with deep, black holes. It looked almost as though someone had shot at it, over and over.

Rebekah stepped forward, examining the flaking paint. "But what does it mean?"

"Les Vainqueurs du Bastille!" the Catacyclist said triumphantly. "Victors at the Bastille!"

"But why?"

He giggled. "I haven't been in a library in years, and you ask me why? Then again, it's not like history changes very much."

"It's the French Revolution," I said, displaying the kind of genius insight that had led me down into the catacombs to begin with.

"Vive la France!" he cried. "It's the French Revolution. You really should be Head Boy with a brain like that. You're going places, young man. Of course it's the French Revolution, but the girl asked *why.* Do you know why?"

"Why what?"

"Why is it here, in a hole in the ground, twenty meters below the street? Why has a monstrous owl lit upon the Bastille? Why is the painting full of holes? Why does it concern the Illuminati? I know, do you?"

I waited. This was going to be good.

He didn't say anything.

"Well?" I coaxed.

"Well, what?"

"What are the answers?"

He thought for a minute and then sat down in the center of the circle, cross-legged, right on the dot.

"Two years ago," he said, "I found a passageway that led directly under the Moulin Rouge. I've also discovered one that opens up right in the middle of Saint-Chapelle—and let me tell you, there are some strange things underneath churches. There's another tunnel that goes into the Opera—you know, as in 'The Phantom of'? It's all overrated. No phantom. No lovely young singers. Yes, there is a big lake under there, but what do I want with a lake?"

This wasn't the kind of explanation I was expecting. "What's your point?"

"Not three days ago, I was under the Pantheon and stumbled upon an art show. Paintings and drawings and sculptures. The place was full of people—must've been a dozen, very posh."

Rebekah sat down across from him. "So?"

His eyes lit up and a crooked smile stretched across his face. "So I see everything! One would imagine that living down here would keep me from learning anything, but I learn *everything,* because I see *everything!*"

"What do you know about the Illuminati?" Rebekah asked, getting excited.

"What do you know about The Great Fear?"

"I've heard of it," she answered. "From history class. Something about peasants burning down manor houses."

"Yes! Exactly! Because they'd heard rumors. After the peasants stormed the Bastille—" without taking his eyes off Rebekah, he gestured to the painting—"the peasants started to hear rumors. They heard that the aristocrats had paid brigands to burn down their crops. So the peasants decided to make a preemptive strike, as it were. They went after the nobles and burned down their houses. They got into the safes and took the documents—the ones that make a noble a noble, and peasant a peasant—and they burned them all. Those were important documents. They were straight from the king."

"It sounds like a regular revolution to me," I said, reluctantly joining them on the floor.

He laughed. "Aha! That's because it's supposed to sound like a regular revolution. But where did the rumors start? No nobles were burning down any crops."

"Where do any rumors start?" I scoffed. "They just start."

"All right, professor, explain this. According to your obviously thorough research of the French Revolution, what was the cause?"

"Well," I stammered, "like you just said, it started because the people didn't like the king, or the class system."

Rebekah came to my rescue. "Rousseau wrote *The Social Contract,* which said that liberty could only be reached by uniting the people and working toward common good."

"Beautiful!" the Catacyclist declared. "Tell me more."

"Um . . . Voltaire wrote about the corruption of the Catholic Church, and about religion in general. He questioned whether religion actually gave people good rules to live by. At that time, when the church was so strong, it was, well, revolutionary."

"Fantastic," he shouted. "Now, the last one."

Rebekah looked confused. "I'm sorry?"

"The last one. Rousseau, Voltaire, and there's a third."

She looked down and thought. I didn't bother thinking, since I knew I wouldn't come up with it.

"You know it," he urged. "Starts with an *M* . . ."

She nodded. "I know I know it."

". . . ends with an *ontesquieu.*"

"Montesquieu," she said, as though she was an idiot for not thinking of it. I don't think I'd ever heard the name. "He was a writer. He said that England had a good system of government, because it was based on giving everyone freedom."

He laughed. "He should have told that to the Americans."

"He also said that France's system couldn't work because it was an absolute monarchy. Well, there were parliaments, but they were nearly powerless."

"Now," he said, imitating a schoolteacher. "Name for me the three estates."

Rebekah smiled. A question she could easily answer. "The aristocracy, the clergy, and the commoners."

The Catacyclist smiled and motioned that Rebekah and I should lean in a little closer to hear. His voice was barely above a whisper. "Now tell me, if these philosophers spoke out against the aristocracy and the clergy, then they were obviously speaking to commoners, right? And ultimately, it was the commoners who revolted, right? But explain this—ninety-five percent of the commoners couldn't read, and of the ones who could, how many knew big words like *absolutism?* Have you ever tried to read something written by Montesquieu? It's horrid. Only the most educated could even understand this stuff, and yet it incited a revolution?"

Rebekah looked confused and stared back him.

I scratched my beard, which still smelled of the tunnel water. "What are you saying?"

The Catacyclist leaped to his feet and pointed at the painting. "Who is storming the Bastille? The commoners! But who is leading them?"

I stared at the mural. There was no one who looked like a leader. Even the flag bearer was just another face in the crowd. Finally, I guessed. "The owl?"

"Of course the owl!"

Rebekah stood to get a better look. "But who is the owl?"

"You know about the Illuminati, right? There are different ranks in it, like ranks in the army or the Freemasons or what-have-you. First rank doesn't have a name, and the only people who are in that rank are the ones who have been in the Illuminati for about a day. They write an essay."

I laughed. "Really?"

"Oh yes," he answered very seriously. "The Illuminati only wants the best and brightest, and they make you write essays and use codes and read books. But that's what you do in the first rank, the essay. The second is called the Novitiate, and you're usually in there for a couple of years. You get your code name. Weishaupt, who started the whole thing, was called Spartacus, and Goethe—you knew Goethe was Illuminati, right?—he was named Abaris. During this time they mostly study and write. See, not all secret societies are fun and games."

"But what about the owl?" Rebekah asked.

"The third rank in the Illuminati is marked by the owl. This is the rank where you really sink your teeth into something. It's an academy of sorts—they study as a group and they have class projects, if you will. They met together twice a month, and they'd read and study, and then as a group they'd carry out some of the wishes of the higher ranks."

"That's why there are all these books?" I asked, pointing to the shelves in the room.

"Yes. I've read these. The Bible, Seneca, Epictetus, Marcus Aurelius, Confucius. They read everything, and this room was one of the academies. But the owl was their symbol—it's the symbol of wisdom. It's the symbol of Minerva, the goddess of wisdom. That's the rank's name: The Brethren of Minerva."

Rebekah was on her feet in a flash, and I yanked the map out of my pocket.

The Catacyclist laughed with glee. "I've got them excited! What is it?"

Rebekah looked at the map and read the words again. "Le coeur peut être vu seulement par les yeux de Minerva."

Reading over my shoulder, he translated. "The heart can only be seen through the eyes of Minerva."

I looked up at the owl. In place of its eyes were two round holes, bored deep into the stone wall.

The Catacyclist seemed in genuine awe. "The heart? Where did you find this map?"

"A friend," Rebekah answered, looking for something to stand on to look in the owl's eyes. "What are these holes?"

"I've never known," he said, amazed. "I thought they were just holes."

I put my eye up to one of the holes in the mural and peered inside. I could see nothing, except that the wall was only a few inches thick, and another wall stood a few inches behind that. Enough light came in through the other holes that I could see, but nothing was written there—just plain stone.

"Here," I said to Rebekah. "Let me give you a boost."

I cupped my hands as a foothold. Rebekah gingerly stepped in and I hoisted her up to the owl. I was amazed by how light she was—she was wasting away.

"What do you see?" the Catacyclist asked, nearly bouncing with excitement.

Rebekah gazed for several seconds before answering. Finally, she stepped down, looking confused.

"It's Latin. *Ut Ipse Finiam.*"

I turned to our guide. "What does that have to do with the heart?"

"The heart is legendary," he said, thinking carefully about the Latin phrase. "The center of the Illuminati. It's the meeting place of the Mysteries—the Presbyters, the Princes, the Magus, and the Kings. All the highest levels of the order."

"Do you know what that Latin phrase means?" Rebekah asked, hopeful.

He laughed, though still deep in thought. "I do, but I don't. I know what it translates to, but I don't know how that's supposed to lead you to the heart."

Rebekah was practically pleading. "What does it translate to?"

"*That I may finish it personally,*" he answered simply. "It's often written on the pyramid." He gestured absently toward the frieze and began peeking in other holes in the mural.

Rebekah turned to the bookcase, as though she might find something there. I looked at the pyramid. It was sculpted in stone, though the carved lines were no more than an inch deep. It looked exactly like the Great Seal. Twelve layers of bricks—the thirteenth would be the all-seeing eye, if it were still there. At the bottom were the roman numerals MDCCLXXVI—1776.

"Wait a minute," I said, jumping for the gym bag. Rebekah and the Catacyclist watched in confusion as I tore through it, searching.

Finally I found what I was looking for and held it up. Edward's antique Scrabble game.

Rebekah's eyes went wide. Our guide smiled anxiously. I fumbled with the letters, carefully arranging them on the triangular board. Finally, they spelled it out: *Ut Ipse Finiam.*

"Where did you get that?" he asked, laughing as I stepped over to the pyramid and pushed the triangle into the cavity in the wall. It was a perfect fit.

"My father's house," Rebekah muttered, stunned.

"Well, it is his room."

I looked at the phrase for a moment, and then turned the crank. Unseen, the small pins under each letter were depressed into the stone frieze.

"It's a key!" the Catacyclist cried, giggling wildly. Rebekah was standing right at my shoulder, watching everything in wonder.

There was a muffled ping, and a small, dusty panel popped open a few feet to the right of the pyramid. Rebekah pushed the tiny door to the side and looked eagerly at the carving behind it.

It was the Black Sun again, at the center of a twelve-pointed star. Above it was a short sentence of French.

Rebekah touched the wall, slowly translating the words. "Enter the ranks of the enlightened."

"Illuminated," the Catacyclist corrected.

She took a step back, bewildered. "What is it?"

The corner of his mouth turned up as he stared. "You've passed the test."

I let out a confused laugh. "We did?"

"Well, no, not you. Someone passed the test." He tapped on the triangular key. "This would have been a gift from the Minerval's superiors. When they felt it was time for him to advance in the organization, he'd receive this device—he became an Illuminatus Minor."

"Is that how your dad got it?"

Rebekah shrugged, gazing intensely at the symbol. "This is it?"

"It's a map," the Catacyclist said simply. "Part of the test is figuring it out."

I looked down at the Black Sun on the floor and gestured to our guide. "Do you know of any more of these? There's the one in the grotto and this one. Maybe this room is a map—you know, a twelve-pointed-star-marks-the-spot kind of thing."

"None," he answered sadly. "And no twelve-pointed stars, at least not with a Black Sun."

"But there are more?" Rebekah asked hopefully.

"Nothing grand. I've found them as graffiti or on tombs. The star is a common symbol for secret mystical groups—it's merely a sign of the zodiac."

Rebekah glanced sadly around the room. "So this is it."

"Yes."

"If no one comes down here," I said, "then how did Edward have this?"

Rebekah shook her head, still staring at the panel. "It was on his mantelpiece. Maybe he didn't even know what it was."

The Catacyclist nodded and chuckled. He was enjoying this much more than Rebekah or I. "Perhaps a gift when he joined?"

She looked at me. We'd found more than I'd expected, and certainly enough evidence to prove part of Isabella's theory. The Illuminati had existed. And more importantly, Rebekah's father had an Illuminati artifact above his fireplace. Edward was linked to them, and everything Isabella had said seemed true.

Isabella had said things would get a lot worse—a lot worse on Tuesday night, to be exact. I could only hope that Rebekah wouldn't fight me anymore. We needed to run.

CHAPTER 26

I COULDN'T GET Rebekah to leave the room for another forty minutes. She checked every single hole in the mural but found nothing. She looked at all the books on the shelves, hoping for clues, but discovered only dusty pages and cobwebs. She even checked the walls and corners, hoping for a secret passage or another hidden panel. Nothing.

While she looked, I clarified a few things with the Catacyclist, picking his brain for more information that would lead us to the heart, but I mostly wound up with an erratic history lesson.

"So the commoners stormed the Bastille," I said, turning to the mural. "The Illuminati were trying to help them get their share of the wealth?"

"Haven't you been listening, boy?" He shook his head, exasperated with my ignorance.

"You said that it was the commoners who revolted in the Great Fear, and it was commoners who stormed the Bastille."

"But the Illuminati weren't doing it for the people," he said, gesturing wildly. "The Illuminati did it for the Illuminati. They saw a way that they could get more control and they dove on it. They couldn't have cared less about the commoners—they were tools, pawns. They were easy to manipulate. If it had been easier to use the clergy, the Illuminati would have used the clergy."

He motioned for Rebekah to join us, and took her firmly by the arm. "Listen carefully. I know your father is your father, and that's terrific. But if this is his room, then you need to remember what I just said: the Illuminati do everything for the Illuminati. He's not your friend anymore. He's not your father."

Rebekah's response was silence.

My flashlight was going dim when we finally left the room and headed back into the tunnel. After climbing over the bone pile—which we did much faster this time, concerned much more with speed than respect for the dead—we paused in the center of the catacomb passage.

"Thank you for that," the Catacyclist said, sounding sincere. "You showed *me* a new secret in these caves—that hasn't happened in some time."

"Where will you go?" Rebekah asked, noticeably concerned.

He laughed. "I must pedal. It's what makes my light work."

"Wait," she insisted. She unzipped the gym bag and pulled a handful of bills from it. "Here's something. Thanks."

The Catacyclist shook his head and mounted his bike. "What would I do with money?"

"You're just going to stay down here?"

"Of course."

"At least let us give you some food."

He conceded, and Rebekah filled a bag with most of our leftover bread and cheese. She tried to give him water, but he insisted he had a supply.

"You know how to get out?" he asked, hanging the bag on his handlebars.

I shook my head. "Not really."

"Go back to the grotto and take the door on the far wall. Follow it until you see a plaque marking the tomb of Henri Tallandier. Behind the tomb you'll find a ladder."

"Thank you."

He smiled and winked at Rebekah. With that he was gone, pedaling merrily down the tunnel, the sound of his bell and whistling brakes growing quieter and quieter until it was gone completely and we were left alone again.

I changed the batteries in my flashlight while Rebekah retied her shoes. We didn't say anything, both apprehensive to discuss what happened from here. Australia was my vote. Rebekah probably had other ideas.

We walked back toward the grotto, following our map and wondering what other mysteries were hidden behind the stacks of bones—and what else the Catacyclist knew. It wasn't as creepy as it had been only an hour before. After climbing over the bones, just seeing them neatly stacked wasn't much of a shock.

When we reached the grotto, Rebekah paused in the doorway, shining her light on the Black Sun. It was bold and oppressive, almost more frightening than the bones we'd passed. It was the symbol of everything that was wrong with our lives. It was the reason we were deep underground, filthy and tired, instead of home.

Rebekah muttered quietly to herself. I couldn't hear what she said.

"Isabella was right." I wanted to say more. I wanted to say that Isabella must have been right about other things too, but I held back.

Rebekah nodded and then headed across the room toward the door.

The second tunnel was narrow, small enough that we couldn't walk side by side. Rebekah took the lead, taking her time around the twisting corners and checking every plaque. This passage was carved straight from the rock, and the walls had been left raw and chiseled. The floor was uneven and strewn with debris. Occasionally the tunnel would widen and we'd find a large stone box and a sign indicating whose remains were left there.

It felt like the burrow of a giant insect, and I wanted to get out of there.

The farther we traveled, the damper the ground became, until we were walking through a few inches of watery mud. Finally, at a tomb flanked with twin statues—chipped and tarnished cherubim—Rebekah translated, "The final resting place of Henri Tallandier, industrialist and philanthropist, 1870." As the Catacyclist had promised, in the shadows of a niche, behind the tomb, was a ladder. I shined my flashlight up.

"Rebekah?" I asked. "You don't mind heights, do you?"

She sighed. "You mean really tall ladders?"

"I mean climbing *really* tall ladders, while water is dripping on you." A drop hit me in the eye.

"I love 'em."

The ladder was made from iron, and it was old. It was bolted into the side of the narrow shaft, but years of erosion—probably from all the dripping water—had loosened its hold. And from my view at the bottom, it looked seventy feet high.

"You want to go first or second?" she asked, eyeing the rickety ladder with a kind of desperate capitulation.

"Whatever you don't want."

"If I go first, you can catch me." She forced a laugh, tightened the straps of the backpack, and began climbing. The flashlight was turned on and peeking out of the pack—we'd be doing this climb with only reflected light.

I opened the gym bag and took out what remained of the bottled water. It probably wouldn't make a big weight difference, but it gave me some peace of mind. Finally, I slung the bag over my neck and shoulder and began climbing.

The rungs were wet.

Rebekah climbed slowly, taking ten or twelve steps and then pausing, either to catch her breath or to shake off her nervousness. Her hand was still bandaged and burned—I knew it must hurt like crazy. The third time she stopped, I dared to look back down—I couldn't see anything, just a deep, black pit. Above me, all I could see was Rebekah and the glow from her backpack.

She waited for a minute and began climbing again.

"Rebekah?"

"Yeah?"

"Do you remember our first date?"

"Does something about dangling precariously remind you of it?"

"No," I laughed. "I just was thinking about it."

"Which one are you considering the first?"

"You know, the first."

"You were my stats tutor," she said. Even in the darkness, I could tell by her voice that she was smiling. "I don't think that counts as a date."

"It totally counts. We went to a football game. I bought a new shirt for it."

"I know you did."

"What do you mean?"

She paused to rest and tried to stifle a laugh. "You left the tag on."

"Thanks for not mentioning it."

"So why did you bring it up?"

"Because that entire thing—the football game, the tutoring, everything—it was a dare."

"Huh?"

"I don't know if I ever would have asked you out. I was terrified. But I talked about you all the time. Finally my roommate told me that I could have the tickets if, and only if, I got you to go with me."

Rebekah laughed and began climbing again. "Really?"

"Yes."

"So, you were too scared to ask me out when the prize was just me, but when the prize was me *and* a football game, then you found your courage? I'm flattered."

My face turned red, and I was glad it was dark. "That's not exactly what I meant."

She giggled. "But it's true."

"Does it matter? The point is that I asked you out."

"Is that all you were going to tell me? That our first date was a dare?"

"Pretty much."

"Then, why right now? Strange timing."

"Because I've been afraid to tell you, and I figured that right now you could easily put it in perspective. You won't get mad, because asking you out on a dare isn't nearly as bad as spending two days in the catacombs."

"Makes sense, I guess."

"Do you have any confessions?"

"Me? I don't know. How about . . . my father is a member of the Illuminati."

"I already knew that."

"That's about it," she laughed, then paused to catch her breath. "I don't do embarrassing things."

"Of course not."

She paused. "Actually, I do have one, but you have to promise not to get mad." Her voice sounded serious.

"Go for it."

"It's kind of a touchy subject."

"Sure."

She didn't get a chance—I heard her shriek, and a split second later I knew why. Somewhere above, something had broken loose, sending gallons of watery mud showering down on top of us. I wrapped my right arm around the ladder and wiped my eyes frantically to get the dirt out.

"Eric?"

"I'm here. You okay?"

"Yeah. Eric, I hate this."

"Me too."

From that point the climb got worse. Whatever had come loose above us was still leaking, sending a constant stream of mud splattering down the shaft. The ladder was more slippery, and we had to climb with our eyes nearly closed to avoid the spray—not that it mattered. The initial downpour had smothered Rebekah's pack, dimming the flashlight and obscuring our way.

We climbed the rest of the way in silence, since every time we opened our mouths, mud and filth ricocheted inside. Rebekah stopped more and more often, and the top was still nowhere in sight. I tried to remember which bag held the portable—and heavy— oxygen, but couldn't. The gym bag felt terribly heavy, but I didn't know if that was because it held the tank, or if it was just because I was tired.

After what seemed like hours, enough time to completely cake us in mud, Rebekah's light disappeared.

"Eric," she called out. "We're here!"

I hurried up the last few rungs, finding renewed strength in her words. The ladder ended, and Rebekah sat at the top in a tiny, cramped passage. She was wiping off the flashlight lens with her sleeve, and I saw that she looked horrible—her face and hair were smeared with dark gray mud.

"You look awful," she said, grimacing as I reached the top.

"You're stunning," I countered, smiling. "We made it."

A warm grin broke across her face, and she pointed behind her. At the far end of the tunnel was a crack of light.

We crawled on our hands and knees, through the stream of running water that had been spilling over the edge from about forty feet ahead. Rebekah was breathing poorly again, but she didn't say a word.

At the end was a square stone slab, to the right of which showed a quarter inch of light. Water was running into the tunnel from underneath the slab.

We pushed with all our might—with the strength of people who have been living in desperation for days. The stone quivered and shifted outward, pouring light and water in on us.

"Rain," Rebekah gasped, elation spreading across her muddy face.

We shoved the stone the rest of the way out and crawled out of the hole, exhausted. Lying on the ground, we basked in the warm Paris rain.

CHAPTER 27

WE WERE IN the Cimetière du Montparnasse, one of the cemeteries built after the heyday of the catacombs. We'd come up through
a slab in the walkway, directly in front of an enormous bronze angel.
Its wings spread toward heaven as it looked down on us.

Rebekah lay on the stones for several minutes, letting the rainwater wash away the mud and memories. It was a downpour. Huge
drops exploded on the walk, splashing us as it fell down and as it
bounced back up.

When she finally stood, her wool sweater sagged on her shoulders,
soaked and heavy. She looked at me and laughed.

I took her hand and we walked happily through the drenching
storm, passing gravestones and monuments, happy to be on this side
of them. As a kid, cemeteries had always scared me, but after the catacombs, these stone tombs looked no more threatening than the apartments and cafés that lined the street.

We ducked under the cover of a small shade tree, and Rebekah
hugged me. I held onto her tightly, never wanting to let go. We had
gone into the belly of the beast and survived. Certainly, we weren't
safe yet, but it felt as though we'd won a major victory just by staying
alive as long as we had.

The rain began to subside, and we could see blue sky in the
distance. Rebekah kissed my cheek, and we sat down on a bench
beside the tree.

"What do we do now?"

She wiped a few strands of wet hair from her forehead, her eyes
watching the street. "I don't know about you, but I need a shower."

"And a dry set of clothes."

She nodded. "Which means that we probably need a hotel."

I opened the backpack and dug to the bottom to find the guide-book. It was only slightly damp. "Any idea where we are?"

"Montparnasse," she said.

I flipped vainly through the pages and then turned to the index. The Cimetière du Montparnasse had a two-page spread.

"Did you know that statue was the *Angel of Eternal Sleep?*" I said, looking at the pictures.

Rebekah laughed. "Sleep doesn't sound too bad right now either."

"But not eternal sleep."

"No."

I read through the hotel section and their listings of amenities that all sounded wonderful. "We have a couple of problems, though. How did Felix find us last time, and also, can we check into a hotel without getting caught?"

Rebekah stretched out the sleeves of her sweater and wrung water from them. "Do you think that all the hotels are linked to some database?"

"I don't know," I said honestly. "But at the Hôtel des Deux Iles, they put our names into the computer, and then the girl showed up. Our IDs are the same ones we got on the island. If he tracked us down there, he could track us down here."

Rebekah looked discouraged. "So what do we do? I really need a bed."

I looked down at the book. I knew that she was right—she was probably feeling much worse than she was letting on.

"Can we sign in with a fake name?" she asked.

I shook my head. "Hotels require ID."

"Maybe cheap ones don't."

"Where are we going to find a cheap hotel in the middle of Paris?"

"Try a hostel."

"Would you be able to rest in a hostel? There'll be a lot of people there—probably noisy."

She grinned. "At this point, if there was a bed in the metro station, I'm sure I could sleep there and never hear a thing."

The guidebook didn't have much to say about hostels, other than to give a couple phone numbers. So Rebekah entered what looked like the most tourist-friendly shop and asked about them. The sales-clerk was more than a little annoyed with our appearance, and our asking for directions to a cheap hostel didn't help. Certain that we were too poor to buy anything from him, he gave us some vague directions and waved us on our way. We tried again at the next shop and got a similar response. Finally, at the third—a small bakery—a woman suggested something called a *café-couette,* a bed-and-breakfast. Rebekah wrote down the directions and thanked the woman by buying one of everything.

We walked another few blocks down the Avenue du Maine before our directions sent us west. The sky was clearing rapidly, and the evening sun was warm and welcome. It was just after five o'clock, Sunday evening.

The café-couette looked just about like every other building on the street—narrow and five stories tall. On the ground floor was an art gallery, and Rebekah and I made our way up two flights of stairs to our destination. There was no front desk, or anything that seemed like a hotel—merely a sitting room. There were already half a dozen visitors, milling around a coffee pot and talking in what sounded like German. They glanced at us when we entered, curious at our appearance, but didn't seem annoyed.

An older woman approached us.

"Avez-vous une reservation?"

Rebekah thought for a moment, translating in her head. "Non. Nous avons besoin de deux chambers, s'il vous plaît."

They conversed back and forth for a few minutes before the woman nodded and smiled, then scurried out of the room.

"All their private rooms are booked tonight," Rebekah told me as we waited. "She's going to put us in a public one—she said there are six beds."

"That okay with you?"

"Of course."

In a few minutes, the woman returned and led us down a narrow hall to our room. It was large and clean, with high ceilings and a row of windows that faced the street. There was a small balcony, and the window was open, carrying in the sweet, post-rainstorm air. I could tell that two of the beds—small, low-to-the-ground mattresses—were already claimed; the blankets were rumpled. A young woman sat in the corner, reading.

The hostess handed a key to Rebekah.

"Oui, où est-ce que nous pouvons acheter les vêtements?" Rebekah asked.

Our hostess walked to the window and pointed to a building across the street. "The Tulip."

Rebekah smiled. "Merci."

"Bon séjour." The woman smiled again and hurried from the room.

"What was that? The Tulip?" I asked.

"We need dry clothes, right?" Rebekah said, grinning from ear to ear. "I'm going shopping."

I took as long a shower as I could and wished that the water heater had been a little bigger. The heat felt terrific, temporarily soothing the aches in my neck and back.

Rebekah had taken some money with her, and I'd brought the rest in the bathroom with me. It was all damp, but I figured everyone would still accept it just fine. My clothes were damp too, however, and I wasn't looking forward to putting them back on. I had no idea how long Rebekah would be gone.

It scared me, to be perfectly honest. A lot of things scared me now. Not only was I scared that she'd run into Felix in the short trip between here and there, but I was even worried that she'd simply have trouble making it back up the stairs. She'd somehow been granted superhuman strength up to this point, and I wondered how long her luck would last. She was sicker than she acted, I knew that.

We needed to get out of Paris.

I got out of the shower and put my clothes back on. Despite the rain, they still smelled dirty. I hoped that Rebekah would return soon.

When I got back to the room, the previously rumpled beds were filled with sleeping Germans. The young woman who had been reading had now moved out to the balcony. I puttered around the room for a few minutes but had nothing to do, so I went outside and sat down.

The young woman looked up from her book. "Bonjour."

Rebekah had taught me a few phrases, but I was too tired to think of them. "I'm sorry. I don't speak French."

"Neither do I," she answered in a purely American accent.

"Where are you from?"

"Corpus Christi," she answered, and then looked out at the Paris skyline. "It's a little different from this."

"I would imagine."

"Where are you from?"

Where am *I from? I have no idea.* I decided to use my old San Juan Island cover story. "Montana. Butte."

"How big is that?" she asked absently.

I had no idea how big Butte was—I'd never been there. But then, if she was asking, she'd never been there either. "About 150,000 people."

"Pretty?"

"Sure."

She turned back to her book and read a few pages. I looked down to the street below, watching the shop windows of The Tulip for any sign of Rebekah.

"Vacation?" the woman asked without looking up.

"Not really. Business."

"What kind of business makes you stay here?"

"I'm a doctor," I replied, as if that explained everything.

"Really?" She looked doubtful.

"Yep."

"You're too young to be a doctor."

"I get that a lot."

Rebekah emerged from the store, but not to leave—she was looking at something on a table in front of the shop. She glanced up at me and waved. I waved back.

"Who's that?"

"Excuse me?"

The young woman pointed to Rebekah and repeated the question. "Who's that?"

"That's . . . she's my . . . Her name is Rebekah—er, I mean, Jennifer."

"You don't know her name? Or you don't want to tell me?"

"No, neither," I said, trying to sound as calm and confident as possible. "Her name is Jennifer. I sometimes call her Rebekah, but that's not her name."

"Makes sense," she said dryly. "And you two are . . . what?"

"Oh, she's my, uh, girlfriend."

"You don't sound so sure."

Rebekah disappeared back into the store, carrying something with her. I hoped she'd come rescue me soon.

"I'm sure," I said, watching the storefront. "It's just that . . ." I don't know what happened. I was talking to a nosy tourist, who I didn't know from Adam, and everything just started to gush. She'd learn better than to make casual conversation with me. "It's just that I proposed to her a while ago, and she kind of turned me down. Not really, like, she didn't say no, but she said that she didn't want to think about it right now. That sounds kind of like no, doesn't it? And then she's never mentioned it since, like it's just something that shouldn't be talked about. I mean, it's not like she said no and walked away—she's still with me, but I don't know what she's thinking. I have no idea."

She stared at me for a few seconds. "Well, good luck with that."

"Thanks."

It took Rebekah another twenty minutes before she emerged from the store, heavily laden with bags. I left the balcony and hurried down the stairs to help her. She enthusiastically told me about all the things she'd bought, and the salesman's reaction to her bedraggled appearance. I listened contentedly, happy that she was happy. Back at our room she sorted through her purchases, handing me the clothes she'd found for me, and then took her bag to the shower.

I changed. She'd bought me a pair of silk pajamas, which she explained were the only pajamas sold in that store. I don't think I'd ever owned anything silk before, with the exception of a few ties, so the pajamas were an entirely new experience. It felt like wearing Teflon.

I sat on my bed. The mattress was a little lumpy, but I knew I'd fall asleep the instant I lay down—consequently I stayed up, waiting for Rebekah.

With two sleeping Germans in the room and a Texan on the balcony, I tried to be discreet as I checked our possessions. The gym bag had gotten wet and a lot of the money was soaked. If we'd had a private room I could have laid it out to dry, but there was no chance of that here. Instead, I moved the soggiest bills to another pocket of the bag. I pulled out what remained of the food. It wasn't much, but it would give Rebekah and me a little something to eat before bed. The Camembert had been in the bag for two days—unrefrigerated. Back in the United States, that would be considered disgusting, but here it seemed par for the course. In France, moldy cheese was considered a return on your investment.

At the bottom of the bag, under the money and bread and old cheese, was the gun. I sat on the edge of the bed, the bag between my feet, staring down at it. Just seeing it seemed to throw all the weight of the catacombs back on my shoulders. It was Isabella's gun—the gun she'd taken from the black-haired girl. And then Isabella had died.

I didn't want to get rid of it. It was the only thing standing between me and Felix, assuming we ever met up again. And if we ever did meet up again, I wouldn't hesitate to use it. Felix would shoot me in the back if he could. More importantly, he'd shoot Rebekah in the back and celebrate afterward. I wasn't going to let that happen.

Below the gun, in the corner of the bag, was the spark plug. I picked it up, turning it over in my palm. It was so small.

"Hey."

Rebekah was almost beside me before I noticed she'd entered the room. I quickly dropped the spark plug in the bag and set a stack of folded clothes on top of it.

She sat down on the edge of the bed. Her pajamas looked almost identical to mine, though I'm sure that she looked better in hers than I did in mine. She was smiling. Tired, certainly, but her hair was combed and straight and she looked almost healthy.

"How are you?" I asked. "You look good."

She laughed quietly, her eyes wide and happy. "I look awful. I'm feeling a little better, though. Better all the time."

"How's your hand?" I asked.

Her smile faded, and she held out her left wrist to show me. "It hurts. This bandage got soaked and dirty—it can't be sanitary anymore. We're going to need to find a doctor."

"We will," I assured her, having no idea how we'd do it. Seeing a doctor meant filling out forms, and filling out forms meant creating a trail Felix could follow.

Rebekah flexed her hand and winced. The bandage was stained black and brown from the rusty rungs of the ladder. She spoke softly, her voice almost void of emotion. "Eric, I don't know if I'll be able to play the violin again."

"You will," I said, doubting my own words. "I've never known anyone who works as hard as you. You can do it."

"Thanks."

I turned and watched the Germans. Both were still sleeping, but I lowered my voice to just above a whisper. "So what's the plan?"

She shrugged listlessly. "We don't have a choice, I guess. We can go to the police, but if the FBI couldn't help us, I doubt the French police can."

"Where should we go? I'm thinking we need to head south, maybe buy a car so we won't have to take the trains. But where from there?"

"I don't know," she said, turning and lying down. "Somewhere that speaks English."

"Australia?"

"I don't know."

I zipped up the gym bag and pushed it under the bed.

"This is it," Rebekah whispered. "This is everything."

"I don't know what else to do."

"Neither do I."

Lying on my bed was the most comfortable thing I'd done in a long time, and my body pleaded for sleep. I rolled over and looked at Rebekah. She lay on her back, staring up at the ceiling.

We remained in silence for several minutes. For the thousandth time, I tried to think of an amazingly clever plan whereby she and I could escape from her father, escape from the N.O.S., and go back to our normal lives. We'd get married—she'd teach violin lessons to the local kids, I'd write the Great American Novel, and we'd live out our lives in peaceful, blissful anonymity.

Rebekah rolled over to face me. "I want to show you something."

She grabbed the backpack and pulled it toward her. Unzipping a side pocket, she pulled out a small, almost triangular piece of metal. It looked more than a little like an undersized tortilla chip, made from jagged steel.

She handed it over to me. "Look at this."

I turned it over in my hands. From end to end it couldn't have been more than two inches long. I couldn't tell what it had come from, or why she would be interested in it.

"Most people collect stamps," I joked, "but this is nice."

She grinned and took it back from me. "It's part of your moped," she said, her fingers running across its scratched surface. "The surgeon removed it from my thigh. She said it was four millimeters from puncturing the femoral artery."

I opened my mouth to say something, but the words stuck in my throat.

"I would have bled to death in less than a minute," Rebekah continued, her voice warm but serious.

I glanced at the gym bag, where I'd dropped the spark plug. Every time I touched it, it was a reminder of what Felix had done—how close Rebekah had come to dying, and how much I hated him for it.

I handed it back. "Why do you keep it?"

"So that I won't forget."

"Won't forget what?"

"It's a miracle," she answered. "I should have died, but I didn't."

CHAPTER 28

DESPITE GOING TO bed early in the evening, Rebekah and I slept late. By the time I awoke, everyone in our room was gone, and the room was filled with sunlight. I rubbed my eyes and checked my watch. It was almost ten o'clock, Monday. According to Isabella, whatever Edward was doing, he was doing it tomorrow night. But I didn't care—we were leaving.

My head hurt a little, and I didn't really want to get out of bed. Instead, I just lay there, watching Rebekah sleep. Her breathing was still a little wheezy, but it was the best it had been in days. She moved slightly, causing a few thin strands of hair to fall across her face. Her nose twitched at the irritation for a few moments, and then she unconsciously brushed the hair away. I thought it was the most adorable thing I'd ever seen. But I'm biased.

She woke twenty minutes later, sitting up and stretching her neck.

"Good morning."

She yawned. "Hi."

"You're cute when you sleep."

Rebekah rolled her eyes and laughed. "Yeah, right. Was I drooling?"

"No, I mean it."

She rubbed her face and stood. "I need to use the restroom."

Rebekah headed off to one bathroom, and I went to another. I was dressed in five minutes; Rebekah took thirty. However, when she reemerged, she looked radiant. She'd pulled her short, dark hair into two stubby pigtails, which made her look even younger than she was, but also seemed to match her newfound exuberance. She wore a casual dress, black with small cream dots. The hem fell right at the knees, showing her slender legs.

On her feet were leather sandals—I worried for a moment that they'd be bad if we had to run again, and then I shook the thought from my head. It wouldn't happen again—I wouldn't let it.

We were too late for the bed-and-breakfast's breakfast, so I took some of the money and headed out in search of food. Just down the street I found a small café and ordered several varieties of breakfast crepes. They smelled better than any crepes I'd had in America.

Rebekah and I dined on the balcony, looking out on the bustling shops below us. Rebekah ate ravenously, finishing everything I brought her, which was twice as much as I expected her to eat.

"You look like you're feeling better," I said, folding my napkin and setting it on the table.

She smiled, embarrassed. "I feel like I haven't eaten in days."

"I can get more if you want it."

"No," she said, her face red. "I'm done."

"Don't feel bad," I insisted. "You're sick."

"I'm really okay."

I looked down to the street. The road was packed with slow-moving cars, and the sidewalks were overrun with tourists.

"You know," Rebekah said as though she read my thoughts, "it seems like a dream."

"What?"

"Everything underground. Just look out there—everything seems so normal. It was like another world, one that no one ever sees."

I nodded. "It doesn't seem real."

"Yeah. We were there just yesterday, and it already feels a million miles away."

"I hope this all ends like that." I laughed to myself and set my napkin on the table. "You know, I'm glad no one was in the cemetery when we popped up yesterday—we probably looked like zombies, crawling out of the ground, covered in mud."

Rebekah nodded absently, watching the city. Suddenly, she leaned down and grabbed a stack of papers from her pack. "Take a look at this stuff. I asked the woman here for some travel information."

I flipped through the papers. Most of them were pamphlets for tourist sites—the Eiffel Tower, the Arc de Triomphe, the Louvre. There was also a metro schedule, and a train schedule for routes to northern Europe.

"I don't know about buying a car," Rebekah continued. "I was thinking about it. We'd have to find a used one that someone is willing to sell. Back in the U.S. there's a ton of paperwork, plus they won't let you drive it off the lot unless you have proof of insurance. That would all be more risky than taking the train."

"I hadn't thought of that," I said, reading a brochure. "What about the bus? Do they have a bus station here?"

"I've seen buses around."

"Listen to this," I said, reading from the pamphlet. "In 1912, a tailor attempted to fly from the top of the Eiffel Tower using a modified cape as wings. He fell to his death."

She grimaced. "That's horrible."

"It says that according to the autopsy he died from a heart attack before he hit the ground."

"I don't know which is worse."

"I'd take the heart attack."

"I'd take the elevator."

I turned the page. "Sixty tons of paint are used on the tower every seven years."

"Maybe Felix is gone," Rebekah said. "It's been two days. Maybe he thinks that we're long gone, and he's headed back to the U.S."

"Maybe. Still, I'd be more comfortable watching our backs."

"Yeah."

I set down the pamphlet and picked up another. "We could take a taxi out of town—take it as far as it would go. From there, we could get a train to wherever we want to go."

"We need to figure *that* out," Rebekah said. "No matter what we do, we'll end up showing our ID to someone—and we'll need a plane eventually."

There were heavy implications with this conversation. We were leaving, and we were starting a new life. We. Us. She and I, together. I needed to ask her. I needed to find out what she had planned. Instead, I read her more trivia.

"The Arc de Triomphe took thirty years to build," I read. "It was started in 1806. When did the French Revolution end?"

Rebekah stared at me quizzically, the question shaking her from her thoughts—probably the same thoughts that I was avoiding. "Huh? Oh. It ended pretty quickly, I think. Just a couple of years later."

"What was in 1805?"

She shook her head. "I don't know. Napoleon?"

"Was he a Revolutionary? I mean, maybe he was associated with the Illuminati that started the whole thing."

"I don't know. The French Revolution didn't go as smoothly as the American. After they overthrew the king, they had a bunch of problems. There was Robespierre in there somewhere, and Napoleon took power sometime after that."

I read through the pamphlet a little more, but it didn't explain it. "So were they better off?"

"What do you mean?"

I put the pamphlet on the table. "I mean, after the Revolution, were the people better off?"

"I think so, but it took a long time to get a stable government. Napoleon was only around for a little while, and then got exiled, and then came back. There were more revolutions later, too."

"So it didn't really work."

"No, I think it helped. The people were rebelling because living conditions were so bad, and they got cleaned up. Paris grew like crazy. Getting the king out of the economy was probably one of the best things that could have happened."

I picked up another pamphlet and began reading. We were post-poning things we had to do, and things we needed to discuss, but it was nice just sitting there, talking. This is what we'd do every day, I hoped, when we ended up on our kangaroo ranch. Summer evenings on the porch, for the rest of our lives.

"Eric." Rebekah's voice was quiet but forceful.

I looked up. She was staring at a pamphlet.

"What?"

Quickly, she pushed the rest of the papers to the side and laid the brochure down. Grabbing a pen, she drew a circle. "Look."

I leaned in closer, but all I saw was an aerial photo of the Arc de Triomphe, and Rebekah's scribbling. "What?"

"The Arc de Triomphe. It's a dot, in the center of a circle."

I looked at what she was tracing. The Arc stood on a round circle of pavement in the center of a massive roundabout. It was a dot in the center of a circle.

"And look," she whispered, drawing more. "A twelve-pointed star."

There was no doubt about it. Twelve roads, all radiating from the arc. They were the cause of the chaotic roundabout—the convergence of twelve thoroughfares, all focused on one point. It was as plain as day. The Arc and the roundabout were the Black Sun, and the roads the twelve-pointed star.

"The heart," I said.

"The heart."

"It was built as a tribute to the revolutionary battles," I said, skimming again through the text. "Commissioned by Napoleon."

Rebekah flipped the pamphlet over, searching for more pictures. "This thing is covered in Revolution artwork."

I sat back in my chair and thought. It was the right time period. It was so . . . huge.

"I want to go," Rebekah said.

I'd been worried she'd say something like that. "Why?"

She scooped the pamphlets and papers into a neat pile, and then looked up at me. "What do you mean *why?*"

"I mean, we already know that the Illuminati is real. We know that your father had an artifact in his house that ties him to them. What more do you expect to find out? The heart will be old and dead, just like the room we saw."

"Eric . . ." She didn't finish her sentence, but stood up and left the balcony. I followed her and watched as she stuffed the pamphlets into the backpack.

"What?"

Her voice was quiet. "I just want . . . I don't know."

I put my hand on her arm, and she turned around to face me.

"I just want to check," she said. "We're giving up so much."

Her eyes were red but devoid of tears. I don't think she was honestly expecting to find anything more definitive than what we'd already seen, but neither of us were about to run without checking. If we left now, it would be forever.

I did my best to offer a hopeful smile. "Maybe we could stop by your dad's house and say good-bye on our way out of town?"

She smiled and looked at her feet. "Let me change my shoes."

We'd packed up, left the café-couette in ten minutes, and had hailed a cab in twelve. It was lunchtime, and traffic was snarled, but we were on our way.

We didn't know what to expect. Could the Arc be the heart? Or was it again underground? I didn't look forward to that prospect, and I hoped I could talk Rebekah out of any crazy ideas.

"So does this mean that Napoleon was an Illuminati?" I asked quietly so the driver wouldn't overhear. He was talking on a cell phone, though, so I doubted he was listening.

Rebekah shrugged. "I don't know. Maybe the designer was."

I held her hand as we drove—her skin was cold, but she squeezed back tightly. Montparnasse was on the wrong side of the river, and the streets were crowded. The cab wasn't moving very fast.

"Have you ever been to Australia?" I asked as we were stopped at an intersection. The Eiffel Tower loomed to the west.

She shook her head. "No."

"One of my friends went on his mission there. He said it was neat."

Rebekah nodded. She wasn't paying attention to my subtle hints.

"Hot sometimes, but neat. Nice beaches."

"Yeah." I don't think she was paying any attention at all.

The taxi took a narrow bridge over the Seine, and we caught our first glimpse of the Arc. It was still a mile off, but unmistakable. Considering the distance, the thing must have been huge.

"What is that?" I asked Rebekah, pointing to an enormous building on the right. It was surrounded by trees and had a rounded glass roof.

She ducked to see out my window. "The Grand Palais," she said. "When I came here before, my father took me to lunch over there." Her eyes lingered on the building until we turned the corner and onto the Champs-Elysées.

And there was the arc. Our driver sped down the avenue, pulling over before reaching the roundabout.

"Il y a un tunnel sous la rue," he said, turning to speak to Rebekah.

"Un tunnel?" She looked stunned.

"Oui. Vous allez sous la rue pour obtenir l'Arc. C'est plus certain."

I climbed out of the car, carrying both the backpack and the gym bag. Rebekah paid the driver and he pulled away, jockeying for position with the other drivers before entering the madness of the circle. I'd planned to ask him to stay—I hoped that this stop wouldn't take long—but he disappeared into traffic almost instantly.

"What did he say?" I asked Rebekah. She was looking all around.

"There's a tunnel."

"Really?"

"I guess it's modern. So people don't get run over."

"Even so."

"Yeah."

We hurried to the tunnel, which looked very similar to a metro station—a long flight of stairs leading deep into the earth. But there was nothing mysterious, just a long, straight cement structure with no noticeable exits. Litter was strewn in the corners, and the place was in dire need of someone to sweep up.

It was all I could do to keep Rebekah from running the entire way.

At the end, we climbed the steps again and were there—standing beneath the towering arch. It was even bigger than I expected, over 150 feet tall. Every surface was decorated. Sculptures and reliefs were displayed on the front and sides, while the interiors were carved with the names of battles and army officers.

A man in an official-looking uniform was standing near the stairs, and Rebekah hurried over to him.

"Do you speak English?" she asked.

"Yes." He was an older Frenchman with a heavy accent—possibly a volunteer.

"Can you answer some questions for us?"

"Certainly." He smiled warmly and waited.

"Is there anything below the Arc?" Rebekah asked. I hadn't expected her to be so forthright about it—I'd planned on a little more snooping.

"Below?" he repeated.

"Yes," she insisted. "Tunnels?"

"There is the pedestrian tunnel, through which you entered."

"But no others? Are you sure?"

"It is a strange question, but you are correct. There were other tunnels below the Arc." The old man waved to another volunteer—a man who looked even more elderly. He nodded to our guide and walked over.

"These people are interested in the tunnels beneath the Arc."

"The tunnels?" the second man replied. "They are not there anymore."

Rebekah took a step forward. "What do you mean?"

He gestured apologetically. "I'm sorry. Several years ago the tunnels were considered a threat to the structure. The Inspecteur Général des Carrières deemed them a danger due to the weight of the Arc, and they were filled."

Rebekah looked heartbroken. She didn't say anything, so I jumped in.

"What do you mean 'filled'?"

"Filled with cement," he explained. "You see, the Arc is very, very heavy, and over the centuries the soil settles and shifts. There was some discussion about those tunnels giving way."

I nodded. "But what *were* the tunnels?"

"Oh, Paris has a great many tunnels beneath its streets. There is a tour offered of the catacombs. I can get you a pamphlet, if you are interested."

"We've been," Rebekah said, clearly shaken up. "But you don't know what the tunnels here were used for?"

Both guides shook their heads, and the second spoke. "This was several years ago. All that I have heard was that the caverns were extensive—including large rooms, not just tunnels. That was the cause for alarm. But they have all been filled, and L'Arc de Triomphe de L'Etoile is more solid now than ever before. Is it not extraordinary?"

Rebekah didn't respond but turned and looked at the chaos and honking horns of the roundabout. The men, confused, addressed me. "Is everything all right?"

I nodded.

"May we answer any further questions? A tour will be starting in just a few minutes."

I looked at Rebekah. She was holding back tears. The Heart had existed—it was real—and it was buried in cement. I reached out and took her hand, and then turned to the volunteers. "Thank you, we'll come."

Rebekah and I walked slowly across the paving stones to where a small group of tourists had congregated. She still hadn't said a word.

"Rebekah," I began, not knowing what to say.

She shook her head. She didn't want to talk.

The tour guide called for the attention of the people. "Mesdames and Messieurs. The Arc de Triomphe de L'Etoile was first commissioned in 1805 by Napoleon Bonaparte, who told his troops, 'You shall go home beneath triumphal arches.' Unfortunately, Napoleon's political demise caused trouble for the project, and it was many years before its completion."

Rebekah pulled me toward her and whispered, "There's nothing. It was here. All of it, and they filled it in."

"I know."

"Eric, this could have been it. We could have found—I don't know—something."

"I'm sorry."

Her tears were flowing freely, and I wrapped my arm around her shoulders, pulling her against me.

"This frieze," the guide droned, "is titled *The Departure of the Volunteers in 1792* . . ."

"Where are we going, Eric?" she asked softly.

"Wherever you want."

"Australia?"

"Australia."

This was it. It was over. The bad guys had won, and we were running.

We followed the tour group. To not follow them would be to take the first steps toward Australia, and we were both afraid.

The guide continued. ". . . which is when Rouget de Lisle first penned 'La Marseillaise,' which is now the national anthem of France. If I may be permitted, this is a rough translation:

Arise children of our fatherland,
For the day of glory has arrived!
Against us, tyranny
Has raised its bloody flag,
Do you hear in the fields
The howling of these fearsome soldiers?
They are coming into your midst
To slit the throats of your sons and consorts!
To arms, citizens!
Form your battalions!
We march, we march!
Let the impure blood of our enemies
Soak the furrows of our fields."

I forced a laugh, hoping to cheer Rebekah. "A little grim."

She nodded but didn't smile.

I looked up again at the frieze on the Arc. The citizens of France were marching to war, led by a winged angel. I thought of the owl in the mural, leading the fight at the Bastille.

Wait a minute. Edward has nuclear weapons. . . . He's part of the Illuminati . . .

"Rebekah?"

"Yes."

"Why?"

She looked at me, and I stared back into her eyes. I led her away from the tour group to a quiet spot inside the Arc.

Rebekah looked hopeful. I didn't think she'd be happy when I was done. "What is it?"

"We know that the Illuminati caused the French Revolution, right?"

She nodded, wiping her eyes.

"But why did they do it? They must have had a good reason."

"I don't know."

"What did Isabella say? Those people Edward met with aren't ideological. They're not trying for a new world order or to save humanity. They're trying to make a buck."

"But what does that have to do with this?"

"Think about it—you said it yourself. The country was far better off without a king, and the people had more money."

She had stopped listening and grabbed my arm. The look on her face was sheer terror. I wondered if she'd figured it out, but then I saw she was watching over my shoulder. I turned.

"First of all," I heard a familiar voice say. "Don't try to run. You're cornered."

Felix.

CHAPTER 29

HE WAS STROLLING up behind me as casually as ever, with no sign of a weapon. I glanced back the other way. The black-haired girl stood twenty feet away, a jacket hanging over her hands. She looked every bit as terrified as the last time I'd seen her, but I knew there was no way around her. She had a gun under that jacket.

My mouth was dry, and I had to force the words.

"Hi, Felix."

"Eric Hopkins and Rebekah Hughes," Felix laughed. "My two best friends. How's Paris?"

"Uh . . . good."

Rebekah's breathing had quickened. I wondered if we'd live long enough for it to pose a problem.

"You guys are getting better at hiding," he said. "Nicole here was actually thinking that you'd left the country."

I looked back to the black-haired girl. Nicole. Her cheeks were flushed.

I turned back to Felix. "How did you find us?" I didn't really care, but maybe if I kept him talking I could think of some way out of this.

"Simple. I don't have unlimited manpower, so I just sent out bulletins. I told the taxi company that you were missing persons, and to please contact me if you turned up. Your driver reported you while you were in the car with him." Felix looked so darn pleased with himself that I wanted to punch him in the eye.

I had the gun in the gym bag, but it was at the bottom, and everything was zipped up tight.

"We can give you money," I said. "Anything you want."

Felix laughed and shook his head. "You forget—I make money. I mean literally, with a press. It's what I do."

"You can't kill us right here," Rebekah said. "There are a hundred witnesses."

"Becky," he said as condescendingly as possible, "do you think that I have traveled all the way from the United States to take a bribe or to be talked out of this?"

"You're an idiot," I said. "You'll risk it all just to kill us?"

"First, I don't think anybody is going to catch me. I'm good at what I do. But second, yes, I'm going to kill you. Of course, I'd prefer it if we went somewhere nice and quiet, but I'm quite content to take care of things right here if need be."

Rebekah's grip was about to break my arm. "Then why—"

I cut her off. "Felix, what if I were to tell you that your entire plan is about to fail."

Rebekah turned and looked at me, confused.

Felix smiled and cocked his head. "And you're going to stop it? How?"

"I'm not going to," I said. "But it's going to be stopped—brought to a screeching halt. How long have you been working on this? Twenty-five years?"

"You're stalling."

"I wish I were." I gave Rebekah a look that indicated that, yes, I knew what I was doing. She didn't seem to believe me.

Felix groaned and leaned against the heavy stone of the arc. "Fine. Tell me how my plan is going to fail. Then I'll shoot you."

"I just realized this myself, which is why we haven't called the police."

"Convenient."

"Are you aware that Edward is a member of the Illuminati?"

A smile broke across his face. "Eric, I was expecting something better."

"No, really. It's true. If you hadn't killed Isabella, she could have told you herself. Why do you think that we're running around here instead of calling Rebekah's dad?"

"I thought you'd had a burst of good taste."

"Well, it's because he's a member of a secret organization, whose goal is to get as much money as possible."

Felix sighed and looked at his watch. "That sounds like him."

"But if you're a member of a secret organization whose goal it is to get rich, and someone is bankrupting the best economy in the world, then that would get your attention."

"So Edward is going to stop me? With what?"

"Are you aware of his business?"

"You mean selling nukes? Yeah."

"And you know the structure of his company?"

"You know, kid, you sound like Edward with all this Socratic-method garbage. If you have a point, just spit it out."

I looked at Rebekah. From the mortified expression on her face, she'd connected the dots.

"Felix," I said, hoping to get it all out in one breath. "The Illuminati has done this before. They started the French Revolution just so that it would save the French economy—turned it over from the king to the free market. Well, Edward is going to do the same thing. He's going to start a war in the United States. He's going to make it look like some other country did it, but he's going to kill a lot of people. And then, just as World War II saved the country from the Great Depression, the U.S. will go to war and the economy will thrive. There will be jobs and industrialization and military service, and Edward will reap the benefits. Felix, Edward's going to set off a nuke."

Felix stared at me for a while, weighing my words and thinking. I expected him to shoot me—*I* wouldn't have believed a story like that.

He folded his arms and frowned.

"So," he said, "Edward wants to get rich. But, if I succeed and bankrupt America, then he won't get rich."

I nodded. "Right."

"So he's got a nuclear weapon somewhere in North America, is going to set it off, make it look like Osama bin Laden did it, and get us into another war."

"Right," I said again. "But he wouldn't blame it on bin Laden. He'd blame it on a specific country—someone we could invade, like North Korea or Iran. And then the American people would get to work building planes and bombs, and everyone would have jobs working overtime, and the economy would boom."

Felix shook his head. "I hate to remind you, but we're already in a war. Remember Iraq?"

"Yeah, but I'm talking about something bigger—a war that mobilizes the whole country. A war that requires us to convert some of our car factories to tank factories. Probably a draft, too."

"And he'd get rich?"

Rebekah spoke up, her voice quiet and pained. This was her father we were talking about—and the potential murder of hundreds of thousands of people. "Maybe he's not doing it so he'd get rich. Maybe it's so that the people he works for would get rich. He's not a very high-ranking member, I don't think."

"And more than just the boost in the economy," I added. "Maybe the Illuminati has invested in defense contractors, companies that make airplanes and submarines and Korean-to-English dictionaries. They're going to do this to get rich. They did it in France two hundred years ago, and they're doing it now."

Felix chuckled. "And you have proof?"

I pointed to the gymbag. "We have proof that he met with five members of the Illuminati three nights ago. And we know that whatever he's planning with them is supposed to take place tomorrow night."

"And why are you telling me this?"

"Because we have a common interest now. We don't want that nuke to go off, and you don't want that nuke to go off."

"But I'm going to shoot you." He almost looked confused, but he maintained his calm.

"You can't." It was Rebekah stepping forward this time. There was fire in her eyes.

He smiled. "No, I really think I can."

"You can't, because if you kill us, your plan will fail. But if you let us live, I'll tell you where the bomb is."

What?

I looked over at her, confused. I was just trying to buy time—she was actually trying to save the world.

"You know where it is?" Felix said. He appeared to be on the verge of impressed.

"Yes." She said it with enough certainty that I almost believed it myself.

"Where?"

"If I tell you, then you'll shoot us."

He stretched his neck, frustrated. "You know, I don't like either of you. I mean, at all. I don't like either of you in the least. Because of you two, some of my best people died. You both pepper-sprayed me—both of you. It doesn't feel good to get pepper-sprayed. And now you want me to believe you that, one, Edward is a member of the Illuminati; two, that he's going to nuke America; and three, that you morons can stop him."

Rebekah waited patiently for him to finish and then replied with a simple, "Yes."

"I wish I'd killed you two days ago."

I smiled. Rebekah squeezed my hand.

Felix had a car waiting, driven—I assumed—by the mysterious third N.O.S. member that the black-haired Nicole had mentioned. He was short and unkempt, with greasy hair and a dirty shirt, and he looked like he'd spent most of his adult life digging through garbage cans.

I sat in the back, with Felix on my right and Nicole on my left. Both of them had guns in their hands. Rebekah was in the front. She had the backpack on her lap, and I had the gym bag between my feet—the revolver was still in there.

Felix ordered the homeless chauffeur to take us to Charles de Gaulle International Airport.

"We have a problem," Rebekah said without turning back to look at Felix.

"I have two big problems," he replied. "But what's yours?"

"We don't have passports. They were left at the hotel."

"Don't worry. Nicole retrieved them."

I looked over at her, but she kept looking straight ahead.

"So, Nicole," I said, "what's it like working for Felix? I imagine the pay isn't very good—he is a communist, after all."

She didn't say anything. Felix smiled.

"Well, for the benefit of anyone who wants to know it—and I'm speaking particularly to Nicole and the hobo driving—Rebekah and I are one hundred percent innocent of everything your boss accuses us of."

Felix laughed. "Great sentence structure, Eric. Kudos."

"We were minding our own business, normal people, and Felix swoops in with his murdering and torture and explosions, and now look where we're at."

Felix patted my knee condescendingly. "Two for two, Eric, ending a sentence with a preposition."

I turned to Nicole. "I can see why you chose terrorism. It's evil, *and* it values good grammar. I had a freshman English teacher you'd like."

"Let me explain something, Eric," Felix said calmly. "I'm not evil. Think about this: if you put one hundred communists in a room with one hundred capitalists, which group do you suppose, statistically speaking, would be nicer?"

"Are you one of the hundred?"

"The communists, hands down. Why?"

Rebekah glanced back, smiling, but I knew she wasn't happy.

I glanced over at Felix. "Pray tell."

"People become capitalists because, well, usually people become capitalists because they're born capitalists, and they think that it's great. They watch James Bond movies and think that they have a pretty good handle on what communism is, and they know that they don't want any part of it. But then they grow up, and they get a job, and they love capitalism, because it means they get a big house with a home theater system and an SUV in the garage.

"But," he continued, "communists are communists solely because they think that the world could be a better place. They see suffering and they want to do something about it. They don't want people living on the streets, or working three jobs, or dying because they can't afford medicine."

I shook my head. "Maybe they become communists because they don't have a big house, and they're jealous."

"Oh, my goodness gracious," Felix said with mock horror. "People wanting a good place to live! Heaven help us!"

Rebekah interrupted. "But anyone can get a house like that if they work for it."

"The old Equality of Opportunity argument," Felix laughed. "I love it. Let's say that you're a poor kid who was born in the ghetto—

Rebekah, I know you can't relate, but maybe you've seen a movie or something. So, you're born in the slums. Your mom is single, and she works two jobs—menial jobs, maybe minimum wage—just to keep you in an apartment and diapers. You grow up, and you go to school—and at school you're more concerned about staying out of the way of gangs than paying attention to your work. Half the kids in your class never show up, and the ones that come disrupt the teacher the whole time. You don't have anyone at home who can help you with your homework because your mom works nights. And you're telling me that kid has a chance? The same chance that a rich kid, in a good school, with a stay-at-home mom or nanny has?"

Rebekah frowned and faced the front. "There are programs. There's a lot of money and assistance available. Anyone can get through school."

"But only if they *want* to get through it. Becky, your reality is different from the reality of poverty. School is great, if you can do it, but some of those kids are working by the time they're eight, just to help with the rent. They turn to crime, not because they're evil, but because they're hungry. And you rich people sit in your nice homes, watching satellite TV on your plasma screens and think, 'The poor are fine—they have programs and assistance.'"

Rebekah didn't answer. I knew there was no winning an argument with someone who had so wholly given his life to an ideology like this, but I tried anyway.

"So communism is the answer? Bread lines and dictatorship?"

"Well, obviously Soviet communism isn't the answer. That didn't work."

"And your way will?"

"It's a step in the right direction. Every time there's a depression we see a resurgence of energy from the lower class. Unions are formed. New labor laws are passed."

"Maybe new laws could be passed without ruining everyone's lives."

"Here's a quote. I'll give a counterfeit dollar to the first one who can tell me who said it—"

"Isn't that somehow against your philosophy?"

"'In the East, a new star is risen! With pain and anguish the old order has given birth to the new, and behold in the East a man-child is born! Onward, comrades, all together! Onward to the campfires of Russia! Onward to the coming dawn!'"

I didn't answer. I had no idea. Rebekah thought for a minute and finally shook her head.

"Nicole? Joe?" The driver shrugged.

Nicole spoke. "Helen Keller."

"No, it couldn't be!" Felix said mockingly. "Helen Keller? Helen Keller the humanitarian? Helen Keller the inspirational writer? Helen Keller, the woman we all read about in junior high and yet know absolutely nothing about?"

I looked back and forth between Nicole and Felix. "Really?"

Felix nodded. "Red as the spot on Gorbachev's head."

"That doesn't prove anything."

Felix ignored me. "Do you know why she was a communist? It was because she discovered that there are more deaf and blind people in the lower classes than in the upper classes. The working class is more likely to have industrial accidents. They eat unhealthy food. They don't have access to medical care. If you're born poor, odds are you'll stay poor."

I couldn't think of what to say. His arguments made a strange sort of sense, but I knew he was wrong—I just wasn't good at explaining why. Felix'd had twenty-five years to develop his philosophy. I hadn't even been alive that long.

I decided to try Edward's argument. "What about greed?"

"What about it?"

"Do you really think that if you bankrupt America, and we're all equal, then everyone will want to be equal?"

"If I thought that, then I would have never tried this. If I thought that people could be persuaded by a lot of political rhetoric, then I would have tried that. What I am doing is forcing them to live equally—they will make it work because they must."

"That's awfully idealistic."

"Is it? What's more idealistic is your girlfriend here thinking that government programs are the answer. As long as the rich can sit back in their leather armchairs, letting the government and charities tackle the poverty problem, America will never solve anything."

Rebekah spoke, her voice almost a whisper. "But it's not right."

"What's not right? Helping the poor? Feeding hungry kids?"

"People are going to die, Felix," she said. She was still looking straight ahead. "How many more kids are you going to starve because their parents have no jobs and the charities have no more money? Bankrupting the country is going to kill people, not save them."

"Oh, Becky." He laughed. "The wealthy Rebekah Hughes suddenly cares about the poor. I'm touched. The thing is, nothing is ever easy. Humanitarianism isn't about protecting every single person in the world—it's about helping the majority of them. Look at the United States dropping the bomb on Hiroshima—they were killing innocent civilians. But they did it to stop the war, and it worked. Yes, people will suffer because of the Novus Ordo Seclorum, but far more people will benefit. It's the greater good that we should be concerned with."

Rebekah didn't flinch. She kept her eyes on the road ahead, her answer simple and quiet. "You can't *force* people to be good. You can only help them *want* to be good."

Felix ignored her words but continued talking all the way to the airport. I made a comment here and there, but Rebekah fell silent. She was right. I knew it and she knew it, and we both knew that Felix would never believe it.

We pulled into Charles de Gaulle International Airport, but instead of turning toward the terminals, Hobo Joe took an access road toward a distant cluster of buildings.

"A private jet?" I asked as we neared the hangar. "That's awfully fat-cat capitalist of you."

He shrugged. "I am Public Enemy Number One in America. That can make it hard for me to get through Customs."

"I thought you just paid people to look the other way."

"I do, but it's hard in the middle of a crowded airport."

The plane waiting for us was smaller and older than Edward's private jet. There was no butler waiting inside to take our coats or help us up the stairs. Instead, there was a pair of nervous French officials, looking very unhappy.

Hobo Joe and Nicole directed Rebekah and me into the plane. I thought about trying to overpower Nicole and run, but Hobo Joe looked a lot meaner and stronger than I felt. He also had Rebekah by the arm.

I did have the gym bag, though, and no one had examined it yet.

The interior of the jet was plain—it looked like it had been a commercial passenger plane until recently, and it still had rows and rows of cramped seats. Rebekah and I were directed to the back and then separated. She sat by the window on the right, and I sat by the window on the left. There were two seats and an aisle between us. She looked at me and smiled. We were still alive.

I mouthed the words, "You okay?" and she replied with an uncertain shake of her hand.

Hobo Joe sat down next to Rebekah. She didn't look pleased—it was going to be a long flight, and he probably didn't smell very good. Instead of sitting next to me, Nicole stood in the aisle behind us, waiting for directions from Felix.

The gym bag was on the floor, tucked under the seat in front of me.

Finally, after squaring things with the men outside, Felix entered and walked toward us. The small flight crew closed the door and began preparations to fly.

Felix leaned on the seat in front of Rebekah. "So, Becky, where to?"

"It's too far to get there in one flight," she said, with more confidence than I expected from her. "Fly, stop in New York, and then I'll tell you where from there."

He smiled. "Becky, for a minute, let's assume that I'm not an idiot."

She smiled back. "Okay."

"You've only spent much time in two places that your old man owns—your house in Utah and his house on San Juan Island, right?"

"And his house in England."

"Well, since you're telling me to fly to America, I'll assume it's not the one in England. So, which is it, Washington or Utah?"

Rebekah glanced over at me, and then back at Felix. "Washington."

"Honestly, you people," he muttered. "Quit playing Super Spies." He left us and walked back up to the cockpit. He was gone for only a few minutes before he returned.

"Nicole," he said, sitting next to me, "get me something to drink."

She nodded silently and headed toward the front of the plane.

"What time is all this stuff supposed to go down?" he asked me, adjusting the chair and leaning back.

"Tomorrow night."

"And why am I not killing you two right now, since I know where the bomb is?"

Rebekah leaned forward to look past Hobo Joe. "Because it's locked, and Eric knows the code."

He looked at me. I nodded that yes, indeed, I knew the code. With every fiber of my being, that code was something I knew.

I had no idea what she was talking about.

"So, Eric knows the code—why shouldn't I just kill you?"

"Because," I said, panicked. "I won't tell you the code if you kill her."

"You wouldn't save all those poor, innocent people from a nuclear weapon, just because I kill your girlfriend? I'm appalled, Eric."

"What if something goes wrong," Rebekah said, trying to remain calm. "My father will be there—you can use me as leverage."

She was volunteering to have a gun to her head. Better than having a bullet *in* her head, I supposed.

He chuckled. "Well, you've just thought of everything, but I still think you're not telling the whole story. Why does Eric know the code, and not you?"

She shrugged and put on her best ditzy expression. "I'm just not good with numbers."

"Felix," I said, trying to reason with him man-to-man. "We're trying to help you here. Couldn't you just forego the killing altogether? You'll get your way, and your plan will be saved. That ought to be worth something."

"We'll see," he replied. "Remember though—I don't like you."

CHAPTER 30

Hours later Felix looked at his watch. "It's going to happen tomorrow night—do you mean Paris time or Washington time?"

"I don't know."

"And you probably don't know what the target is. How do you know the bomb is still there?"

"It's our best chance."

"Then I guess we'd better hurry."

The flight was long. We got off the ground shortly after three in the afternoon, and we were chasing the sun the entire time, which made the flight seem even longer—the sun simply wouldn't set. Two hours into the trip, Rebekah asked if she could use her oxygen mask while she slept. Hobo Joe emptied her backpack, inspecting all the medicine, flashlights, and food. Satisfied that it was all fairly innocuous, he let her put on the mask.

I wished I could talk to her. In a few minutes, she was asleep.

"She needs a doctor," I told Felix.

"So do a lot of people."

"For being a communist, you're not very nice."

Felix laughed. "You know, this plan of Edward's isn't half bad. He could make a lot of money."

"Don't tell me you're thinking of joining him."

"Of course not. But it could have really worked. Do you have any knowledge of economics?"

"Not much."

"That's because you're stupid. I'd almost forgotten. Well, economists track something called transfer payments—basically, how much money the U.S. government gives other countries, and how much they give us. I'm sure you can guess who does more of the giving."

"The U.S."

"Right. They love to throw their weight around and earn brownie points with the world. Anyway, this number is always huge in the negative—the U.S. gives out tens of billions of dollars more than it takes in. Except for one recent year: 1991. Any guesses why?"

"I don't know. The Gulf War?"

"The Gulf War. The U.S. went to war in Iraq, and in the same year netted somewhere around twenty-six billion dollars."

"Why?"

"Because war is good money. Edward's onto something."

Four hours after leaving Paris, Nicole brought us something to eat—not much, just sandwiches in plastic wrap, but I was starving. After she'd passed them out and gotten Felix a refill on his drink, she headed back up to the front of the plane.

"She's your personal stewardess?" I asked Felix, my mouth still full.

"Just contributing to the overall objectives of Novus Ordo Seclorum," he said, grinning.

"She doesn't look like a communist."

"Not ugly enough?" he said with a laugh. "Not fat and wearing a babushka?"

"Something like that."

"You have to realize that some people just think I'm right. Normal people."

"She thinks you're right?"

Felix smiled. "She will. Right now she just thinks that she doesn't have much of a choice."

"Huh?"

"No, she's not here against her will. She just got in a little over her head and is sorting things out." He seemed awfully amused with himself.

"What do you mean?"

"She worked for one of my counterfeiting operations. She had no idea what it was all about—didn't know what the N.O.S. was. She was just trying to get through college and wanted a little extra money on the side. She got hooked up with one of my people in Philadelphia and helped us to fabricate the money. In December, when you and Becky screwed everything up, Nicole's office got investigated by the police."

"And she came to you for help?"

He laughed. "Better than that—Nicole assaulted a police officer with a deadly weapon. She shot a cop."

I looked back down the aisle to where she sat, quietly eating her sandwich.

"After that, she was in, whether she wanted to be or not. Even so, she's a quick learner and she follows directions. She believes it now, for the most part."

"And you had her following me?"

"That was your fault, actually. I'd set her up with something nice and easy. She couldn't stay in Philadelphia, not after the police were chasing her. I set her up in Friday Harbor with a nice money-laundering gig. I never planned to use her, but you made it so easy."

"Money laundering? She worked in an antiques shop."

"A lot of my people run this kind of shop. It's perfect. Almost all buying and selling of antiques is done with cash—large amounts, too. I had someone deliver the counterfeits to her, and it was simply her job to spread them around. She'd go to estate sales or auctions and buy armoires and paintings and whatever else, and pay with cash—counterfeit cash. She got to live the dream—shop all day. It wasn't a bad life."

"And then we showed up on the island."

"Something I never expected. Once you walked into her shop—thank you, by the way—she called me, and I had her follow you."

"So, she planted the bomb."

Felix stared at me for several seconds before bursting into laughter. "No, Eric. Nicole didn't plant the bomb."

* * *

It was around nine hours before we landed. I'm not sure what city it was—everything was dark. We'd been flying over land for too long for it to be New York. We were on the ground for a little more than forty-five minutes and then up in the air again.

I slept a little bit on the second leg of the flight. I don't think Felix ever did, and I never saw Hobo Joe bat an eye. Nicole came back a few more times, mostly whenever Felix needed something.

I was sore and I was tired, and I was sitting next to a terrorist who wanted to kill me. As a rule, I don't like flying. The bouncing doesn't bother me, nor does the takeoff, but in the sixth grade we learned about airfoils and lift and drag and thrust, and I just have a hard time believing that something as heavy as a jet can be held in the air simply by differential air pressure. I have no faith in the concept.

No faith. It was becoming a regular thing for me.

I had a pistol in the bag—the Great Equalizer. It was the one thing that gave me even a little confidence about facing down Felix. And it terrified me. Rebekah said that it wasn't right—that you couldn't fight fire with fire. Using a gun would make me no better than those I was trying to stop.

I didn't believe it. If the moment presented itself, I'd shoot Felix in the back the first chance I got.

They all claimed to be in the right. Felix was bankrupting the economy so that the country would improve—better care of the poor, less suffering. Edward was selling nukes to prevent war. And he was nuking the United States to save the economy.

Rebekah just wanted it all to stop. So did I. But what was right? Was there something inherently wrong about using the gun? I'd be stopping Felix. I'd use it to stop Edward if I could. Granted, you're not supposed to shoot people, but isn't it justified if you're saving someone else? Isn't that self-defense?

The scriptures say you can fight to defend your family. Police officers fight to protect others.

But on the other hand, when the oxen carrying the ark of the covenant stumbled, and Uzzah put forth his hand to steady it, he was killed on the spot. He was doing the "right" thing—the ark was slipping, and he was trying to save it. But the Lord had commanded them to never touch the ark. This example contradicted my previous ones, leaving me all the more confused.

But I still wondered: did the end sometimes justify the means?

* * *

It was still dark when we arrived in Seattle. I felt terrible.

Once again, the plane landed on a runway off by itself in a far section of the airport. We were led to another car—a newer-model sedan—and once again Rebekah and I were kept separate. Nicole drove, since she was more familiar with the area than Felix or Hobo Joe.

One of our captors put the gym bag in the trunk.

Just north of Seattle, Felix ordered Nicole to pull over at a rest stop.

"Eric," he said, turning to me. "Get out."

"Why?"

"Because I'm going to shoot you."

Rebekah screamed. "What? He's the only one who knows the code!"

Felix laughed. "Just kidding. My fellow pinkos and I have things to discuss, and you two have a tendency to listen in and meddle." He pointed out the front window to a picnic table. "You two just go sit over there and wait. Of course, if you try anything stupid, I *will* shoot you."

Hobo Joe opened the door and let me out. I met Rebekah in front of the car and, taking her hand, walked to the table. The car doors were shut, leaving us in silence and blinded by their headlights.

"Hi," I said, sitting down.

She sat next to me, and I put my arm around her waist. "Hi."

It was chilly. I hadn't noticed it until we got out of the car, but there was a very light, misty rain. Rebekah was still wearing the new black dress she'd bought, and goose bumps appeared on her knees and calves.

I pointed. "Maybe you ought to start wearing warmer clothes all the time. You know, just in case."

She smiled. "I like being optimistic."

"How are you feeling?"

"Other than cold?"

"Yeah."

"Tired, mostly."

"You're a liar."

She laughed softly, and the little dimple appeared in her cheek. "My hand is burning. I think it's really getting infected."

"And your breathing?"

"Same. I'll be okay."

"So," I said, keeping my voice down in case they opened a window. "You know where the bomb is?"

"I hope so. That house was huge."

"You think it's in the house?"

She shrugged. "I actually do. I know it's a long shot, but that house was something more than just a house. Did you see the power lines that went into it? And all the monitors everywhere?"

"I don't know the code."

Rebekah grimaced and laughed. "I know—I made that part up. Maybe we can fool Felix into thinking I meant the security code."

I shook my head. "No—there is a place for a code. In the basement, there's a vault door. It's hidden in a closet."

"Really?"

"Yeah. The way you were talking, I thought you knew."

Rebekah laughed. "I was totally making it all up."

"So you didn't have a plan?"

"No, but I do now. I think we have two possibilities. Either we get away from these guys and go to the police, or we get to the house and get the attention of one of my father's people."

"Get their attention? And then what?"

"My father doesn't know that we know what he's up to. All we have to tell him is that we went to Paris—a romantic getaway or something—and that Felix found us."

"I took you to Paris on a romantic getaway and got you mixed up with Felix? He'll have my head."

Rebekah laughed grimly. "It's better than us getting to that vault door and you not knowing the code, and Felix killing us both."

"True. But if we have your dad's people help us, you know what that means."

She nodded. "Yeah. We'd end up with him again—never going back to real life."

"Right."

"Let's try to get to the police."

"I agree. Any plans?"

"No. They've been watching us like hawks."

"We're going to be getting on the ferry. Maybe we can contact the ferry's onboard security—it'll be a public place, so Felix can't have his guns out."

"Sounds good."

The car door opened and I heard Felix's voice.

"All right you lovebirds, back inside."

Rebekah and I stood, but before I could take a step, she put her arms around me. We hugged tightly for a few seconds. Felix yelled something, but I didn't care.

Rebekah let go and then kissed me. It was far too short.

"Just in case," she whispered. She was trembling.

In an hour and a half, we were back in Anacortes, the small town north of Seattle, where we could catch the ferry to the San Juan Islands. The sun was coming up, but the sky was still overcast and gray.

The ferry yard was basically an enormous parking lot. Lines of white paint marked lanes for taking vehicles onto the large boat, and Joe followed the directions of the attendants as they guided him to the right place.

"Well," Felix said, yawning. "This is where Joe will be leaving us. He has a great many things to do today, and we should all wish him well."

No one did.

"But before he goes, Nicole, head into the shop up there and see if you can find me something to eat. And coffee. I'm falling asleep."

She nodded and left. Hobo Joe got out of the car and opened the trunk to get his things. I felt like looking back to make sure he wasn't looking in the gym bag, but I didn't want to give anything away.

I heard him rummaging around.

It was just me and Rebekah in the car with Felix. This might be the best chance we got. Unfortunately, before I could think of anything, Joe opened the door.

"Hey," he said simply. He was holding my bag.

Felix reached over and took it. The top was unzipped and the money was exposed.

"Whoa," Felix laughed, opening it all the way. "Where in the world did this come from?"

I didn't know what to say, and Rebekah was quiet. Felix looked at us, expecting an answer.

"I've been saving for a while," I said.

He pulled out some of the American money and held it up to the light. "This is the real deal. Is this Daddy's money?"

Rebekah didn't answer.

Felix dug down in the bag, counting the stacks. "There's a lot here. You guys decide to cut and run?"

"It's Isabella's," I finally said. "It *was* Isabella's, before you shot her."

"This hers too?" He found the gun.

He pulled it from the bag and checked to see if it was loaded.

"This isn't her gun," Felix laughed. "This was Nicole's. She'll be so happy to get it back. So tell me, Eric—were you going to try to use it? Wait till I wasn't looking and shoot me?"

I did my best to play it cool. It was hard, since every muscle in my body was tense. "I was going to take you to the nuke, and then you were going to see that I wasn't such a bad guy after all and decide to let me go."

"Which is why you tried to hide that it was in there, right?" He reached past me and handed the weapon to Hobo Joe. "Do me a favor, kids. I know what I'm doing here, and you don't. Don't try anything stupid."

Nicole returned ten minutes later carrying a small paper sack filled with donuts and four cups of coffee. Rebekah and I took the former and declined the latter, and Felix made several comments about our religion.

We boarded the ferry, slowly, in a long line of cars. There were two levels of parking, and we were directed up a curved ramp to the right. The upper level was two lanes wide and extended the length of the boat. There were large openings in the steel hull, and we could see the cold, blue water of Puget Sound.

We waited ten more minutes before the ferry started to move.

"Are we going to get out?" I asked, hoping he'd let us go up to the passenger cabin.

"Nope," he answered.

"I've been sitting for an awfully long time—the plane, then the ride up here. I need to stretch my legs."

"I've been sitting just as long as you have, and I think I'll be okay."

The ferry churned on. It was gray and dismal outside, threatening rain. The ferry made a stop, but it wasn't our island.

"I need to go to the bathroom," I told Felix. I really did.

"You went on the plane."

"I need to go again."

"Do you always sound like you're six years old?"

"I really have to go."

"Eric, you make me tired."

"Felix, you make me need to use the bathroom."

"Fine. Nicole will go with you. Nicole, check the bathroom to make sure no one else is in there. If he tries to talk to anybody, shoot him." He reached into his pants pocket and pulled out a collapsible knife. "But, Eric—check your watch. If you're not back in this seat in four minutes, Becky's going to have an unfortunate accident."

I looked at Rebekah as I got out of the car. She gave me an encouraging smile.

I didn't have a plan. Actually, I had expected Felix to come with me—then I might have been able to do something.

Nicole walked behind me, up the long flight of steel steps.

"We're innocent, you know," I said, keeping an eye on my watch.

She didn't reply.

"Rebekah is really sick—she needs a doctor."

Still no answer.

We reached the top of the stairs and entered the passenger cabin. There were rows and rows of booths and benches, filled with travelers. Outside on the deck were dozens more, watching the water for whales and otters.

Nicole hesitated at the bathroom door.

"You'll pull a gun on a helpless invalid, but you won't go in a men's restroom?"

She frowned and directed me to push the door open. I did so, and she followed. No one else was there.

"I'll wait outside."

I could jump her, I thought, take her gun, and then go back down to the car. She wasn't strong—I knew that much from the last time we'd fought. I could easily overpower her.

When I reemerged from the bathroom, she was standing ten feet away from me. I took a step toward her, and she took a step back. I should have tried it before.

"Don't," she said quietly, jerking her hand a little bit inside her jacket pocket.

Gun. I nodded and turned back toward the stairs.

"You don't have to do this," I said, listening to the metallic sound her hard-soled shoes made on the steps. "Felix explained what happened—you don't have to work for him."

No answer.

"Think of it—you turn him in, and the FBI would be falling over themselves to make a plea deal with you. You might not even serve time."

Nothing.

Just before I opened the heavy door to the parking area, she spoke.

"Unless I talk, and he gets away. Then they'd make an example out of me, like they did with Paul Arbogast."

I turned to look at her. Her face was emotionless, and her lips were frozen in a thin line.

"I'm sure that you have information on someone else, some bigger fish. How about Joe? Or whoever delivered counterfeit money to you? At the very least, you could expose the breach of security at the airport."

She looked at her watch. "We need to get back."

Rebekah was fine. Felix looked amused, as always, and checked the time. "Thirty seconds to go. Eric, you're fast."

"I try."

CHAPTER 31

THE FERRY DOCKED at Friday Harbor, and a wave of emotion washed over me. This was the place where I'd proposed to Rebekah. It was also the place that she'd almost died. The last time she was on the island, we'd been surrounded by acrid smoke and the twisted metal of my moped. And now I was about to drive back to the scene of the crime—sitting next to the man who'd planted the bomb.

I wondered again, as I had many times, what had happened to the ring.

Nicole drove the car a few blocks into town and parked in front of a hardware store.

"This is where she gets out," Felix announced. "Nicole is going to take care of a few things for me here—make sure that we can still get out of here if push comes to shove, which it might."

I half expected her to look my direction as she stepped out of the car, but she didn't. She just left, taking her bag and walking away.

"Becky, you're going to drive now. And Eric, you get up there with her. That way I can shoot either of you, if necessary."

I opened my door and looked at him. "Felix, you have such a way with words."

"Well," he replied, "I am a very smart man. Now, Rebekah, you switch seats first, and when you're all buckled in, Eric can switch. I don't want you both out of the car at the same time."

Rebekah switched, as directed, and then I moved to the passenger seat. She reached over and took my hand. It was her right hand—bandaged and infected—and I could tell it hurt her. I rubbed the back of her hand above the bandage with my thumb and let go. She smiled.

"Aw, that's sweet. Having you two so enamored with each other makes my job that much easier—either one of you could have run and let the other die," Felix said. "Let's get going."

Rebekah turned north and began heading out of town. It'd been a while, but she still remembered the way. Rain had begun to fall, making the island look even greener and more beautiful than it already was.

"So," Felix said, "is your daddy's house here as big as his house back in Utah?"

Rebekah didn't answer.

"One swimming pool or two?"

She glanced over at me, confused.

Felix didn't know what the house looked like.

"You've never been there?" I asked.

"I know it's a big tourist site, but I don't get around much."

"You'll like it."

I faced forward, watching the trees buzz past as we neared the house. Felix didn't know where the house was and he'd said Nicole hadn't placed the bomb. So . . . who had?

Rebekah pretended to check the rearview mirror and looked straight at me. It was only for a split second, but I swore she tried to mouth something.

I tried to get her to do it again, but Felix moved to the middle seat and was leaning forward.

"So," I asked him, "what's the plan when we get there?"

"I'll have to see what it looks like," he answered. "And it will depend on if anyone is home."

"And if they are?"

"Well, I didn't come all this way to leave empty-handed. Neither did you, though. You might have to ask yourself who you'd rather shoot."

"You'd give me a gun?"

"Probably not. Maybe Becky—I bet she has better aim."

"You've never seen me shoot."

"I'm sure you're a regular Annie Oakley," he said, leaning back into the seat. He yawned loudly.

Rebekah glanced over again. With her eyes, she pointed to the dashboard in front of me. I looked down, but didn't see anything—except the glove compartment. Maybe she'd seen something in there while she was in the passenger seat.

I turned back to look at Felix. He was looking awfully relaxed, leaned back in the center seat, his seat belt loose around his waist and his shirt untucked. He held the gun lazily in his hand, resting it on his knee. I wondered if he was going to fall asleep. That'd be awfully convenient.

"What's Joe doing?"

"Turn around, Eric."

I faced the front. "What's Joe doing?"

"He's going to make sure that the Coast Guard is far away from the islands."

"Really? How?"

"Create a disturbance of some kind. He may not look like much, but he's good at what he does."

The turn for Limestone Point Road was coming up, but Rebekah wasn't slowing down. I didn't know what she was doing, but Felix didn't seem to notice. She blew past the road without a second look. Felix didn't know where we were going. Neither did I, but at least Rebekah was on my team.

"How much farther is this place?" Felix asked, leaning forward, his head right between us.

"A mile," Rebekah answered. "Maybe a little more."

I wondered if I could hit him in the head and how quickly he could respond. Before I got the chance, he leaned back.

Immediately, I popped the glove box open. It was empty.

"What are you doing?" Felix snapped, the weariness gone from his voice.

"Just bored."

"Be bored later. Bored people who do stupid things get shot."

"Right."

Rebekah was driving toward Roche Harbor. The road got a little curvy, and Rebekah slowed down. She glanced over at me and mouthed something, but I only got the last word: *yourself.*

"He lives in here," Felix said, watching the cabins peeking through the trees. "Not bad, but I expected something a little more grandiose."

"I don't think you'll be disappointed," I said.

Rebekah adjusted the rearview mirror. She was looking at Felix.

She turned the car down the steep hill toward the harbor, and we could see the marina to our right. It was usually bustling with life, but was almost deserted in the rain.

"Ah," Felix said. "A place for his yacht. Convenient."

Rebekah glanced over at me again, and I understood her loud and clear. "Brace yourself."

That couldn't be good.

I checked my seat belt.

We made the final curve. There was a short straightaway, with cars parked on both sides of the street. Straight ahead of us was the Hotel de Haro.

Rebekah gunned the engine, mashing the pedal to the floor.

"Someone's following us," she shouted. "Look!"

Felix spun around in his seat. I stared straight ahead. I hoped she knew what she was doing.

The road curved just before it got to the hotel, turning to the right and up the hill. At the curve was a series of heavy stone pillars, with guardrails between them. She steered for the first one.

Felix turned back and screamed for her to stop, but it was too late.

She hadn't been looking at the glove compartment—she'd been pointing to the passenger-side air bag.

This could kill her.

We hit.

The front of the sedan crumpled around the pillar, and the air bags exploded. Everything went black for a minute, and then white.

I opened my eyes. White smoke had filled the car and was pouring out of the broken windows. The windshield was gone, and Felix was lying awkwardly between the two front seats, only his legs still tangled in the back seat belt. He was unconscious. Rebekah was hunched over, coughing violently.

I yanked off my seat belt and kicked the door open. The dashboard had been jammed into me, and something had smashed my knee and hurt like crazy. I hobbled around to the driver's side, rain splattering down around me.

I tugged on Rebekah's door for what seemed like forever. Groggy, she pushed on it from her side, but it was stuck tight. I saw Felix roll his head—he was bleeding from his nose and chin. I put my foot on the car for better leverage and yanked the door open.

Her seat belt wouldn't come off either, and I helped her awkwardly climb out of it. She was in serious pain, and every movement seemed to make it worse. I offered to pull her arm over my shoulder and help her walk, but she refused, keeping her shoulders hunched and her arms folded tightly across her chest.

"Where to?" I asked, my arm around her back as we hurried away from the scene. This was her plan, and I hoped she had an escape route.

Rebekah simply pointed to the marina. We crossed the street and were descending a set of steps and were out of sight before anyone arrived at the car to help.

"Over here," Rebekah wheezed. Even saying two words seemed to knock the wind out of her. She was still coughing, shuddering with pain.

Instead of heading toward the larger yachts and sportfishers, Rebekah led me into the small maintenance area on the left. The water around us danced with falling rain as we hurried along a short pier.

"There's one." Rebekah pointed to a small dinghy with a simple motor. It was no more than eight feet long, nothing like the other boats in the marina. A single oar rested in the bottom. She forced a smile. It was a maintenance boat with just a regular pull-cord motor—it didn't need a key.

I helped her down into the dinghy. She sat in the front, huddled over in pain. I noticed that blood was running down her leg.

I stepped down into the boat and untied the moorings.

She was getting soaked.

I pulled off the sweater that she'd bought me in Paris and wrapped it over her shoulders like a shawl. In her current condition, I didn't think she could move enough to put it on.

"Thank you," she whispered, shuddering.

"You're going to be okay."

I yanked the cord to start the motor, and it turned over on the first try—they must have been good maintenance people.

CHAPTER 32

I STEERED SLOWLY out of the Roche Harbor Marina. Looking back at the shore I could see a small group of people standing around the car. None of them were looking our direction.

The rain was coming down steadily, and there were already two inches of water in the bottom of the boat. I wasn't a big boater—I got the motorboating merit badge in Scouts, but I could only remember driving a boat for about half an hour—so I had no idea whether a little rainwater would sink us. My anxiety only increased as we left the marina and moved out into the open waters of the Sound. The sea got choppy, and our tiny dinghy was battered back and forth.

My knee throbbed, and I could already feel a swollen lump on the front of my shin—peanuts compared to Rebekah. The cut was on top of her right leg, a few inches above the knee—apparently there were more sharp things under the dashboard of the driver's side than the passenger's. I helped her tear a sleeve off the sweater, and she wrapped it around her leg, tying it in a rather horrible makeshift bandage.

But even the cut was nothing.

Forget anything you've ever seen on TV about air bags. You've watched the crash test dummies dive head first into the steering wheel, only to be protected by a plush bag of pillowy softness—wrong. The bag comes hard and fast, and it feels like you've been hit across the face with a two-by-four. In her case, the bag detonated out of the steering wheel; it was not only big enough to catch her head, but sent every bit as much chemically explosive force into her chest. If jogging or standing up too fast was enough to knock the wind out of her already-bruised lungs, blunt trauma had to be much worse.

She sat on the middle seat, huddled over, arms folded. Her eyes were squeezed shut, and every breath looked like it took Herculean effort. She was white as a ghost, and freezing cold.

"We need to find somewhere to stop," I said, watching the shore. Among the rocks there were small piers where homeowners tied up their personal boats. About a mile more and we'd be at Edward's house.

She shook her head.

"Rebekah," I said as sternly as I could manage, "we're going to stop."

"No."

"You need a doctor. And I don't mean it like I mean you need a doctor for your hand—you need a doctor or you could die."

She spoke through clenched teeth. "Eric, I knew what would happen when I did it."

"I know, and we made it—we got away from Felix."

"No—it's not about that."

I turned the boat toward shore. A wooden home with big glass windows was only a few steps up from the pier.

"Eric," she pleaded, looking up at me. "We need to stop my father. People are going to die."

"I'll drop you off and get you inside, and then I'll go. We'll call the police."

"Joe was diverting the Coast Guard, and Nicole's probably doing the same thing to the police. *We* need to stop him."

I wiped water from my face and brushed at my soaked beard. "What if the bomb isn't even there? What if they took it from the house a week ago? What if it was never here to begin with, and that's just some glorified gun safe?"

She looked me in the eyes. A bruise was forming around her nose and cheekbone. "We need to try."

I lost it. Normally, rain would have hid my tears, but not like this—it wasn't just a drop rolling down my cheek, I was sobbing.

I turned away, looking at the houses passing us by where Rebekah could go and get warm, where we could call the paramedics. We were nothing, bouncing out on the water, helpless, with only a few old boards between life and drowning. And only a few final moments between life and nuclear war.

"Rebekah, I can't lose you."

I wanted nothing more than to take her in my arms, keep her warm in the rain, and help her breathe, but I couldn't let go of the rudder.

She smiled, weeping.

"Rebekah, you're . . . you're everything. When I'm with you, you're all I think about. When I'm away, all I want to do is get back. And when I think of you . . . like this . . ."

"Eric." Her chin trembled, and she put her hand to her mouth.

I whispered. "It's not fair."

She shook her head. "No."

"I love you."

"I love you."

We didn't stop at the pier. I steered us gently back away from the rocks and toward Edward's house. Rebekah closed her eyes and breathed.

My hands were shaking, and I was glad I had the rudder to hold on to.

She then opened her red, puffy eyes. "I need to ask you something." She was trying hard to smile, but it looked difficult.

I nodded.

She didn't say anything. The winds and surf were calming, leaving us with a steady stream of heavy, perfectly vertical rain.

She smiled again—this time genuinely. "This will sound stupid." I could barely hear her.

"I'll answer it, whatever it is."

"I need . . ."

There was a row of rocks in the water, and I turned the boat to steer wide of them.

"You need what?" I asked, trying to sound positive. "A doctor? A drink? A foot massage?"

"All three," she answered, smiling but hesitant.

"Well?"

"The bomb went off," she finally said. "The doctors said I was next to the moped. The last thing I remember was sitting on the couch—I don't remember going back outside."

I'd been expecting this conversation, though that didn't mean I was prepared for it.

"You're wondering why you were next to the moped?"

She coughed, and I could almost see the pain shoot through her body. It was a few minutes before she calmed down. "I'm wondering what happened—what was said. You proposed to me."

"I did."

She paused, smiled, and then blurted out, "Did I say yes?"

I exhaled. All this time, all these weeks, she'd been wondering if she was engaged.

"You said you'd think about it."

She cringed. "I did?"

"You did. You tried to give me the ring back, and I wouldn't take it. You set it on the moped. You know the rest."

Rebekah shook her head, and tears started falling again.

I wished I could hug her. "This is what you were going to ask me on the ladder, when we were climbing out of the catacombs."

She nodded. I don't know how girls can laugh and cry at the same time, but they do and she did.

"Um . . ." I stammered. "I know this isn't a good time, but the offer still stands. I don't have the ring anymore—"

The answer was immediate. "Yes. I don't care about a ring."

Well, sometimes you just have to let go of the rudder.

* * *

I cut the motor as we approached Edward's house. Using the boat's solitary oar, I succeeded in spinning us around twice before we got headed in the right direction. Slowly and silently, we passed the rocks that formed Edward's private harbor and paddled to shore.

As bad as I'd expected Rebekah to be, she was worse on her feet than I'd imagined. She stumbled getting out of the boat, stepped into a foot of water, and nearly fell face-first. I caught her, then wrapped her in my arms and helped her toward the long stairs that led up to the deck. I helped Rebekah lie down on the first level, and then carefully and quietly limped up the stairs to the second. My knee ached.

There were lights on in the house. From the angle of the deck, and the arrangement of the thick fir trees that speckled the hill, I couldn't see much, but there was no hiding the warm glow that emanated from the living room.

I moved around the deck, trying to see inside and wondering whether anyone inside could see me. Satisfied that I was sufficiently hidden, I detached the umbrella from the table and hurried back down to Rebekah.

"Someone's there," I said, setting it up over her. I was only wearing a thin T-shirt—now sopping wet—and wished there was something else I could give her to warm her.

She took my hand and smiled. "Don't do anything stupid."

"This is already stupid."

She chuckled softly. "Be careful."

"I will."

She was my fiancée. Wow.

I kissed her and left. Instead of using the stairs, I clambered over the railing and into the thick ferns and ground cover. With each step my leg throbbed, and it felt like my knee would give out, but I kept climbing, slogging through the muddy underbrush. After a few minutes I paused, resting underneath a tree.

I could see inside. Not much, but enough to know that the lights weren't left on just to keep potential burglars away. There were people inside—two, at least. The first I recognized right away: Reuben. He was standing behind the couch, talking to someone else.

Time was a luxury I didn't have. I had no idea about the extent of Felix's injuries, but I knew that as soon as he got to the hospital he would call Nicole, and she'd be on her way here. Felix might not have known the location of the house, but one of them did—somebody had planted the bomb.

I moved to the front of the house, crouching low to stay obscured behind the plants. There were three vehicles in front—a Cadillac, Reuben's motorcycle, and Rebekah's black Honda Civic. The damage had been repaired.

And it hit me: this was where it happened—where the bomb had gone off. I stared for a few minutes, trying both to remember every little detail and to block it all out. I didn't know where to go from here—Felix was supposed to make up the plan and stop the bad guys. Well, the *other* bad guys.

Edward's house had a huge security system. There was no chance of me finding a window cracked open or a door ajar. Even if there was, there were people inside, and they carried guns. I was outside and carried nothing more than a swollen knee.

I took a deep breath, trying to inhale some courage. Rebekah needed help, but first all I had to do was thwart the Illuminati and stop a nuclear attack. Then we could go to the hospital. Easy.

Ignoring my knee, I jogged out toward the cars. Reaching the far side of the Cadillac, I crouched down behind it and I looked in the window—an old coffee cup, a newspaper, a crumpled-up paper bag, and a CD case. Apparently someone liked Led Zeppelin.

The doors were locked, so I moved to the Civic—same kind of stuff, except a little more clutter. *Nothing to see here, folks.* I hobbled back across the driveway and into the bushes.

I waited. I didn't know what else to do. I was outside and they were inside. Maybe they wanted to hold off on killing thousands of people until the rain subsided. Maybe the bomb had already left, and they were just hanging around, watching the news.

I was soaked to the bone, my hands becoming numb and useless. I was about to head back down the mountain and get Rebekah when the door opened.

I lay flat. If I could have burrowed, I would have.

McCoy appeared first, followed by Reuben, who carried what looked like a briefcase, except that it was three or four times as wide. The sides were polished metal, and the handle was sturdy and black. *The bomb.* They slogged through the rain, popped open the trunk of the Civic, and placed the case inside.

The next man out of the house was someone I'd never seen before. He was big and wide and looked like he belonged in the Mongol Horde. He waited on the porch, watching the other two and staying out of the rain. Reuben said something to McCoy, to which the latter nodded. They closed the trunk.

And then Edward appeared. I hadn't expected him at all, but as I thought about it, it made a little sense. Edward was in the Illuminati—who knew if the others were. They were all part of his nuke-selling group, and probably more interested in their own skewed version of world peace than in saving the U.S. economy via war. They wanted to prevent war, for goodness sake. Edward was going to be running this show, and the others might not know a thing about it.

Or they might. I really had no idea.

Edward shook McCoy's hand and then Reuben's. Genghis—which I'd settled on calling him—left the shelter of the porch and joined the rest in the driveway, oblivious to the weather.

It was now or never. Stop them, or the bomb goes off and everyone dies.

Or, I'd try to stop them, and they'd turn around and shoot me. There were four of them.

The door was open.

Reuben and Genghis got into the Civic. Edward and McCoy stood by the car door—one last pep talk.

I pulled myself back up to my knees, and then carefully to my feet.

My first step was bad—my knee was weak and I nearly fell—but I gathered my strength again and raced for the door. I sloshed through the mud, grateful for the sound of the pounding rain around me, and grateful that the men were in such a serious discussion. I jumped up onto the porch, my muddy feet sliding on the stone, and I was in the front door.

I dashed into the kitchen. Every light in the house was on, and from the looks of things, the men had just finished an early lunch. I reached for the phone.

I would call the police, the fire department, the Coast Guard, Marine Toxins, and every other number on the emergency-contacts list—I didn't care what Nicole and Hobo Joe were up to, someone would respond. I'd call the paramedics and tell them to bring a helicopter and the best doctors in the state—and to stop by the Mayo Clinic on the way, maybe.

I wouldn't call anyone, actually, because the phone wasn't on the wall. It was cordless, and it was gone. I searched the counters, but saw nothing. Nothing by the microwave, nothing behind the toaster. Nothing even in the fridge—I checked, because I've put the phone in the fridge before.

Peeking my head into the hall again, I couldn't see anyone coming. I ran down the stairs to the living room. No phone on the table, or by the TV, or with the motorcycle keys under the lamp. It was gone. I thought about pushing the button on the phone's base, but then it would beep and beep, and everyone would know I was there.

There was a creak and a thud. Someone had closed the door. I froze for about half a second and then darted into the basement hallway. There were footsteps upstairs—not loud and excited, but steady. Only one person, and he didn't know I was there.

I checked every room in the hallway for a phone, but there was nothing. The last door was the bedroom with the vault. Quietly, I turned the knob and entered.

The closet that had been obscuring the door was empty—all of the coats had been taken out and laid across the bed, revealing the secret door. It was closed and locked, just like the last time I'd seen it, but now it made sense. The last time I'd been here, I'd thought it was just another symbol of the eccentricities of the house, but now I saw what it was. There were carvings of birds all right—owls. Four of them, perched on the winding branches of a leafy tree. In the center—what I had thought was a perch—was an unfinished pyramid, hovering over the words *Ut Ipse Finiam.* "*In order that I might finish it personally.*"

But it was locked, and there was still no phone. And the guys with the bomb were getting away.

I peeked back out into the hall and crept to the living room. I could hear a voice from upstairs. Holding my breath, I climbed slowly and silently to the top of the stairs.

"They're gone," McCoy said into the phone.

I held my breath, staying out of sight.

"Right," he said, then waited. "Yeah, the ferry's probably a little late with the weather, but they assured me it was still running . . . Yes . . . Okay . . . I'm not sure what he has planned—it's all very hush-hush, but yes, they took it."

I didn't have to hear any more. I was down the stairs in an instant, stopping only long enough to take Reuben's motorcycle keys from the living room and two coats from the bed before sneaking out the back door.

* * *

"Hey," I said, bending down and shifting the umbrella slightly.

Rebekah looked up. Her eyes were slightly unfocused, and her skin had a distinct blue tinge.

"Here." I moved the umbrella completely and helped her up. Gently, I helped her into a heavy lambskin coat—it had to weigh half as much as she did. I'd only grabbed a thin windbreaker for myself—she needed warmth more than I did.

"What did you find?"

"They're leaving. They left. They're heading for the ferry."

She nodded.

"I tried to call the police—and the paramedics—but I couldn't get to a phone."

"It's okay. I'm feeling better."

"You are such a liar."

It took us more than ten minutes to climb up the rest of the road. Rebekah shaking with every step. The bleeding from her leg had stopped, but she looked awful.

I climbed onto the BMW motorcycle, and Rebekah very gingerly got on behind me. She wrapped her arms tightly around my waist, and I turned the key.

The winding driveway was not what the bike was made for. At the top of the hill, I pulled slowly out onto the pavement and looked both ways.

I closed the choke fully and eased on the throttle. About the time the needle was getting in the red and my blood pressure was reaching critical, I dropped the choke. Limestone Point Road transformed into an impressionist painting, and we were out of there.

CHAPTER 33

"Where are we going?" Rebekah yelled into my ear, clinging to my back as we rocketed down the road.

"I'm going to drop you off at the clinic," I said loudly with all the authority I could manage. "You need a doctor."

Rebekah didn't answer, which I took as a good sign.

"From there, do everything you can to get the police. Have them call the FBI or the Coast Guard."

"Where are you going?"

"He's getting on the ferry. I'm going with them."

"Is that safe?"

"Is anything safe?"

"Staying together would be safer."

"For who?"

She didn't answer. I was worried, though. If the ferry was intercepted and Edward cornered, he might just detonate the bomb from wherever he was—he could just as easily say that it was the North Koreans' plan that was thwarted and that the bomb was set off in the wrong place. Either way, there would be a nuclear explosion in United States territory, and people would die, and there would be a war.

I slowed for the turn onto the highway. Rebekah's grip around my waist tightened.

"Are you warm enough?"

She laughed. "I could use a pair of jeans."

"I could use a hot tub."

"That sounds nice."

"I could also use something good to eat, and a shower, and seventy-two hours of sleep."

Rebekah was quiet. Puddles of water had formed in the street, and I slowed a little to keep control of the motorcycle.

"Where do you want to go on the honeymoon?" she asked.

I paused. It was a great question—a divine question. A question I'd prayed I would one day hear. It was fitting, given our relationship, that she would ask it as she was on death's front porch, getting ready to knock on the door, and I was trying to think of the best way to stop a nuclear attack.

"I don't know," I said, laughing. "Paris."

"Ugh."

"I still haven't seen the part above ground."

"I'll buy you a picture book."

"So I guess England is out, too."

"Yeah."

"You're the world traveler. Where do you want to go?"

"Somewhere quiet. Somewhere far away."

I came up behind a brown station wagon and slowed down, looking for an opportunity to pass. It was speeding. "I'm going to ask Felix to be my best man."

"Nicole can be my maid of honor."

"I know where I can get a nice gold ring with a big ruby in it."

"I wonder what happened to my ring."

"I don't know," I said. "Probably in the forest somewhere or blown out to sea. I'll get you a new one."

With the outskirts of Friday Harbor in view, I downshifted and pulled out from behind the car to pass. It was going twenty-five miles per hour over the speed limit, but a speeding station wagon is no match for a BMW RT 1200, and I had places to be.

It happened both intensely fast and excruciatingly slow—it was only an instant, less than two seconds, but it seemed like the video camera in my brain was set on slow motion.

I checked my speed as I passed. We were doing a hair under seventy in a thirty-five-mile-per-hour zone. And there was water on the road, so it was Reckless Driving as well as Driving at an Excessive Rate of Speed. Plus, neither of us was wearing a helmet, and just half an hour before we'd fled the scene of an accident. And the motorcycle was stolen. If there'd been a cop on the road, he would have pulled us over and beat me with his billy club.

There was a puddle in front of me, and I juked around it even though it was exactly the kind of thing that I would have normally buzzed straight through. But Rebekah was sitting on the back, with bare legs and a serious case of everything, and spraying her with cold rainwater wouldn't really help.

The station wagon was going faster than I thought it was—I think it was speeding up just so I couldn't pass. Fortunately for me, the BMW motorcycle eats station wagons for breakfast. I launched forward.

And as I pulled ahead, I glanced into the window to see exactly who had foolishly thought they could outrun me and the bike.

Felix. He didn't look good. In fact, he looked horrible. From his nose down he was covered in blood, and his face was bruised. His left hand, which he was using to grip the steering wheel, was wrapped with a crude cloth bandage, not unlike the makeshift compression bandage around Rebekah's leg. His polo shirt was stained. When he realized who I was, his face contorted momentarily and I saw his teeth—he was missing two.

He swerved wildly. I dodged to the side, avoiding his bumper, and then opened the bike up.

The road came to a T, the left leading through town toward the ferry, and the right leading to I didn't know where. I slowed just enough to not die, and turned right.

"Where did he get a car?" Rebekah asked, her fingers digging into me.

"He's going to come after us," I said, my heart falling to my stomach. "He probably thinks that there is no nuke—that we made it all up to get away from him."

In my mirror I saw the station wagon skid around the corner and follow us. I took the first road I came to—a small, wooded residential street on the left. I'd hoped that Felix wouldn't be able to see where we'd gone, but the street was long and straight, sloping gently up. I revved the engine, doing at least twice Felix's speed.

I took a left on Park Street, which turned out to be just as straight and open as the last, and with fewer trees. I looked for side alleys, but everything was gravel and dirt, and I didn't want to risk riding through mud.

"Just go to the ferry," Rebekah urged. "Take me with you."

"What about the clinic?"

"If Felix misses the boat, I don't want to be here on the island with him."

We flew past the island's small high school and turned right by the post office. The marina was close. Felix was a hundred yards behind us when I turned.

We were getting closer to the center of town, and traffic was increasing. I maneuvered onto the center line and cruised past the line of cars waiting at a stop sign. They honked at me, but I didn't care. Just as I was turning I heard a whole lot more honking, accompanied this time by screeching tires—Felix wasn't waiting his turn.

It was a straight shot down to the marina, and I let the RT 1200 do its thing. Being pursued by police wasn't really a big worry. The honking behind us grew more and more distant.

One block before Front Street I pulled the motorcycle to a stop. I was illegally parked, but couldn't have cared less. I helped Rebekah down, and she took my arm as we walked quickly away. There was a narrow alley between two stores, an art gallery, and a restaurant, and we limped as best we could. If we'd had more time and my knee hadn't been inflamed, I'd have picked up Rebekah and carried her— she was in far worse shape than I and shouldn't have had to walk at all, let alone hurry through the rain.

At the end of the alley was a long flight of stairs. Rebekah took them one at a time, trying hard not to show the pain on her face as she moved her bleeding leg. Her breathing had been bad the entire time we'd been on the bike, but it was getting faster and shallower all the time.

Across from us was the ferry waiting area—more than half the cars had already loaded onto the boat, and there was no sign of Reuben, Genghis, or Edward.

We hobbled down the steep slope to the ferry dock. Foot passengers didn't have any special accommodations—we simply walked next to the cars as they drove slowly toward the boat.

I glanced at Rebekah's leg—the rain had washed away the blood, but the bulky bandage was clearly visible hanging out from her dress.

Hopefully no one would notice, and if they did they could just assume it was an odd fashion statement. Even so, we both looked horrible. Despite the lack of blood on her legs, her shins were speckled with grime from the wet roads, as were my pants—and we were both soaking wet.

We kept our faces down. It was common practice on the ferry to leave your car as soon as you were loaded, and there was a very good possibility that any of Edward's traveling companions were already up on deck.

A bell rang, but I didn't know what that meant.

We crossed the threshold of the dock and stepped onto the ferry's heavy steel deck. It was nearly full already, with only a few more cars trickling in. Rebekah and I limped along the inside wall, eyeing the densely packed lanes for either the Civic or the Cadillac. We couldn't see either, but there were still two other possible areas on board.

Another bell rang. I looked back at the dock. The last few cars were loading—and in the back was a brown station wagon.

CHAPTER 34

THE FERRY HAD been underway for twenty minutes, causing Friday Harbor to disappear into the rainy mist. I sat on the floor of the vehicle area, in between the cold steel hull of the boat and a dark green minivan, trying my best to stay out of sight. Rebekah lay next to me, her head in my lap.

The wound above her knee was oozing again, trickling diluted pink droplets down her wet leg. The pressure bandage on her hand was fraying and loose, revealing the pink, burned skin underneath. She could barely breathe.

I needed to get to security—I needed to find a policeman or get to the captain and have him radio for help. I was on a boat with one member of the Illuminati, his two bodyguards—Rueben and Genghis—and a terrorist with a score to settle. Also on the boat was a nuclear weapon. And my fiancée, who was dying.

She looked up at me. I wanted to say something, but I didn't know what. I wondered if there was a life raft nearby, and if we could just hop in and float all the way to Australia.

As gently as possible, I lifted Rebekah's head so I could move. She winced and rolled over. "Where are you going?"

"We need to stop the ferry before it gets to Anacortes."

"I'm coming with you."

"Not this time."

Standing, I scanned the area for other people, but didn't see anyone. I checked the doors of the van, but they were all locked. I moved to the next, and then the next. On the fourth—an older-model Jeep Cherokee—I found the passenger side open. I hurried back to Rebekah and picked her up.

She was light and limp—conscious but almost unresponsive. My knee nearly shattered.

I carried her to the Jeep and helped her into the backseat. She lay down, welcoming the soft seats. Digging in the back, I found an old picnic blanket and wrapped it around her.

Before I left she grabbed my hand. Her voice was raspy and cracked. "Be careful, Eric."

"I will."

"I love you."

I nodded and smiled. "Me too. I mean, I love *you* too, not me." *Way to ruin the moment.*

Rebekah smiled softly, closed her eyes, and let go of my hand.

* * *

I added one more quick prayer to the thousands of silent prayers I'd offered that day—perhaps quantity would make up for something. I wandered through the cars, trying to maintain a nonchalant, innocent appearance while crouching low to keep out of sight. I looked something like a man with severe stomach pain, who constantly checked his shoelaces, all the while admiring the view. James Bond, I wasn't.

There was a curved ramp at the end of the narrow two-lane parking area, which led to the back of the boat and the main four-lane vehicle section. The very last car was the station wagon, empty. I peered in the windows and saw a bloodstain on the seat. I'd hoped to find the gym bag there—maybe he'd brought it with him as he fled from the paramedics—but there was no sign of it. There was a woman's purse, though, most likely belonging to the real owner of the car.

I'd only walked a few dozen yards more before I came upon the Cadillac. As before, there was very little inside, and all four doors were locked. Even so, it confirmed all that I had set out to confirm—the ferry needed to be stopped.

I crept along farther. The occasional car was still occupied with reading or sleeping commuters, but the place was mostly vacant. The ferry's engines churned loudly, echoing around the large metal belly of the boat, and the floor was slick with water dripping from the cars.

I saw the Civic. It was ahead of me by about forty feet and in the far left lane. My first thought was to get to it, smash in the window, and do whatever I could to get rid of the bomb. But the car was occupied—two people, probably Genghis and Reuben—remained in the front seats, guarding the deadly device in the trunk.

There was nothing I could use as a weapon, and they were certainly armed. I remembered from my last ferry trip that there was a large ax at the top of the stairs next to the fire hose, but I was sure that if I went after them with an ax, they'd shoot me before I got within ten feet. It wasn't a very clandestine weapon.

There was nothing more to do down there—I had to go up and notify the captain or find a cop.

The stairs were behind me, and I backtracked along the wall to the heavy metal door. There was a small window of reinforced glass, and I peered inside—the stairwell was empty. I opened the door and started up.

I remember, as a kid, thinking that I'd like to be a police officer when I grew up, and I'd often pretended to be a soldier. After this past week, I'd be content with a good old nine-to-five desk job, talking on the phone and using a computer, and doing nothing more dangerous all day than risking a paper cut from my notepad. Even better—I should just work from home and never step foot outside.

The stairs were long and steep, and the walls narrow. Each footstep clunked metallically up and down the stairwell; I must have sounded like an elephant. And my knee hurt like crazy.

I reached the top and peeked through the tiny window.

I jumped back and nearly toppled down the stairs (which would have been a really stupid way to die, given the much more glamorous alternatives I was facing). Felix was right there, not ten inches from my face.

He was leaving the bathroom, his face freshly washed. His shirt was soaked, but the bloodstain was still visible. He walked slowly, grimacing with every step, and as he got farther from me I saw that he was using a cane—I had no idea where he'd come up with that. There was another unwashed stain on his right pant leg.

I was about to open the door, sneak past him, and get up to the captain, when he sat down at a booth. He was still facing away from me, but Nicole, sitting opposite him, was looking in my direction. I didn't think she'd seen me, but there was no way past her.

Great. Current tally—Illuminati: 3, Terrorists: 2, Innocent College Kids Who Just Want to Get Out of This Alive: 2.

I stood at the door for a few more minutes, wishing that Nicole would leave, but getting no indication that she would. She and Felix kept right on talking. Nicole was showing him something—images on the display of a digital camera. Both of them were visibly upset, and I couldn't say that I blamed them. Finally, Felix stood. He leaned on the table for a second, gritting his teeth before having to walk on his bad leg, and then turned toward me.

I ducked down, kicking myself for standing so close to the window. I wasn't sure if he'd seen me, but I wasn't going to risk it. I scrambled down the stairs, hopping most of the way to keep weight off my swollen knee. At the bottom, I yanked a fire extinguisher off the wall. It was heavy and awkward, but I could also use it to hit someone in the head. I would have preferred a baseball bat, but none presented itself.

Crouching down again, I made my way into the mass of cars, trying to watch both ahead of me toward the Civic, and behind me toward the stairs and Felix. There didn't seem to be movement in either direction.

And there I was again, back in the vehicle area, with no plan and nowhere to go.

There were other sets of stairs—at least four, I thought. Maybe the others would be clear.

I looked at my watch. The boat would be reaching Anacortes in twenty-five minutes. I didn't have much more time.

Reuben's motorcycle keys were still in my pocket, and I pulled them out to look at them: long and semipointy. They weren't great, but they'd have to do. Figuring that if I couldn't stop the boat, I could stop the Civic from leaving the boat, I decided to use the keys to puncture the Civic's tires. It was a long shot—I had no idea if I could ram a key through the rubber—but I didn't know what else to do.

If my knee hadn't been swollen and pulsing with pain, I would have probably crawled all the way to the Civic. Instead, I just crouched and waddled, clumsily packing the fire extinguisher along with me.

The closer I got, the more nervous I became. My palms were sweating, and my throat seemed like it was closing up. I wanted to run away and I wanted to vomit. I wanted to go hide in a corner and wait for the ferry to reach Anacortes, at which point I would run from the boat, screaming for police. Surely that would work, wouldn't it?

I was nearing the Civic. I could hear the radio—they were listening to music.

The tires looked new and not the least bit ready to pop. I stared at them for a long time—could I puncture the tires without them getting out of the car and shooting me? Should I even care? This was a nuke we were talking about—hundreds of thousands could die.

Was I ready to take one for the team?

Trembling, I moved next to the car, positioning myself at the back tire on the passenger side. I chose the best key on the ring—it was two and a half inches long, with a pointy tip and a thick plastic end. I prodded the hard rubber with it—there was a little give, but it wasn't going to be easy.

I looked at the side mirror. I couldn't see the passenger, which meant he couldn't see me.

I flexed my hands, trying to get them to stop shaking.

I pressed the key into the rubber and began to push.

The door opened.

I snatched the keys up in my hand and dropped to the floor. It was the driver's side door, and under the car I could see his feet. He wasn't going anywhere. The music was loud now—something hip-hop that I didn't recognize. Silently, I pushed the keys back into my pocket and then gripped the fire extinguisher, ready to use it as a weapon.

I never got a chance. There was a loud pop—the kind of sound that gets mistaken for a firecracker by people who have never heard a real gunshot before, but a sound that I'd heard far too many times.

My first thought was that I'd been hit—who else would have been the target?—but looking underneath the car I saw that the driver was no longer on his feet. It was Genghis, lying on the steel deck of the ferry. There was blood.

I scrambled around to the back of the car, my shoulders and head against the trunk. Another two shots were fired, and I heard the car's back window shatter. Small pebbles of safety glass showered down on me. It was a few seconds before Reuben began returning fire, but he did, and the noise was deafening.

It was a cacophony of bullets, some shattering glass, others pinging off the steel walls of the ferry's interior, ricocheting wildly. The hip-hop was blaring.

The shooter was either Felix or Nicole. I was sure of that. And judging by the modus operandi—waiting until the victim opened the door and then firing without warning—I guessed it was Felix.

Reuben opened his door and jumped out. Keeping low and quiet, I moved to the driver's side of the car. I wasn't there to fight Reuben, but I certainly wasn't on his good list, and under the circumstances I was sure he'd shoot first and ask questions later.

Genghis was in front of me now, face-first on the floor. I looked quickly to see if there was a gun in his hand, or any weapon better than my fire extinguisher, but I couldn't see anything. I had to look away or I would have been sick right there.

Reuben was on the move, heading toward Felix, it seemed. The gunfire was lighter now, only here and there as the two men glimpsed each other between the parked cars.

I didn't waste any time. Stepping over the body, I reached inside the open driver's door and popped open the trunk. Then, as fast as I could, I rushed to the back of the car and peeked inside.

It wasn't exactly a suitcase nuke, but it was close. I grabbed it, and nearly dropped it immediately. It was a lot heavier than I'd expected.

I had it out of the trunk and was making my way for the stairwell when I realized that there were no more gunshots. I turned and looked, spotting a dash of motion between two vehicles, but I couldn't tell who it was. I didn't wait to find out.

Hoisting the bomb in my right hand and the fire extinguisher in my left, I hobbled to the stairway door. Each step sent burning darts through my knee—if I hadn't been gritting my teeth for a dozen other reasons, I would have done it for the pain.

I threw the door open and stepped through. There was no obvious way to block it, and no lock, so I hurried up the stairs. My knee felt like it was about to collapse, but I forced myself to run. I was careful, though—I didn't want Reuben to get the bomb back, but I knew stumbling and dropping it might be worse.

Just as I reached the top of the stairs, I heard the door at the bottom open. I turned and emptied the contents of the fire extinguisher into the stairwell, filling it with a cloud of white smoke. I stepped outside the door, tried to regain my breath, and waited.

I looked around the cabin—rows and rows of passengers had turned to stare. Whether out of fear or curiosity, none of them moved. I set the bomb down and took the extinguisher in both hands.

A man in a business suit called over. "Is there a fire?"

I was about to answer—to tell him that people were shooting each other down below, and to call security—but I didn't get the chance. The door opened.

Cutting through the carbon-dioxide fog billowing into the cabin, I swung the fire extinguisher.

Reuben, blinded by the cloud, never saw it coming. It hit him square in the abdomen and knocked him flat.

I dropped the extinguisher and grabbed the bomb.

I looked back at the businessman, who was staring, open-mouthed.

"Could you call the police, please? Thanks."

Across the cabin, a hundred people pulled out their cell phones.

* * *

I ran for the deck, but before I was halfway to the door I saw Edward. He was standing outside, watching me as I ran toward him.

I planted my foot, trying to stop, and my knee buckled. I fell, dropping the bomb with a nauseating thump. Edward opened the door.

"Eric."

I didn't answer. I stumbled to my feet and grabbed the nuke.

"Eric!"

I ran the other direction—there was more than one door on this boat. All I had to do was get outside and throw the bomb overboard. Problem solved. No bomb, no war—just a lot of people who had guns who were really, really upset with me.

I passed the stairwell again. Reuben was still there, unconscious on the floor.

I was trying my best to run, but I nearly fell every third or fourth step. I passed the bathrooms, and I passed another stairway door. I was nearly outside when I collapsed completely. My knee felt like mush—like the joint didn't even exist anymore, like the femur and tibia were grinding against each other.

Rolling onto my back, I looked down the length of the boat. Edward was closing fast. Suddenly a face appeared beside me.

Nicole.

I scrambled, trying to get up and grunting in pain.

"Here," she said, grabbing my arm. She put her other hand around my waist and helped me stand.

I looked at her, confused.

"Come on," she said urgently. She picked up the bomb. We walked toward the door.

"Where's security?" I said, nearly delirious with pain.

"Downstairs, chasing Felix."

I glanced back. Edward wasn't far. "Nicole, hold on." I reached over and took the bomb from her. "Get upstairs to the captain and make him stop the ferry. We can't get to land."

"But—"

"Go," I insisted, pushing her away. Edward paused as she ran, but only for a moment.

I shoved the door open and stepped out onto the deck.

The air was cold, and the blowing rain stung my face and hands. I hobbled to the side of the boat, each step ripping apart my knee and sucking the breath out of my lungs. The railing was tall and sturdy. Below me to the right was the front of the ferry, the steel deck where ferry workers waited to unload. Below to my left was the water. I leaned against the rail, trying to find the strength to lift the bomb up and over.

Anacortes was a mile away.

Edward opened the door behind me.

CHAPTER 35

I WAS BENT over, trying to pick up the bomb. My body felt weak and useless.

"Eric," Edward said. "Don't do it."

I glanced at him. He had a gun pointed at me.

"You're insane," I said. "Crazy."

I tightened my grip on the bomb. All I needed was two seconds to yank it over the railing and throw it into the water.

"I don't expect you to understand."

"I understand, all right," I said. "You want to start a war to save the U.S. economy. Very noble, except that you're going to kill thousands of people. Millions maybe."

Edward looked surprised.

"I know who you work for. I know you're Illuminati."

He laughed, but his face was deadly serious. "Who told you? Isabella?"

"She died because of you."

"She died because of Felix Hazard and the N.O.S. Are you saying she was running away from me?"

"And with good reason, it looks like."

"She could have stayed."

"So she could be just like you? Killing people?"

"She's killed people before. The important thing is the reason why you kill."

"The end justifies the means?"

Anacortes was getting closer. I could see the massive parking lot and the waiting dockworkers. Other Illuminati could be there, for all I knew, waiting with an emergency getaway.

I looked back into his eyes and felt my strength ebb away. He didn't mind killing, as long as there was a good reason. Maybe this nuke wasn't the first bomb he'd ever used.

"You make it sound so cliché, Eric. Don't you remember anything we talked about?"

"Yeah. Greed is good."

"You think I'm the only one who will make money off of this? Why do you think the economy improves during wartime? It's because we'll need to hire 50,000 people to build new tanks, and 50,000 people to build airplanes. Those 100,000 people suddenly have good jobs, working overtime. And then they build houses and pump money into construction, and they buy new cars and pump money into the auto industry. And with all the new weapons and houses and cars, factories will need to improve their businesses to keep up, and technology leaps forward."

"And you get a big cut off the top."

"So what?" he yelled. "The war will generate trillions. If I'm giving them that, what's so wrong about taking a little bit of it back?"

Behind Edward, a crowd was forming at the window. I kept telling myself that security would get there soon. I wondered how many of them were still alive. I didn't even know how many there were to begin with.

"What happened to world peace?" I said. "What happened to selling nukes to prevent war? You're setting off a nuke now to start a war."

"It's not my preferred method," he said, frowning. "But you do what you need to do. Besides, what do you think will happen when the economy fails? Every two-bit dictator and terrorist will want a piece of the crippled United States. War is inevitable—I'm merely deciding who's going to win."

I glanced back at the Anacortes dock. It was getting closer. Nicole hadn't been able to stop the ferry.

"You can't get away," I said, stalling. "There'll be police at the dock."

"You underestimate my influence," he replied coldly.

"Look at all these witnesses." I pointed at the crowd, hoping he'd look away, but he didn't. "They've seen you, and they've seen the bomb. They can put two and two together."

"They can do whatever they want," he snapped, "but there will be a war."

I stared at him. His face was white, and his overcoat was soaked. His black hair streaked down his forehead, and rain bounced off the barrel of his pistol.

His face was Rebekah's. The eyes, the mouth. He looked like her, and I hated him for it. She was good and pure, and he was evil and dangerous. It was because of him that she was down in the back of that Jeep, struggling for her life.

"Your daughter agreed to marry me," I said quietly.

He paused. "What?"

"We're getting married."

Edward didn't answer.

"I wanted to fight you. I was carrying a gun for a long time. She told me not to."

He smirked. "She's my daughter."

"It has nothing to do with you, Edward," I said angrily. "She wanted to do the right thing. That's why she's here on this boat and not in the hospital—because she wants to do what's right."

"Can't you see that she was wrong, though? You *should* have had a gun. You could have killed me and gotten rid of the bomb like you'd wanted."

"Maybe," I said, looking down at the bomb. "I don't know."

The boat was getting closer to the shore, and security hadn't come. I tightened my grip on the bomb.

"Don't do it, Eric."

I'm going to do the right thing.

I yanked the bomb off the deck. It was heavy and clumsy, and with my bad knee I almost fell over trying to adjust for the weight. Every muscle ached. My bones felt like cracking. I got the nuke up to the railing.

And then Edward shot me.

I didn't have time to think. I didn't have time to move. As the bullet hit my stomach, hot, grotesque pain ripped through my body. My grip failed and my body seized. I collapsed.

And the bomb fell off the railing. Back onto the ferry. And my vision blurred.

I grasped my side, trying to focus. Edward was standing over me, picking up the bomb. I tried to say something, but I couldn't force my mouth to speak.

"A lot of good it did you," he said. He lifted the nuclear weapon.

Bells sounded all over the boat, and a voice came over the PA telling the crowds to evacuate. Edward ran to the railing and looked over the side. Enormous rafts were inflating in the water. He took a step back.

"Leave the bomb and go," I urged, gasping for each word.

"No," he answered, his face solemn.

"Don't—" I began, but couldn't finish.

"You don't understand these people," Edward said calmly but forcefully. "I can't fail. Not like this."

I wanted to say that I did understand these people, which was why I was lying in a puddle of blood, but I hurt too much to speak.

Edward knelt down and opened the box. It wasn't much to see. No countdown timer, no red and blue wires, and no gears and flywheels. It was just a big, black cylinder nestled in foam. There was a small keypad and a digital readout.

"Edward," I gasped.

"I can still make it look like an attack."

"There are witnesses . . ."

"Not for long." He ran a nervous hand over his face as he surveyed the buttons.

He stared at the bomb for probably half a minute, which seemed like an eternity there in the rain. Not the good kind of eternity either—no angelic choirs and heavenly mansions and all-you-can-eat buffets where the food is always fresh and soda is included. No, this was the Dante kind of eternity, where the rain doesn't stop and I shake from my hands to my chin to my heart, shivering at the thought that I might not have the chance to bleed to death. I might blow up first.

It was the kind of eternity where Edward realized that no matter what he did, he was going to die, and the kind of eternity where I knew the same thing.

It was the eternity of having succeeded—I didn't give in, I resisted the Dark Side, I tossed the Emperor down the air shaft—but Rebekah still couldn't breathe.

Rebekah was still on the boat. She was going to die.

I tried to move, but everything burned.

The door opened unnoticed amid the bells and sirens. It was Felix.

He was unarmed, I assumed, or else he would have simply shot Edward. He looked terrible—his clothes were torn and stained, and his chin was bleeding again. Our eyes connected, but I wasn't about to announce him. Edward was going to kill us all.

Without warning, Felix raised his cane and brought it down across the back of Edward's neck. Edward splayed out on top of the bomb, long enough for Felix to strike a second time, smacking Edward's gun hand. The weapon bounced away. Edward leapt to his feet.

"Felix."

"Eddie."

"I thought you were dead."

"Close."

"You can't stop me," Edward said.

Felix laughed. "I just did. I can do it again."

The two stood several feet away from each other, the bomb in between.

"You're a delusional fool," Edward growled.

"Because I believe America might have a chance?" Felix swung the cane, and Edward dodged it.

"Because you think it needs one."

"Not everything needs to revolve around your pocketbook."

Edward lunged for Felix, but Felix sidestepped and struck Edward on the side of the head with the cane.

"Spare me the philosophy lesson." Edward took a few steps toward the gun, and Felix countered.

Felix swung the cane and missed. "You're not an ideologue, Eddie. But you're going to blow yourself up? For what?"

"I'm dead if I don't."

Felix stared at him, almost bewildered. "And you're going to kill all these people just because your friends will come after you? You're dead either way—let them live."

I couldn't believe it. For once, I was agreeing with Felix, and he seemed sincere.

"At least I'll kill you!" Edward lunged for Felix, and though Felix batted at Edward's arms, it was useless. The two men fell to the ground, and I knew it was over. Felix had been through a car accident and was having trouble walking—he couldn't survive an all-out brawl.

I stretched out my arms and tried to pull myself toward the bomb. Electricity blazed through my stomach—I'd had no idea how much I used my abdominal muscles until there was hole in them. I stretched out again but still couldn't drag myself forward. I was getting dizzy and couldn't keep my eyes focused. I was bleeding to death.

Edward was hitting Felix now—kneeling on his chest and punching him over and over in a frenzy.

I looked back at the dock—it was only a half mile away, and the entire place was lit up with flashing lights and emergency vehicles.

Felix struggled to defend himself, but Edward showed no mercy.

The door opened again.

Edward stood and kicked Felix a few times in the side. Felix wasn't moving. Edward, keeping his eyes on his victim, walked to the gun.

He didn't see his daughter step out onto the deck.

CHAPTER 36

SHE WAS WALKING gingerly, trembling as she crept behind her father to the bomb. Her eyes met mine and she smiled. It was weak and unconvincing, but she did it anyway. I gestured for her to hurry.

Edward knelt down and looked Felix in the face. He was completely unresponsive.

Rebekah didn't bother with the case—she reached in and pulled out the bomb itself. It was heavier than she expected, and she took a few steps backward. She readjusted her grip, but the bomb had been sitting in the rain and the metal surface was slick.

She almost dropped it, but grabbed the edge just before it fell.

She'd caught it with her burned hand and let out a tiny, almost imperceptible grunt.

Edward spun around.

"Rebekah."

She didn't say anything, but backed over to the railing.

"Don't," he said, shaken. "That's what he tried." He held his gun aimed at his daughter's head.

"Edward!" I shouted. "Don't."

He waved her toward him. "Come on, honey."

She took a pained breath. "Don't call me that."

"Give it to me."

"Why?" she demanded. "So that you can kill us all?"

"Rebekah," he stammered, shaking his head. He was confused, but he wasn't lowering the gun. "I wanted you to be a part of everything—all that I have."

"I can't believe you," she said, seething. "You're my own father."

"I've never done anything but protect you. When you got mixed up with Felix, I came. I sent Isabella first, but I came, and I got you out of there."

I reached for the railing. Using just my arms, and trying to keep my abdominal muscles relaxed, I pulled myself up into a sitting position. "And you blew up Rebekah."

Edward glared at me and then turned back to his daughter. "Give it to me."

She turned her head slightly toward me but kept her eyes on her father. "*What?*"

With the pain in my stomach, I wouldn't have thought I could feel anything else, but my head felt like it was being crushed in a vice. "He planted the bomb, not Felix."

Edward yelled exasperatedly. "I saved your lives—both of you!"

"You wanted Rebekah in your organization," I said, "but not me."

"That's because you're an idiot! Now, Rebekah, give me the weapon." He took another step toward her. She was struggling to hold the heavy bomb. She looked so weak—I was amazed the rain itself didn't knock her down. The news had stunned her, and her face was blank.

"It was Reuben that took us out of Utah," I said, struggling for the breath to speak. "Everything on the island was fake."

"It wasn't fake," he snapped, taking another step toward her. "It was so I could protect you. I had to tell you it was the FBI so that you'd go."

"Felix didn't know we were on the island until later."

Edward didn't answer but stepped closer to Rebekah. The barrel of the gun was only a few feet from her chest, and her fingers were slipping off the bomb.

I shouted, and every muscle in my body seized. "Edward! Felix didn't plant the bomb on the moped. He didn't even know we were on the island until two days before the bombing. He's never been to your house. All that stuff Reuben told me about tracking the bomber to Montana—it was a lie."

Rebekah stared at him, shocked and terrified. Her voice was gone. "Tell me it's not true." Edward leaped forward and grabbed her arm. The heavy metal cylinder dropped from her hands and hit the deck. I tried to jump toward them but only made it a few inches.

Rebekah scrambled for the nuke, and her father roughly shoved her away—sending her tumbling violently onto the hard floor. She lay on her back, panting for breath.

Carefully, he inspected the edges of the cylinder, frowning at a small dent. Then, gently and cautiously, he picked the bomb up and placed it back in the case.

I couldn't do anything.

Edward pulled a handkerchief from inside his coat and wiped rainwater from the keypad and display.

"You wanted me out of the picture," I said, my raspy voice barely more than whisper. "You cut all her ties to home. Your daughter would turn to you for help. You planted the bomb."

He pulled a small, laminated note card from his pocket, read it, and then laid it next to the keypad.

"You didn't mean to hurt her, but you did."

Edward paused, turning his head toward me but avoiding eye contact.

"Look at her, Edward."

He turned back to the bomb.

"Look at her!"

Slowly, Edward's head turned toward Rebekah. She was flat on her back, struggling for each tiny breath. Her face was bruised and purple. The cloth around her leg had loosened and streaks of crimson ran across her knee and onto the deck.

"Is that your kind of protection?"

Edward turned back to me. His face was hot and red. "That wasn't me—that was you."

"Me?"

"You can't leave well enough alone," he growled. "You couldn't be content with being safe. She had everything she ever needed with me. Money, safety, doctors. And then you took her away from all that."

"I didn't take her away," I answered. My eyes were completely unfocused, and the world around me was getting dark. "She came because she wanted to—because she wanted to do what was right."

Edward closed the case over the nuke and stood. "Fools only strive to make a great and honest hive."

"You told me greed is good. Your greed is killing your daughter."

He shook his head and picked up the case. He stared at Rebekah.

I could barely hear him as he moaned the words, "She wasn't supposed to get hurt."

There was a low rumble and the ferry shook. I turned my head and looked through blurry eyes at the dock. We were a few hundred yards away, but getting no closer. The boat had stopped. Anacortes was a mass of flashing red and blue, and I could hear the rapid chop of a helicopter.

I turned back to Edward. He was gone.

Next to Rebekah was the bomb.

I leaned over and tried to crawl. My arms had no strength—I could hardly move them, let alone pull myself. Planting my feet against the rail, I tried to push toward Rebekah, but my knee gave way.

My eyes were wide open, and I lay on my back staring at the clouds—they were dimming to black. Raindrops pattered against my face.

I felt something touch my hand.

"Eric."

Her voice was broken. I rolled my head to look at her, but saw only darkness.

"I love you."

CHAPTER 37

I HAVE FOUR distinct memories of the next twenty-four hours.

The first was of intense pain. It shocked me enough that I opened my eyes and could see, if only for a moment. There were two men in front of me, both wearing dark blue. One had his hand on my stomach, and I can only imagine that he had just discovered exactly where I'd been shot. He said something to me, and I said something back. It could have been anything but was probably along the lines of "ouch."

The second memory was of a big, white room, where a dozen people wore masks.

The third was of a hallway and four policemen. Agent Harrop was there. I was lying down.

The fourth was of Rebekah. She was smiling. This one could have very well been a dream.

* * *

I woke up in the dark. There was the strong smell of a hospital, and the TV was on.

It was a baseball game. St. Louis was playing somebody, and I didn't care at all. I cared even less than I usually cared about baseball, which was very little.

I wanted to move my head, but it didn't share the same desire, so I kept watching the game. Somebody struck out.

"Hello?" I finally said. My voice didn't sound like it belonged to me—it was low, weak, coarse, and scratchy.

Someone muted the game. I saw a face.

"You're awake?" It was Special Agent Jeff Harrop.

I nodded.

"Good. I've got some questions." He pulled a Palm Pilot out of his suit coat.

"I'm fine, thanks." I was really angry, but my whispery voice couldn't satisfactorily express it.

"What happened out on that boat?"

"Where's Rebekah?"

"She's here," he said. "What happened with Edward Hughes?"

"*Here* here? Like, in the room?" I slowly forced out. I tried to move my head again and managed about a quarter turn. I still couldn't see much.

"Here in the hospital. What—"

"Is she okay?"

There was another voice. "She will be." The voice walked into view. He was an older man, with white hair and a careworn face.

"Who are you? The doctor?"

"I'm with the state department." He sat on the edge of the bed. My stomach hurt.

"And she's okay?"

"She's in the ICU. The medical team doesn't know how she lasted as long as she did. Did you know that pulmonary barotrauma kills seventy percent of those who have it? She should have never left the hospital in the first place."

"That wasn't her choice," I said, clearing my throat, relieved to hear a semblance of my real voice return. "It was her father's."

He smiled. "That's the way it sounds."

"She can talk?"

"A little bit. We've also been in contact with a Nicole Benson."

"Nicole stopped the ferry."

He nodded. "She also shot a police officer, among a dozen other things."

"But she quit running. That ought to count for something."

"It does," he said, deeply serious. "How *much* it counts is up to a judge to decide."

"Where's Felix?"

"In another hospital. His injuries were severe, but he will stand trial."

"Did you hear that Isabella was killed?"

Harrop nodded. "We understand that it was Felix who shot her?"

"Yes," I confirmed. "And what about Edward?"

The man gestured to Agent Harrop. "I believe that's what the FBI was here to ask you about."

"You mean you didn't catch him?"

Harrop shook his head, but it was the older man who answered. "We recovered the nuclear device, and Rebekah explained why he'd tried to use it. But he's gone."

"What about Reuben?"

"Who?"

"He was on the boat too—one of Edward's men."

"There was a shooting," the older man said. "Several members of the security team were killed, as well as some civilians."

"He was upstairs—I left him by the stairwell."

Harrop scribbled into his Palm Pilot.

I lifted my head. It weighed a hundred pounds. "Reuben is the guy who took us to the island in the first place. He's Edward's right-hand man," I said in frustration. How could they have slipped through the cracks? "You know he was Illuminati, right?"

The older man looked uncomfortable with the term, but he nodded. "That's what both of the young ladies have told us."

"And you believe it?"

He chuckled grimly. "Yes, I believe it. There's nothing mythical about the group—we've had our eye on them for some time."

"So," Harrop said, getting back to his initial question, "what happened with Edward on the ferry?" He was poised with the Pilot stylus, eager for the answer. The older man folded his arms and stared at me.

"He left," I said simply. "He set down the bomb and he left."

"But why? Rebekah told us that he was going to set it off anyway—he was going to start the war, even if it meant suicide."

I leaned my head back. "I think he just finally got it. You can't do wrong and be right."

The older man nodded and stood up. He appeared to be deep in thought, and Harrop waited, watching.

Finally, the older man spoke. "The government has a favor to ask, Mr. Hopkins."

I'd watched enough movies to know what was coming next. *It is the official position of the government that none of this ever happened. The last thing the country needs now is this kind of disaster. Our enemies will have a field day with this—we've revealed a weakness. If this hits the papers, the tenuous hold we have on the economy will snap.*

"What is it?"

"Talk about this."

Huh?

I stared for a minute. "What do you mean?"

"Agent Harrop here will ask you some questions, and the federal prosecutors will speak with you, but as soon as you can, talk to the press. Talk to the *New York Times* and the *Wall Street Journal,* and do an interview with *60 Minutes.* You'll get book deals, and I want you to sign them. There'll be movies, and I want your story in every cineplex and marquee in every state in the union."

"But why?" Even Harrop looked confused.

"You saved this country," he said. "You saved it when you stopped Edward Hughes from setting off that bomb. But you're going to save it again when people learn about what you did. I don't need to tell you about the economy, Eric. What this country needs right now is to learn that we can stand up to evil and fight it. We need to see that terrorists aren't running things here.

"Eric, every time that someone spends a dollar, they worry that it's fake. Well, we have Felix in custody now. And we have Nicole Benson—and she's being very cooperative, giving us names and outlining the organization of the N.O.S. People are going to start getting arrested, and the counterfeit money is going to dry up. And you're going to be the man who stands up in front of the country and shows them that there's nothing to be afraid of. You've fought, and not only did you live—you won."

I stammered, trying to think of what to say. My voice was getting stronger. "But won't everyone be afraid? I mean, yes, we'd be telling them that the terrorists were defeated, but we'd also be telling them that the terrorists almost succeeded."

He shook his head and smiled. "People aren't afraid of monsters, Eric. They're afraid of the dark—of the unknown. Give them something to fight and they'll fight it."

I nodded. "What about Edward?"

"I can't make any promises," he said. "I can tell you that we'll be keeping a closer watch on the Illuminati. Rebekah gave us some good information. I'm sure you'll give us more, and that will help. The FBI can offer you protection, of course, but ultimately, you might have a hard life. I'm sorry. You've made some real enemies."

"That's not very optimistic."

"I'm just being honest with you. But I need to go, and Agent Harrop has some questions for you. We'll talk again."

I nodded.

"You'll be all right," he said, opening the door. "You've been through worse."

* * *

The debriefing with Harrop took the better part of the morning, and we hadn't even touched on a quarter of what we had to discuss. When the nurse brought the lunch tray, Harrop excused himself to make a phone call, only to return a minute later and tell me my parents had just arrived at the airport and were on their way. Then he offered to let me take a break from the questioning.

It took four times punching the nurse's call line, and twenty minutes of further argument, but I finally got someone to help me into a wheelchair and cart me across the ICU to Rebekah's room, which wasn't far. The route was lined with police officers.

Rebekah was awake and her face was beaming. The nurse parked my chair next to the bed.

I took her hand. "Hey."

Her cheeks were red, and as she grinned her dimple appeared. "Hey."

"You look good."

"Someone shaved your beard."

I nodded and ran my hand over my chin. "I'm grateful. I hated that thing."

Rebekah's room was almost pure white, and even though only a few of the lights were on, everything seemed to glow.

She squeezed my hand. "They told me you were in surgery."

"I guess," I said.

"How do you feel?"

"Better."

"Me too."

"How's your hand?"

She frowned. "They're going to work on it some more."

"They didn't catch your dad. Or Reuben."

It was strange, sitting there in the hospital room. We weren't hiding anymore. I'd spent so long being nervous that it was hard not to keep one eye on the door. I'd grown accustomed to doubt—were any of the FBI agents actually working for Felix? Had the police intentionally let Edward go? Were we really safe?

And yet there I was, not using a fake name and not denying anything. And Rebekah was alive and she was holding my hand. And we were going to be married.

There were no guarantees, of course—just because we'd won didn't mean we'd always win.

She laughed quietly. "Were you really going to throw the bomb overboard?"

I smiled, realizing how ironic it was that my fiancée's dad had shot me. Not many engagements start like that. "I tried. I wasn't fast enough."

A silent, happy tear rolled down her cheek. "Thanks for always taking care of me."

"I love you."

I sat next to her for an hour, until a nurse came delivering medicine and Rebekah was too tired to stay awake. I went against the nurse's orders and stood up, just long enough to kiss Rebekah goodbye. My stomach stung and ached and burned, and I didn't care at all.

My parents were back in my room. My mom was nearly hysterical—she'd spent the last few weeks thinking I was in the Witness Protection Program and was stunned to hear the truth. They sat next to my bed, hanging on every word of the story. The only thing that got them off the subject was when I told them I was engaged.

Eventually the doctors shooed my parents away, and they retreated downstairs to find something to eat. The nurse brought me my dinner tray, and I was left alone.

It was quiet and warm, and I felt safe. My body ached, and I felt like I could sleep for weeks, but I was calm and content.

On my tray, next to the carton of juice, between my plate and my napkin, was a small slip of folded paper. Scrawled on the front in ink was a rough circle with a dot in the center. I opened it.

Eric—

Though our minds differ on many issues, there is one subject on which we agree. You have never done anything without Rebekah's happiness in mind. I have always loved her, and always will, but I believe you will give her something I never could. I give you both my blessing.

Epilogue

I SWITCHED OFF the TV. There wasn't much worth reporting anymore, but the news kept trying for new angles on the story, struggling to one-up the other networks. By now, most of the story was known. Rebekah and I had been interviewed and interviewed, and had been asked every question imaginable. We'd appeared together on *Larry King*. I'd stood with Matt Lauer in Rockefeller Square while Al Roker gave the weather report. Rebekah sat on Oprah Winfrey's couch, describing terrorism from a woman's point of view, after which Oprah surprised her with a makeover.

CNN was teeming with analysts—former CIA officers, nuclear physicists, and a whole troop of conspiracy theorists who'd never gotten the time of day from the mainstream media before (though the producers became a little more exclusive again after one theorist listed Ted Turner as an eighth-level Illuminati).

And then there were special guests—human-interest stories. Fox News interviewed my parents. *Newsweek* had a three-page article about the cataphiles. MSNBC somehow tracked down the Parisian waitress whose shoes I'd bought for two hundred euros. She said she'd used the money to pay her late college tuition, and hailed the sudden windfall as a heavenly miracle.

But despite the different stories, the one common thread that connected them all together was that the N.O.S. was collapsing. The distribution of counterfeits was slowing to a trickle, and the dollar was on the rebound.

I stood up from the couch and stretched. It had been two and a half months since I'd gotten out of the hospital, and I was recovering nicely. I still had some abdominal pain once in a while, but my knee was almost completely healed, and the doctors had said I would be back to full health in no time.

I walked to the phone and dialed room service. Even as I was ordering dinner, I knew that the FBI was listening in on the line. I didn't mind so much anymore.

Outside the hotel room door was Agent Jeff Harrop, patiently acting as a bodyguard. He checked every elevator before I went in, arranged for secure vehicles, and monitored the phones. Working with him was a bigger guy named Steve Reinhold. Harrop told me that other agents referred to Steve as Reinhold the Rhino, which was a much more comforting name than Jeff. Someone back in Washington was looking out for me.

I opened the curtains and stepped out onto the balcony. The bright lights of Sydney, Australia, spread out before us, reflecting on the harbor. Rebekah stood next to me, watching the sunset and playing the violin.

"How's it coming?"

Rebekah grimaced. "Better than a week ago, I guess."

The new pressure bandage on her wrist and hand was smaller. There would be permanent scarring, but movement was coming back a little more every day.

"It still hurts?"

She nodded but smiled, setting the instrument on the balcony table. I put my hands on her waist and pulled her toward me.

"Do you know how much I love you?"

Rebekah grinned and kissed me.

It had been a small, beautiful ceremony. No reception, no throwing the bouquet. Six days ago, my father and grandfather had served as witnesses as Rebekah and I knelt across the altar of the Salt Lake Temple. I loved her, and nothing was going to separate us again. What was bound on earth had been bound eternally in heaven.

The good kind of eternity.

TO THE READER

In the months leading up to *The Counterfeit*'s release, two conspiracy-theory websites offered insight into the events and codes within the book, as well as led readers on a multi-state hunt for the truth. The first website, an online novella (trialofthecentury.blogspot.com), illuminated the actions of the characters prior to the first pages of the novel. The second website (www.theunknownpatriot.com) offered readers clues to follow and puzzles to solve that would help them uncover the conspiracies found in *The Counterfeit*. The final clue is found within the pages of *The Counterfeit* itself.

If you are purchasing this book immediately after its release, then you may still be able to crack the code in time. The first individual to solve the ancient code and email the translation to the author (robisonwells@msn.com) wins the grand prize; the next ten people to email the answer will be entered into a drawing for second prize.

Regardless of when you are buying this book, you may still be interested in the aforementioned websites and the author's other works. Please see the author's bio at the end of this book for more information.

ABOUT THE AUTHOR

Robison Wells lives in the scenic Salt Lake Valley with his lovely wife Erin and their two crazy children, Holly and Sam. Rob graduated from the University of Utah with a degree in Political Science and an emphasis in International Relations. And, since a PoliSci degree and a nickel will buy you a tall cup of jack squat, Rob works in the wholesale lumber industry as a structural designer. *The Counterfeit* is his third novel.

The Counterfeit is actually a sequel to Mr. Wells's 2005 novel, *Wake Me When It's Over.* While we're certain that you would enjoy this prequel, it is not required reading for those wishing to immerse themselves in the world of *The Counterfeit.*

For more information, please visit Robison Wells' website at www.robisonwells.com, or write him via email at robisonwells@msn.com, or through snail-mail at Covenant Communications, Inc., Box 416, American Fork, UT 84003-0416.